Saving Iris

KAREN VICKERS

Books by Karen Vickers

Remember Me

First printed in 2025 by Ingram Spark

Saving Iris
© Karen Vickers 2025

ISBN: 978-1-7638644-2-9 (Paperback)

A catalogue record for this book is available from the National Library of Australia

Dedication

To everyone who loves nothing more than to curl up with
a good book, a hot drink, and your favourite snack,
this book is for you.
Read for the story
Read for the passion.
Read for the adventure.

Chapter 1

"Lyla!" a young girl's voice called out in the distance. "Lyla, where are you?"

Taking in the warmth of the afternoon sun, Lyla startled in surprise, her heart skipping a few beats. She sighed deep in annoyance, as the shrill voice of her little sister in the distance, disturbed her.

Today marked Lyla's eighteenth birthday, and right now, she did not want to be disturbed.

Inhaling as deeply as her corset allowed, Lyla tried to block out her sisters voice. Gently caressing the lush green grass beneath her fingers, Lyla concentrated on the sun warming her exposed face and arms and willed the feeling of calm to return and lull her back into a rested state.

Ignoring her sisters call, Lyla lay down with her eyes closed, her heartbeat steady, and drank in the sweet, perfumed air. The calming scent of the pine trees, lavender bushes, and lemongrass growing in the gardens surrounding her, brought back a barrage of childhood memories.

This was always her favourite part of the estate, filled with so many memories of growing up with her siblings. Wadding in the lake with her papa, chasing the birds and squirrels through the trees, and picking wildflowers for their mama.

Feeling settled once more, Lyla listened to the mallard ducks quacking lazily on the pond in front of her, and she smiled as a light breeze teased the loose hairs peeking out from beneath her bonnet and tickled the pale skin of her neck.

"Lyla!" The voice drew nearer, laden with irritation. "The guests are arriving soon. You need to get ready!"

Sighing, knowing her little sister would find her any second, Lyla opened her eyes and allowed herself one final moment to take in the beautiful turquoise blue of the cloudless sky above, before her alone time was over.

For years, Lyla waited patiently, even eagerly for this day, but now that it was here, she suddenly feared it. It had arrived all too quickly, and she felt like she needed a few more months, or even another year to be truly ready.

Wishing she could stay exactly where she was, her calm demeanour rapidly faded as she recalled all the challenging work she had been required to put in to become a society lady and a confident bride.

The endless hours of learning the correct etiquette rules and how to carry herself, had they paid off? Would her family see her differently after tonight?

Unlike previous birthdays, her eighteenth brought with it immense pressure and responsibilities. Knowing how her loving parents had dedicated their time and energy to find their daughter the right suitor, Lyla was not sure if she was ready for this day. Was she even in the right place mentally to be in this important position?

What if she was not strong enough? What if she did not choose anyone?

Whatever would her dear mama think? Whatever would her papa say if all the guests left, and she remained alone?

Rolling to her side, Lyla sat up just as Iris, ran around the garden bed, and stopped in front of her shiny blue shoes.

"What are you doing out here? Mama will throw a fit if you have dirtied your dress," Iris said, glaring down at Lyla, her hands perched firmly on her small hips.

Although Iris was six years younger than Lyla, and the youngest of four children, she was an overly confident and smart young girl. In her eyes, Lyla wasn't an older sister to look up to—she was competition. It was no secret that Iris strove to be prettier and smarter than her. Her little sister found satisfaction in telling Lyla off if she had not made enough effort with her appearance, or in her behaviour.

Rolling her eyes, Lyla stood up carefully, re-adjusted her silk bonnet over her blonde hair, and glanced over Iris's head towards the glassy still water of the pond. She knew once she left this household, Iris could finally take the centre stage she seemed so desperately to be on.

Iris always ensured she was the centre of attention. Always fussing about in her pretty dresses, playing the pianoforte perfectly and checking that their parent's attention was solely on her—much to Lyla's annoyance.

"My dress is fine, Iris," Lyla commented, finally turning her attention to Iris's pretty, freckled face, before smoothing over the large ruffles on her dress with her hand. "It's not like anyone is going to look behind me anyway." Lyla turned around slowly, the thick, sapphire blue silk taffeta swirling around her legs, as she made sure the hem of her elegant Victorian ball gown hung straight and low to the ground.

Iris stepped forward and brushed off some dried leaves and loose blades of grass before she straightened the matching silk and lace bow at the back of Lyla's waist.

"I still think you should have worn the other blue dress; this one makes your skin look too pale," Iris sighed as she stretched up to brush more of Lyla's hair back under her bonnet.

"Well, it is too late now, isn't it?" Lyla mocked. "If the guests are already arriving, there is no time to change." She looked at Iris and smiled widely. Even though Iris could be a little annoying and overbearing, Layla knew deep down she would miss her when all of this was over.

"Come on," Iris said, finally grabbing Lyla's hand and pulling her back around the garden bed, to the expansive manor, Lyla called home.

Lyla had spent her entire life here — it was her safe place. The home she had watched her siblings grow up in as well. What would life be like once she moved out and began her new life, in a new house? Would she miss this place, her family, the privacy of her bedroom?

With her nerves taking hold, Lyla held her bonnet firmly on her head as she allowed Iris to lead them towards the old and worn kitchen door at the back of the manor. If the guests were already arriving via their carriages at the front of the manor, it would be unseemly for Lyla to scamper past them.

Stepping into the kitchen, the bustling noises from the brightly lit room, felt overwhelming after the peace of the garden. To add to the chaos, the aromas of Lyla's birthday feast overpowered her sensors, and Lyla felt her stomach churn as a fleeting wave of nausea rushed over her—her nerves getting the better of her.

Holding her breath and ignoring the agitated looks from the cook and servants, Lyla followed Iris into the servants' back corridors, up the worn narrow staircase, and towards the main ballroom, her hooped dress brushing lightly against the walls.

Slipping through the concealed door, Lyla and Iris discreetly entered the ballroom and stepping onto the polished herringbone floorboards, Lyla let go of Iris's hand and paused, taking in the beautiful room. While the servants had prepared the room earlier that morning, Lyla avoided it, not wanting to ruin the surprise, and now, it was better than she could have imagined.

Lyla took a moment to take it all in before the room filled with guests. The soft glow from the candle chandeliers hanging from the ceiling sent a warm shimmer across the white and silver silk curtains adorning the large windows and brightened the green walls and colourful oil paintings that hung around the room.

Several dark mahogany chairs, embroidered with black and red brocade with white and silver silk bows tied around their backs, lined the walls for the guests to sit on during the ceremony.

At the far end of the room stood a large red, carpeted platform, which for grand events like this would normally be filled with musicians, but today it stood empty except for an elegant, throne-style chair at its centre.

Turning her attention to the steps leading up to the platform, Lyla offered a gentle smile as she observed her parents standing and waiting anxiously for her arrival.

It was now or never.

Just as she began walking across the floor, Iris spoke, diverting her parents' attention in her direction.

"I found her!" she exclaimed loudly, staring at her parents with pride.

"Lyla!" her mama exclaimed, as she turned and rushed towards her, the hem of her pale lime green and white lace ball gown swishing silently on the floor as she moved. As her mother gently cupped her face in her hands, Lyla closed her eyes, relishing in the warmth of her mother's touch. "You know just how to make me fret, my child."

"Sorry, Mama." Lyla opened her pale blue eyes and gazed into her mama's. Eyes the same shade as hers.

Lyla's father stepped closer, gently taking Lyla's hand. "My dear child. You just might be the death of my nerves," he spoke tenderly. Turning to her father, Lyla smiled nervously.

"Sorry, Papa. I didn't mean to worry you; I just needed a moment to myself."

"I know this is a big day. I have never forgotten the day I met your mama, on her Flowering Day." He smiled tenderly at her mother, who blushed and smiled lovingly back, and Lyla felt a sliver of hope push through her nerves. Returning to Lyla, he continued. "Remember, every decision you make today, is yours to make alone. Trust your heart, and your head. I know you will do the right thing." He squeezed her hand gently.

"But what if I don't like any of them?" Lyla asked, turning back to face her mother.

"Then we try again in a few months' time. Your happiness is especially important to us and this family."

Dropping her hand from her father's, Lyla sighed wearily and smiled, hoping to convey a small amount of confidence. The pressure she faced to make the right match bore down on her, setting pulse racing.

With trepidation, Lyla's eyes shifted to the ballroom doors. While lying on the grass before Iris rudely interrupted her, Lyla had wished and prayed, her future husband would walk through these doors tonight.

Now, within a few minutes, she would stand on the platform and select a man from those her parents had handpicked and invited to her Flowering Day.

As per tradition, passed from generation to generation, each daughter on the day they turned eighteen, took part in a Flowering Day Ceremony. During the late afternoon, they were presented with five suitors. Young men their parents nominated as a potential husband.

During the evening, it was the daughter's responsibility to engage with each gentleman, become acquainted with them, and participate in dances. At the conclusion of the ceremony, she was expected to select one individual, the man she would marry, and in most ceremonies, a suitable match was typically achieved.

Then, after an engagement lasting a few weeks, the daughter would marry her match and move to her own household. Historically, the semi-arranged marriages were remarkably successful, which only added to the burden Lyla felt as the eldest of three daughters.

Despite her nerves, Lyla knew she *needed* to make a choice tonight, both to help her family and to provide a leading example to her two younger sisters. Regardless of her mama's words, Lyla knew she wouldn't allow her parents to search for other suitable young men. They had already spent the past three months meeting and discussing potential marriage ideals with many families, and finally, organising this large party, just for her.

Removing the pins and slipping off her bonnet, Lyla handed them to Iris and asked her to place it in her room and watched as she hurried to the ballroom doors. Glancing back at Lyla, Iris gave her a slight shake of her head in disappointment and called out.

"You still should have worn the other blue dress," she said before slipped out the ballroom door, leaving Lyla alone with her parents.

Turning her attention back to her mama, Lyla gently took her hands in her own, and pulling her closer, kissed her mother's cheek. Tonight, she would make her parents proud.

By the time the clock struck ten, Lyla would be a young lady, with her future husband by her side.

Taking a deep breath, she let go of her mama's hands and took her father's outstretched arm. Hitching up her skirt, together they ascended the three stairs of the platform, and stood before the large, deep purple, high-backed chair awaiting her.

Releasing her father's arm, Lyla ran her fingertips over the velvet and wood armrest. Closing her eyes, Lyla tried to picture her mama sitting in the same chair so many years ago.

Had her mama been just as nervous as she was?

Taking another deep, slow breath, calming her nerves, Lyla turned to face the empty room.

Flicking her eyes to the ornate grandfather clock standing beside the grand doors, Lyla watched as the brass hands aligned on the five and twelve. Abruptly, the clock chimed, each ring reverberating through her chest.

As Lyla counted the five rings, her nerves intensified, and feeling her courage seep from her legs, she sank into the chair. Finally, after all these years, her Flowering Day ceremony was here.

Chapter 2

As the final chime of the clock marked the ceremony commencement, Marcel, the door attendant, opened one of the large, white, and gold wooden doors. As per tradition, Lyla's three siblings entered the ballroom, and Marcel silently closed the door behind them.

Jonathan, the sole survivor of three sons, the younger two sadly passing away in infancy, strode towards the platform in a new dark green, tailored suit, and a proud grin. At sixteen, he was a little taller than Lyla, and a good-looking young man, a younger version of his father.

Standing before his older sister and parents, Jonathan bowed low before rising and winking at Lyla. She could see the twinkle in his eyes as he tried not to laugh at the formality of the moment before he placed a single white carnation on the top step.

"Thank you, Jonathan," she said, suppressing her own giggle. Standing tall, he stepped back, making way for their sister, Emily.

Dressed in a bright yellow satin and white lace dress that swayed gracefully around her feet, Emily looked much older than her fifteen years. Her dark blonde hair fell in perfect ringlets over her shoulders as she smiled up at her sister.

Only a little shorter than Lyla, they were both very much alike. Creative, musical, and funny, both sisters could more often than not be found curled in the library, their noses buried deep in a book. Of her three siblings, Lyla knew Emily would be the one she would miss the most.

Stepping up to the platform, Emily curtsied low, before placing another white carnation next to Jonathan's.

"Thank you, Emily," Lyla said, as Emily stepped back, and moved to stand by her brothers side.

Next, Lyla watched as Iris approached, her shoulders back, and chin high, her smile tight and perfect. Her delicate pale pink, satin dress, adorned with pearls and small embroidered white flowers, swished softly, as she walked, her matching flat pink shoes, soundless against the wooden floor. Arriving at the platform, Iris curtsied low and placed a third white carnation on the step.

Lyla beamed with delight, seeing the three flowers laid down before her. White carnations, her favourite flower.

Straightening, Iris widened her eyes and wriggled her shoulders at Lyla, pushing out her chest a little, motioning to her to sit taller in the chair.

"Thank you, Iris," Lyla said, straightening her back slightly as she gave Iris a slightly exasperated stare. Iris smiled defiantly and moved to stand at Emily's side.

Marcel then opened the door again and allowed the rest of Lyla's family members to enter. Entering the ballroom as a group, were Lyla's grandparents, aunts and uncles, and cousins, who each approached the platform, bowed, or curtsied, and laid a colourful flower on the middle step.

Her childhood friends entered the ballroom last to watch Lyla pick her future husband, their expressions bright with excitement. Although Lyla was not the first of her friends to have her Flowering Day Ceremony, she knew they were all extremely excited for her, nevertheless.

In fact, two friends, Katelyn and Gabriella, arrived to support her, their arms entwined with their husbands as they walked into the grand room. As each guest approached the platform and placed a flower, a carpet of colour blooms covered the bottom step. The seriousness of the procession caused a giggle to rise in her throat, and Lyla had to minimise eye contact with them to keep it from erupting.

Finally, the guests stood in a semi-circle around the ballroom, and with all eyes on her, Lyla tried her best to maintain her poise and posture.

Last to approach Lyla were her parents, both laying a white rose at her feet, before taking their places on either side of the chair. A serene calmness fell over the room, the only sound coming from the grandfather clock.

As each tick matched the rhythm of her heart, the feeling became overwhelming, and Lyla took a deep breath and focused on the sweet, perfumed air permeating around her. Roses, carnations, sweet peas, daises, snapdragons, and marigolds of all assorted colours, blanketed the stairs before her, a symbol to signify Lyla was finally a lady.

As the clock chimed five-thirty, and on the final strike, Marcel opened the door again, and the first suitor entered the ballroom, followed closely by his parents.

The young man stopped a few feet from the threshold and glanced up at Lyla.

"May I present, Mister Bram Lawson," Marcel called out.

Bram was tall and thin. His black hair was pulled neatly back and bound at the nape of his neck. His dark, midnight blue coat, trimmed with silver thread and adorned with five pearl buttons, hung low over his black, woollen trousers.

The collar of a light green, silk shirt, poked out at his throat and Lyla noticed that he held a bright pink rose in his hand.

Bram locked eyes with Lyla briefly before he lowered his head and bowed. Lyla watched the young man, noting her first impressions on who could potentially be her future husband.

Straightening, he approached Lyla, stopping a few feet away from the base of the platform. With a closer look, Lyla could see he was a handsome man, fair skinned, with chestnut brown eyes and thin lips.

"It is an honour to meet you, Miss Pierson," he said in a low, deep voice, which caused Lyla's breath to catch in her throat.

"The honour is mine," Lyla responded nervously, discreetly repositioning her sweaty palms.

Bram stepped forward and placed the rose onto a small wooden table at the foot of the stairs covered in a delicate white, lace cloth. Stepping aside, Bram's parents then approached, adding matching roses to the flowers gathered at the base the stairs.

"Thank you for your gifts," Lyla nodded in approval and watched as Bram's parents moved back to join the other guests. Moments later, Marcel opened the door once again, and another young man entered the room.

"May I present, Mister Duncan Saddler."

Duncan lumbered through the doors and immediately bowed low, keeping his eyes on the floor. As he stood, Lyla was shocked to see that he was tall and well rounded. As he approached, his footsteps heavy, Lyla couldn't help but notice he seemed to struggle to maintain eye contact with her.

His emerald-green jacket, fit snuggly over his bulky frame, and his dark blue trousers, were too short for his long legs. He shuffled loudly towards her as though nervous, and only once he reached the stairs, did he raise his gaze. Lyla smiled softly, noticing the small beads of sweat forming along his hairline, causing his brown hair to stick to his skin.

"It is an honour to meet you," he said, his voice breaking into a high pitch.

"The honour is mine," Lyla replied as her eyebrows shot up, and she forced her composure to return.

Duncan pulled a yellow daffodil from behind his back and hastily placed it on the table beside the rose before making way for his parents. With smiles that were a little too wide, his parents placed their daffodils on the steps before the trio stepped aside.

Lyla's gaze followed Duncan and his mother, noting as she quietly scolded him, her expression filled with disappointment. Knowing how nervous she felt, a feeling of compassion rushed through her, and Lyla flashed him a sympathetic smile. Finally, Duncan took his place next to Bram, while his parents moved over to the wall, his heavyset mother opting to sit down immediately.

As the door opened again, Lyla felt relief at the distraction and turned her attention to the front of the room.

"May I present Mister Winston Stuart."

Winston stood erect, his expression proud as he stared unflinchingly towards Lyla. As he studied her, she found no hint of emotion in his eyes before he stepped forward and bowed low, sweeping his left hand before him.

Lyla stared at his deep red jacket, with a hint of gold thread at the edges. A white collared shirt peeked out of his black and red embroidered vest. Trailing her eyes down his black trousers, Lyla was impressed. His outfit was a stark contrast to the white and frost-green tones of the ballroom.

Straightening, he walked confidently to the platform, stopping only a few steps away from Lyla.

"It is an honour to meet you," he said in a dry, deep voice.

"The honour is mine," Lyla repeated.

As Winston stepped forward, Lyla stared at his dark green eyes, her breath temporarily caught as he returned her stare. Eventually breaking the intense gaze, Winston presented a beautiful crimson red rose, which he placed besides the daffodil. Backing away, he bowed again and moved to the side so his parents could place their roses on the ground. Looking at his parents, Lyla smiled to herself when she noticed all three had the same golden blonde hair and green eyes. They were an attractive family.

Following suit, Winston took his place beside Duncan as his parents backed away.

Three down, two more to go.

Once again, Marcel opened the door, and the next suitor entered.

"May I present, Mister Noah Valdez."

Lyla glanced towards to door, and her breath hitched as a strikingly handsome young man entered. Her heart skipped a beat, and she clasped her fingers together, trying to maintain her composure.

Cloaked in a long coat of deep purple velvet adorned with bright blue stitching and gold buttons, Noah bowed deep and held his position longer than the previous three.

His chestnut brown hair, with a hint of ginger, fell around his face, causing a flutter of butterflies within her stomach. Slowly straightening, he smiled broadly at Lyla, showing off his white teeth. She returned the smile, but only for a moment, before she restrained herself. She could not pick her suitor purely on his good looks.

Moving swiftly towards Lyla, his black silk trousers and highly polished shoes gleamed as he crossed the floor.

"It is an honour to meet you," he said, his voice deep and masculine.

"The honour is mine," Lyla replied, her voice catching in her throat.

Noah stepped forward, holding a blue iris. He placed it on the table and gave Lyla a polite nod before stepping aside. Noah's mother then placed two Iris flowers on the stairs, smiled sweetly, and moved away to join Duncans parents, while Noah took his place alongside Winston.

Sensing movement from the corner of her eye, Lyla glanced slightly to the right, where her siblings stood and tried hard not to laugh. Lyla saw Iris's eyes were wide, and she grinned wildly at her, nodding her head enthusiastically. Of course, Iris would approve of Noah Valdez; he just handed her, Iris's favourite flower.

Finally, Marcel opened the ballroom door for the last suitor.

"May I present, Mister Damien Olsen."

Damien stepped through the doors, followed closely by his parents and Lyla's eyes widened in shock, then dropped quickly to the floor. As Damien bowed, Lyla flicked her eyes quickly to her father, standing beside her. He did not meet her gaze. Turning back, Lyla watched as Damien strode across the room to stand before her.

She stared at his dark, sapphire-blue jacket with gold trimming, which surprisingly matched the colour of her dress. A pale blue shirt peeked out above the lapel, and his black pants hugged his muscular legs. Yet, he failed to impress her.

"It is an honour to meet you," he said cooly, a slight cocky grin tugging at the corner of his lips.

"The honour is mine," Lyla replied, refusing to meet his gaze, instead staring at his unruly black hair tucked behind his ears.

Damien stepped forward and placed a white carnation on the table. Trying desperately not to roll her eyes or sigh with contempt, Lyla scoffed at his poor attempt to impress her. Matching her dress and presenting her with her favourite flower would *not* win her favour. Smiling once more, he held Lyla's gaze and with a slight incline of his head, Damien stepped aside for his parents as they placed their carnations.

For the last time, Lyla thanked her potential suitors and their parents for their gifts and felt relieved. This part of the ceremony had ended.

After Damien moved away from the platform and joined the other four men, a quiet hush enveloped the room as Lyla's father stepped forward.

"Thank you all for attending Lyla's Flowering Day and thank you very much to the five men of honour, for coming." He glanced over at the men and nodded in approval. Each man nodded back, a sign of respect and grace.

Turning back to the crowded room, he continued. "This is a moment that my beautiful wife and I have been looking forward to for many years, and just the first of the Flowering Day celebrations that we will have in this family."

He turned and glanced at Emily and Iris, who both smiled eagerly. "It does not seem that long ago that I was in this very position and meeting Grace for the first time. How fast the years have gone." With a pause, he looked tenderly at his wife, who blushed and blew him a kiss.

"So, without further ado, please join us for dinner and an evening of music and dancing. We will all gather back here at nine forty-five for the ringing of the bell at ten. Hopefully, Lyla," he placed a tender hand on her shoulder, "will have picked her suitor."

Applause erupted, quickly followed by excited chatter as Marcel opened the large double wooden side doors, which led into a spacious and elaborated decorated dining room.

The aromas which Lyla had smelt in the kitchen earlier, now wafted into the ballroom. Platters of roast meats, fish and vegetables, cakes, sweets, ale, and wine, filled the buffet tables, encouraging the guests to enter.

As the guests and family members made their way through the doors, Lyla quickly stood and grabbed her father's arm as she glared up at him. "You picked Damien Olsen as a potential suitor?" she whispered in frustration.

"He comes from a good family Lyla," he said gently, yet his brow furrowed at her reaction.

"Damien Olsen is a bully, Papa. He spent most of his teenage years teasing Jonathan! Why would you think I would want to marry him?" Lyla hissed.

"I doubt he is that boy anymore, Lyla," her mother said sweetly, trying to calm Lyla down. "He would have changed."

Lyla looked past her parents and saw Jonathan had not moved from the same spot he had stood during the introductions. She scanned his face, noting the fearful look in his eyes before she turned back to her mother, her tone resolute.

"A leopard does not change its spots; Damien … Mr. Olsen will always be that boy!"

Chapter 3

Marching into the dining room, refusing to walk with her parents, Lyla took in the enormous oak table in the middle of the room draped in a fine white silk and lace tablecloth. Laden with generous platters of food, and large vases of flowers, several guests had already gathered around it, generously filling their plates.

Ten small tables were spread around the sides of the room, set out with fine china plates, silver cutlery, and crystal glasses.

The warm glow from the candle chandeliers and the wall sconces, radiated off the walnut wall panels, giving the room a peaceful and inviting ambiance.

Lyla sighed as she scanned the faces of the guests. Watching each suitor enter the main room had turned out to be easier than she thought. Although, hearing Damien's name being called out and seeing him enter the ballroom, had caused Lyla's heart to stop for a beat or two in surprise and then anger, yet she had survived it.

Centring herself, and willing what nerves still lingered to dissipate, Lyla focused on the new task at hand. She needed to seek out each of the suitors, get to know them as best she could, given the limited time she had, and hope she'd find a connection. A spark or intuitive feeling, to let her know she'd found her future husband.

And she only had four hours, to make the choice.

Weaving her way through the colourful dresses and tailored suits, Lyla smiled when spoken to, engaged in conversations with those who sought her out, and looked hesitantly for the five men she needed to get to know.

Well, four men, if she did not count Damien.

Just the thought of him striding through the ballroom doors was enough to make her eyes roll. The fact that he was arrogant enough to even accept her parents' offer offended her. Not only had he endlessly teased her brother but had also gone out of his way to tease herself and her sisters. Lyla did not believe a boy like him could change his ways.

Bypassing the food, the rich aroma's still overwhelming, Lyla weaved her way towards the drinks table, feeling like everyone's eyes were fixed upon her. Suddenly, Iris ran up beside her, slipping her small hand into Lyla's.

"Well, that was exciting!" she exclaimed, smiling up at her sister.

"Was it?" Lyla replied and squeezed her hand.

"I think the man who presented the iris should be your husband." Her smile widened. "Plus, he's very good looking." Iris smoothed out the skirt of her pink dress, while brazenly staring across the room towards Noah.

"Of course you would choose him," Lyla whispered in her sister's ear, her voice teasing. "But I have not made up my mind yet, and if I do not choose him, maybe you can pick him when you have your Flowing Day."

"But … he'll be too old then!" Iris moaned, her face suddenly scrunching up. Lyla laughed.

"Well, as much as I do love your company, and you telling me what to do, I need to get on with the next part of the ceremony. How about you grab something to eat and sit with Emily and Jonathan?" Kissing Iris gently on the forehead and letting go of her hand, Lyla inhaled slowly and straightened her dress.

Smiling to herself, remembering she was now an official adult, Lyla grabbed a glass of wine off the table and made her way over to the closest suitor.

Trying not to laugh at the irony, Lyla approached Noah and his mother.

Upon seeing her approach, Noah stood abruptly, pushing his chair back. He seemed as nervous as Lyla felt as he quickly handed his napkin to his mother. As she reached the table, he bowed slightly.

"Please, you don't need to do that," Lyla smiled, waving for him to straighten. "Please, sit back down."

"After you." Noah stepped aside, pulling out the empty chair next to him, and Lyla, sweeping her dress out of the way, gracefully accepted.

"Lyla, please meet my mother, Brianna Valdez," Noah said, as he sat himself back down.

Lyla stretched her hand forward and took Brianna's white, silk-gloved hand in hers. "Nice to meet you."

"And you. And I must apologise for my husband's absence; he is unwell and was unable to make the trip."

"Oh, I do hope he feels better soon." Lyla squeezed Brianna's hand, in a show of concern.

"Thank you. He really did want to be here."

"It's okay. I am sure there will be another chance for us to meet. Thank him very much for the flower, though."

"I hope you liked it!" Noah pipped in. "I wasn't sure what your favourite flower was."

Lyla smiled. "It was beautiful. They all were. I don't think I have ever seen so many diverse types and colours in one day, like I have tonight."

"Yes, it was a splendour to see them all," Brianna said, taking a small sip of her wine.

"The iris certainly is a pretty flower, but it is not my favourite, I'm afraid. Though I will admit," Lyla said as she leaned closer to Noah. "You have won my little sister over. Her name is Iris, and the iris is her favourite flower."

"Duly noted," he smiled. "And which one is Iris?" he asked, his eyes sparkling with mischief.

"The young girl over in the corner, wearing the pink dress, and watching you intently." Lyla giggled.

Noah glanced across the room and peered at Iris, who turned a bright shade of pink, which matched her dress, and quickly turned to talk to her brother.

Unable to contain themselves, Lyla and Noah laughed, his light-heartedness putting her at ease and she felt some of the tension from her shoulders lessen. Feeling a little less nervous, she took a sip of her wine.

"If you'll excuse me, I'd like to sample more food from the table," Brianna said as though sensing the growing intimacy between the two.

"You never told me your favourite flower," he asked politely after he watched his mother walk away.

"Oh, it's a carnation."

"Ah, any particular colour?" he asked, his head tilted to the side like he planned to make a mental note to remember it.

"White, actually." Without meaning to, Lyla glanced over at Damien, who was watching from another table. He gave another slight nod, and Lyla smiled politely in return before quickly turning her attention back to Noah.

She caught Noah's gaze flick between herself and Damien, but he said nothing. Instead, he smiled and positioned himself in front of her. "Are you still nervous? I know I am."

Lyla smiled. "Yes, I am, I don't know how I'm going to do this," she confessed as she took another sip of wine, the tart flavour lingering on her tongue.

"Slowly," Noah said with a gracious smile. "You have a few hours."

"Indeed, I do."

They sat for a moment, an awkward silence suddenly rushing between them. "So, I guess I need to ask all the boring questions first," Lyla said abruptly, holding the stem of her wineglass delicately.

"Of course," Noah pushed his half-eaten meal aside. "Well, where to begin? I am twenty-one, and I work at a bank, like my father, but that is not where I want to stay. I am hoping to obtain a large property of my own to grow crops and farm cattle and currently have an eye on a spectacular manor."

"Wonderful. Is it far from here?" asked Lyla.

"No." A small smile crossed his face. "Not far at all."

"Do you not enjoy banking?" she asked, her eyes flicking to his hair.

"No not at all. Besides, there is so much more money to be made working the land." Pausing for a moment, Noah redirecting the conversation. "Do you remember we used to play together, when we were young?" he asked.

"We did?" Lyla drank deeply from her glass and looked at Noah curiously.

"Yes, many years ago. I think I might have been about eight years old. Our mothers have known each other for a long time."

"Forgive me, but I don't remember that."

He laughed. "It was a long time ago, and you are a few years younger than me." He winked at her. "We left and moved across the country when I was ten. My grandmother became quite ill, and my mother wanted to look after her."

"Oh, is your grandmother well now?"

"No, unfortunately she passed away a few months after we arrived. I fear my father has the same illness now. We moved back to our manor about a year ago, hoping the weather might be more suitable for his health." As Lyla noted the tears welling in his eyes, Noah quickly looked away, and she felt a pang of empathy for him.

"I am so sorry to hear that," she said softly as she reached out and placed her hand tenderly on his.

"No, please forgive me," Noah said as he rested his other hand on top of hers, gently pressing down. "I should not be ruining the mood of the evening with my sad stories."

Lyla shook her head. "You've not ruined anything. Thank you for being honest with me."

They sat together a little while longer, talking again of their childhood before she glanced across the room and her eyes settled on Duncan Saddler.

"I'm not ready to call it a night with you yet, but I must keep moving."

"Understandable." Noah stood and held the back of Lyla's chair so she could stand. Smiling politely and excusing herself, but promising to return later to chat more, she made her way to where the three Saddler family members sat.

"Good evening," she said as she approached the table. Duncan fumbled with his napkin before standing up too quickly, knocking his chair over behind him. The loud clatter it made as it hit the floor drew the room's attention.

"So sorry," he mumbled as he turned awkwardly, trying to stand the chair up. His father, shaking his head in bewilderment, leant over and picked it up for him, placing it a safe distance from Duncan's side.

"It's okay, accidents happen," Lyla said kindly, then waited expectantly for Duncan to introduce his parents. When he said nothing, Lyla cleared her throat and extended her hand to Duncan's father, who accepted it gently.

"Richard Saddler and my wife, Emily," he smiled courteously, but Lyla could tell from the flush in his cheeks that he was embarrassed. Not wanting to draw attention to it. Lyla took Emily's hand and squeezed it softly.

"Wonderful to meet the three of you. Thank you very much for coming today," she remarked politely. When Duncan remained silent, Lyla sat herself down in the empty chair and placed her half-empty glass on the table.

Richard, with a slight look of contempt, tugged slightly on Duncan's green jacket, prompting him to sit back down. Unable to sit, Duncan spun around, eyes wide in fear, searching for his missing chair. Seeing it off to the side, he fumbled briefly for it, his sweaty fingers slipping over the backrest before pulling it over, and plodding himself at the table, giving Lyla nervous sideways glances.

Smiling respectfully, allowing Duncan to settle, Lyla prompted a conversation with his parents.

"I hope your trip here was pleasant. I'm not sure how far you had to travel."

"It was, thank you," Richard replied. "We only live a few hours away."

"Your parents' manor is beautiful," commented Emily. "Much grander than ours."

"Thank you. I do hope you get a chance to walk through the gardens; Papa has done a splendid job lighting up the grounds."

"Well, that, sounds like a wonderful idea to me," Richard said, standing and offering his hand to Emily.

As they left, Lyla turned to Duncan.

"How are you going?" she asked.

"Um ... good," he replied, as he pushed his uneaten food around the plate.

"Are you enjoying the night?" Lyla tried again, knowing he was not, but needing to try anything to get him to talk.

"It's okay," he replied, his hazel eyes darting to her face and back to the table.

"Do you enjoy reading?" Lyla asked hesitantly, struggling to keep any conversation going.

"No," he replied quietly.

Noticing beads of sweat reforming across his brow and feeling the tension at the table, Lyla could see Duncan clearly did not want to be there. Not wanting to make him or herself any more uncomfortable than they were already, she decided her time would be more beneficial elsewhere.

"Thank you for coming tonight, Duncan, and please thank your parents. I know you have all come a long way."

Swallowing deeply, he nodded as Lyla stood, leaving her empty glass on the table and noticed his expression lightened as though the weight of the world, suddenly lifted off his shoulders.

"I hope you will save at least one dance for me tonight," she asked hopefully.

Standing quickly, and loudly knocking his chair over again, he nodded sharply, then turned away, his attention diverted to the chair on the floor.

Lyla walked away from the table, smiling politely at those watching. She felt slightly perplexed as to why her parents would choose someone like Duncan. With no confidence, or ability to talk to her or even look her in the eye, for longer than a few minutes, her brows furrowed in confusion.

Was he there because they could not find anyone else? Were there only four potential men who accepted her parents offer?

Shaking the thoughts from her head, Lyla moved to the main table and grabbed a small bunch of grapes. As she popped one in her mouth, Lyla crossed Duncan off the list, her night was looking easier than she thought.

The five possible suitors had now been reduced to only three.

Chapter 4

Bram Lawson's dark brown eyes locked onto Lyla's as she moved slowly away from the buffet table. With a sweet smile, still eating her grapes, Lyla sashayed her way across the room, to Bram and his parents.

"Good evening," he said, his deep voice polite and confident.

He extended a hand to Lyla and, placing hers in his, he promptly brought it up to his mouth. Carefully, he pressed his lips onto the back of her hand. Lyla was a bit surprised by the motion, but a warm feeling coursed through her skin, and she lowered her face to hide the flush in her cheeks.

"May I introduce you to my parents, Eric and Jacinta Lawson." He motioned to his parents, who both stood and greeted Lyla with affectionate smiles.

"Pleasure to meet you both," Lyla smiled as she extended her hands to them.

"Please sit down." Eric motioned to an empty chair, but before Lyla could move, Bram quickly stepped beside her, pulling the chair out, so she could easily move her dress under the table.

No sooner had Lyla sat when Eric wasted no time in talking. "So, if you pick my son, when do you think the wedding will be?"

"Eric!" Jacinta exclaimed, shocked at her husband's briskness.

"Father!" added Bram and glanced at Lyla, a deep shade of red flushing his cheeks.

"Please forgive my husband's rudeness. Sometimes he doesn't think before he speaks," Jacinta added through gritted teeth.

Eric sighed. "Apologies, but I was hoping if you chose Bram tonight, we could have the wedding at our manor. The garden would be the perfect place. The flowers will be in spectacular bloom in a few weeks, and it would have to be done relatively quickly. I have to go overseas on business."

Lyla's eyes widen slightly in astonishment. She had not considered having the wedding at her future in-laws' manor.

"Thank you very much for your offer, but I was planning to have the wedding here," she replied, hoping it would not upset Eric.

"That's fine. It was just a thought." He turned to Bram's mother and gave her a polite yet downcast smile.

"I'm sure your garden is wonderful, and I would love to see it," Lyla added quickly, seeing the disappointment in his face.

"And perhaps you shall," Jacinta added. Turning to Eric, she placed a tender hand on his arm. "I think the dessert table is calling us, dear."

With a polite nod, Eric and Jacinta left the table, allowing Bram and Lyla to talk alone.

"I'm so sorry about my father," Bram uttered, a hint of shame in his tone. "He can be a little forward."

Lyla sighed softly. "It's okay. This is an important night. My decision does not just affect me and my family. I'm sure he meant it well." Lyla fidgeted with her fingers, having nothing to do with her hands.

"Have you had any dessert yourself yet?" Bram asked.

"No," Lyla shook her head. "I haven't really eaten much at all tonight."

A look of dismay crossed Bram's face. "Wait right here," he said and stood abruptly. Dashing off, Lyla watched as he approached the large table, covered in cakes, jellies, fruit and cheeses, and brought back a small plate of food. Placing it in front of Lyla, he promptly sat back beside her.

"Can't have you passing out on us during the dancing because you were too busy to eat." He smiled warmly at her.

"Thank you," she replied, touched by his actions.

Trimming off a mouthful of Battenberg cake with her fork, the sweet apricot and marzipan cake, one of Lyla's favourites, she continued talking. "So, what do you do for a living?"

"I'm a clerk at my fathers' shipping company but would very much like to run my own business one day."

"Your own business?" Lyla inquired.

"Yes," he replied. "I have it all worked out." A look of pride gleamed in his eyes as he explained his plans. "I want to buy a few cargo ships of my own. Of course, starting with one and buying a few more once the business takes off, but I wouldn't work from the city. I want to live near the sea, close to the harbour, where I could manage the boats easier."

Lyla swallowed in surprise. "You want to live near the ocean?"

"Yes," he said with a smile. "I would love to watch my children and my wife enjoy the salty ocean air. I think it would be a great place to raise a family."

Lyla smiled. She had only been to the ocean a few times in her life. It was a long trip and far from home and posed big decision to make, if she were to pick Bram.

While finishing off her dessert plate, Lyla and Bram spoke about their thoughts on marriage, children, and their general likes and dislikes. Lyla smiled when Bram mentioned his love of horses. Although she did not ride them, she loved to be around them, nevertheless.

Glancing towards the dining room clock, Lyla noticed that time was passing by, and she still had two more suitors to talk to.

"I'm sorry to have to cut this conversation short, but I really do need to move on," she said, pushing her empty plate aside.

"I totally understand and hope we can talk more when we dance later tonight," Bram replied.

Lyla smiled sweetly as she stood. "I would like that very much." As she turned from his table, her eyes locked with Damien's. She had wanted to speak to him last, but now that he was staring straight at her, and motioning for her to sit next to him, Lyla conceded.

Making her way towards him via the drinks table, Lyla grabbed a glass of red wine, and navigating around the room, finally reached Damiens table.

In unison, Damien, and his parents stood.

"Lyla, may I present my parents, Arthur and Leona Olsen," Damien said as they both welcomed her.

With a gracious smile, Lyla thanked them both and, adjusting her dress, sat down at the table.

"How has your evening been?" asked Leona.

"It has been wonderful so far," Lyla replied, noting her hair was the same colour as her son's.

"Your parents have organised a wonderful Flowering day," said Arthur. "I can only hope one day we do something this grand as well for our daughter."

"I'm sure it will be lovely," Lyla replied and smiled tenderly at him.

"Well, I can see the night is pushing on. We will give you both some privacy." Leona stood, pulling on Arthur's arm. "Come on, my love, the garden awaits us."

Leaving Lyla alone with Damien, a wave of panic rushed over Lyla, and her palms became sweaty at his proximity. Unsure of what to talk about, Lyla took a deep sip of the red wine, the flavour bolder than the white wine she'd drank before and started with the basics.

"What do you do for a living, Damien?"

Damien scoffed slightly at her bluntness but answered her question dutifully.

"I work as a clerk in a high-end textile business in town. I'm hoping one day to open my own business, something where I sell goods like material and tailoring supplies."

"That sounds like a very busy job," Lyla commented.

"It is, but I wouldn't keep me from having a family or a wife."

Lyla blushed again. The thought of having children hadn't been a primary concern for Lyla until tonight when she realised how it important it appeared to be to her suitors. Feeling nervous again, she sipped her wine, unsure what to say.

"Happy birthday by the way," Damien said, breaking the silence.

Lyla frowned slightly and turned to look at him. "Thank you," she replied. "Do you know, you're actually the first person to say that to me tonight."

"I'm very sorry to hear that," he said with a hint of sorrow. "Well, in any case, I do hope that it's been a wonderful day so far."

Lyla nodded. "It has been," she said politely. "Very different to any others I've had." She smiled in humour.

"Did you receive any presents other than many, many flowers?" he continued.

"This dress actually." Lyla smiled and glanced down at her dress, a present gifted to her by her parents.

"And it is a beautiful dress. It suits you well," he added with a smile and Lyla felt surprised by his sincerity. Feeling the heat in her cheeks, Lyla turned away, hiding her face.

"Apologies, I didn't mean to embarrass you." Damien said, resting his hand on hers.

Turning back and gently slipping her hand out from under his, she grabbed her glass and took a long sip, finishing the wine. Returning the glass to the table, Lyla took in his coat and glanced back at her dress.

"Was it by chance that your suit matched the colour of my dress?" she asked bluntly, the wine making her feel a little bolder.

Damien stared at her for a moment before a sheepish grin crossed his face. "Would it be a bad thing if I had enquired about its colour?"

"I'm not sure, to be honest," she replied, and giggled as a brief sense of dizziness came over her.

The uncomfortable silence washed over the table again, and once more Lyla was at a loss for words. Fidgeting with the stem of her glass, Lyla licked her lips and smiled quietly when she could feel Damien staring at her.

"So," he said, once again breaking the silence. "I don't mean to push the subject, but how is it going with picking a suitor? Have you narrowed it down to one of the five of us?"

Another pang of guilt passed through Lyla as she glanced towards Duncan, Damien quickly following her gaze. What had her parents thought, picking him? Had there truly been no other suitor for her? The thought of standing next to Duncan, dressed in a splendid white dress, watching him stare at his feet instead of her, made Lyla laugh.

"What's so funny?" Damien asked.

"Sorry, I just had a silly thought about him," Lyla blurted out.

"Well, I mean, look at him. He looks like a fine catch to me, and I hear he has a great bug collection," Damien said with a chuckle.

Feeling the effects of the wine making her head spin, Lyla felt light as a feather. Although she had only consumed two glasses of wine, it was the first time she'd consumed this much, and she felt pleasantly happy.

Chuckling beside Damien, Lyla felt a new sense of ease wash over her. She had not expected to be laughing with the very guy who tormented her as a child. Until a moment of clarity washed over her, and realising her error, she turned to Damien. "Stop, that's not funny," she said abruptly.

Damien stopped laughing and ducked his head.

"Apologies, Lyla, I did not mean to make fun of him." As though sensing the tension, Damien changed the subject. "So, if you pick someone tonight, what are your plans for the wedding?"

Lyla glanced at him with a thrilled smile, the jesting towards Duncan already forgotten. So far, during the interactions she'd had with the other three suitors, none of them had asked her what *she* hoped would happen.

Feeling another mild rush from the wine, Lyla relaxed in her chair as she turned to face him.

"I would love to have the wedding here, in the ballroom. I have some great ideas on how I would like to see it decorated. Plus, the convenience of being at home to get ready."

"Of course," he said, listening intently. "Did you decorate the ballroom today?"

"No," she replied. "Although I did tell Mama the general idea for the colours. I am hoping to be fully involved with the wedding plans."

"I'm sure it will look wonderful." He smiled at her and held her gaze longer than necessary. Feeling the warmth in her cheeks intensify as they reddened, she turned and glanced across the room towards her parents.

Deep in conversation with Bram's parents, Lyla smiled softly.

"And your plans for after the wedding — is there a place you would like to go to spend some quality time with your new husband?" Damien asked, bringing Lyla's attention back to him.

"Oh, I hadn't thought about that. I assumed I would just move into our new house and begin my life as a wife."

Damien played with the fork on his empty plate. "If you picked me," he paused, "I would take you to London. Have you been to London before?"

Lyla's face brightened with excitement. "No, I have never been. My father always promised to take me, but with his work and the trip taking so long, it never happened."

Damien grinned in return. "Well, it would be my honour to take you, if I should be the lucky man."

Lyla dipped her head as an overwhelming feeling of guilt washed over her. Had she crossed Damien off her list too quickly? Could he have changed his ways after all, and could Lyla forgive him for his childhood behaviour?

Swallowing a lump in her throat, Lyla could not forget the torment nor the look in Jonathan's eyes when he saw him. If she picked Damien, she knew she needed to consider any risk there might be to her brother.

Glancing away, Lyla caught sight of the clock once more, and realising the time, knew she needed to keep moving.

"Thank you for talking to me, Damien, but I really must press on. One more suitor to go." She smiled, but it did not reach her eyes. As she stood, Lyla reminded herself that a leopard does not change its spots.

Chapter 5

Winston stood up politely and bowed his head as Lyla neared.

"So sorry to keep you all waiting," she commented, coming to a stop at the table.

"Not a problem. One of us has to be the last suitor for you to meet," he smiled gracefully. "May I introduce my parents, Marcus and Bethany Stuart." He waved his hand in their direction.

Marcus stood and took Lyla's hand, his large fingers dwarfing hers. "Pleasure to meet you, my dear." His voice was deep like Winston's, and his eyes were the same shade of green. With their similar suits, it was evident that Winston was just a younger version of his father.

"The pleasure is mine," Lyla replied, releasing his grip as she sat down, and turned to Bethany. "I absolutely love the necklace you are wearing." Lyla pointed to the gold and pearl necklace, which rested elegantly at the base of Bethany's neck.

"Thank you," Bethany replied with a smile as her hand instinctively reached for the pearls, which she stroked fondly. "They were a gift from Marcus on our wedding night." She smiled lovingly at him.

"Well," Lyla turned to Marcus. "You have excellent taste, sir."

Looking back at Bethany, Marcus smiled. "Yes, I certainly do." Lyla could see the love between Winston's parents, something she herself hoped would happen within her own marriage as the years passed.

Chatting to Winston and his parents, the time passed quickly. Simple conversations about the weather and Winston's thoughts of his future put Lyla at ease. The four of them got along very well.

After a few more minutes of talking, Marcus and Bethany excused themselves and left the table so Lyla and Winston could talk in private.

"Where would you like to live?" Winston asked, turning in his chair to face Lyla.

"Somewhere close to my family, I think, but not too close as to be … in their pockets, if you know what I mean."

"Would you move closer to the coast? I hear that the summer months there are wonderful."

"Oh, it had not crossed my thoughts of moving so far away." An interesting thought crossed her mind. Fancy chatting to two suitors who both wanted to live by the ocean. "Do you like it there?" she asked.

"I have been to visit the coast a few times over the past years, but have never lived there, although, with the work I wish to do, it could be a good opportunity."

"And what work would that be?" Lyla's interest peaked.

"I would like to run a shipping yard. My father and I have spent many years sailing, and I am well educated in boats and cargo."

Lyla's eyes widened and a small smile spread across her face.

"Does that please you?" Winston asked.

Lyla shook her head. "Sorry, it's just." She paused and her eyes flicked towards Bram briefly. "You're the second suitor tonight who has expressed an interest in working with boats, or should I say, wanting to own their own shipping company."

"Ah, it seems I have competition in more than one way." he smirked. "The shipping industry is very popular at the moment and would be a good company to own," Winston added. "The ocean is so vast and the opportunity to send goods to other countries is growing quickly."

"Sounds intriguing." Lyla said. "Personally, I have only been on small boats, on the lakes, never anything big enough to go out on the ocean."

"I think you would like ocean life. It would be a wonderful place to raise children."

Lyla choked slightly at the reminder of having children.

"Did I say something wrong?" he asked curiously, noting her reaction.

"No, not at all. Having children was not something I had thought would happen so soon after marriage, but it seems to be something everyone wants to know tonight."

"Do you not wish to be a mother?" he frowned.

"Yes, oh very much so. I just thought I wouldn't need to think about it for a few more years. I wanted to enjoy my marriage and my husband alone for a while first." Lyla blushed, feeling foolish. "Do you want children?"

"Yes, the sooner the better," he replied sheepishly. "I want boys to work alongside me, as I did with my father.

"No girls?" she asked, watching his blonde moustache as it twitched under his nose. Seconds later, Winston absently scratched his moustache and ran his fingers over his mouth, the movement stirring a dizzy and surprising wave of desire through her.

"A girl or two would be nice too. Especially if they looked like their mother." He smiled at her, causing her cheeks to grow hot again. All the talk of the future and children Lyla's head spinning more than the wine.

Deep in conversation with Winston, Lyla was shocked when the loud clinking of metal on glass, interrupted their conversation and a deafening silence, filled the room.

Glancing around, Lyla saw her father standing at the buffet table, a spoon and glass fixed firmly in his hands.

"Apologies for the interruption, but it is now seven thirty and the next step of Lyla's celebration has begun. If everyone is ready, we shall return to the ballroom for the dancing. Suitors," he said with a mischievous wink, "get ready to sweep my daughter off her feet!"

The room erupted in a round of laughter and cheers, and everyone stood, leaving their empty glasses and plates on the tables, as they meandered their way back to the large ballroom.

When Lyla finally stood to leave with Winston at her side, she felt a small pang of disappointment. Half the ceremony had now passed, and knowing she had to make an extremely hard decision in only two and a half hours sent a fierce wave of nerves coursing through her.

Before she left the dining room, Iris ran up to her side, grasping her sister's hand again.

"Oh, I can't wait for my Flowering Day," she expressed with such happiness.

"Are you enjoying yourself?" Lyla squeezed her sister's small hand.

"Oh, very much so." She paused, looking at Lyla tenderly. "Now that you have met all the suitors, do you know who you are going to pick tonight?"

Lyla and Iris slowed their walk down, taking advantage of being the last ones to make their way to the ballroom.

"I'm not sure yet."

"Oh, please pick Noah. He is such a gentleman," she said, and the flush in her cheeks didn't escape her older sister's notice.

"Oh, you really do like him, don't you?" Lyla smiled, a small laugh escaping her red lips.

"Well, he did promise me a dance tonight." Iris straightened her shoulders and stood a bit taller.

"Did he now?" Lyla said, her eyes alight with mirth.

"Do you think if you didn't pick him tonight, I might truly be able to on my Flowering Day?"

Lyla stopped walking just as they reached the ballroom doors. "I thought you said earlier he would be too old for you."

Iris's blush deepened, and she lowered her head, breaking eye contact. Lyla took both her hands in hers.

"I know you are only twelve, but when you turn eighteen, and if he is available and attends your Day, you would be very welcome to pick him." She leaned forward and placed a small kiss on Iri's forehead. "I must go again. Save a dance for me?" Iris nodded eagerly.

Lyla turned and stepped through the large doors and stopped beside her awaiting father, her eyes wide as she took in the changes which had taken place during dinner.

The flowers which carpeted the platform stairs, had been collected, placed into vases, and sat atop small tables dotted around the room. The large throne chair and the table holding the suitors' flowers had been pushed aside to allow for a small orchestra that began playing the opening of a quick waltz. Several guests wasted no time gathering on the dance floor and spun gracefully around the room.

Holding onto her father's arm, Lyla followed him onto the dance floor, where he placed his hand on her waist and twirled her around. Before long, the dance floor was full, and the music became more upbeat and rhythmic.

As she danced, Lyla took in the mirage of colours around her as the satin, silk, and lace gowns flowed and shimmered beneath the glow of the chandeliers. Between the beautiful dresses and endless flowers, the room was a rainbow of delightful colours set off against the men's dark suits. The scene before her was the most spectacular Lyla had ever witnessed.

"Are you enjoying the night?" her father asked over the music.

"Very much so."

"Are you still nervous?"

Lyla giggled. "Yes, I am unfortunately."

"It will pass once you have made your decision." He spun Lyla faster and faster, through the dancers. The skirt of her dress flowed out around her, her head spinning just enough to see the room shimmer, making her laugh.

"I know you will make the right choice tonight," he said tenderly.

"I hope so, Papa."

As the music slowed while the musicians seamlessly eased into the next song, Bram appeared at their side.

"Good evening, sir, would you mind if I cut in?" he asked politely. Her father smiled, happily stepping aside as he passed Lyla's hands into Bram's.

"Thank you, sir," he said as he placed his left hand softly onto Lyla's waist. As the music started up again — a simple violin sonata — Bram pulled Lyla in closer, and they danced into the centre of the room. "Are you still enjoying yourself?" he whispered in her ear, his warm breath ticking the skin on her neck.

Lyla's eyes closed briefly as a pleasant shudder surged over her shoulders. Inhaling slightly, to clear her mind, Lyla took in the sweet orange blossom and woody scent of Bram's cologne. With a small sigh, she smiled. "Yes, yes, I am."

"I hope you aren't feeling too pressured into making a choice tonight?"

"No, I think I will be okay. Although I do feel for you boys knowing my decision will upset at least three of you."

As she pulled back and glanced at his face, she found his brown eyes wide.

"Three of us? I thought there were five suitors!"

Lyla glanced over to where Duncan was dancing slowly and awkwardly with his mother. "I don't think Duncan wants to be here, so I don't believe he will be very disappointed if I do not pick him," she said honestly. "So that will leave three of you, unless you do not wish for a union." She looked earnestly at Bram, but a light teasing smile lingered on her lips.

"I would be honoured to be picked tonight, if it is your decision." The intensity of his gaze made her heart skip. Bram was a close contender for her top pick. Only one year older than her, and with their fathers work colleagues, Lyla could see that a marriage between them could be beneficial. Bram's future would follow suit in his father's business, which was a career Lyla knew well.

Lyla could feel the warmth of his hand through the layers of her dress, and his grip was strong yet light. Having only really danced with her papa and Jonathan in the past, being this close to Bram, and knowing she would be dancing close to four other men tonight, Lyla blushed at the thought of the close proximity to the men.

Bram confidently led her across the dancefloor in a way that made her feel as though she was floating. They danced together through two more songs as the orchestra beautifully evoked emotions through its violins and cello. Twirling around the room, Lyla felt her heart soar.

Just as the song ended, Winston stepped forward. "May I have the next dance?" Bram politely stepped aside and picked a new partner himself, leaving Lyla to dance on.

"I think you are about the right height for me," Winston joked as he looked down at Lyla. He grabbed her hand and twirled her out and back in.

"Is that so?" she questioned, a look of mirth on her face again.

"Yes, too short and I would be looking over your head the whole time. Too tall, and I would feel less like the man in the relationship."

Lyla laughed. "This is an interesting way to look at a future partner. I did not realise my height might be an issue."

"Like I said, you are the right height, so it is not an issue for me, unless you think I am too tall or too short for you?"

"It honestly wasn't something that crossed my mind." With that thought, Lyla glanced casually around the room, locating each of the other suitors. During her earlier discussions, she never noted the height differences between the five men.

At five-foot, six inches, Lyla was of average height, the same as her mother. Dancing with Winston, she noticed that the top of her head was level with his nose. Bram was slightly taller. She realised if she were to dance with Duncan, he would tower over her, as he was well over six foot. Daring a look at Damien, she could see he was about the same height as Winston, and Noah was the shortest of them all, but still taller than her.

Bringing her attention back to Winston, they danced effortlessly across the floor, weaving in and out of the other couples. Lyla took the opportunity to take in his features up close. With his blond hair, and fair skin like hers, and his green eyes, meant that if she were to pick him, any children they might have would look just like them.

Winston was an excellent dancer—seamlessly transitioning tempo as the music played, swinging and sashaying her across the floor.

"You dance very well," Lyla commented, unable to wipe the smile from her face.

"Thank you," he replied, pulling her a fraction closer and Lyla's heart skipped a beat. "My mother believes all men should know how to dance and sweep a lady off her feet." A sheepish grin spread across his cheeks.

"Well, I very much approve of her opinion," Lyla said, her own smile widening.

"Do you like the theatre?" Winston asked, lowering his face closer to Lyla's.

"Yes, I do," she replied, taking in the sweet scent of Winston's aftershave—musky, with a hint of pine and wood.

"I would very much like to take you, given the opportunity. There is a new show on that I think you might like."

"That would be wonderful if the opportunity arises," Lyla smiled again, noting how at ease she felt with Winston. The music changed again, and Lyla and Winston danced on. Although they spoke little, Lyla felt impressed with how comfortable she was with him. Both Bram and Winston had certainly made good impressions.

"If you will excuse me," Lyla said as the song ended. "I'm in dire need of some refreshments."

"I'll happily escort you," Winston smiled, offering his arm before leading her to a large table, where glasses of fine wine, ale and juice were available.

Finishing a refreshing glass of ginger beer, knowing she'd had enough wine for one night, Lyla smiled at Winton. "As much as I've enjoyed our time together, I really should move along," she said, a hint of sadness in her tone.

"I completely understand. Find me later if you wish to dance again." Winston bowed slightly and, with no objection, made his was over to Lyla's mother, who stood not too far away. She watched as Winston asked her mama to dance, smiling to herself as her mother blushed and accept his hand. She gazed lovingly as Winston led her mother to the dance floor and proceeded to waltz her across the floor.

Glancing around the room, Lyla's attention was diverted as her eyes settled on Duncan, standing at the far end of the room. He was alone and looking extremely uncomfortable, keeping his eyes downcast as he shuffled from foot to foot as though desperately trying to blend in with the wall behind him. With a sigh, Lyla straightened her dress at the waist and walked over to him.

With so many people in the room, it was hard to walk without someone wanting to stop her to talk, and Lyla smiled, nodded, and answered politely as she pushed her way through the crowd.

After a few slow minutes, she approached Duncan, who looked mildly shocked to see her standing in front of him.

"Would you like to dance, Duncan?" she asked tentatively, holding out her hand to him.

He smiled shyly and extended his hand forward, placing it carefully into Lyla's. With a small nod, Lyla led the way, Duncan following behind. Stepping onto the already crowded dance floor, Lyla was right in assuming that Duncan would tower over her.

Awkwardly, and seemingly more than a little unsure of himself, Duncan placed his hand so lightly on Lyla's hip that she couldn't be certain that he was even touching her. His other hand felt cold and clammy, covered in a light layer of sweat. Stepping closer to him, Lyla breathed in his sweaty body aroma. Noting the moisture gathering around his collar, Lyla tilted her face to look away slightly, grateful for the fresh air that blew into the room from two large open doors leading outside.

In the back of her mind, Lyla again wondered why her parents would have picked Duncan as a suitor. She tried to make small talk, but he was so shy that trying to engage him caused Lyla to grow a little frustrated.

"Is there anything you are passionate about, Duncan?" Lyla tried one last time.

"Well, yes," he replied nervously, with a slight squeak in his voice. "I study entomology."

Lyla smiled but shook her head slightly. "I must admit, I am not sure what that means."

"I study bugs and insects, and own an enormous collection at home," he said, his face finally glowing with pride. "If you were ever interested, I would be happy to show it to you."

"Oh," she said, understanding Damien's comment about the bug collection. "That would be a wonderful thing to see," Lyla replied, happy to see Duncan smile for the first time that night.

They danced together for two more songs, trying to avoid tripping over each other's feet. Yet, when the third song picked up the tempo, Lyla thanked Duncan for the dance and politely excused herself. Knowing she had confirmed he was not in the running to be her suitor, she felt that she'd done her duty towards him but didn't want to waste any more of their time.

With an expression that Lyla could only interpret as relief, Duncan left the dance floor and returned to his place against the wall.

With time rapidly passing her by, Lyla knew there were still two more gentlemen awaiting their dance, so she pushed on.

Scanning the crowd, Lyla finally located Noah talking with her brother. Although they appeared to be deep in conversation, she knew time was of the essence, and she forced herself to politely interrupt. The alternative was dancing with Damien, but she still hadn't worked out how to deal with that dilemma yet.

Despite his politeness and the ease with which they had talked—as though he really had changed—Lyla still could not shake the vivid memories of how he used to tease her and her siblings.

So, walking around the outskirts of the ballroom, passing the guests, Lyla made her way over to Noah.

"Shall we?" Lyla asked as she smiled up at Noah.

"Yes, please," he smiled, nodding at Jonathan as he accepted her outstretched hand and escorted her onto the floor. The orchestra played a soothing waltz, and Lyla and Noah danced effortlessly amongst the other dancers. With his hand placed gently on Lyla's back, Noah pulled her in carefully as he leaned down to murmur in her ear.

"How has your night been so far?"

Lyla smiled softly. "Fairly good, actually." She looked into his blue eyes as he smiled back.

"I hope you are enjoying the dancing and food. Despite what happens at the end of the night, I do hope it has been a special birthday for you to remember."

"I cannot compare it to any other. It has certainly been the best yet." Lyla smiled softly to herself as she inhaled the sweet scent of his aftershave. Unlike the other three men she had danced with, Noah's aftershave reminded Lyla of being in the garden. The scent of lavender and pine lingered at his throat, instantly putting her at ease. Although she had not been opposed to the scent of the other three men, besides Duncan's sweaty aroma, the familiarity in Noah's aftershave gave Lyla a sense of belonging.

With a mischievous grin, Noah spun Lyla around and giggled with glee.

"What?" Lyla asked, noting his smile and unable to hold back her own.

"Even without knowing who the other suitors were, I didn't think for a second I stood a chance. Yet here, dancing so closely I feel it in my heart that I just might … possibly … be your chosen one," he replied.

Lyla's heart skipped a beat as a flutter of emotions she could not fully understand rushed through her.

"That is very presumptuous of you," she teased. "The night is not yet over."

"That is true," he replied. "But there is something about how I feel with you in my arms. It's like … you belong." Noah smiled and spun her round. Despite the song ending, and a new sonata beginning, Lyla remained in his arms.

Lyla could feel the warmth in his firm yet tender hold on her hand as they moved through the other dancers. Feeling extremely comfortable with Noah, she understood what he meant and began to struggle with the decision she inevitability needed to make. Even with one suitor left on her dance card, despite not being high on her list, Lyla could not decide which man led the pack.

Trying hard to remain in the moment, Lyla looked back into Noah's eyes. Noah seemed like a good fit and having known each other in the past could be a good thing. A little history, something to tell friends and family, that they might have been destined to be together from an early age. Plus, knowing their mothers were friends assured her that their families would get along very well.

Then again, a marriage to Damien could prove successful too. Despite his past, he came from a respectable family. He was only two years older, worked as a clerk in a high-end business, with many positive plans for his future, and tonight, he had proven himself to be a gentleman. Polite, respectful, and courteous—nothing like he was before.

Plus, a point she had not considered prior to the night commencing, was the role of attraction in her decision. Lyla had not thought looks would be a reason to pick one suitor over another. Yet, seeing Damiens face in her mind, and the handsome man he had grown into, she shook her head slightly, trying to free herself of the image.

"Are you alright?" Noah asked, his expression filled with so much concern that Lyla giggled.

"Yes, I'm fine, just a silly thought went through my head, that's all."

"Not about me, I hope!" Noah asked nervously.

"No, not at all. There is just a lot going on up there."

"I bet there is. I am sure you will make the right choice, but I do not envy you, for the position you're in."

"Tradition is hard to turn away from," she sighed.

"Yes, and you still have two more sisters who will need to go through this too."

Lyla glanced across the dance floor to where Iris danced with their father, and Emily danced with Bram. They looked happy dancing together. It was nice to see him trying to get to know her sister, knowing they could potentially become family.

"Out of curiosity, what happens to you and the other suitors if I don't pick you?" Lyla asked as she turned her attention back to Noah.

"You really want to know?" he said, slowing their dancing down.

"Yes, I do."

He looked her straight in the eye, his voice becoming stoic and serious. "We lock ourselves up in our rooms, and stay there until we die, withered old men, denied of all love and hope in our lives!"

Lyla's eyes widened, and her mouth fell open as she stopped dancing, lost for words.

"I'm joking," Noah laughed, giving Lyla's back a slight nudge. "You should see your face!"

"I really believed you then!" She gave him a gentle slap on his shoulder, only causing Noah to laugh harder as he pulled her gently back into the dance.

"So, what does happen then?"

"We go back to what we were doing, and we wait till the next offer comes up. We marry women of lesser class or standing, those who cannot afford a lavish Flowering Day like this or if we are not chosen, we remain alone for the rest of our lives."

"Does that happen a lot?" Lyla pushed.

"What, that some men are never picked as the suitable husband?"

"Yes."

"Yes, it does."

The very thought made her feel sad as she unwittingly cast a glance in Duncan's direction. "What becomes of them?" Lyal asked softly.

"They continue working and many seek … *other* types of companionship." Lyla frowned, not quite understanding his meaning. "Some frequent the … Gentlemen's Clubs," he said discreetly.

"Oh, I see, Lyla replied.

"It is a hard time for men, and it is understandable that women in today's society get to pick the suitor they believe will secure a good profitable marriage, but most unwed men eventually die alone, some never marrying, nor having children to continue their bloodlines."

"Oh, that's sad."

"That's just how it is unfortunately. Most men do marry, Lyla. As do most women, just not always into influential families or arranged marriages."

Lyla continued to dance with Noah for another two songs, their chatter casual. Eventually, her eyes fell upon Damien, where he stood watching, patiently waiting for his turn.

Casting her eyes on the grandfather clock, Lyla was shocked to see and hour had past, and she stopped dancing. "I do hate to end this, but I must move on. One more suitor, unfortunately," Lyla said as she forced herself to release Noah's hand.

"I completely understand." He bowed low and turned around politely, leaving Lyla standing at the edge of the dance floor.

Chapter 6

Before Lyla took one step in Damien's direction, Jonathan appeared before her.

"May I have this dance, please?"

"Thank you, Jon, but I really do need to dance with Damien."

"I know, but please, just one dance with me," he asked, his blue eyes pleading. "Please."

"Is everything alright?" she asked as she stepped back onto the dance floor.

Jonathan looked at her, and then over to Damien. "Please," he begged as he took her hand and swept them both up in the dance. "Please don't pick him!"

Lyla didn't need to ask to know who he referred to. "I know what he did to you, Jon, what he did to all of us," she said softly.

"So, you have already made up your mind regarding him?" he asked, the hope in his voice evident.

"I can't say for now," Lyla replied and felt Jonathan's hand tighten around hers. "I have to give him a chance, like all the others."

"So?" he swallowed thickly. "You are saying he has just as much chance of being your husband as the other four?"

"Maybe," she replied, knowing it wasn't what Jonathan wanted to hear.

"And what happens if he just goes back to treating me like he used to?" he mumbled, though Lyla could feel the tension coming off him in waves as he whirled her across the floor. "I don't know if I can handle having him in my family!"

Lyla sighed. "He seems to be a different person now. He has grown up since then."

Jonathan shook his head. "I don't trust him. You can't seriously think he's the right person for you! Please, I am begging you. Please do not pick him!" A glint of moisture beaded in the corner of his eyes, and Lyla felt overwhelmed as she glanced towards Damian.

He was still watching her, and when their eyes met, he frowned slightly. Lyla smiled weakly at him and turned her head back to her brother.

"I am so deeply sorry for everything he put you through, but I must dance with him. I've yet to make up my mind on who I am going to pick. But whoever I do choose," she paused, looking tenderly up at him. "I do hope I have your blessing."

With a curt nod, he abruptly stopped dancing, and with a quick bow, stormed off the dance floor. Within seconds, Damien stood at her side.

"Just one or two songs is all I ask," he said, his tone polite but emotionless.

"It would be my honour," Lyla replied, forcing a small smile on her face, and Damien stepped forward and took her hand in his. He placed his other hand around her waist and, as a new piano sonata began, he led them across the floor.

Jonathan had a point, but she needed to make a wise choice tonight, and it had to be her decision alone.

"Is everything okay?" Damian asked.

"Yes, everything is fine," Lyla replied with her sweetest smile, however disingenuous.

"No worries." He turned his head slightly, looking away from her.

Lyla felt the discomfort ebbing from Damien, which did little to abate her concern. She'd seen him watching her interaction with her brother and would have obviously noticed he was not happy.

"My brother … has concerns," she breathed, feeling the need to explain.

"I thought as much. I would be too if my sister were having her Flowering Day."

Lyla looked at him but could not hold the gaze for long. "Would you tell her not to pick a suitor?"

"I would if a suitor were not a good match for her. To protect her." He looked at her, slowing their dance down. "Is this what Jonathan did?"

Lyla swallowed slowly. "Something like that."

A small smile crept onto his face, and he let out a small chuckle. "Did he ask you not to pick me?" he questioned, a hint of amusement in the tone, but Lyla could see he was offended.

Lyla paused for a second, but Damien pulled her back into the dance, as though not to arouse any suspicion of the tense moment between them. She turned her head away from him, not wanting to look into his dark blue eyes, but as she did, she caught a whiff of his heady cologne.

The spicy yet woody scent, with a hint of citrus, immediately relaxed Lyla. Visions of being outside, in the orchard, flicked through her mind, as if she were remembering a specific event, but could not place the memory.

"I will not be offended, milady, if you do not pick me. There are some fine young gentlemen here, who would make great a match, besides me," he said, pulling her from her thoughts. As she looked up at him, their eyes locked in an intense gaze as he smiled at her. "Although, I'm not sure what it is I have done to make him ask you to not to pick me."

Lyla's eyes widened a fraction, the thoughts of his cologne forgotten in an instant. "Really?" she exclaimed a little too loudly and dropped his hand. Damien looked a little stunned as they abruptly stopped in the middle of the dance floor.

"Forgive me. I am not sure I know what I have done to offend you," he said quietly, as his hand fell from her waist. "I have tried to engage in conversations with him and your sisters, but to no avail."

"Unbelievable! You are … infuriating!" Lyla hissed and spinning on her heel, stormed off towards the dining room, where she marched out the far doors to a large outdoor veranda.

"Lyla. Please stop," Damien said, sounding bewildered as he followed closely. Stunned that he'd dared to follow her, she spun around to confront him. Gently, he placed a hand on her arm as he stared at her, his expression full of sincerity. "What have I done to offend you and your brother?"

"You can stop the games, Damien. You know what you did!" she said, her head pounding with frustration. With wide eyes, he opened his mouth before closing it again, diverting his gaze to where his hand still rested on her arm as he released her. "Forgive me, but I honestly do not know my error," he whispered, as though not wanting to draw attention.

"All these years, did you really think we would all just forget?" Lyla clenched her fists at her side and stared hard into his blue eyes as the rage from her past brimmed.

"Forget what?" His eyes searched hers as he took a step closer to her, closing the gap.

Lyla spun on heels; the skirt of her dress swishing as she took a few steps away from Damien.

"Please, Lyla. Please tell me what I have done. I am at a loss for words," Damian said as he quickly cut in front of her, forcing her to halt her steps, his expression pleading.

"Have you truly forgotten what you used to do to my poor Jonathan all those years ago? What you did to my dear sisters and me?" Lyla felt the hot sting of tears, which only infuriated her further.

Damien's eyes softened as his gaze ran over her face as though he could somehow find the answers there. "What did I do? Please, Lyla!"

"Every time you and your family came to visit, you incessantly teased and tormented Jonathan, and when you weren't harassing him, you teased me and ridiculed my sisters!" As her breath caught in her throat, Lyla hung her head in embarrassment and anger, yet she could feel the intensity of Damien's eyes upon her.

"I ..." He paused, prompting Lyla to look up as he swallowed thickly, his Adam's apple rising in his throat. "I am so sorry." He shook his head and reached out for Lyla, but she stepped backwards. "I was a foolish young boy. Forgive me Lyla. It would never have been my intent to hurt you or your siblings."

"Intent or not, it is exactly what you did!" she snapped. "And clearly, Jonathan still fears you!" Lyla turned away from Damien and leaned against the banister, which ran the length of the veranda. A single tear rolled down her cheek.

Without looking up, Lyla felt Damien move beside her. As he placed his hand next to hers, but not close enough to touch, a breeze blew past Damien, bringing with it, the alluring scent of his cologne. The aroma stopped her heart, and she squeezed her eyes tight and turned away - it was all she could do to refrain from looking at him.

"I swear on my honour, I have changed. I am no longer the ignorant and thoughtless boy I once was, and I am ashamed of my past behaviours. Never would I do anything to hurt you, your sisters, or your dear Jonathan again." He moved his hand ever so slightly, so the tip of his index finger rested against her little finger.

Before she could stop herself, Lyla opened her eyes, and as she turned to face him, another tear ran down her cheek. Without hesitation, Damien lifted his hand and brushed the tear away with his thumb. Lyla's breath hitched at his touch, and she closed her eyes again, her heart thundering in her chest.

"Please forgive me for any wrongdoing I did to you and your siblings. I am so deeply sorry to have hurt you all," he pleaded as his hand brushed the skin along the top of her arm. She shuddered slightly at the touch. Dropping his hand to his side, he hung his head. "I understand if you don't pick me tonight." He stepped a few paces away from her. "I will not be offended."

Lyla looked at him, unsure of what to say or do. How could he have forgotten all those moments in the past? Now that he claimed to have grown into a mature man, could he really be a different person?

Lyla's thoughts swam. Unsure if it were the wine, the excitement of the night, or Damien's apology for the things he could not remember doing. Staring into the nights sky, Lyla focused on controlling her breathing. Feeling a calm wash over her, Lyla released the banister, and she turned to face him.

"I will accept your apology, Damien, as you appear to be genuine, but I am not the only person you need to apologise to. You will need to seek forgiveness from Jonathan, Emily, and Iris, but I am not sure if you will get it from them." She held her hands together, resting them gently on her dress.

"Yes, yes, I can do that," he replied softly.

Her head still a wash of confusion and unsure of what she wanted to do next, a sense of relief washed over her as she noticed Bram stepping through the doors. Making eye contact with him, she sighed as he approached.

"There you are!" he said as he sauntered over to them. As though sensing the tension between them, Bram moved to Lyla's side. Placing his hand gently on her lower back, he spoke to her directly. "Is everything alright?"

"Yes, fine, thank you. Your timing could not have been more perfect." Lyla squared her shoulders, wiped away the moisture beneath her eyes, and turned to face Bram. "Shall we?" She held her hand out to Bram. With a slight frown crossing his forehead, he shifted his focus to Damien, but Damien said nothing. Instead, he gave Bram a polite nod and an uneasy smile.

Returning his gaze to Lyla, Bram extended his arm out for Lyla to hold. Lyla tucked her hand into the crook of Bram's elbow and together, they disappeared through the doors, leaving Damien alone.

Chapter 7

"Would you care to dance again, or perhaps you would prefer a glass of wine?" Bram suggested.

"A glass of wine would be wonderful." She steadied her posture again as they walked over to the buffet table.

"Is everything alright with Mister Olsen?"

"Everything is as it should be," Lyla replied as she grabbed a glass of white wine and took a deep drink. Bram looked a little perplexed but smiled anyway.

"I can't say I understand your meaning," he confessed. "But at least the night is almost over."

"Is it?" Lyla replied, her eyes wide as she looked towards the grandfather clock — it was eight forty-five.

Had the time really passed so quickly?

"Will you excuse me for a moment? I need to find my mother." Lyla said abruptly and placed the glass back on the table. Not waiting for an answer, she strode back into the ballroom and found her mother sitting with her sisters.

"Mama," she said as she leant forward. "May I please have a little chat with you?"

"Of course, my dear." She stood and squeezed Iris's hand. "I will be back soon." Clasping Lyla's hands in her own, her mother smiled and walked with her to a small sitting room, just off the ballroom. It was a small space, beautifully decorated in light blue and silver tones. Pulling Lyla over to the ornate mahogany sofa, her mother sat her down and squeezed herself next to her.

"Are you getting nervous?" she asked, placing her hands on Lyla's knee.

"I have been nervous the whole night, Mama."

"And I suppose a little anxious, too?" her mother said, her eyebrows raised slightly.

Lyla nodded. "How …" Lyla paused. "How did you know father was the right choice?"

"I'm not sure." Her mother paused as well. "It wasn't an easy choice, truth be told."

"Really?"

"Yes. At the end of my night," Lyla's mother straightened and smiled sheepishly. "I had two suitors, whom I was very much … attracted to. It was only as I stood up at the table that my heart chose your father's flower."

"Have you ever regretted your decision?"

"Never in a heartbeat." She grasped Lyla's hands in hers. "Tell me, my child, what is the issue you have?"

"I … I do not know who to pick!" She lowered her eyes, suddenly feeling like she had let down her parents.

Her mother smiled. "If you cannot choose tonight, then we can try again in a few months. If there is not a suitor you feel one hundred percent comfortable with, we can find new ones. Your father and I have never wanted you girls to marry, just for the sake of it. We both want you all to be completely happy in your choices."

Lyla's heartbeat faster, and she smiled with relief. "Thank you, Mama." She leant forward and placed a small kiss on her mother's cheek.

"Come on, it must be almost time." Her mother stood, pulling Lyla up as well.

"At least one more hour, Mama," she replied, glancing at the small clock perched on the mantel over the fireplace.

Straightening her dress and fixing her hair in the mirror, Lyla sighed deeply. The night *was* almost done, and she still had time to dance with the suitors again if necessary, or family, but she would need to face her suitors one last time.

Returning to the ballroom, Lyla danced with her grandfathers and uncles, her father again, and once more with Bram, Winston, and Noah, keeping her distance from both Duncan and Damien.

In between the dancing, small plates of food were placed on the tables in the room, and Lyla nibbled on the light sandwiches, pastries, and fruits, knowing she had eaten little that night. When she was not dancing or eating, Lyla made sure she was with company, chatting to her friends as they questioned her.

Who was in the lead? Who was definitely not a contender? Who did they think she should pick.

Continuing to mingle, Lyla caught up with her sisters, aunts and uncles, grandparents and parents of the suitors, anyone to keep her distracted from Damien and Jonathan, who she knew, would have seen the commotion.

At nine fifty, the orchestra wrapped up its last song, and the dancing stopped. Standing on the platform, tall and proud, Lyla's father clinked two glasses together, grabbing everyone's attention.

Once everyone turned and focused on Albert, he addressed the room. "Thank you all for coming to Lyla's Flowering Day Ceremony. It has been a wonderful night of friendship, food, and dancing. We would like to extend our sincere appreciation to the five suitors and their parents for graciously accepting our invitations and joining us this evening." A small round of applause erupted, as Albert smiled and nodded to the five men around the room.

"I would like to thank our families for joining us tonight, and to Lyla's friends. I am aware that some of you have come from quite a distance. For that, we are eternally grateful." There was another round of applause as everyone cheered.

"But the moment has finally arrived when Lyla needs to make her choice." An apprehensive hush fell over the room. "As traditions go, Lyla will pick one flower from the five she received today. The suitor who presented that flower will be deemed the lucky husband-to-be." With a broad smile, Albert turned to Lyla. "If everyone could please move to the centre of the room, we shall get the final part of the night underway."

Passing the glasses to a waiter, he motioned for Lyla to join him. Lyla carefully lifted the front of her ballgown as the crowd parted, allowing her to make her way over to the platform. With a deep breath, she ascended the three stairs and faced the crowded room. While she watched on, the five suitors gathered in a line at the foot of the stairs.

While her father had been talking, the orchestra had discreetly moved off the platform and now, just to the right of Lyla, only two steps away, stood the table with the five flowers. A pink rose, a yellow daffodil, a red rose, a blue iris, and a white carnation.

Lyla looked at all the faces glancing up at her and an overwhelming sense of fear pulsed through her.

Suddenly, the grandfather clock struck ten. Lyla's heartbeat thundered in time with each chime. Closing her eyes, Lyla breathed in as deeply as she could as her father kissed her on the forehead.

"All the best, sweetheart," he whispered before leaving the platform to take his place beside his wife.

Opening her eyes, Lyla smiled tentatively at her parents. The moment that they had all been waiting for had finally arrived.

Glancing down at the five suitors, she nervously looked at each of the men she'd spent the night getting to know.

Bram, the first on her left, stood completely still as he met her gaze with a gentle smile and a soft nod. He had made her feel happy, relaxed and at ease throughout the night and Lyla returned his smile tenderly.

Bram was a desirable choice.

Next, she trailed her eyes over Duncan, who was still shuffling from one foot to the other, not daring to look at her. Despite the attempts to engage in conversation and dance with him, Lyla knew he has not one of her choices, but in her mind, she wished him all the best, hoping one day he would find a suitable wife.

Sighing softly, she moved her eyes to Winston. He stood tall and proud, the middle suitor of the five, a confident look on his face that put her at ease. Lyla smiled softly as their eyes locked. She had enjoyed their conversations, his wit, and his plans for his future, despite the possibility of moving to the ocean. Lyla found him attractive, and he was one of her top choices. He returned her smile, his eyes bright and hopeful yet Lyla was still unsure who to choose.

Next, Lyla looked at Noah, who seemed to be holding his breath, and she smiled in the hopes it would help him relax. Funny, polite, a pure gentleman. Easy to talk to, a good dancer, and despite her not wanting to judge people by their looks, there was no denying he was handsome.

Seeing her smile, Noah released his breath and smiled back nervously.

Three potential choices, three potential husbands to be.

Finally, her eyes settled on Damien, standing at the right end of the row. His fixed stare didn't make her feel as uncomfortable as it had when he first walked into the ballroom, but there was still a hint of uncertainty around him. After leaving him out on the veranda, she had not watched where he had gone. Had he apologised to her siblings? She was unsure. Lyla nodded slightly to him, which he reciprocated.

Lyla looked down at the table with the five flowers. All she had to do was walk over and pick up the flower that belonged to the man she would now choose to be her husband. The man she would marry and spend the rest of her life with. Once she held the flower in her hand, the decision would be final.

Taking two bold steps forward, she closed the gap. Her heart was beating so fast, she worried everyone could hear it. With her right-hand hovering over the table, the room fell into a deep silence. All eyes were on her.

Realising she was holding her breath, Lyla forced herself to release it as she decisively lowered her hand and gently grasped the stem of a flower with her delicate fingers. Gracefully, she raised her hand and turned towards the five suitors.

In one fluid movement, four of the suitors took two steps backwards, leaving the owner of the flower standing alone.

Chapter 8

First, Lyla met Duncan's gaze and smiled. With an exceptionally large sigh of relief, Duncan's shoulders dropped, and for the first time that night he smiled back and gave a simple nod of gratitude.

Lyla's eyes then trailed to Bram, and a touch of sadness crossed her heart. Bram was visibly upset, the sorrow in his eyes unmistakable, but he politely smiled and bowed. Although she thought he would make a wonderful husband, she knew in her heart the relationship would not be as fulfilling as she wanted.

Turning her head to the right, Lyla next looked at the suitor at the end of the line. With a kind smile, she nodded her thanks to Damien — a thank you for attending the night, but also an acknowledgement that she hadn't chosen him. Damien gave Lyla a slight shrug of his shoulders, then bowed low, swinging his hand in front of himself in acceptance.

As the last of the unchosen suitors, Noah looked up at her, his smile strained as he nodded his acknowledgement, yet the grim expression on his face told her he was not happy with her decision. As their gaze lingered, Noah raised his eyebrows slightly and tilted his head as though willing her to change her mind. With a sorrowful smile, she did not.

Finally, Lyla turned and looked most tenderly at Winston. The wide smile on his face made her heart skip a beat; all the confirmation she needed that she'd made the right decision. With trembling hands, Lyla moved to the top of the steps and held out the deep red rose that Winston placed on the table only a few hours ago.

"Winston, would you be my suitor, my friend, my lover and my husband, till death do us part?"

Stepping forward, Winston climbed the two steps and accepted the rose, his fingers brushing against Lyla's, sending a tingle of warmth through her skin.

"It would be my honour."

She smiled up at him, taking in the way his dark green eyes sparkled with happiness. Everything else faded away as he moved closer and placed a hand tenderly on her cheek before bringing his lips to hers. A kiss to seal the offer.

Suddenly, the room erupted in cheers, laughter, and clapping. Her parents rushed forward and wrapped Lyla and Winston in a group hug. Lyla's Flowering Day ceremony finally ended, and it had been a success.

"Welcome to the family, Winston." Lyla's father gripped Winston's hand, shaking it with enthusiasm.

"Thank you, sir."

"Oh, sweetheart, I'm so happy for you," her mother whispered in Lyla's ear.

Lyla and Winston turned to face the room as everyone gathered at the bottom of the platform. Slowly, Lyla and Winston made their way down the stairs and into the arms and hands of Lyla's family and friends.

Moving through the crowd, they accepted hugs, kisses, and praises of "congratulations," "well done" and "what a smart match" ringing in their ears, including a tight embrace from Bethany.

"Oh, welcome to our family," she said, squeezing Lyla. "Marcus and I are so happy you picked our son."

"Thank you," Lyla replied, unable to take the smile off her face. Not only was Lyla happy with the choice she made, but she was also happy his parents were so loving and welcoming.

Moving away, Lyla watched Iris run towards her, and leaning down, embracing her little sister tightly.

"Oh, I would have preferred you picked Noah, but Winston is a rather good-looking man," she said into Lyla's ear.

"Well, I'm glad you sort of like my choice," Lyla giggled. Iris pulled back and stared up at her.

"I am very happy for you," she said with a tender and sincere smile before turning to Winston, offering her hand. "And welcome to our family." Winston shook her hand in thanks. "Treat her well, or you might have to deal with me!" Iris said firmly.

"Iris!" Lyla's eyes widened and despite her cheeky smile, knew Iris was only half-joking.

"I would never dare hurt her, but I consider myself well warned, milady," Winston replied with a stoic bow. Iris broke out into a fit of laughter, and Winston and Lyla joined in.

"Forgive my little sister," Lyla said after they all composed themselves. "She can be a little strict and pushy."

"What can I say? Someone here has to act like the adult!" Iris said with a shrug, and Winston laughed again as he turned to Lyla.

"I'm not worried. I have two younger sisters of my own, and I know how bossy they can be." Winston smiled and touched Iri's cheek. "Before you know it, we will be like a true family, and you will love me as a brother."

"Perhaps!" Iris shrugged again, but this time, a smile broke out on her face, and she ran quickly away to her mother.

Lyla rolled her eyes and shook her head slightly. "I worry about her sometimes," she said to Winston.

"Well, from what I've seen so far, I don't think you will have anything to worry about." He squeezed her hand tenderly.

Despite Lyla's parents arranging accommodation for each suitor and his parents to stay the night, the first guests to leave right after the ceremony, were Duncan and his parents. As she watched, her parents thanked Duncan and his family for coming, but Lyla could see from the way Duncan shifted from one foot to the other once again that he could not wait to get out of there.

Over the next hour, Lyla and Winston mingled with the guests, but it quickly became apparent to Lyla that some of the other suitors' parents were less than happy with her choice. Yet, she tried not to let it dampen her spirits.

Seeing her father talking to Bram and his parents, Lyla excused herself, and as she went to join them, her heart sank when she saw the sadness in Bram's eyes.

"Such a pity you did not pick my son; he would have made a marvellous husband." Eric stated, his tone noticeably firm.

"I am sorry," Lyla said, feeling overwhelmed.

"Father, please," said Bram and pulled Lyla aside. "I am so sorry about him."

Lyla smile half-heartedly, "It truly was a hard decision to make Bram, and I am sorry it wasn't you."

"Nothing to be sorry about. I had a one-in-five chance, and it wasn't to be. I wish you and Winston an incredibly happy and successful marriage," he said, his voice shaky.

Lyla could only nod, unable to imagine what the suitors must feel, knowing her rejection of them couldn't be easy.

"Please, you're welcome to stay the night," her father insisted kindly. "Rest up and then leave in the morning."

"Thank you," Bram said solemnly. "You're too kind, but I think it would be best for us to take our leave now." He shook Lyla's father's hand, and without another glance at her, Bram led his parents out of the ballroom and the manor to their awaiting carriage.

Before Lyla could process how she felt about Bram's departure, Damien approached and gave her a small hug, his cologne enveloping her again.

"Damien," Lyla said but fell short on what to say.

Stepping back, Damien smiled and broke the silence. "I wanted to let you know, I spoke to Jonathan and your sisters and apologised for my behaviour towards them as well. My behaviour as a young boy was inexcusable. Understandably, Jonathan was reluctant in his acceptance, but your sisters accepted my apology gracefully."

"Thank you. That means a lot to me, and to them." Lyla's heart swelled, and she suddenly felt a rush of tender emotions towards Damien. He was no longer the young bully she remembered.

Grasping Lya's hand tenderly, Damien offered his blessings. "I do wish you both all the absolute best. If things do not work out between you, I can always be your backup. I'll be waiting," he said with a playful wink.

"Well, thank you for the backup plan, but I doubt I will be needing you anytime soon." A humorous smile touched her lips, and she kissed Damien gently on the cheek. "What will you do now?"

"Go home, return to my job, and wait for the next exciting offer to come my way." Suddenly, the humour fell from his expression as he looked into Lyla's eyes, holding her gaze. "I truly am sorry for all the things I did in the past," his voice softened.

"Thank you, Damien."

"Well, it is time for me to take my leave." He bowed low, dropping his head down. Lyla looked at the back of his head, his muscular shoulders, and his back. A sudden thought crossed her mind. Had she crossed him off her list too quickly? But then, given the limited time she'd had to get to know each suitor, could she be blamed for not picking the right person?

"You are welcome to stay the night. My parents have rooms available," Lyla offered before she swallowed thickly, her palms suddenly sweaty.

Damien straightened and opened his mouth to speak just as Winston joined them.

"Thank you, but it really is just a short distance from here." With a swift movement, Damien extended his hand to Winton, congratulating him on winning Lyla's heart.

"We all had the same chance, Damien. But I am incredibly grateful she picked me," Winston grinned as he placed his other hand tenderly on Lyla's back.

"Yes, we did. You are indeed a lucky man!" Damien withdrew his hand and smiled once more at Lyla. "Milady," he said curtly, as he turned swiftly on his heels and walked out of the ballroom, joining his parents.

Lyla watched Damien walk away from her, his dark form eventually passing through the doors and disappearing from her view. She knew she should not have felt a pang of sadness with his departure, and yet, she wished he could have stayed longer.

Just before the night ended and all the guests left, Lyla found Noah deep in conversation with Jonathan in the foyer. Not wanting to interrupt them but knowing she needed to say goodbye to all the suitors, Lyla walked up to the two of them and politely disrupted their chatter.

"My apologies for interrupting you both, but I do need to talk with Noah."

"No interruption at all. It was nice to talk with you, Noah." Jonathan shook Noah's hand, politely excused himself, and walked away.

"Please, sit." Noah motioned for Lyla to sit beside him on the bench seat. "Congratulations on your choice," he said respectfully as she sat.

"Thank you." Lyla smiled nervously at Noah. "I am sorry I didn't pick you," she said quietly.

"Are you saying this because you regret your decision?" Noah asked, an eyebrow raised.

"To be honest, it was a hard choice," she admitted, feeling her cheeks grow warm.

"So, I was in the top two then?" He smiled tenderly.

"Yes." Her blush deepened. "I know my sister would have approved."

Noah laughed. "Yes, she did express her disappointment to me." Lyla looked wide-eyed at him. He laughed again. "It's okay. Sometimes things happen for a reason. Winston clearly possessed something I don't. I will try not to hold any ill wishes against either of you." Lyla noticed the change in his tone, the playfulness fading as she looked into his blue eyes. Realising she'd held his gaze longer than she should of, she blinked, turning her head away. Noah placed his hand tenderly on her knee, which sat so close to his.

"There is still time, you know, if you feel you have made the wrong choice!" She looked swiftly back at him, her brow furrowed slightly.

"My choice is final," she said, hearing the sliver of doubt in her own voice.

"Is it?" he questioned, again captivating her with the intensity of his stare. Lyla couldn't deny the pull she felt toward him. He leaned in closer to her, his breath tickling her cheek. "It should have been *me* you picked tonight. Winston will not make you genuinely happy," he whispered, his hand squeezing her knee painfully.

"I'm sorry?" Lyla frowned as she felt her breath hitch in her throat, surprised by his firm grip.

Noah shook his head slightly, his eyes narrowing. "We were getting along so well. You made me feel like I was the one," he replied with a growl.

Under the increasing intensity of his stare, Lyla felt uncomfortable. Forcing herself to look away, she shuffled to the end of the bench, creating more space between them. Noting her change in posture, Noah removed his hand from her leg and ran his fingers through his brown hair, drawing Lyla's attention back to him as she watched the ginger highlights shine from the lantern light above them.

"I mean it, Lyla. I would have been your perfect husband. You really should have chosen me!" There was no smile. Instead, his expression remained firm and slightly hostile.

Lyla's breath hitched again, and she frowned, trying to understand Noah's sudden change in behaviour. "I don't understand what is happening."

Noah shook his head again. "You have made a big mistake tonight, Lyla. You will regret this moment," he added, his voice beginning to rise in volume.

Lyla's heart skipped a beat, and she felt a tremble in her hands. After a few moments, she smiled politely. "I am sorry you do not support my choice, but my decision is final!" She spoke firmly and then stood. "I wish you all the best, Noah." Lyla turned on her heels and hurried away, her heart pounding.

Terrible thoughts rushed through Lyla's head as she crossed the foyer. What had happened? Did Noah just threaten her? Did he really believe he would be a better choice?

Warm tears sprang to her eyes as she tried to understand why this fine, polite gentleman she spent a pleasant night with, a man she considered being the one she could have married, would change to someone so hostile and aggressive.

"Lyla. Lyla!" Noah called out as she passed through the doors and returned to the ballroom. Despite hearing her name being called, she did not turn around.

Chapter 9

By the time Lyla reached her father and Winston in the ballroom, her heartbeat had slowed, and she'd wiped away her tears. Smiling as if nothing had happened, Lyla slipped her arm around Winston's.

"I think I am done for the night," she said, as a small fake yawn slipped from her mouth.

"Yes, I dare say. It has been a long night," her father piped up, acknowledging the late hour, and he turned to Winston. "Your family are welcome to stay the night."

"Thank you, sir. We would be incredibly grateful as it's a long journey home."

"Then think nothing more of it. We have rooms prepared for everyone. Shall we inform the others?" Her father asked, taking Lyla's hand in his. She nodded and looked tenderly towards Winston, noting the happiness reflected in his brilliant green eyes as he placed his hand tenderly on her lower back. Together, the three of them walked from the ballroom and into the large sitting room, where her mother and Winston's parents sat.

"Marcus, Bethany," Lyla's dad smiled as he addressed Winston's parents. "As the hour is late, I have two rooms prepared for you."

"Thank you, Albert. That would be most convenient." With a firm handshake and a nod of approval, Marcus stood, offering his arm to Bethany.

Albert motioned to one of the servants standing near the door. "Please show Mister Winston and his parents to their rooms. They're staying the night." The servant nodded in confirmation and waited at the door for Winston's parents.

With another brief hug for Lyla, both Marcus and Bethany followed the servant, and disappeared upstairs. Winston lingered in the sitting room while Lyla's family said their goodnights and goodbyes to those not staying.

Before long, Lyla, Winston, and her parents were the only ones left. Albert stood tall and proud as he looked at Winston.

"We are thrilled Lyla chose a suitor tonight, and we are both most pleased she picked you."

"Thank you, Sir. As am I." Winston bowed his head humbly.

"Now come the next steps," Grace said as she took her daughter's hand.

"Indeed," Albert said. "The two of you shall court for the next three weeks, while we arrange your wedding. During this time," he paused, looking from Lyla to Winston. "You will need to decide where you wish to reside after the ceremony. Although it's not customary for the married couple to live with their parents, Grace and I would be more than happy to have you stay here until you find suitable housing. We could make the guest house up for you. Consider it our wedding gift." He smiled tenderly at Lyla, and she saw a small tear in the corner of his eye.

"Thank you, Papa." Lyla stepped forward and hugged her father. She knew how hard her wedding would be for him. As the first-born child, Lyla was aware of the sweet spot her father had in his heart for her.

"That is a very generous offer of you, Sir," Winston added as he stepped forward and shook Albert's hand. "But it will not be necessary."

"Oh!" Lyla exclaimed.

Winston smiled at her. "I was going to keep it a surprise, but I acquired a small house close to here. Although it's not as grand as this house or my parents,' I was hoping it would do for myself and my future bride, until a proper manor is available."

Lyla reached forward and clasped Winston's hands. "It sounds wonderful."

"Well then, now that's sorted, I'd say it's high time we all got to bed," Grace said, stifling a yawn. "Again, welcome to our family, Winston." She kissed him gently on his cheek, followed by another hug for Lyla. "We shall see you both in the morning for breakfast."

Albert and Grace left as a second servant motioned to Winston to follow him to his awaiting room. Before leaving, Winston turned to Lyla, taking her small hands in his.

"I am very honoured you picked me tonight, and I will do everything in my power to make sure I am deserving of your love and affection." He lowered his face and kissed each of her hands before looking back up into Lyla's eyes. Leaning forward, he allowed his lips to just graze across hers, bringing forth a flush of pink to her cheeks. "Good night, my sweet Lyla."

"Goodnight, Winston."

Standing alone in the sitting room, Lyla let out a deep sigh and closed her eyes. She had done it. Her eighteenth birthday had ended, her Flowering Day ceremony successful.

Opening her eyes, Lyla slipped off her shoes and, carrying them in her hand, made her way back into the ballroom and walked towards a vase of flowers.

Lowering her face, she inhaled the sweet fragrances, taking in each unique scent from the colourful flowers. Feeling her heart soar with love from the emotional day, Lyla spun across the floor, her dress billowing out around her. With a little giggle and a smile, she could not erase, Lyla rushed out of the ballroom and made her way to the grand staircase.

Ascending the stairs, Lyla saw Emily standing at the top, still in her ball gown. Throughout the ceremony, Lyla had not had many chances to talk to her and was now eager to see her sister.

"Emily, why aren't you in bed already?"

"I wanted to catch up with you. I feel like we have not seen each other all night," she said, linking her arm through Lyla's.

"I know the feeling," Lyla replied, suppressing a giggle as they both hurried to Lyla's bedroom. Closing the heavy wooden door behind them, Lyla looked around the room. The covers on her bed cover were pulled back, the curtains drawn, and the candles lit.

"I might need to call Meg," Lyla said, dropping her shoes on the floor.

"No need. I sent her to bed. I will help you undress," Emily replied, and moving in front of Lyla, she started unbuttoning the bodice of her dress. Slipping off the bodice and draping it neatly over one of Lyla's Bergere chairs, the cream and apple green stripes a soft contrast to the deep blue material of Lyla's dress. Continuing, Emily moved behind Lyla, carefully untying her layered skirt.

"How are you feeling now that the night is over?" she asked.

"Exhausted, to be honest," Lyla replied. Allowing the skirt to slip to the ground, Lyla stepped forward, over the skirt and let Emily pick up the heavy material. "Oh, that feels better. That gown is beautiful, and Mama chose well, but it weighs a tonne."

"Yes. A small price to pay to look good," Emily giggled quietly. After draping the skirt over the bodice, Emily untied the corset around Lyla's waist. "Did you recognise Mr Olsen when he first walked into the ballroom?"

"Damien? Yes, I did." She turned to face Emily, her corset now free, and hanging in Emily's hand. "And I was very shocked that Mama and Papa picked him." She took the corset and placed it over the skirt. Turning back to Emily, she grabbed her hands.

"I saw Jonathan's face; the poor boy was aghast. I thought he might faint, right there and then."

"Yes, so did I," Emily replied. "Mr Olsen was so mean to all of us." She let go of Lyla's hand and turned her around, led her to the vanity table, sat her down and began pulling out the pins in her hair. "Did you know he came to apologise to us all for his past behaviour? Even Jonathan," she said, with a hint of surprise still in her tone.

"Yes," Lyla replied. "I know. I asked him too. He claimed he had no recollection of how he had behaved all those years ago and after I reminded him, he apologies to me."

"You asked him to apologise to us?" Emily exclaimed, as she continued to let Lyla's hair down.

"Yes." Lyla looked at her sister through the mirror. "Just before I danced with Damien, Jonathan asked me not to pick him during our dance." Emily's hands dropped to Lyla's shoulders, and Lyla brought her hand up and placed it on her sister's. "Damien must have seen our conversation and asked if everything was all right when he danced with me. I told him Jon had asked me not to choose him, and when he questioned why, I reminded him of his behaviour. Apparently, he had forgotten."

Emily's eyes widened, before a look of clarification crossed her expression. "Is that why your dance ended, and you stormed off out of the ballroom?"

Lyla turned in her chair. "Did you see that?"

"The whole room saw it." Lyla blushed and was grateful for the low candlelight.

"Oh, my goodness," she said murmured. "I didn't think anyone heard us." Her hand covered her mouth as she recalled the argument. "Is that why Bram came out?"

"Possibly," Emily replied and began combing Lyla's hair, draping the large curls over her shoulders. "Either way, I am grateful that he sought us out and apologised."

"Did Jonathan take it well?" Lyla asked.

"I think so. He seemed incredibly quiet afterwards. I don't think Iris remembered him at all."

"And you?" she asked, turning back to Emily.

"I accepted his apology. I think he has changed."

Lyla slipped her stocking off and threw them onto the chair before she motioned for Emily to turn around.

"Come on, your turn." Standing, Lyla carefully assisted Emily in removing her dress, corset, bustle, and overskirt. "Do you think I made the right choice, picking Winston?" she asked, curious to know what Emily thought of him.

"He seems like a lovely gentleman. Spoke kindly to me and danced well," she replied, gathering her clothes from the floor. "What made you choose him in the end?" Emily asked as she stood in her chemise, bloomers, and stockings.

"I think I had the best connection with him," Lyla said confidently. "I felt the most relaxed with Winston. Of course, Bram was a close choice as well." She stepped closer to Emily, taking her clothes from her arms and draping them on the second Bergere chair. "Meg can put these away tomorrow." Grabbing Emily's hand, she took her to the bed, and they climbed on, sitting close together.

"What about Duncan?" Emily giggled. "He seemed like a lovely man." She tried to suppress the laughter, but looking at Lyla's face, she rolled onto the bed, clutching her stomach, unable to contain it.

"What on earth were Mama and Papa thinking when they picked him?" Lyla laughed aloud. "Were there no other suitors?"

"He was clearly uncomfortable. I felt sorry for him," Emily said, wiping the tears of laughter from her eyes.

"As did I." Lyla smiled. It was nice to sit with her sister and laugh about the night's events. With so much pressure on Lyla to make the night a success, she'd forgotten to enjoy herself. Feeling the most relaxed she had all evening, Lyla lay beside her sister, covering her mouth as she yawned and rolled onto her side.

"I do hope I have made the right decision tonight."

Emily slid over to Lyla's side and placed her hand tenderly on her shoulder. "I think you have." Leaning down, she kissed Lyla tenderly on the cheek. "Good night, *Mrs Stewart*," she said playfully.

Lyla grinned. She liked the sound of that.

"Good night, Emily."

Emily slipped off the bed and, walking quietly, sneaked through the bedroom door. By the time she made it to her own room, Lyla was fast asleep.

Chapter 10

As the heavy red velvet curtains were drawn back, the morning sunlight flooded Lyla's room.

"Good morning, miss," Lyla's handmaid, Meg, said, as she tied the curtains back and opened the window, allowing the cool morning breeze to drift into the room.

"Hmmm, good morning, Meg." Lyla stretched out her legs, arching her back and inhaling deeply.

"Congratulations on your ceremony last night," Meg commented, picking up the clothing Lyla and Emily left on the chairs, placing into a basket for washing.

"Thank you." Lyla opened her eyes and sat up, allowing the bedding to fall to her waist.

"How does it feel to be engaged?" Meg opened the wardrobe and started sifting through the many dresses inside.

"Exciting." Lyla smiled. "I was so nervous, Meg." Pulling the bedding off, she swung her legs over the side of the bed and watched Meg pick out a flowing yellow summer dress.

"Yes, I know. I watched you pick up his rose. He was so happy."

"You saw?"

"Yes." Meg ran to Lyla. "Please do not tell your parents I watched, or Marcel. He will be angry I was there." Her green eyes pleaded with Lyla.

"I won't tell anyone. Anyway, I am glad you watched; you have been by my side for so many years, I was upset believing you were not there." Lyla kissed Meg's hand.

"I do hope I get to stay with you." Meg moved over to the mirror and motioned for Lyla to sit in the chair. "After you get married and move out, that is."

"Of course you're going to come with me." Lyla sat down and looked at Meg through the mirror. "I would be lost without you."

Meg smiled broadly as she started brushing Lyla's hair. "How would you like your hair styled today, Miss?"

"Down I think, with the yellow comb and silver earrings."

Meg nodded and got to work, brushing Lyla's hair till it shone. For the past eight years, Meg had served as Lyla's handmaid. Seven years older than Lyla, she joined the family once Lyla turned ten. It was the age when all young girls received their own handmaid, or a valet for the boys.

Over the years, Meg became Lyla's confidante and close friend. She knew all of Lyla's secrets and desires and had become a vital person in her life. Lyla could not imagine starting her day without Meg at her side.

"We are going to have to design your wedding dress now," Meg said as she twisted a small portion of Lyla's hair into a bun atop her head, then slipped the yellow pearl comb into it, pinning it into place. Meg then arranged the rest of Lyla's hair to hang loosely down her back.

Lyla admired her reflection, her eyes bright and twinkling with excitement. "You know what?" She suddenly turned in the chair. "I have not thought of a wedding dress. I was so focused on just getting through the Flowering Day ceremony, I totally forgot about what I would need to do next!"

Meg smiled with excitement too. "I hope it was okay, but I gathered all of your flowers from the ballroom last night and brought them all in here." She motioned to the three large vases in the room.

"These are all my flowers?" Lyla gasped, embarrassed that she had not noticed them already. The three vases were overflowing with colour. She walked up to each one, dropping her face into the flowers and breathing in the individual scents. "I can't believe how many I got."

"There were a lot." Meg motioned over to a small vase standing on the bedside table, next to where Lyla slept. "This one is from Winston."

"Thank you, Meg." Lyla walked back to her bed, picked up the dark red rose, and pressed her nose into it. Closing her eyes, she breathed in deeply. "Everything is going to change now, isn't it, Meg?"

"Yes. Yes, it will, but they will all be positive changes." Meg walked over to the dress she picked out. "Come on Lyla, you need to get dressed. Breakfast will be called soon."

Within ten minutes, Lyla was wearing the yellow day dress. The sheer see-through yellow lace hung softly over a darker yellow satin skirt. The bodice hugged Lyla's chest, with the yellow lace flowing delicately over her shoulders. A modest dress, but well fitted, showing off her pale skin.

The silver earrings, a present for her sixteenth birthday, now hung from Lyla's ears.

"Here, one more thing." Meg leant over, opened the jewellery box, and pulled out a simple yellow and white pearl necklace. Draping it around Lyla's neck, completing the outfit.

With another glance in the mirror, Lyla studied her reflection. She no longer saw the young, innocent eighteen-year-old girl she saw yesterday. Instead, Lyla now saw a mature young woman, recently engaged.

Moments later, a bell sounded through the manor, signalling that breakfast was ready. As Lyla turned from the mirror, there was a knock at her door.

"Come in," she called as she faced the door.

"May I come in?" asked a voice cautiously as the door cracked open.

"Yes," she replied curiously, glancing at Meg.

The door opened further, and Winston stepped through the doorway. Abruptly, laying his eyes on Lyla, he stopped in his tracks. Lyla watched his eyes widen, as he noticed the morning sun shining onto her dress.

"You look like you are glowing!" he exclaimed.

"Do I?" She looked down and gasped at the way the sun's rays shone directly onto her dress, the light reflecting off the silk skirt. She grinned widely and looked from Meg back to Winston. Meg dropped her head, not leaving the room, but trying to be invisible.

"If this is how I am going to be seeing you every day, I will be one very happy man."

Lyla giggled. "I'm pretty sure this is just a one-off thing."

"Hm, I hope not." He stepped further into the room but did not approach Lyla. "I was hoping to escort you down to breakfast."

"Thank you," she replied before her smile faltered.

"What is it?" he asked, his brow creasing.

"You do know, you're not really allowed in my room … without an escort." She glanced behind Winston, but a small smile tweaked at Lyla's lips.

"I got your father's permission to fetch you … without the escort. Plus, he told me you were not alone, that your handmaid would still be in here." To that, he glanced in Meg's direction, nodding politely.

Meg nodded in return. Quickly jumping in, Lyla introduced Winston to Meg.

"Winston, please, this is Meg, my handmaid."

"Pleasure to meet you, Meg." He bowed low.

"And to you, Mr Stuart." She curtsied.

"Please, call me Winston." He smiled before turning back to Lyla.

"So, are you ready?"

"Yes."

"Well then, let us not keep them waiting!" He offered his arm to Lyla, who happily stepped forward and placed her hand on it. Giving Meg a small wave goodbye, they left the room.

Together, they walked along the corridor, down the grand staircase, and back into the dining room, which was now set out for breakfast. The room was returned to its normal setting, with the small tables and extra chairs for the guests last night gone, and the large dining table back in the centre of the room, surrounded by ten chairs.

The room looked amazing. A crisp white cloth draped over the table topped with a delicate white lace runner. Atop the runner, stood three small vases with fresh flowers from the garden. Completing the setting were white porcelain plates, crystal glasses, and silverware at each family member's place.

Along the side wall, a long buffet table was laden with platters of bacon, sausages, eggs, and porridge, with added platters of fruit, cheese, and bread. The warm aroma drifted towards Lyla, commanding her attention. Taking in the sight and seeing the added platters of fruit, cheese, and bread, Lyla's stomach rumbled.

Taking her seat at the table, Lyla's mother, father, and her three siblings were already seated before their plates waiting to be piled with food.

"About time! I am starving!" whined Iris.

"Iris," Grace said patiently, giving her youngest daughter a light scowl. "Manners, please."

Iris sat back, rolling her eyes before shooting Lyla a look of irritation.

Not long after Lyla and Winston sat down, Winston's parents walked in and joined them.

"Good morning, all." Albert called out to everyone. "I hope you slept well."

"Very much so. Thank you." Bethany slid into the chair that Marcus pulled out for her. "The room was lovely."

"I'm glad you liked it." Grace smiled from across the table.

"Well, without further ado, shall we?" Albert motioned to the buffet table. Immediately, Iris grabbed her plate and took off towards the food.

Marcus leant in low and spoke softly to Bethany. "Shall I get you some food?"

"Please, and a glass of wine."

Marcus made his way over to the buffet table and started placing food on two plates. Winston turned to Lyla.

"I would offer to do the same for you, if you wish, but I'm afraid I don't know what food you like."

"That's okay. I'm happy to serve myself," she replied with a smile as she reassured him with a pat on the hand. Together, Lyla and Winston both moved over to the buffet table. Winston and Lyla filled their plates and returned to the table to join the others.

"Will you stay long with us today?" Grace asked Winston's parents.

"Business, unfortunately, is calling me to return, so we shall all have to leave this morning," Marcus said between mouthfuls of delicious food.

"Winston and I could stay for a few hours," Bethany offered. "I'd love the opportunity to get to know Grace better."

"Unfortunately, not my dear. I will need the carriage to head into a meeting this afternoon."

"You're more than welcome to visit anytime, Bethany." Grace smiled warmly. "We could even lend out our carriage to fetch you."

"Thank you, Grace." Bethany smiled, and Lyla could see their mothers were going to get along very well.

Breakfast passed with exciting chatter about upcoming plans, the courtship of Lyla and Winston and, of course, the upcoming wedding.

"Shall we say, Saturday, three weeks from now?" Albert offered.

"I think that would give us enough time to work with." Marcus agreed. Lyla met Winston's stare as they smiled. With the wedding date set, Lyla knew the time would fly, and there was so much to do.

"Shall we have the wedding at our place?" Marcus offered. "After all, you had the Flowering Day here. We would be honoured to repay the favour?"

"Oh!" Lyla exclaimed. All eyes turned to her. "I was hoping to have it here in the ballroom. I have so many ideas already," she said meekly.

"Of course, of course, after all, it is your day," he replied, but Lyla could tell from the slight frown that she'd offended him.

"But your offer is wonderful. We could have it at your manor," Grace pipped in.

"Oh no, no, no. I have learnt, once a woman makes up her mind, one must never talk her out of it," Marcus said with a serious tone. Bethany looked at him, raising her eyebrows.

"And who taught you that, Marcus Stuart?"

"The most wonderful wife in the world!" he replied quickly and chuckled, and everyone joined in. Lyla felt like she really had made the right decision. Her family and Winston's family were getting along so well.

After breakfast, the Stuart family made their way outside, to take their carriage back home.

"We would be honoured to have you all come over within the next few days, to meet the rest of our family," Bethany said as she held Grace's hands. "My children would love to meet yours and I am sure they will all get along famously. My youngest daughter is the same age as Iris."

Grace beamed. "We shall organise it soon. I think I can speak for us all when I say we're looking forward to extending our families."

Winston helped his mother into the carriage and turned to Lyla, gently moving her aside before grasping her hands and bringing them to his lips.

"I am so incredibly happy you picked me. I cannot wait to start courting you and organising our future together." He smiled, and Lyla could see the strength of his feelings in his eyes.

"Me too." Lyla lent forwards, placing her lips to Winston's cheek.

""I will return shortly," he stated. He responded with a gentle kiss on her cheek and entered the carriage and sat beside his mother.

"Albert, Grace." Marcus bowed low, then climbed onto the front of the carriage, next to the driver. "Until next time." He tipped his hat.

As the carriage started off, Winston leant out the window, laughing.

"Lyla! You are glowing again!" Lyla looked back down to her dress. Once again, the sun light was shining through the lace and onto the yellow silk material.

"You look like an angel!" Iris stated from the manor stairs.

"Well then, I guess this means … you are my angel!" Winston called out, as the carriage passed through the main gates.

Lyla's smile shone as brightly as her dress.

Chapter 11

A few minutes after Winson left, Jonathan sought out Lyla and enveloped her in a big hug.

"What was that for?" Lyla asked.

"I wanted to thank you for not picking Damien. I know he apologised to me, to Emily and Iris, but I was so happy when I saw you reach for Winston's rose."

Lyla was silent for a moment as her thoughts drifted back to the way she'd felt watching Damien leave the night before. "I think he is a different person now," she finally said with a quick shake of her head.

"A simple apology does not wipe out the times of torment and teasing we all endured, Lyla," he said quietly.

"I know, but at least he apologised. He could have been very rude about it all."

Jonathan nodded in agreement. "Congratulations, by the way. Winston seems like a good man. I do hope the best for you both," he said, walking back into the manor with her.

"Thank you, Jon. It does mean a lot to have your support." He nodded politely, and excused himself, leaving Lyla standing alone in the grand foyer.

The rest of the day passed quickly for Lyla. Returning to the pond, she sat on the grass, where she'd sat just the day before.

How things can change so much in such a short space of time! Yesterday, I sat here a young girl, and today I sit here as a mature bride to be.

Staring at the mallard ducks swimming in the pond, Lyla lost herself in their swift movements across the flat surface of the water. She realised she saw them in a different light as she admired their gracefulness, their beauty and how they moved together in small groups. They had a purpose in life, a reason to keep moving all day, just like her.

A small wave of fear and trepidation suddenly washed over Lyla, and her eyes widened. Now that she was engaged, every day from this moment until the wedding would be filled with appointments.

Lyla and her mama would need to appoint a seamstress to make her wedding dress, chat to the gardener to organise her flowers, and discuss the menu for the wedding feasts with the cook. All while looking like she was confident and poised yet knowing deep down, she would be flailing like the mallard's legs, hidden beneath the water.

Falling back on the grass, Lyla inhaled deeply to calm her nerves as she gazed in wonder at the soft, white clouds floating effortlessly through the blue sky, changing shapes before gradually fading away.

Eventually her thoughts drifted to Winston, running over the short time they'd spent together last night. Recalling how she'd felt as he'd guided her across the dance floor in his strong arms, brought a smile to her face. Then, the look of pure joy on his face when Lyla held up his rose melted away her worries. She had made the right choice.

Closing her eyes, she listened to the breeze rustling through the trees behind her—the sound relaxing and hypnotic. Before long, Lyla drifted off into a light sleep.

Winston returned the next day on horseback and spent the morning and afternoon walking through the garden and sitting by the pond with Lyla, getting to know her better.

"Tell me," Winston asked as they gazed over the calm pond. "What's your favourite dessert?"

"Hmm, tough one," Lyla replied, tilting her head in thought. "I do love a Bakewell tart, but I would say bread and butter pudding would be my favourite."

"Oh yes, I do like Bakewell tarts." Winton smiled and nodded his head. "And roasts, any preference?"

"Oh, definitely roast goose, with plenty of vegetables and Yorkshire pudding." She turned to Winston, enjoying the chance to get to know each other. "And you?"

He returned her gaze, his expression one of contentment. "Goose is good, but I prefer beef, with plenty of Yorkshire pudding smothered in gravy."

Lyla giggled and relaxed back against the bench they sat on. How happy she felt, spending time discovering more about the man she would marry in a few weeks.

"Do you enjoy reading?" she asked.

"I do like a good poem now and then, but not so much the books you ladies seem to get lost in." Lyla nodded respectfully. "But don't let that stop you from reading them," he teased.

"Oh, it won't." She giggled again, the sound drifting off with the breeze. "I am hoping to have a beautiful library in our house one day."

"And I would be more than happy to create one for you."

"Do you have staff ready for us?" Lyla asked as she slipped her hand through Winston's arm after they left the bench and began walking along the edge of the pond.

"Of course. Just a small team. A cook, a kitchen hand, a butler, two housekeepers, a gardener, a stableman, my valet and of course your handmaid, Meg, if you wish her to come with you.

"Oh, yes, please! She means everything to me."

"Done. She will have a room to herself, not large, but it will be private."

"Thank you." She smiled tenderly at Winston; confident he really had thought of everything.

Continuing to stroll around the garden, enjoying the warm light wind that teased their hair, they talked about how they could decorate, and style their new house, with Lyla leaning more towards, mint green, silver, cream, and baby blue colours, while Winston envisioned colours of forest green, navy blue, walnut and gold.

"Perhaps we should wait until we move in. That way we could better see the options and how they may look," he suggested, smiling at Lyla.

"Perhaps you are right," she replied, not wanting to argue with him before they had even wed.

They changed the subject to which parties they would host as newlyweds, or if Christmas should be held at their place, a grand event, to officiate their marriage.

Walking arm in arm around the large stone fountain, chatting like old friends, Lyla was very much at ease with Winston. The more time they spent together, the happier she was with her decision.

Not long after Winston departed, Lyla lay on a scarlet velvet chaise lounge in the candlelit library, her favourite room in the manor, and attempted to read a book. Although Lyla tried not to think about anyone other than Winston, she grew agitated when random thoughts of Noah kept drifting into her mind.

Knowing she wouldn't get through the pages, she slammed the book closed and paced the ornate room, desperate to distract her mind. It did not help when Iris intruded, interrupting her thoughts, and plopped down onto the chaise, next to her book.

"I am not saying that Winston is not a kind man, and that he would not make a good husband, I just think you should have chosen Noah," said Iris, picking up the book and leafing through the pages.

Resisting the urge to walk over and snatch the book from Iris's hands, Lyla sat back down and sighed. "I made the right choice, Iris," Lyla said wearily, but she couldn't help feeling a little worried. Iris didn't know about the last conversation she had had with Noah. In fact, she had not spoken to anyone about it. Not even Meg.

That conversation with Noah still lingered in Lyla's mind, so much so that she'd slept restlessly most of the night, tossing and turning as his words played over and over in her mind. How could he have turned so quickly?

His temperament had changed so fast. A charming gentleman throughout the night, and then a vindictive and aggressive brute at the end.

Even though he was long gone, Lyla couldn't shake it off, and she didn't know why.

Chapter 12

Lyla was kept so busy with wedding plans that she hadn't realised an entire week had passed since the Flowering Day ceremony, until Winston arrived early one morning, complete with horse and carriage.

"What are you doing here?" Lyla asked, not remembering if they'd made prior arrangements.

"I am taking you out for the day to see the ocean, if you would be up for the ride!"

Lyla beamed. "Oh, Winston! That would be wonderful. I will, however, have to check with my parents."

"It has already been organised," her mama piped up as she appeared behind Lyla.

Lyla spun around and frowned. "What!"

"Winston asked us the last time he was here. He wanted to surprise you." She smiled warmly at her daughter.

Lyla turned back to Winston. "Well, aren't you a sneaky gentleman!" She turned back to her mother. "And who will be chaperoning me?"

"I will. It has been too long since I last visited the ocean. I hope you don't mind," Grace added.

Lyla smiled widely. "Of course not, Mama." She stepped forward and gently kissed her mother's cheek.

Glancing down at the pale ice, green day dress, adorned with small pink and yellow flowers that Meg had selected for the day, Lyla realised she hadn't questioned the choice. Nor did she question why Meg piled her hair high on her head, and covered it with a soft woven bonnet, and slipped flat silk ballet shoes on her bare feet. Yet, as she looked over at Meg and found her grinning at her, Lyla realised she'd been in on the secret too—quickly confirmed by a wink from her handmaid.

Propping her hands firmly on her hips, she glared at the three of them with amusement. "Well, I am not sure if I can trust any of you again," she joked, but grinned as they laughed in response.

"Shall we then?" Winston stepped forward and gently placed his hand on Lyla's back.

"Lead the way, sir," Lyla replied, stepping towards the door. Guiding her gently outside, the three of them approached Winston's readied horse and carriage and introduced them to his stableman, William, who sat patiently at the front.

The day was perfect for visiting the beach. The sky was a vibrant shade of blue without a single cloud.

Helping Lyla and her mother into the carriage, Winston soon followed, sitting himself opposite Lyla, and once the three were settled and comfortable, Winston tapped twice on the roof and with a jolt, the carriage moved.

The trip was smooth and comfortable, and a slight breeze came through the carriage windows, tickling the hairs at Lyla's neck.

"Shall we use this opportunity to discuss the wedding day?" asked Grace.

"Yes. I meant to ask you, Lyla, you said you would like to get married in the ballroom of your manor, is that still your plan?" Winston said, taking her hand in his.

"Yes," she replied, giving his hand a gentle squeeze.

"That would be nice. You and your family could stay in the guest house the night before," added Grace.

"Thank you." He smiled warmly at Grace. "Well, that settles it. The wedding shall be at your manor. In the morning if you wish," he added.

"Yes please. The weather is warming up, and I do not want to be in my wedding dress in the heat of the day." Lyla added, content that the wedding plans were effortlessly falling into place.

An hour later, the carriage pulled off the main road and onto a smaller track, which meandered its way through the countryside. Through the open window, Lyla and her mother breathed in deeply. The breeze was scented with the salty smell of the ocean, and Lyla closed her eyes, picturing the water lapping against the sand.

It was not long before the carriage came to a stop, Lyla relieved the bouncing journey had ended. Winston opened the door, pushed the stairs down and climbed out. Reaching back into the carriage, he gently took Lyla's hand and assisted her out. The view that stretched out before her took her breath away.

The beach extended about twenty meters or so, from the gravel road they stopped on before the white, bubbly water of the crashing waves lapped across the white sand.

Stepping aside, she allowed Winston to assist her mother out, and grinned at her, like an excited child. Standing side by side, the three of them gazed out over the vast blue water. Only a few white clouds dotted across the horizon.

"Oh, this is a wonderful spot, Winston," Grace said, beaming with happiness.

"I have two blankets, plus a picnic basket. Shall we head to the beach?" asked Winston.

Lyla nodded enthusiastically. It had been a few years since she had been to the beach. Growing up, they did not get too many opportunities to travel the distance, and her parents could only take them all at least once a year. Moving across the sand, old memories flashed through Lyla's mind.

Running across the sand, Jonathan close behind, laughing. Emily splashing Lyla and Iris. Papa chasing Jonathan into the water. So many fond moments happened here.

With a grin, Lyla placed a hand on top of her bonnet and took off running toward the water's edge, laughing.

"Lyla!" her mother called out to her. "You will get your dress and shoes wet!" Upon hearing this, Lyla flicked off her ballet slippers and hitched her dress halfway up her calves and continued to run across the sand, squealing and laughing in delight.

Grace smiled and glanced over at Winston. "Good luck with that one!" She said in humour.

Winston grinned and turned to Grace. "I'm sure this is going to be an adventure." It did not take Winston long to place the blankets and picnic basket down, remove his shoes and socks, roll the cuffs of his trousers up his legs and take off running after Lyla.

Lyla squealed in delight as he reached her, and hand in hand, they ran towards the crashing waves, quickly retreating before the water could reach their bare feet.

Grace felt her chest swell with pride as she watched the young couple frolicking in the waves, smiling fondly while reminiscing about the times she and Albert visited the beach to do the same thing.

It did not seem that long ago that she had had her own Flowering Day, and she still treasured the memories of her courting weeks, getting to know Albert. She reflected on how fast time had flown by. Now it was Lyla's turn to take this new road. There was no doubt in Grace's mind that her eldest daughter had chosen a wonderful young man to marry.

After playing chase with the water, skimming stones into the waves, and tiring themselves out, Lyla and Winston made their way back to Grace and plopped down heavily next to her.

"It is quite warm in the sun," Lyla said, trying to cool herself down with her silk and paper fan. Even though she was only wearing a light cotton dress with short, capped sleeves, being out in the sun, avoiding the cool water, Lyla overworked herself, and now sitting down, small beads of sweat formed at her hairline.

Winston, on the other hand, succumbing to the heat, removed his coat and loosened his collar.

"Here. Have something cool to drink!" Grace said as she brought out a large bottle of ale from the picnic basket. Together, they sat and watched the waves ebb and flow, as they enjoyed the picnic lunch of sandwiches, cheese, fruit, and cake that Winston's cook had prepared for them.

The rest of the day breezed by, like the cool wind blowing off the ocean.

Chapter 13

Over the next week, yards and yards of white and ivory silk, satin, brocade, and intricate lace were delivered to the house as Lyla, her mother, Meg, and a seamstress designed the perfect wedding dress.

A modest corset and rear pannier covered with a full white satin, and lace underskirt was made for Lyla. The brocade bodice with matching brocade and lace elbow-length sleeves was trimmed down the centre with delicate lace and pearl buttons, which enhanced Lyla's slim waist.

A half skirt, created with ruched layers of white silk and satin, trimmed with lace and a long-looped train, finished off her dress. Completing the ensemble, Lyla's veil, made from tulle and lace and trimmed with matching pearl buttons, now hung in a corner of her room, draped in a sheet, protecting the exquisite masterpiece.

Stunning jewellery, embellished with pearls, diamonds and rubies, were sent from Lyla's grandmother and her aunt, as well as a few items from Winston's mother. Lyla felt overwhelmed with the number of earrings, necklaces, and bracelets that now lay on her dresser, sparkling in the sunlight.

The entire manor was abuzz leading up to the wedding day. With so much work to be done both within and outside the manor, there was no time to be idle, and attendants, valets and staff were constantly ducking and weaving from one room to another. Furniture in all the rooms needed dusting and cleaning, and the staircase balustrades, wooden table and floors were polished until they gleamed. Bedrooms, which had only just been used a few weeks ago, were all turned over again, linen washed, curtains cleaned, and rugs beaten free of dust, to ensure they were ready for family members to return.

Lyla's father hired more staff to assist with the catering, the flower arrangements, and the general running of the manor, ensuring all the guests would be well looked after on the day. Lyla had never seen so much happening within her home. The atmosphere, the hustle and bustle, quickened her heart rate and heightened her excitement.

Each morning, the cook prepared new culinary dishes and presented them to the family to try out, and by the end of two weeks, a brand-new menu was created to cater for the many mouths that would be there in one weeks' time. Palestine artichoke soup, boiled fowl with bechamel sauce, raised oyster pie, braised ham, French pheasant pate, and salmon with mayonnaise. For dessert there was fruited jelly, custard, Swiss meringues, pineapple creams, and ornamented trifles, and new wines, liqueurs, ginger-beer, and lemonade arrived by the crateful.

For the wedding cake, Lyla had decided on a single-layered fruit cake, covered with almond paste and white frosting and embellished with a wreath of orange blossoms.

The stables were freshened up with fresh straw, and the water trough scrubbed clean and refilled with fresh water, awaiting the many horses that would arrive at the end of the week.

Not a place or room was left out, including the garden. The trees and bushes were trimmed. The large fountains in the front and back gardens were emptied, cleaned, and scrubbed, then refilled with fresh water. The main driveway to the manor was methodically swept and cleaned of branches and debris. As the first wedding, Albert was adamant it would be the perfect day for his daughter.

During his visits with Lyla, Winston kept her updated with his own preparations, making sure the small house he had purchased a year ago, was now ready for Lyla and himself. Although it was only a small five-bedroom house, with a large kitchen, formal lounge, small ballroom and garden, Winston wanted to make sure Lyla would fall in love with it the moment she saw it. Lyla had no doubt that she would be comfortable there while Winston went to work each day, and it also helped to know that she would only be a two-hour carriage ride from her parents' manor.

"Will I be able to come visit you?" Emily asked one afternoon, while they were enjoying some tea and cake in the sitting room.

"Of course. I would never say no to you or Iris. And I dare say I will need the company when Winston starts to work at the docks."

"Is he really going to manage a cargo ship?" Emily asked curiously.

"Yes, he has plans to buy one in the next few months, and then, if all goes well, he wants to buy another."

"But doesn't that mean he won't be home very often? The Docks are at least two days away from here."

"Yes, I know," Lyla sighed and looked out the sitting-room window, into the garden beyond.

"Does that worry you?"

Lyla shook her head but then glanced at Emily. "We have discussed this at length. Winston is hoping once the cargo ship starts trading, he will be able to hire a second to run the business, so he can be home with me, and hopefully, our children."

Emily's eyes widened. "Are you … with child?" she whispered.

"Oh, good grief, no!" Lyla blushed and giggled. "We are not married yet."

Emily rolled her eyes. "People still … do it … before they get married, you know."

"Emily Pierson!" Lyla hissed. "I hope you are not implying that you are not … pure!"

"Of course I am, Lyla. I'm only fifteen years old!" Emily said, scrunching her face up with disgust. "When have you ever seen me alone with a man?" She quickly lowered her voice and looked around the room, making sure no one was listening.

"Be still my beating heart!" Lyla placed her hand on her chest, feeling her heart beating faster under her rib cage. Glancing back at Emily, they both collapsed into a fit of laughter. "I shall miss seeing your face every day."

"And I shall miss yours."

It was not far from Lyla's mind, the memory of sitting with Winston at her Flowering Day ceremony, when he mentioned his desire to move closer to the ocean in order to run his business. That would mean the small house Winston bought for her would have to be sold and a new one purchased near the docks.

Lyla closed her eyes briefly, saddened to know she would soon be living two days coach ride away from her loving family, but still blessed to have picked a wonderful man.

Chapter 14

With only a few days until the wedding, Lyla's mother decided her daughter needed an afternoon to escape everything happening at the manor, to help clear her head and calm her nerves. There was a large and beautiful lake that was only a short carriage ride away, and, since she needed a chaperone, Lyla convinced Meg to accompany her.

Wearing a beautiful green lace and chiffon dress and matching bonnet, Lyla sat in her papa's open Victoria carriage with Meg, its retractable roof pulled back to allow the ladies to watch the scenery pass by.

In a few days, she would be Mrs Winston Stuart. No longer a young girl. No longer the eldest child of Albert and Grace Pierson, but Mrs Lyla Stuart. She smiled to herself.

"Thinking of something good?" Meg enquired.

"Just daydreaming of becoming Mrs Stuart."

"I am so happy for you. It is exciting."

"Yes, yes, it is." She sighed softly and looked at Meg. "Are you ever going to get married, Meg?"

"I can't say. I admit it has crossed my mind a few times, but I have always put you first," Meg replied honestly.

"Can you … get married? Or would you have to leave the household?"

"I can if I meet someone who wants to marry me. And it would be up to the owner of the house and the head butler if I would be allowed to stay."

"Oh, I would allow it," Lyla said quickly. "And you wouldn't have to leave."

Meg smiled. "That is truly kind of you to say so, but if I live with you as your room attendant, it will be your husband who would need to give me the permission. It would be his house, and not yours."

"Fiddlesticks." Lyla flicked her hand in front of her face, dismissing Meg's comment. "I would convince Winston. He has already granted you permission to come with me after the wedding. I would not be able to survive if you were not by my side, husband, or no."

Meg laughed. "You are too kind to me."

"Not as kind as you have been to me, Meg."

Holding hands and admiring the view, the carriage soon slowed and entered through a pair of large black wrought-iron gates and along the path that would lead to the lake. Plenty of other folks were already there, enjoying the sunny day. Families with young children, couples walking arm in arm, and ladies accompanied by various dogs of different breeds.

Waiting for the carriage to come to a full stop, and the coachman to lower the steps, Lyla and Meg disembarked the carriage and strolled towards the huge blue lake, holding their parasols high.

Finding an empty bench along the gravel path, which meandered its way around the lake, Lyla and Meg sat down and watched the ducks swimming lazily across the smooth water.

"I didn't think to bring a bag of seeds to feed the birds," Lyla said, with a hint of sadness.

"Not a problem, Miss, I would be happy to share mine." A male voice spoke just to Lyla's left. Lyla turned her head slightly, and a pair of black shiny shoes came into her vision. As she lifted her eyes, she saw an extended hand, cuffed by a dark blue jacket sleeve, holding a brown bag.

Her parasol, although shading her from the sun, was also hiding the face of the male, who now stood next to her.

With a simple backwards movement, Lyla tilted the parasol behind her, revealing the face of the kind gentleman, who offered to share his bag of seed.

Lyla's eyes widened in shock as a pair of blue eyes stared back at her. Eyes she instantly recognised.

"Good afternoon, ladies." The gentleman's voice was deep and masculine.

Lyla's froze as she took in the young man's features. Handsome, with a straight nose, a light stubble growth on this jaw line and deep brown hair, with a hint of ginger.

"I do not believe we have met," he said as he extended his free hand towards Meg, seemingly oblivious to Lyla's shock.

"I'm Meg," she replied and took his hand gently, smiling at the handsome stranger. "We may not have met before, but you seem familiar?" The man glanced quickly at Lyla, then back to Meg.

"It is lovely to meet you, Meg. I am Noah Valdez."

Meg's smile widened. "Oh, yes! You were one of Lyla's suitors." She turned to Lyla, her smile still on her face, until she saw Lyla's withdrawn and stoic expression. Although Meg did not remove her smile, the emotions behind it disappeared. Meg turned back to Noah. Slowly, she pulled her hand out of his grip.

"Well, fancy meeting you here at the lake, Mister Valdez," Meg said, trying to lead the conversation.

"Yes, what a pleasant coincidence. It is lovely to see you again, Lyla, or should I say … Mrs Winston Stuart?" He looked at Lyla with interest, pulling the conversation back in his direction.

"I am not Mrs Stuart yet, Mister Valdez," Lyla informed Noah curtly.

"Please, call me Noah. There is no need for the formality." Lyla smiled but did not make eye contact. "May I join you?" He motioned to the space on the bench.

Not wanting to be rude, or cause a scene in public, Lyla moved over slightly toward Meg, allowing Noah to sit next to her.

As though ignorant of the chilly reception from Lyla, Noah continued to talk. "You both look lovely today. That shade of green certainly suits your eyes," he said to Lyla.

"My eyes are blue, not green," Lyla said politely, yet firmly.

"Yes, they are, and a lovely shade of blue as well." He held her gaze. Lyla blinked and turned back to look out over the lake. "So, I take it the wedding is still going to go ahead?"

"Of course, it is," Meg stammered as a small crease of uncertainty crossed her forehead.

"And when is the special day?" Noah asked, his gaze still locked on Lyla.

"Why do you want to know, Noah?" Lyla said, turning back to look at him, a hint of annoyance crossing her face.

"Just curious." He smiled at her, but the smile did not reach his eyes. "Bird seed?" He held the bag out. Lyla did not take it.

"I do not think it is a concern of yours to know when my wedding day is." Lyla returned her focus back on the ducks, bringing her parasol down slightly, trying to block Noah out. It did not work.

"I was just making sure, you know, if you …" He leaned in close to her, whispering in her ear. "If you might have changed your mind." His breath on her neck sent an unpleasant chill down Lyla's spine, as did the familiar scent of his cologne.

Lyla stood up quickly, so fast Meg startled, and Noah moved back as well. She took two steps forward and spun on her heels to face Noah.

"Mister Valdez, I shall say this once, and one time only. I plan to marry Winston this Saturday, and there is nothing you can say or do that will ever change my mind. And in the rare chance I might change my mind and decide … not to marry Winston, *you*, Noah … would be the last person I would then ask! Now if you will please excuse us, we have better places to be!"

Lyla extended her hand towards Meg, who quickly grabbed it and stood up, looking at Lyla with a curious frown but held her tongue. Lyla turned to face Noah one last time.

"Goodbye, Mister Valdez!" she said, then spun back around, looped her arm in Megs, and they both walked swiftly along the path, leading them back to the carriage.

Despite Meg's confused glances between Lyla and Noah, Lyla did not turn back, nor did she glance over her shoulder. Instead, she walked tall and with as much confidence as she could muster, praying he was still sitting on the bench.

Picking up her speed, pulling Meg along, Lyla was grateful Noah did not follow her, or call out to her, but seeing his eyes narrowed, and his face became still when she bid him farewell, Lyla could see that Noah Valdez was not a happy man.

Chapter 15

"What was that all about?" Meg asked once they climbed back into the carriage.

"Nothing." Lyla wiped a tear away from her cheek.

"Um, I think not. Tell me what happened, Lyla!"

"Noah … Mister Valdez … is not happy I chose Winston instead of him. He believed *he* was the better choice," Lyla replied, looking out the carriage as they travelled away from the park.

"Okay, fair enough, but did you have to be so rude to him?"

Lyla spun her head quickly to look at Meg. Another tear ran down her cheek. "You do not understand."

"Then tell me." Meg leant forward, placing her hand tenderly on Lyla's knee. Lyla flinched a little at the touch. "Lyla. What happened?"

Lyla paused a moment, trying to work out how to explain her dislike of Noah to Meg. "At the end of my Flowering Day Ceremony, when I was saying goodbye to Noah, I may have told him … I was sorry I did not pick him instead." She paused.

Meg sighed, "Did you want to pick him as your suitor?"

Lyla nodded. "Yes. At the end, it was between him and Winston."

"I see, but you will need to explain more, because right now, I am still a little confused."

"Noah informed me while we were sitting together, I still had time to change my mind. He believed I was going to pick him, and he was … angry when I picked Winston instead. He believed I had … led him on during the night."

"Had you?"

"I am not sure. Like I said, it was a tough choice. I really did think he could be the one."

"And he is obviously still upset with your decision, then."

"I guess so." Lyla looked out to the side, watching the trees pass by.

"I am still not sure though, why you spoke to him so rudely today."

Lyla slowly turned back to Meg and held her gaze.

"While talking, he … threatened me. Told me I would be sorry for not picking him. He grabbed my leg and squeezed it so hard that it frightened me. I couldn't understand it — he was such a gentleman during the night but then turned so abruptly. And today once again he questioned my choice."

Meg's hand travelled to her mouth, and her eyes were wide in horror. "Lyla! Did you tell your father or Winston?"

"No," she replied quietly.

"Then why didn't you say anything to me! Why didn't you tell me he laid a hand on you?"

"I didn't want to think about it. I was in such a happy place with Winston, and I thought once I walked away from him, he would just leave. This is the first time I have seen him since."

"And clearly, he's still not happy. I do wish you had told me, Lyla."

"What difference would it have made? He went back home with his parents. I assumed he would just get on with his life."

Meg sighed heavily. "Well, let us hope that will be the last time we see him."

"I hope so," Lyla smiled weakly.

"Have you thought about how you would like to wear your hair for the wedding?" Meg asked as Lyla removed her bonnet and tossed her hair loose. Lyla appreciated Meg trying her best to distract her.

"Well." Lyla's mood perked up, and she turned to Meg. "I was thinking of a braided coiffure style. I know it's old and outdated, but I do think it will look wonderful with the veil."

"Hmm, it is an older style for sure, but I think you're right." Med turned Lyla's head slightly away and ran her fingers loosely through her long hair. "A braided bun would be the perfect place to attach the veil, and the side braids would frame your face beautifully." She pulled Lyla's face back and smiled.

"We will also need to organise what clothes to pack for your wedding night and for the next few days, until all your clothes are brought to your new house," added Meg, before she raised her eyebrows. "Where will you be staying on the night of your wedding, anyway?"

A sheepish grin spread across Lyla's cheeks. "Winston bought a house a year ago, knowing he wanted to get married. It's not far from here. We'll stay there, and he has given you permission to come live there too and continue as my handmaid."

"Wonderful." Meg smiled and clasped Lyla's hands in hers. "I will be sure to bring as much of your clothing as I can fit in the carriage with me when I arrive."

By the time they returned to the manor, Lyla had put the incident with Noah behind her and was back to her cheerful self. Keeping busy, Lyla walked through the gardens, and picked a few flowers to give to her mama, before retreating to the library to finish her book.

After dinner, Lyla returned to her room and sat at her dresser, watching in the mirror as Meg sectioned off a large portion of her hair. Attempting a wedding updo, Meg braided and twisted her hair into a bun at the base of her neck. "Meg," she said suddenly, turning to grab her hands. The remaining loose hair around her face fluttering with the movement. "Please do not tell anyone about Noah. There's nothing to be done about it, and I would like to forget about the whole thing."

"I promised not to say anything about the incident, or what happened on the Ceremony night, but that doesn't mean I'm not concerned," Meg replied honestly.

"Thank you." Lyla turned back around, studying her reflecting in the mirror.

Once she and Winston were married and living in their new house, she would get on with her life, and hopefully Noah would get on with his. There was no reason for her to think otherwise.

Chapter 16

Finally, after three weeks of preparation, the day of the wedding finally arrived. Meg entered Lyla's room and swiftly opened the curtains, flooding the room with light. Turning on her heels to walk towards Lyla's bed, Meg was surprised to find the bed empty.

The sheets and covers were thrown back, indicating the bed *had* been slept in, but Lyla was not in it. Glancing at the small chair that sat near the bed, Meg noticed Lyla's slippers and dressing gown were also missing.

"Lyla!" she called out, walking towards the small washroom attached to Lyla's bedroom. She knocked on the closed door. "Lyla. Are you in there?" There was no reply. "Lyla?" Meg knocked again before opening the door. The washroom was empty as well.

Her brow creased with confusion, and feeling a little embarrassed to find she could not locate her ward, Meg quickly left Lyla's room to search for her. Descending the grand staircase, she made her way to the kitchen. Lyla was known to sneak down there in the mornings to eat with the cook.

Stepping into the large busy room, she glanced around, trying to spot Lyla's blonde hair.

"Looking for Lyla?" the cook asked.

"Yes, has she been here?"

"No, not this morning," the cook replied, going back to kneading dough for bread.

With a quick smile of thanks, Meg turned back, wondering where else to look. It unnerved her a little that she couldn't find her, but Meg told herself there were still plenty of places within the manor Lyla could be.

Continuing to search the house, Meg heard voices coming from the sitting room, and as she rushed through the doors, Meg came to a halt when she saw Lyla curled up on the spacious bay window seat with Iris.

Sighing with relief, she walked up to the two girls. "What on earth are you two doing here?"

"I couldn't sleep," Lyla confessed.

"Neither could I!" piped Iris. "I was way too excited."

"I was worried for a moment. I thought you had gotten cold feet and run away," commented Meg, trying her best to keep her tone light as she stared at Lyla.

"Oh, I am sorry. I was just nervous, and when I heard the birds singing, I got up. I was making my way down to the kitchen, but I ran into Iris, and we ended up here watching the sunrise."

"So, you don't have cold feet?" Meg teased.

Lyla laughed. "No, not that I am aware of. I do hope Winston doesn't either."

"You're lucky you didn't run into him this morning. You know it's bad luck to see the groom before the wedding!"

Lyla and Iris giggled. "He's in the guest house. Why would he be in the manor, anyway?" asked Iris.

"Who knows, maybe he likes to sneak into the kitchen in the morning too." Meg laughed with Lyla.

"Will you be in the new house after the wedding today?" Lyla asked Meg as she slipped off the seat and grasped Meg's hand.

"Yes. I will be travelling to the house in a separate carriage, along with yours this afternoon. How else would you be getting out of your wedding dress?" Then she leaned forward and whispered to Lyla, not wanting Iris to hear. "Unless you want your husband to undress you!"

Lyla blushed and covered her mouth. "Meg! You cannot say that!"

Meg laughed. "He would be in his right place to do so. He will be your husband then."

Lyla blushed deeper. "I'm not even sure if he would know how to undress a female, especially one wearing as many layers as my wedding gown." She giggled again.

"I guess not. Then you are lucky I shall be there to help you out. Now, we need to start getting you ready."

Lyla pulled Iris closer and kissed her on her head before she cupped Iris's face with her hands and stared into her eyes. "For what it's worth, even though you irritate me dreadfully, I will miss you the most."

A tear sprang from Iris's eye. "And I will miss you." Iris ran from the room and headed upstairs to get dressed.

"Is she okay?" Meg asked, and Lyla sighed.

"While we watched the sunrise together, Iris told me that although she was happy about my marriage, the house won't be the same without me. She even questioned who she was going to boss around once I'm gone."

"She has a fair point there," Meg smiled, and Lyla nodded.

"Emily never listens to a word Iris says, and Jonathan will only put up with her for so long before he retreats. Do you know Iris even suggested our parents could have another baby!"

"She certainly is eager to have someone to boss around, isn't she?" Meg chuckled.

"I told her that, hopefully, I will have children of my own soon enough, and that with full aunty rights, she can boss them around to her heart's content. She loved the sound of that. Though it didn't stop Iris from trying to persuade me to live in the guest house until she is old enough to attend her own Flowering Day."

"I think it's safe to say she's going to miss you," Meg said softly.

"I know, and I'll miss her too. Yet, I know for Winston's sake, it's the best thing for us to move into the house he bought," Lyla said.

"Do not fret, Lyla. She will be fine without you. I am sure she will find a way to boss Emily and others in the household. You know how stubborn she is!" Lyla giggled, knowing Meg was right.

Meg grabbed Lyla's hand. "Shall we get you ready for this wedding?" Her eyebrow arched up.

Lyla nodded. "Yes. Why not?"

Together, they walked arm in arm up the staircase. Entering her bedroom, Lyla came to an abrupt halt, her jaw dropping open at the sight before her.

Standing in the middle of the room, on the dressmaker's dummy, stood Lyla's wedding dress. Meg had moved it from the corner of the room earlier and removed the protective sheet, allowing the morning sunlight to shine onto her dress.

With the window open and the curtains pulled back, a slight breeze drifted through, provoking the many layers of lace and silk to flow and dance like it was floating off the ground. The dress looked magical, like it had a life of its own as it glittered against the light.

It looks like something an angel would wear.

Lyla walked up to the dress and gently caressed the intricate lace. "Do you think I will look as beautiful in this dress as it does now?"

"No, of course not!" Meg replied. Lyla looked up at Meg, a shocked scowl on her face. Meg laughed. "You will look more beautiful!"

Lyla shook her head. "Don't scare me like that." Moving away from her dress, she sat down at her dresser and looked at her reflection in the mirror. Studying her face, the small pert nose in the middle, the light spray of freckles across her nose and her blue eyes, Lyla stared, for the last time, at the face of a young unmarried girl.

Meg laughed. "Let's get this hair done." She grabbed Lyla's brush and pulled it through her long hair before separating it off into two sections.

"Do you think Winston is as nervous as I am?" she asked Meg through the mirror.

"Did he seem nervous last night at dinner?" Meg asked as she braided the front section, weaving the hair from one ear to the other, across the front of Lyla's head and pinning it down. The braid sat high like a natural crown and glimmered where the sunlight caught it.

"No, he seemed very much at ease," Lyla replied, admiring Meg's work. Lyla and Winston had enjoyed a romantic dinner together the night before to celebrate their last dinner of being unmarried.

"Well, I dare say, from the way I have seen him looking at you, he will get through this day, nerves or not. Knowing you chose him to be your husband should be enough to ease any nerves."

Meg always found a way of calming Lyla down. "But what if he gets cold feet and decides he is not right for me? He could still back out of this arrangement."

Meg stopped what she was doing and knelt next to Lyla. "Lyla Pierson! Did you not hear a word I just said? If he *were* going to back out, which I don't believe he'd do for a second, he would be foolish in doing so. You make a wonderful couple. Any man would be lucky to have you, and you, who had the chance to pick someone else …" Lyla blushed, remembering how close she had come to picking another suitor. "Chose him."

Meg stood back up and, gathering the back section, brushed it into a smooth ponytail before braiding the full length. Twisting the braid around into a large bun, Meg pinned it firmly at the nape of Lyla's neck. Admiring her hair in the reflection, Lyla watched as Meg abruptly turned away, but not before she noticed a tear roll from Meg's eye.

Calling out to Agnes, Grace's attendant, who'd offered to assist dressing Lyla, Meg got Lyla to stand and removed her dressing gown. Helping her change into her wedding undergarments, stockings, and shoes, Agnes tied the corset tight, to pinch in her waist, and adjusted the underskirt, making sure it sat correctly and centred over the bustle. Finally, Meg and Agnes slipped on her wedding apron and bodice, both fussing over the pearl buttons. For the last step, Meg slid the comb of the lace veil, embossed with pearls, into Lyla's hair.

Moving to face Lyla, Meg stepped forward and handed Lyla a small box she removed from the pocket of her skirt.

"What is this?" Lyla asked curiously.

"A small wedding gift from all the ladies in the house."

Lyla looked at Meg with surprise. "You didn't need to get me anything."

"Most of us have watched you grow up from a baby, and we are all so proud of you. We could not let you go without giving you something."

Lyla looked down at the small silver box in her hand and slowly pried off the lid. Lying on a cushion of blood red velvet, lay the most beautiful necklace and earring set Lyla had ever seen.

A delicate string of light pink and white pearls shone in the sunlight. At the base of the necklace was a large silver pendant encasing a shimmering opal. Two matching earrings sat on either side. Lyla looked at both Meg and Agnes, completely lost for words.

"Thank you," she finally managed to whisper.

"Our pleasure. We all know this is not as opulent as the jewellery you received from your family, but we hoped you would wear them today," replied Meg, wiping away a small tear.

"Oh yes please," Lyla nodded enthusiastically.

"Here, let me." Agnes stepped forward and took the box from Lyla. Carefully, she clipped the earrings onto Lyla's lobes and, picking up the necklace, positioned it gently around her throat, clasping it at the back of Lyla's neck.

Lyla placed her hand on the necklace and looked at the two ladies. "Thank you so much. It is wonderful." Lyla then turned to look at her reflection in the large oval mirror.

Lyla gasped in shock, and her eyes widened as she took in her reflection. Turning her body left and right, Lyla watched how the lace and silk swirled around her body, and as her eyes sparkled with moisture, a single tear ran down her flushed cheek.

"Oh, come now." Meg rushed towards Lyla, a small handkerchief in her hand. "You don't like the dress?" she queried.

"It is ..." Lyla swallowed the lump in her throat. "I am ... beautiful!"

"Of course you are, my love. This day and every other day I have raised you." Lyla looked over her shoulder through the reflection to see her mother standing in the doorway. She turned quickly, the back of her dress taking a few seconds longer to rotate.

"Mama," she gasped with surprise. She had not heard her bedroom door open.

Grace walked elegantly towards Lyla, her own pale blue silk and taffeta dress flowing behind her. "You are the most beautiful bride I have ever seen." She kissed Lyla on her cheek, brushing away another tear from her daughter's cheek.

"Come now. If you keep crying, you are going to ruin this stunning dress of yours." She took Lyla's hands in hers.

Lyla stared into her mother's blue eyes. They were slightly red, like she had been crying. "Everyone is ready. It is time for you to head downstairs." Her voice cracked a little, and Lyla picked up that something was not right.

"Mama. Are you okay?"

Grace smiled weakly at Lyla. "Just so happy to see you looking so beautiful."

"Thank you, Mama."

"This is an especially important day, Lyla. Not just for you, but for the whole family." She started helping Lyla put on her small white silk gloves. "You are so strong, and you always make the right decisions. Today is one of those days. I know you will do the right thing. Your father and I are proud of you," her voice quivered. She leant forward, kissing Lyla one more time, then quickly turned on her heels and walked out of the bedroom.

Lyla watched her leave, then looked at Meg with confusion. "That was strange. Did she seem a bit ... sad to you?"

Meg nodded softly. "I thought she would be happier. You are the first of her daughters to get married, maybe she is not ready to let you go so soon." Meg moved behind Lyla and fixed a few stray bits of hair that had fallen loose and readjusted the veil. Moments later, there was a gentle knock at the door.

"Come in!" Lyla called out.

Emily and Lyla's best friend and bridesmaid, Katelyn, quickly entered. Lyla's face brightened, and she grinned at the two girls.

Emily seemed to float into the room, her dress of soft pink silk and lace swishing silently around her. The bodice showed off her tiny figure well, and the small veil, trimmed with pearls, offset the curls in her blonde hair. In her hand, she held two beautiful bouquets of white carnations and white roses. Katelyn's dress was similar, but in a darker tone of pink.

Rushing to her side, Emily gave Lyla a gentle yet tight hug. "You look stunning," she said tenderly.

"Thank you," Lyla replied while glancing over Emily's shoulder. "Where is Iris?"

Emily's eyes clouded over, but she quickly smiled and fussed over Lyla's dress. "Do not worry about Iris. This is your day."

"I do hope she won't be late," Lyla said, and turning back to the full-length mirror, smiled at the reflection before her.

Katelyn also started fussing over Lyla's veil, making sure it sat correctly in her hair. Although Meg had already fixed it in, Katelyn kept herself busy and avoided looking into Lyla's eyes. The tension in the room changed from the moment Lyla's mother had entered, and Lyla could not pinpoint the reason.

After a few minutes, there was another knock on the door. "Come in." Lyla called out, overwhelmed with the fussing. The door opened, and Albert walked slowly into the room. Once he laid his eyes on Lyla, he stopped, and his eyes teared up.

"You look … beautiful."

Lyla turned around carefully so as not to catch the veil on the back of her bustle.

"Thank you, Papa." She smiled widely at him. He smiled back at her, but she could see the smile did not touch his eyes. Lyla frowned a little. Both of her parents didn't appear as happy as she believed they should be. What if they did not approve of this marriage? What if they had changed their minds and deemed Winston unsuitable?

"May I please talk to my daughter alone," he said to Meg, Agnes, Emily, and Katelyn. Agnes quickly curtsied to him and quietly left the room. Emily and Katelyn glanced quickly at Lyla, smiled awkwardly, and left as well.

Lyla's frown deepened. "Papa," she said as she grabbed Meg's hand, preventing her from leaving. "What is wrong?"

Albert looked at Lyla, and his chest rose with the large breath he inhaled. His eyes quickly shifted to Meg's face, and Meg, seeing he wanted her to leave, tried to pull her arm out of Lyla's grip.

"No, you stay with me!" she said to Meg. Lyla sensed something was not right. She looked her father in the eye. "Has something happened?" She swallowed hard. "Has Winston decided he does not wish to marry me?"

Albert took two steps towards Lyla but then stopped. His shoulders drooped a little. "I do not want to alarm you, and I wish I were coming here with better news." His hands found each other, and he began to slightly clench them. "Iris is … missing," he said quietly.

"Iris?" Lyla questioned, but a small sigh of relief escaped her lips when she realised Winston still wanted to marry her. "What do you mean, Iris is missing?" Lyla looked sideways at Meg, who shook her head in confusion as well.

"We cannot find her."

"But I saw her just a few hours ago. Where could she have gone?" Lyla took a step towards her father, but he stepped back, keeping the same distance between them. "Papa!"

"We looked everywhere. But ..." a tear fell from his eye. Lyla took another step closer, but he held up his hand to stop her. "Lyla. I am so sorry."

Lyla turned once again to Meg, her mouth agape. Meg's expression mirrored her own. Lyla went to remove her veil, but her father quickly walked up to her and placed his hand on hers.

"No, leave it there. The wedding must go ahead."

Lyla shook her head. "I will not get married if Iris is not there! We need to find her!"

Albert sighed again, but this time, Lyla could see he was desperately trying to hold himself together. "You must get married, Lyla. For Iris's sake and for her safety, and we need to go. Now."

Lyla took a step backwards. "I do not understand what is happening!"

Another tear ran down Albert's cheek. "Iris has been ... taken. This we know for certain." Lyla stumbled as her knees gave out. It was only Meg, stepping quickly to grasp her elbow, which prevented Lyla from falling to the floor.

"By whom?" Lyla whispered as Albert and Meg escorted Lyla to a chair.

Albert glanced over Lyla's head to Meg. Meg still refused to leave Lyla's side. He closed his eyes and dropped his head.

"Lyla, please." Her father pleaded. "Trust me."

"Papa." Lyla shook her head again. "If Iris has been taken, we could postpone the wedding and get married another day."

"No. It must be today. Everyone is downstairs, in the ballroom, waiting. Please, Lyla."

Meg grasped Lyla's hand as tears fell down her cheeks.

"You will understand more, I promise, but we must go ... now!"

Lyla stared at her father, unable to keep her anger and frustration from her expression. She shook her head. "I do not understand how getting married is the right thing to do, when my sister has been taken away!"

Albert moved closer to Lyla and got down on his knees. "I know how hard it is for you to comprehend things right now, but to get Iris back, the wedding must go ahead. Everything you need to know will be revealed to you after the wedding."

He stood back up and offered his hand to Lyla. After a few moments, she looked down at her dress, and then into the mirror that sat on the small table. This is not how she pictured her day to go, but trusting in her father, as he had never given her a reason not to, Lyla took his hand.

"Do you promise we will get her back after I get married today?"

Albert nodded. "Yes, I promise."

Accepting his word, Lyla stood and clasped her father's arm.

Chapter 17

When Lyla retired to her bed the night before, the air throughout the manor smelt sweet, perfumed with the scent of Winston's ceremony red rose, and Lyla's white carnations which had arrived at the manor that morning.

In preparation for the wedding, the staff spent the day positioning them throughout the house. Large vases sat on tables, at the top and base of the grand staircase, and throughout the dining room, turning the manor into an indoor garden.

Yet as Albert escorted Lyla through her bedroom doors and out into the main hallway, she frowned. The scent in the air had changed.

As Lyla and her father made their way to the top of the grand staircase, Lyla tightened her grip on her father's arm as she tried to work out what was different. Albert gripped her arm as though sensing Lyla's trepidation as he began walking her down the stairs.

Seeing Emily and Katelyn waiting at the foot of the staircase gave Lyla a small sense of normality in the confusing situation, but that quickly faded when Lyla's gaze fell on only two groomsmen.

During the third week of their engagement, Winston introduced his three groomsmen to Lyla and her family. Two of his close friends and his younger brother, but Lyla frowned upon the realisation that the two men below were not the men she had previously met.

As they reached the foyer floor, the men nodded respectfully to her in greeting as she and her father passed.

"Papa?" Lyla said, but squeezing her hand, Albert ushered her across the foyer towards the closed doors of the ballroom. Glancing over her shoulder, Lyla saw Emily and Katelyn following close behind, their hands resting softly on the arms of the two mystery men by their sides. She felt a pang in her chest knowing that Iris should be there as well … but she was not. Fear settled in her chest, making it hard for her to breathe.

Albert hesitated and turned to face Lyla. Emily took the opportunity to fix her veil, making sure it hung neatly over the bustle of her dress, then handed Lyla her bouquet. Lyla watched as she silently took her place back beside the stranger. Lyla's sorrow deepened when Emily refused to make eye contact with Lyla. With a gentle squeeze of her hand, Albert brought Lyla's attention back to him, and he held her gaze firmly.

"No matter what you see, please do not react. This wedding must take place. Promise me, Lyla."

Her eyes widened as she wondered what he could mean. "Papa, you are scaring me." Lyla squeezed his hand as her heart raced faster.

"I need you to trust me, Lyla. Everything will be fine. You just have to say your vows, and we will get our Iris back."

Lyla nodded tentatively, but her thoughts swam with confusion. She knew there was so much her father was not telling her, but Lyla would do anything to ensure Iris's safety. Albert turned to face the door and set his shoulders as he nodded to the two door attendants, and stepping forward, they reached for the door handles.

It was time for the wedding to proceed.

As soon as the doors opened, a small orchestra situated at the far end of the room started playing the bridal waltz.

Lyla's eyes widened in delight as she took in the ballroom for the first time. The room had been transformed into a stunning wedding chapel, with rows of chairs filled with family and friends lining either side of a beautiful ruby red carpet. The carpet ran the length of the aisle towards the platform where, a mere three weeks ago, Lyla met her five suitors and chose Winston.

Instead of the throne she previously sat on, a beautiful wooden pulpit stood in its place before a clergyman wearing his finest white and yellow robes.

Guiding her gently along the red carpet, Albert led his daughter down the aisle, her bridesmaids and the two groomsmen following behind. With her thoughts racing, and her heart thundering against her chest, Lyla allowed herself to glance around the guests filling the ballroom. Despite the beautiful music, the room had an eerie sense of calmness, which only set Lyla further on edge.

Although the guests turned in their chairs to watch her approach, Lyla noted the solemn expressions on the faces of her family, wondering why they didn't seem happy to see her. A few smiled at her as she passed, but they didn't feel genuine to Lyla, while others just appeared confused.

To her relief, many other guests, family, and friends of Winston's she had not met, smiled at her. Smiles of happiness and pride, of joy and well wishes Lyla expected to see from her family and friends on her wedding day.

The hush in the room began to make Lyla's hands sweat. Inhaling deeply, she did her best to push aside her worry and fear, knowing once she set her eyes on Winston, everything would be okay, and her heart and anxiety would slow. With a confident smile, she shifted her glance towards the end of the aisle and looked at the man she was about to marry.

The groom stood with his back to her, dressed in a stylish dark grey suit, with deep brown hair neatly resting above his shoulders. Lyla gasped aloud. The morning sunlight streaming through the open windows highlighted and enhanced the flecks of ginger in his hair. Lyla's forehead furrowed in confusion. That was not the shorter, blond hair of Winston.

As Lyla and her father approached, the groom finally turned around and Lyla froze, her feet unable to take another step, her mouth dropping open in shock.

"Papa!" she exclaimed quietly.

"Please, Lyla," her father whispered, gripping her arm tighter, pulling her forwards. Glancing over her shoulder to where her mother and Jonathan sat, Lyla found neither of them would make eye contact with her, and her mama was silently crying.

A surge of butterflies flittered through Lyla's stomach, and her knees went weak as Albert ushered Lyla to the end of the carpet. When the bridal waltz ended, Albert presented Lyla to the groom. Yet Lyla was at a loss for words as she took in the features of the man standing before her.

It was not Winston who stood at the pulpit waiting to marry Lyla, but a man she thought she would never see again.

Standing tall and proud, with a grin that turned Lyla's blood cold, was Noah Valdez.

Chapter 18

Albert slowly placed Lyla's hand into Noah's outstretched palm. Time seemed to slow as she watched her father smile grimly at Noah, his expression devoid of happiness. Noah wrapped his fingers around Lyla's hand, squeezing it tenderly. She fought against her repulsion as her hand instinctively tried to jerk out of his, a motion that did not go unmissed by Noah.

Blinking rapidly, Lyla hoped the scene before her was nothing more than a terrible dream that she would soon wake up from. Instead, Noah remained before her, his blue eyes taking in her dress and veil as though he wanted to devour her. It sickened her to know that only a few moments ago she'd admired her angelic appearance as a bride, and that it was Noah who looked so pleased.

His smile widened, but Lyla did not smile back. She was too confused, knowing his expression was what she'd envisioned Winston greet her with. Her heart sank. Where was Winston? Had he changed his mind? And why was Noah standing there in his place?

"You look amazing," he whispered, and the sound of his voice sent a shiver down her spine.

Lyla was speechless as she turned to her father, her eyes pleading with him to explain what was happening. Without hesitation, though not meeting her gaze, Albert stepped forward and placed his hand on top of Lyla's and Noah's.

"You have our blessing from this day forth," he spoke with conviction before he leaned forward and planted a small kiss on Lyla's cheek through the veil. Straightening, he squared his shoulders, and with a nod to the clergyman, he turned and walked off the platform. As he took his seat beside his wife, Lyla watched as he took her mother's hand tightly, placing it in his lap.

Emily quickly fixed Lyla's train, tucking it neatly at her side, before standing behind her and Katelyn moved beside her. Despite having her sister and best friend by her side, Lyla felt alone, confused, and scared. Unsure of what to do next, she forced herself to meet Noah's gaze and searched his face for answers. But before he could say anything, the clergyman spoke.

"We are gathered here today in the sight of God to witness the holy union of Noah Valdez to Lyla Pierson. If any person objects to this marriage, may they speak now or forever hold their tongue."

A nervous shiver ran through Lyla as she carefully looked around the room, hoping someone would speak up and end her nightmare.

No one stood up.

No one spoke.

When she looked at her family, her confusion only intensified as they kept their heads down, avoiding her gaze. None of them opened their mouths, none of them interjected or stood. Instead, her papa nodded just once, his eyes pleading for her to continue.

Sliding her gaze to the other side of the aisle, Lyla's eyes fell on Brianna, Noah's mother. She beamed at Lyla, her smile full of adoration and affection.

Lyla blinked heavily, her mind rolling deeper into the dark void before her.

Did no one else in the room understand that Noah was not meant to be standing in front of her? Had everyone forgotten she'd picked Winston's rose and not Noah's iris?

As Noah gently squeezed her hand, bringing her back from the edge of madness, Lyla's eyes moistened as an overwhelming sense of numbness enveloped her. Slowly, she turned back to face him. The movement felt sluggish, like she was moving through water.

The clergyman, accepting no one objected to the marriage, spoke once more and, in a daze, Lyla turned to face him, her eyes falling to his mouth. Although she could see his lips moving, his voice sounded slow and far away.

"Marriage is a sacred covenant and shall not be taken for granted. It is a union founded on love, trust, and fidelity." He turned to Noah. "Noah, will you please repeat after me." Noah squeezed Lyla's hands again, and she turned to him, her breathing shallow as a wave of dizziness took hold. He locked eyes with her and repeated the clergyman's vows.

"I, Noah Valdez, take you Lyla Pierson, to be my wife, to have and to hold from this day forward, for better or worse, for richer, for poorer, in sickness and in health, to love and to cherish, and I promise to be faithful to you until death parts us."

The clergyman then turned to Lyla. "Lyla, will you please repeat after me." Lyla glanced again towards her father, desperate for him to stand up and do something. Instead, he only nodded and gave her a weak smile.

Swallowing hard and fighting back the tears which threatened to be her undoing, she turned back and stared at

Noah. Feeling everyone's gaze on her, she slowly repeated the clergyman's vows.

"I, Lyla Pierson, take you Noah Valdez, to be my husband, to have and to hold from this day forward, for better or worse, for richer, for poorer, in sickness and in health, to love and to cherish, and I promise to be faithful to you until death parts us."

"As those before us are our witnesses, let Lyla and Noah now exchange rings."

Noah's best man, the gentleman who had walked beside Emily, stepped forward, and placed a simple gold band into his right hand and took the glove off Noah's left. At the same moment, Emily, having passed her small bouquet to Katelyn, moved towards Lyla, gently removed the glove on her left hand, and took her bouquet. Carefully, she placed a matching gold band in her free hand. At no point did she dare look at Lyla.

"Repeat after me," the clergyman said to Noah.

"With this ring, I thee wed, in the name of the Father, the Son and the Holy Spirt." By the time Noah repeated the words, he had slid the ring down Lyla's finger. Gently, he squeezed her hand again, the sensation tingling through Lyla's arm.

The clergyman then turned to Lyla. "Repeat after me."

"With this ring …" her voice faltered, but she continued. "I thee wed, in the name of the Father, the Son and the Holy Spirt." Though Lyla spoke the words, they meant nothing to her. After pushing the wedding band, on Noah's finger, Lyla tried to drop her hand, but Noah held on tight.

"The marriage between these two is witnessed by all in this room. May we grant them a happy marriage and a blessed and long life together. You may now kiss the bride."

Noah dropped Lyla's hands and carefully lifted her veil over her head. Cupping her face in his hands, he leant towards her. Lyla stiffened and pulled back slightly, and Noah tightened his grip. Moving in closer, his lips almost touching hers, he whispered.

"If you want to see Iris again, you will kiss me!" Lyla's eyes widened as the realisation dawned on her exactly who was responsible for Iris's disappearance. Sighing in defiance, letting her shoulders slump, Noah closed the gap and kissed her gently. Feeling the warmth and pressure on her lips, Lyla accepted the kiss but refused to return it.

"May I present to you all, Mr and Mrs Valdez," the clergyman spoke boldly, and soft applause echoed around the ballroom.

Pulling herself from his grasp, Lyla and Noah turned and faced the guests. With a large, over the top smile, Noah clasped Lyla's elbow and escorted her back down the aisle and out of the ballroom, passing their family and friends. As soon as they walked through the doors and into the foyer, Lyla yanked her arm free and stepped away from him.

"What is this game you are playing? Where is Iris? Where is Winston?" she hissed at him, her frustration and fear turning to rage.

"Ah, so many questions—and such anger." Noah stepped closer to her again, lowering his voice. "Let us save the questions for later, my dear wife. We have the wedding breakfast to attend."

Hearing the rest of the bridal members approaching, Noah grabbed Lyla's hand again and, before she could question him further, he escorted her through the house to the dining room.

Chapter 19

Despite the numerous questions running through Lyla's mind, she had to acknowledge the dining room looked amazing.

The main table was laid out with twenty beautiful china plate settings, cutlery, and crystal glasses. Four smaller tables, the same ones they used at her Flowering Day Ceremony, were also set up for the guests, laid out the same.

Inhaling deeply, desperate for the agony of the morning's events to dissipate, the perfumed scent she had detected when she left her bedroom, returned.

Scanning the room, Lyla noticed four large vases placed in each corner, brimming with flowers, but as Lyla inspected the arrangements, she finally understood what was wrong.

Intermingled with her white carnations, baby's breath and soft silver ferns, were blue irises.

A realisation suddenly came to her. The scent in the air was different because the red roses that had arrived yesterday—the roses which represented Winston—were missing.

Swallowing thickly, the numbness in her heart returning, Lyla allowed Noah to lead her to the main table where he pulled her chair out for her, acting like a perfect gentleman instead of one who had threatened her family. Standing behind his own chair with his hand resting firmly on the nape of her neck, Noah watched patiently as the guests entered the room and found their nominated place cards.

It was at that moment that reality finally sank in, and Lyla felt completely helpless. As she watched the guests enter, she saw her parents, grandparents, aunts, uncles, cousins, and friends, yet the only person she recognised among the other half of the guests was Brianna.

Thoughts overwhelmed her as she scanned the room. How did this happen? How did things change so dramatically? Only the day before, she had walked through the room, making sure everything was in its place and that all the name cards were correctly laid out. Now unfamiliar faces stared at her from where Winston's family and friends were supposed to sit.

Yet, they smiled at her, offering greetings and well wishes. They all seemed to look at her as if nothing were out of the ordinary, like Lyla had picked Noah from the very start.

Lyla's parents sat at the end of the table to her left and Noah's parents at the end to his right. Next to her sat Emily and Katelyn, and next to Noah, his two groomsmen. Lyla noted the chair and setting for Iris remained, and the setting on the other side, which would have been for Winston's third groomsman, his younger brother, was now occupied by a third groomsman who Lyla did not know.

Opposite her and her bridesmaids, sat her grandparents and three elderly guests that Lyla assumed were Noah's grandparents, sat opposite him and his groomsmen. Family members and friends occupied the remaining tables.

Despite all the people in the room, Lyla felt incredibly alone.

Feeling overwhelmed, Lyla dropped her eyes to the table, and her gaze fell onto the most beautiful wedding cake she had ever seen. A single layered fruit cake, covered in white frosting and embellished with orange blossoms, with a single ribbon of white silk wrapped around it. Yet, with everything that was happening, Lyla could not fully appreciate its beauty. She felt numb, confused, and scared — she needed someone to explain what was happening.

Ten minutes later, after all the guests were seated, a hush fell over the room. Using this moment, Noah addressed the room.

"Thank you all for being here today to witness the union between Lyla and myself. We are both honoured to have your blessings. Please enjoy the feast."

Brushing his fingers along the back of Lyla's neck, causing a shiver to rush down her back, Noah finally took his seat. Leaning in to whisper in Lyla's ear, his warm breath tickled the fine hairs on her neck, sending another shiver through her.

"I meant what I said earlier. You look beautiful."

Lyla closed her eyes briefly, trying to control her breathing as she placed her hands on the table. Noah placed his hand tenderly over hers, a portrayal of the perfect couple. Lyla concentrated on sitting still and lowered her eyes to the plate in front of her.

Taking their cue, Lyla's bridesmaids stood and raised their glasses towards the room. "To the bride and groom," Katelyn said, raising her glass above Lyla's head.

"To the bride and groom," the guests replied, toasting the newlyweds.

Placing her glass down, Emily, with Katelyn assistance, pulled the wedding cake towards them, removed the silk ribbon from the cake, and began cutting it into smaller pieces. A silent hush remained over the room as Lyla watched the knife slice into the cake over and over, each feeling like a slash to her own heart instead. Once the cake was cut, each slice carefully boxed, and put aside for the guests as they left, the breakfast food was served, and the feast began.

Throughout the meal, Noah tried to engage Lyla in conversation, but keeping her composure, Lyla only answered what she needed to, to keep up the facade. Family members at the other tables questioned Iris's whereabouts too, forcing Lyla and her parents to lie and say that she was unwell to hide the awful truth.

"I do hope she feels better," Lyla's grandmother said. "She is missing a wonderful event."

Lyla's grandfather, never one to hold his tongue, turned to Albert. "I thought Lyla picked that Winston fellow at her Flowering Day. Did I miss something?"

"No, father," Albert said calmly. "Winston was … unable to marry Lyla, so Noah was her next choice." Lyla's breath caught at the comment.

Could Papa be telling the truth? Had Winston changed his mind after all and decided he was not worthy of this marriage?

Pretending she never heard her father's comment, Lyla continued eating, chewing her food without tasting it, as confusion swam through her mind. Suddenly, a bitter thought struck her hard. If what her father said was true, and Winston had told him he no longer wanted to marry her, Noah would not have been her second choice! Risking a sideways glance, Lyla looked towards her father, but he never raised his eyes from his plate.

The end of breakfast could not have come any faster for Lyla, and finally, Emily and Katelyn escorted Lyla out of the dining room and into the small sitting room, to wait for the end of the reception. The moment the door closed behind Emily, Lyla broke down and started to cry.

It was by far the worst day of her life.

"I am so sorry." Emily rushed to her sister's side, clasping her hands, and kissing them.

"I … I do not understand what is happening?" Lyla blurted out between sobs. "Where is Iris? Where is Winston?" She turned to Katelyn.

"We don't know," Emily responded tearfully.

"How could they both just not be here?" Lyla asked as she sank down in a chair, yanking the veil from her hair and throwing it to the floor. "Tell me, please! What happened this morning after I saw Iris?" Lyla pleaded.

"Papa came to me … to us, not long before we came to you. He told us that things had changed. He said Winston was unable to marry you, and Noah would be marrying you instead. I questioned him about it, but he pleaded with me to follow his lead. He said not to say anything to you, to let him tell you."

"But he never said anything about Winston not being there, and he certainly did not tell me Noah would be standing in his place!" Lyla stood abruptly and started pacing the small room. "And Iris?"

"Papa just said she was unwell and couldn't make it."

"Unwell!" Lyla stopped in her tracks.

"Yes, that's what he told us," Katelyn said, coming to stand next to Lyla.

"He told me she was missing. Missing! Not ill!" Her voice rose in anger. Katelyn's face slackened, and she moved to a seat by the window. Lyla looked hard into

Emily's face. "At the end of the ceremony, when Noah leaned in to kiss me, I didn't move. Noah whispered to me, told me I had to kiss him, or I would never get Iris back. It was him, Emily. Noah took our Iris!"

Tears streamed down Emily's cheeks. "No, Noah wouldn't do that. Mama told me Iris was unwell but refused to let me go to her room. Why would Mama lie to me?"

"To keep her safe, I guess." Lyla resumed pacing, her wedding gown swirling around her ankles each time she turned. "What am I meant to do?"

Emily stared at her. "You did what Papa asked. You married Noah. Now we wait, I guess. But I don't know why Winston no longer wanted to marry you. The last time I saw him; he looked so happy."

Lyla stopped again and quickly returned to Emily's side. "When was the last time you saw him?"

"Yesterday afternoon. I was walking in the garden with Iris when we ran into Winston and his brother. We were all so excited for today."

"And he gave you no indication that he wanted to back out?" Lyla asked desperately.

"No. None. In fact, he said he could not wait to be your husband."

Lyla's head swam as her emotions overwhelmed her. What would have made Winston change his mind? He had seemed so happy when they had lunch together the day before.

Why would Noah have stepped up and taken his spot? Where was Iris? Did Noah hurt her?

With so many thoughts rolling over each other, Lyla felt a mild headache take hold, and she rubbed her temples, trying to subdue the throb.

A gentle knock on the door alerted the three ladies, and Lyla's back stiffened. Meg opened the door and entered the small room. "It is time to go, Lyla. Noah is waiting for you." Her eyes were puffy and red from crying.

"I shall not go with him!" Lyla said defiantly, her hands forming tight fists.

"Lyla, I don't think you have a choice," Meg said as she walked over and picked the veil up from the floor. Approaching Lyla, she stood behind her, sliding the comb of the veil back into Lyla's hair. "I do not know the full story of what has happened, but I do know …" She paused as though she was unsure if she should continue.

"Please, Meg," Lyla said.

"I just know that if you want to see Iris again, you must go with Noah."

Lyla turned around slowly, staring at Meg. "You do know something though! Meg, tell me what you know!" Lyla grasped Meg's hands, her heart racing again.

Meg's shoulders raised as she inhaled deeply. "It's only what I have heard. Iris is missing. After hearing she was ill, I went to her room, but her handmaid informed me she hadn't seen Iris since she dressed her this morning. Iris left her room, talking about picking some flowers for you but hasn't been seen since."

"Where could she be? And where is Winston? I am so confused."

Meg squeezed Lyla's hands. "Do you remember the last conversation you had with Noah, and then with me?" Lyla's brow creased as she thought back to the last time she saw him. It was at the lake just a week ago, yet with everything unfolding, she struggled to recall the conversation. "You told me Noah threatened you. That he said you would be sorry for not picking him. Remember?"

Hearing this, Emily rushed to Lyla's side. "What do you mean he threatened you?" she asked, her voice full of concern.

"Not now, Emily." Lyla replied, brushing her off. But then suddenly, the pieces fell into place. "Noah took Iris as leverage to make me marry him!" she said, staring at Meg.

"Yes, I think so," Meg responded.

"And Winston?" she asked. "Do you know what has happened to him?"

Meg shook her head. "No one has seen him or his family today."

Lyla swallowed the bile rising in her throat. Her Winston was gone, and no one knew where he was. Her sweet little sister was missing, and Noah was responsible. Lyla looked at Emily, at Meg and then at Katelyn.

"Do you think Noah is the reason why Winston is not here?" she asked, her voice quivering and her eyes beginning to well up again.

"I don't think he has hurt him!" Katelyn said, coming to her side.

"What if he chased him away? Threatened him?" Lyla asked.

"He was so nice at your Flowering Day. I can't see him being able to hurt someone," added Emily.

Lyla began pacing again, despite her legs feeling weak. "I guess there is only one way to find out, isn't there?" Lyla said as she looked at the three girls again. "I am going to have to leave with him, aren't I?" she whispered.

"Yes, Lyla. You must," Meg said tenderly, giving her a gentle hug.

"I need to talk to Noah, find out why he has done this to me, to Iris, and tell me where Winston is. I fear what he might be thinking."

"Do you think he might have told Winston you didn't want to marry him? So, he could step forward?" questioned Emily.

"I do not know," Lyla sighed deeply, allowing the air to fill her lungs and her head to clear. Straightening her bodice,

Lyla tugged slightly at her skirt. Then, summoning every ounce of courage she had, Lyla turned toward the door.

"For Iris and Winston!" she said boldly.

"For Iris and Winston," Emily whispered.

Chapter 20

Stepping courageously into the foyer and out the front door of the manor with Emily, Katelyn, and Meg not far behind, Lyla walked past Jonathan, her mother and her father and stood beside Noah. Maintaining her resolute stance, Lyla looked him straight in the eyes.

The dutiful and obedient bride.

Slowly, she moved her gaze from Noah to his family, who stood at the base of the stairs, smiling and looking like they were happy with the arrangement. Lyla wondered if they truly knew what was going on.

Everyone in her family, though, looked sombre and quiet, diverting their eyes, too scared, nervous, or even confused to meet Lyla's. So, she did her best to control her breathing and swallowed deeply. Lyla knew she would have to be incredibly careful with what she did next.

"Once again, thank you all for a wonderful day," Noah spoke out, reaching over and clasping Lyla's hand in his. She flinched at his touch but did not withdraw her hand. "It is wonderful to be accepted by you all. I hope to make Lyla proud." He leaned over, gently tilting his head down, and kissed Lyla on the cheek. She closed her eyes for a fleeting moment, fighting the urge to run away. Releasing her hand, Noah placed his on her back. Once again, she flinched at the contact. Even though his touch was warm through her dress, it did not put her at ease.

"Lyla and I would like to welcome you all to our house next weekend for a picnic lunch. Invites will be sent out in a few days."

Feeling bewildered, Lyla turned and looked at Noah, the man who stood so calmly next to her, inviting their family over like a gentleman should, like a newly married couple were meant to. Yet all the while, he held her dear sister hostage, just to make Lyla marry him. Blinking back the tears, Lyla looked away, wanting to find solace in the garden beyond the house.

At the sound of footsteps crunching on the gravel, Lyla turned and saw her father approach. She could see he wanted to say something, but Noah stiffened, and he pressed against her back so firmly that she staggered half a step forward. As she straightened, Lyla met her father's stare as he glanced quickly from Lyla to Noah. Turning to face Noah, she saw the pursed lips and darkened stare directed at her father, silencing him.

Albert dropped his head slightly and smiled weakly. "Welcome to our family, Noah. It will be an honour to visit you both in a week," he said politely.

Noah's face broke into a smile, and he turned to Lyla. "Come, my beautiful wife, we have a new house to get to."

Guiding her by the waist, Noah led her towards a large black and mahogany carriage. Assisting her up the steps, he carefully pushed her train in after her before he followed, taking his place beside her. As soon as he closed the door, he tapped on the roof, signalling the driver to proceed. With a jolt, the carriage took off, the wheels grinding over the gravel, around the large fountain in the front yard and down the long driveway, taking Lyla away from her family.

Even though the carriage was big enough for four people, Lyla slid herself across the seat, desperate to distance herself from Noah and his familiar cologne. In the confined space, the aroma of lavender and pine, became overwhelming, making Lyla feel unwell.

Noticing the movement, Noah turned slightly to lean back into the corner, enabling his body to face hers.

"Did I tell you that you look beautiful?" he asked, his deep voice filled the carriage.

"Why are you doing this?" Lyla asked, the tears she had held off for so long finally sliding down her cheeks. Noah leant forwards and wiped the tears away, but Lyla pulled back and turned her face from him. He dropped his hand slowly, as a small laugh escaped him.

"You didn't answer my question." Lyla turned back to stare at him and found him gazing at her lovingly as she frowned back.

"Do not frown, Lyla. It does not suit your beautiful face."

"Why?" she questioned.

"Why what?" he asked, his tone calm and peaceful.

"Why are you doing this? Where is Iris? Where is my sister?" Lyla's voice trembled.

He smiled at her, his white teeth peeking out between his lips. Lyla's breath hitched. She could not deny the fact that he was a very handsome man, or that his beauty had taken her breath away when she first saw him. Yet now, as she stared at her husband, he was far from the gentleman she had met a few weeks ago, and his good looks were now nothing but vulgar and menacing.

"If I tell you she is safe, will you calm down?"

"Where is she, Noah!" Lyla's voice raised.

Noah tilted his head slightly, studying her face, and his eyes narrowed slightly. "You seem to be very concerned about your sister, Lyla."

"Of course, I am! Why would I not be?"

"I would have thought you might have been more concerned with why Winston was not standing at the pulpit this morning." He clasped his hands and rested them in his lap. Lyla's eyes widened a little as she swallowed the lump forming in her throat.

"Winston," she whispered as her breathing quickened.

"Have you forgotten him already? Is it feasible, he was *not* the man you were meant to marry after all?" Noah smirked, his voice mocking and cold.

"What have you done with him?" Lyla's voice shook with fear.

"What makes you think I did anything?" Noah's brow creased, but his eyes darkened in humour.

Lyla closed her eyes and took a few deep breaths. When she opened them again, Noah was still staring at her. His head still tilted, he rocked gently from the movement of the carriage.

"Where is Winston, Noah?" Lyla urged, her palms beginning to sweat.

He fiddled with the cuff on his white shirt, pulling it slightly out of his coat sleeve. Lyla could see he was trying to avoid the question, and he did not look at her when he spoke.

"Would you be content to know he died with honour?" he asked, his voice cold and unemotional. Lyla gasped loudly as her hand shot to her mouth.

"No, no." She shook her head. Fresh tears rushed from her eyes, and her stomach churned.

"I gave him every chance to walk away." His blue eyes roved over the shock on her face.

"I don't understand. Did you … kill Winston?" she whispered.

"Unfortunately, yes." He shrugged like it were nothing. "He refused my offer and challenged me to a duel. I guess the better man won the fair bride," he replied, the mocking tone in his voice striking Lyla in the heart.

Grateful she was sitting down, and struggling to get in full breaths, Lyla's body slumped with grief, and she turned her face away from Noah as tears streamed down her cheeks.

"He put up a good fight," Noah continued. "Got a good jab at my left arm, but I guess I am better with a rapier sword than he was."

Lyla couldn't see through the tears. "Do you expect me to thank you for killing the man I chose to be my husband?" she choked, her breath fogging up the window.

"No. But I do want you to see; I was always the better choice for you." His voice deepened a little as he sat up straighter in the seat.

Lyla sat still, letting the carriage rock her gently. She continued to stare out the window at the trees and scenery passing by. Looking but not really seeing anything.

"It was not meant to be like this," she said quietly. "I did not choose you. Why could you not accept that?" She suddenly spun around, glaring at Noah, her hands clenching into fists.

"I don't think you were looking at the grander picture at your Flowering Day, Lyla."

Lyla frowned. "What grander picture?"

"Your family loved me," he said confidently. "Iris warmed up to me very quickly and even Jonathan was content in my company. I watched you all night. It was a simple choice, really. We both knew there were only two men in the room who held your attention. I am not sure what Winston had over me, but I *do* know he was bad for you, and eventually, you would have regretted your decision. I am here to make sure you truly get the best husband you deserve."

"How would you know what I want?"

"That is the role of a good husband, Lyla. To predict his wife's needs at all times." He sat back smugly.

His arrogance stunned Lyla, and she shook her head in disbelief. "And Iris? How does she play a part in this?"

"Would you be shocked to know Iris wanted you to pick me instead? She was terribly upset when you let me leave the manor on your Flowering Day!"

"That is not news to me. She told me how she felt."

"Did she tell you she ran after me, begging me to stay?" Lyla's eyes widened with shock. "Ah, she did not. Interesting!" He smiled again, his cockiness overwhelming. Lyla diverted her eyes once more.

During the ceremony, every time Noah smiled, it softened his face and enhanced his beauty, one factor Lyla took in while making her decision, but now, turning away from him, it was all Lyla could do, to try to stop her heart from skipping a beat, and her face from flushing. She was beginning to dislike his smile.

Squeezing her eyes closed, Lyla focused on her breathing, desperately trying not to bring up her breakfast.

"Where is Iris?" she pleaded again.

"She is safe, and she will be returned to your family. In time."

"Did you hurt her?" A single tear ran down Lyla's swollen face.

"Absolutely not!" he exclaimed. "What kind of monster do you think I am?"

"The kind who will duel an innocent man to death!" she spat back at him.

"You know this is all your fault," Noah said, his voice softening. "You forced me to do something I had not planned and … well, there was a price to pay. If you had just picked me in the first place, then Winston and Iris would be safe right now."

When Lyla did not respond, Noah shrugged his shoulders. "As I said before, I gave Winston the chance to walk away. He refused and challenged *me* to duel. It would have been ungentlemanly of me *not* to accept. He also chose the weapon. How was I to know he was not particularly good at it?"

Lyla blinked, her fingers now spinning the gold band on her left hand. "And what offer did you present him with? Did you just ask him to step aside?"

"No. I offered him money. More money than I think he would have ever earned in a month. He refused."

Lyla stared out the window again, trying to put all the pieces together. "When did this happen? Your offer?" Lyla asked, turning back to face him.

"Two days ago," he replied casually, brushing his hand over his pants.

"And the duel?"

"Late yesterday afternoon, just before sunset. He picked the time and location too. It was his challenge." The sound of his voice irritated Lyla, the deep tones filling the carriage, choking her. Especially the way he spoke to her calmly and respectfully, as if they were having an ordinary conversation.

"So, you murdered him, and then the next day, just walked into my house and married me? Have you no guilt, no shame?" she asked, the bitterness filling her stomach, sending another rush of bile up her throat.

"It would have brought shame to your family, had you walked down the aisle to find no one at the end to receive you," he replied truthfully.

"So, what? Do you think you did my family a favour? Married the poor bride, whose fiancé you killed!" she asked spitefully, the anger in her voice rising again.

Noah raised his eyebrows, seemingly shocked at her reply. "He chose his path. *I* have no guilt about his death. *I* did not murder anyone. He challenged me, and he lost." Noah's voice deepened further, and his eyes darkened. "As I said before, this is *your* fault. Don't blame me for choosing the wrong suitor."

Lyla blinked, unsure of what to say. "He chose his path?" her voice trembled. "I don't believe you gave him any other option. You should have just walked away and let us be!"

"I could not." He looked at her sternly. "As I said to you before, and I'll say it again for the last time, it should have been me from the very start." He pointed to himself, his voice rising in anger. "He would have failed you as a husband. I will be so much better."

The tension in the carriage thickened, and the resentment Lyla felt towards Noah became intolerable.

"Better! Ha, well, *husband*!" she emphasised loudly. "You are off to a horrible start, and by the way," Lyla turned her body away from him, "You need to wear a different cologne, this one makes me feel ill," she said as she opened the window, inhaled the fresh air, and closed her eyes.

After ten minutes without another word between them, and having no idea where they were heading, Lyla eventually turned to face Noah and broke the silence. "I still don't understand what Iris has to do with this. Why did you take her?"

Noah blinked slowly, his gaze shifted from his window towards her. "I guess …" he paused. "I did not think you would marry me so eagerly."

"Eagerly!" Lyla sat up straight, his comment not what she was expecting. "You think I married you without hesitation?"

"It looked that way." Noah shrugged. "You certainly didn't put up a fight." He tilted his head again, the smug expression returning briefly.

"I did it to save my sister!"

"Yes, your sister. Someone whom you were leaving anyway. Someone who would have gotten on with her own life after you left. Winston, on the other hand — you didn't even ask about him once, not until we got into the carriage … until *I* had to remind you, he was not there."

Lyla huffed; frustratingly aware Noah was right. Not once had she thought to question Noah about Winston not appearing at the wedding. She was so shocked upon seeing Noah standing at the pulpit and then preoccupied with doing what she had to do to ensure Iris's safety. She hadn't had the headspace to consider what had prevented Winston from being there in the first place. Not until she was in the sitting room.

"I know you are angry now," Noah said as he leaned forward and placed his hand tenderly on Lyla's knee. She shifted slightly, but the weight of his hand sank through her wedding skirt, and she paused. "I know you care for me. I see it in your face every time you look at me."

"I do not care for you," she replied calmly, and picking up his hand, removed it from her leg. Flipping it over quickly, Noah curled his fingers around hers. His soft skin seemed to melt into hers. Lyla glanced down, the movement shocking her. He brushed his thumb slowly over the back of her hand, and a warm tingle ran up her arm, through her neck, and into her face, causing Lyla's cheeks to flush with colour. Her heart raced.

"See. You respond to my touch — I can feel your pulse quicken in your wrist."

In frustration at her reaction, Lyla yanked her hand out of his and turned her back to him again, tucking her hands against her chest. "After what you have done to Winston and Iris today, I will never love you." She kept her face turned away from him as she spoke.

Noah observed his wife's shoulders rise and fall with every breath. He watched as several strands of her hair escaped from beneath her veil, stirred by the breeze entering through the open carriage door. A smile brushed his lips as the vanilla and sweet pea scent of her perfume reached him, realising it was the same one she wore when they danced at her Flowering Day.

Trailing his eyes down her back, he took in the smallness of her waist and how the wedding dress hugged her body. Noah had not lied to Lyla, when he told her she looked beautiful.

When Noah turned to greet Lyla at the end of the aisle, his own heart had skipped a beat, she had been a vision he honestly did not think he would see.

He knew Lyla would have been confused with Winston not being there, and the look on her face to seeing him instead, confirmed his suspicions. Confusion, shock, hate, and fear had flashed through her eyes.

Despite her reaction to Winston's unfortunate death, and her anger towards him in the carriage, Noah knew she would eventually see the truth and, in time, realise he was the right suitor for her.

Sitting back, staring at Lyla, his smile widened. Everything he had planned was falling into place.

Winston was gone, Iris would go home tomorrow and his new life, with Lyla by his side, had begun. What could go wrong.

Chapter 21

For the next half an hour, Lyla sat in silence, rocking gently with the motion of the carriage. Her attention remained fixed solely on the outside world, but again, her mind was still too foggy and full of thoughts to appreciate the scenery. She was grateful Noah had stopped talking, yet she could feel his watchful eye on her. It was not until they turned down a narrow road that Noah spoke gently.

"Welcome to your new home."

Upon hearing his words, Lyla focused her vision, but seeing only trees and an open field, turned to peer through the right-hand window, next to Noah.

Through the tall, slim trees edging along the curved driveway, a large white manor appeared. It didn't match her own home in size, but it wasn't a small house either. Four massive ornate white stone pillars reached up from the ground to the second story, and a grand stone staircase fanned out in front of the house.

A small breath caught in Lyla's throat—it was prettier than she imagined. She leaned closer to the window, getting a better look at the house. Soon the carriage turned towards the manor, obscuring Lyla's view.

As the carriage finally came to a stop at the base of the stairs, Noah quickly opened the door and stepped out.

"Wait here," he said, his voice composed and polite. Closing the door, Noah walked around the back of the carriage and opening the door next to Lyla, he extended his hand. She sat there for a moment, wanting to decline his offer, but knew she couldn't get out of the carriage without help. With a disgruntled sigh, Lyla carefully placed her hand in his, ignoring the warmth of his skin on hers.

Stepping onto the compacted gravel driveway, Lyla waited patiently as Noah pulled the veil and train out behind her, allowing the train to pool elegantly to her feet. Carefully Noah held the veil off the ground as he stood beside her, and Lyla felt his eyes on her as she looked up at the manor in awe, taking in its simple elegance.

Lowering her gaze, she glanced at the five staff members who had gathered at the base of the stairs to greet the newly wedded couple.

Still holding the veil, Noah placed his free hand on her lower back, just above her bustle, and encouraged her to walk towards the house.

As they approached the stairs, Noah introduced the staff. "This is Callum the gardener, Maryan the cook, sisters Penelope and Regina the servants and William the head butler."

Lifting the front of her dress, Lyla walked up the stairs, acknowledging each person as they passed, but forgetting their names immediately.

"Welcome to your new home, Mistress," William said and bowed as they came to a stop at the top of the stairs.

Releasing Lyla's veil, letting it fall behind her and cascade down the steps like a waterfall, Noah approached the two grand white wooden front doors. Grasping the handles, he opened the doors and swung them inwards, revealing the interior of the manor, the house the butler had just called, *her home.*

Stepping through the doorway with a hint of trepidation, Lyla's eyes widened in wonder. Polished white marble tiles spanned the foyer floor, while a grand white marble staircase stood in the middle of the room, branching off in two directions at the halfway landing. A deep blue carpet runner, the same colour as Lyla's Flowering Day dress, trimmed with gold stair rods, hugged the steps all the way to the top.

The house was bright and airy. Natural light streamed through two large windows, which stood on either side of the front doors. Taking a small breath, Lyla noted the air was perfumed with a sweet familiar aroma, and when she looked at a round table on her left, she saw a large vase with white carnations and blue iris flowers.

"I hope you like them," Noah said. "Our flowers. You can have fresh ones every day if you like." Lyla turned her head away from them — she felt nothing for the pretty blooms.

Edging her forward, Noah took her hand. "Let me show you to your room. I am sure you would like to take your wedding dress off."

Lyla's eyes flicked to his face. Suddenly, she thought of Meg. "I have no one to help me take it off, and I have no other clothes to change into."

Noah stopped in his tracks. "Ah, yes. I will make sure your lady-in-waiting arrives this afternoon with your belongings." He turned his head quickly and nodded to a young gentleman, who was standing by the doors. The young man, who Noah did not introduce, walked over, and Noah whispered discreetly to him before he pivoted and promptly left through the front door.

"Please. Your room is upstairs," he said as he took a step towards the staircase. "Unless you would like to take a tour of the house first?"

She shook her head. Her room, where she could finally be alone, was the only place she wanted to be right now. "Is this your house?" Lyla asked as she hitched the front of her wedding dress and slowly ascended the staircase.

"Yes. I acquired it a few weeks ago as a wedding gift to you. I do hope you like it," Noah replied, walking in unison with her.

She paused on the steps and looked at him, her brow creasing for a moment. A few weeks ago! How long had he been planning this? She thought to herself. Maintaining her composure, Lyla relaxed her brow before she continued to climb.

"It is very grand," Lyla said, trying to silence her thoughts.

"It is not as big as your home, I do admit. In fact, it's minor compared to most manors, and there is still some work I would like done to the ballroom and the guest bedrooms. I was hoping you might like to be involved in the decorating of them."

Lyla stopped halfway up the stairs, her hand slipping from her dress. "You are allowing me to decorate this house?" she asked in surprise.

"Of course. It is your house as well. I want you to be comfortable in it. When your parents and my parents visit, I would like them to see how much you love it too."

"Your father!" Lyla suddenly blurted out.

Noah stopped one step above her. "What about him?"

"He was at the wedding."

"Yes, he was." Noah frowned.

"At my Flowering Day, he couldn't make it. Your mother said he was unwell."

He nodded. "He still is unwell but wanted to be there for our wedding."

Lyla's forehead creased again. "You say that like your family knew I would marry you!" Lyla questioned him, not moving from the step.

"I may have told them to be prepared." He held his hand out to escort her further up the stairs, but exhaling through her nose, Lyla picked up her dress again with both hands and continued without him.

Feeling the anger surging within, Lyla took a slow breath to dispel it and changed the subject. "Is Iris here?"

"Let's talk about her later," Noah replied, another small smile crossed his lips. "We have more important things to talk about."

Reaching the landing, Lyla stopped and released her dress, letting it fall around her. She inhaled deeply, her lungs pressing harshly against her corset. Calming her temper, she dared to look back into Noah's blue eyes.

"Right now, Noah, the only thing I wish to talk about, and the only thing that *is* important to me, is the whereabouts of my twelve-year-old sister, who you kidnapped this morning, on the day of my wedding!"

"Kidnapped is a strong word." He raised his eyebrows at her.

"Well, what would you call it then?"

He tapped his fingers on the top of banister. "I didn't kidnap her, not really. Iris came willingly." He shrugged his shoulders and blinked slowly.

Lyla's eyebrows raised. "Meaning?"

"I didn't have to force her to leave with my man. She freely climbed into the carriage."

"Where. Is. She. Noah!" Lyla said through gritted teeth, her fingers curling into fists.

"As I said before, she is safe."

"Take me to her then!" Lyla said, her voice raised as she abruptly turned to walk back down the stairs. Reacting just as quickly, Noah took two large steps, closing the gap between them and grabbed Lyla's wrist, his grip painful around her slim bones.

"I promise you. She is safe for now, but if you start to create … a problem," his fingers tightened, "you might put her at risk, and I am sure you do not wish that to happen."

"Are you threatening me, Noah Valdez?" Lyla's voice quivered as she spoke.

"Yes. I guess I am," he replied, his blue eyes darkened like a storm about to break.

Lyla's heart raced again, but this time, it was in fear. "Let me go!" she said, trying to pull her wrist free.

Noah breathed in slowly, keeping his grip on Lyla's wrist. "All I ask is that you give this marriage a go. If you walk away from me now, the shame you will bring on your family would be … unforgivable. You understand we are married until death parts us. Those are the vows you spoke to me this morning, were they are not?" His voice was stern; it sent a chill through her.

Lyla stared at him, her own blue eyes burning with anger and hate. "Then hopefully, your death comes before mine!" she said, stepping closer to Noah.

Noah's face tightened in rage, and he used this opportunity to turn on his heels and pull Lyla up the stairs on the left side of the landing.

Struggling to pull herself free, Lyla almost tripped up the stairs as her dress caught under her shoe. Frantically, Lyla pulled the front up to prevent standing on the delicate silk and lace underskirt. Not stopping to assist Lyla, Noah dragged her the rest of the way up the stairs and down the hall to a large bedroom.

Storming through the open doorway, Noah finally let go of her wrist as he flung her toward the bed. Turning abruptly and moving back towards the doorway, he growled at her, his voice deep and angry.

"I hoped you would not cause this much trouble. As my wife, I do expect that by dinnertime tonight, you will have composed yourself and will present a better image in the dining room. Until then, Lyla."

He stepped through the doors and closed them loudly, the sound crashing through Lyla's chest. Before Lyla could even take a few steps, she heard an audible click as Noah locked the doors, trapping her inside.

<h1 style="text-align:center">Chapter 22</h1>

Screaming in anger, Lyla collapsed to the floor, unable to breathe. Tears streamed down her face—tears for her poor Winston, tears for her dearest Iris, tears for her broken heart.

After a few minutes, breathing slowly to compose herself once more, Lyla got to her feet and looked around her new bedroom.

An ornate four-poster bed stood in the middle of the room, adorned with soft sheer cream curtains tied to each post. A pretty quilt of soft pink, with cream, and gold flowers embossed into the silk, lay across the bed. Feeling the weight of the veil, Lyla pulled out the comb and tossed it onto the bed, the veil half pooling to the floor.

Raising her eyes to the wall behind the bed, Lyla stared in awe at a large tapestry depicting the countryside. A beautiful scene intricately created in bold colours so realistic, Lyla felt like she was gazing through a window.

Turning away from the tapestry, Lyla took in the rest of the room. A walnut dressing table, trimmed in gold, stood to the left of the bed, its oval mirror reflecting the pretty room and her image. No longer feeling like a beautiful bride, Lyla closed her eyes and turned away.

Opening them, Lyla noticed a small door leading off the side. Feeling like this might be a way out, Lyla rushed to the door, and grabbing the handle, twisted it hoping it would be unlocked. The latch opened, and Lyle pushed the door in to reveal a small washroom. Sighing with disappointment, Lyla closed the door.

Standing against the wall next to Lyla stood a tall, old-fashioned bowfront walnut armoire, and a smaller matching bowfront three-drawer chest. Moving in front of the armoire Lyla ran her fingertips across the smooth wood, leaving light smudges in the varnish. Clasping the bronze handles, Lyla swung the two doors open, revealing enough room for her clothes.

Closing the door and taking another deep breath, Lyla ambled across the room and sat in a light cream and peach velvet brocade, armchair positioned in front of a large window. Having nothing better to do, Lyla stared outside, her body feeling tired, her mind overwhelmed.

Despite it feeling like an eternity, only three hours had passed since Noah had locked her in her room when Lyla finally heard the door unlock. Not wanting to look at Noah, she kept her eyes focused on the garden outside her window. It was not until she heard Meg's sweet voice say her name that she turned her head.

"Oh, my sweet Lyla." Meg rushed to her side.

Although Lyla had stopped crying a fair while before, fresh tears sprang from her eyes as she embraced Meg.

"I want to go home." Lyla's youth and innocence poured out of her, and she looked to Meg like she was a young girl again.

"We both know that's not possible." Meg brushed back the loose hairs around Lyla's puffy face.

"I cannot stay here. He is a monster," she blubbered through the tears.

"I would not call him a monster, Lyla."

"He killed Winston!" Lyla said abruptly through her tears. Meg's face paled, and she looked at Lyla with shock.

"No," she said, shaking her head. "He would not do that!"

"Well, he did. Winston is dead because Noah could not accept my choice. And he kidnapped Iris to make sure I would marry him." She turned her head back to the window, heavy with grief and sorrow.

"Oh, Lyla, I am so sorry." Meg said, placing a tender hand on her shoulder. "I admit he seemed to be a charming man when I met him, but to do these things — oh my dearest Lyla, your heart must be broken."

"Do you see now why he's a monster?" Lyla said, returning her gaze to Meg.

"Yes," Meg replied, then frowned. "Lyla," she said and sat in the chair opposite. "After you and Noah left, your father told us Iris was taken and that she would be returned after the wedding, but she has not been seen since this morning. Have you seen her yet?"

"No," Lyla replied quietly. "He refuses to take me to her. I have no idea where she is, and he threatened to hurt her if I didn't give this marriage a go."

"Oh," Meg relied quietly "I see."

Pushing the tears away, Meg blinked her eyes, as she turned away from Lyla and looked around the bedroom. Noting Lyla was still in her wedding dress and the quilt across the bed untouched, her frown deepened.

Leaving Lyla to sit by the window, Meg walked over to the foot of the bed and picked up Lyla's discarded veil. Folding it carefully, Meg placed it on the bed and turned back to face Lyla.

"Lyla, I'm not sure what Noah's intentions are, but for now, can I help you out of your wedding dress? Your things arrived with me." Before Lyla could answer, there was another knock at the door.

"Hello, Mrs Valdez, I have your belongings," a male's voice called from the other side. Moving swiftly, Meg opened the door to find two young men standing in the hallway with three cases. Peering past Meg, Lyla recognised the young man who Noah had spoken to after they entered the house, but the other young boy, Lyla had not seen before. Motioning them in, Lyla watched as they carried the heavy cases in and placed them near the wall. As they left, a young maid, one of the sisters, whose name Lyla had forgotten, appeared holding a silver tray carrying a fresh pot of tea, a plate of sandwiches and some fruit.

Meg took the tray from her and nodded her thanks. The maid took a sideways glance at Lyla, curtsied politely, then closed the door behind her, and it locked once again.

Walking back to Lyla, Meg placed the tray on a small circular table beside her and sat back down.

"Why was the door locked?" Meg asked as she poured Lyla a cup of tea.

"Because apparently, I am a prisoner in *my* new house." Lyla replied spitefully, her gaze still fixed out the window.

Meg placed the teacup close to Lyla. "You should eat," she said quietly.

Lyla, ignoring the food and the tea, turned to look at Meg. "I feel like I have been in this room forever. Why did it take you so long to get here? Should you have not been directly behind us when we left?"

"Apparently Noah ordered everyone not to follow you, that if anyone did, Iris would not come home. We were instructed to wait until a footman arrived with Noah's carriage. I assumed that was when Iris would come back, but the carriage was empty. After it was loaded with your belongings, I was brought here, but again, no one else from the family was allowed to come with me."

"So, no one other than you, knows where I am?"

"*I* don't even know where we are. The curtains were closed in the carriage for the entire journey, and the young boy who just brought your cases in, sat with me to make sure I didn't try to look outside."

"Oh God, I really am a prisoner in my own marriage!" Lyla's face crumbled. All thoughts about marriage and how special this day was meant to be, was now just a shattered fantasy.

Seeing Lyla refuse the tea, Meg smiled. "Come. Let me help you get changed. You must be uncomfortable now in your bustle."

Lyla stood and followed every direction Meg gave her. She stepped out of the wedding gown and into in a pale green day dress. Throughout the process, Lyla did not speak. Meg patiently stayed by her side until Lyla sat back down in the chair and went straight back to staring out the window.

While Lyla sat, her broken heart beating weakly, Meg busied herself removing Lyla's clothes from the cases she brought with her and placed them in the large armoire and drawers. The wedding dress, she folded neatly, placed it into one of the empty cases, added the veil and closed the lid.

Pulling a few books out as well, Meg stacked them on the chest of drawer, yet Lyla still did not move. The food remained untouched, the cup of tea, now cold.

As the sky darkened, there was a gentle knock at the door, and Meg, closing the book she was reading, calmly walked over, pausing just before the door.

"Yes?" she called out.

"Dinner is ready, Mrs Valdez," a young male's voice echoed from behind the door.

"Thank you, we are ready." Meg replied, looking at Lyla, hoping she would stand.

The door unlocked, and the face of the young footman came into view. "If you would both follow me." He pushed the door open wide and waited patiently for Meg and Lyla to follow. Yet still, Lyla didn't turn away from the window.

"May you give us one moment please," Meg asked the footman. He nodded curtly. Meg walked to Lyla and placed her hand on Lyla's shoulder.

"For Iris and Winston," she whispered. Only then did Lyla turn away from the window and look at Meg.

"For Iris. Winston cannot be helped anymore," she said quietly, her voice cracking at the mention of his name.

Standing for the first time in hours, and giving her back a small stretch, Lyla and Meg followed the young man along the corridor, back down the grand staircase and turned left at the landing. Having barely acknowledged the sun had set, Lyla noticed the foyer was lit with numerous white candles and wall sconces, bathing the room in a soft glow.

Despite the warm, cosy vision, Lyla flinched slightly at the emptiness of the house. It was nothing like her home, full of laughter, and familiar sounds. Following the footman, the only sound Lyla heard came from their shoes on the marble tiles.

<h1 style="text-align:center">Chapter 23</h1>

"Ah, my wife has arrived." Noah moved away from the lit fireplace and walked briskly towards Lyla. Tenderly, he took her hand in his, brought it up to his lips and placed a gentle kiss on the back of it. "Please, sit down." He guided Lyla to the oak dining table and pulled out a chair for her.

Lyla watched Noah, his demeanour calm and friendly, his face relaxed and his eyes glowing with pride. Gone was the man who had growled at her, thrown her into her room and locked her in like a prisoner.

"Once again, you look beautiful," he said. She smiled weakly in response as she sat and glanced at Meg, waiting for her to sit as well. Noah gently placed his hand on Lyla's shoulder, and turning to Meg, smiled and nodded.

"Thank you for helping Lyla change, your help is most appreciated. If you follow Matthew, he will take you down to the kitchen. Your dinner awaits you there." Her eyes darted quickly to Lyla. "It is all right," he said, giving Lyla's shoulder a tender squeeze. "She will not be harmed and is perfectly safe in my company."

Lyla nodded once, but her eyes conveyed a slight sense of worry. Meg smiled politely, her own eyes reflecting Lyla's concern, but with a slight curtsy, she turned on her heel and followed Matthew.

Brushing his thumb along Lyla's exposed neck, Noah squeezed her shoulder once more, then turned and strolled to the opposite end of the table, pulled out his chair, and sat down. Within a minute, the side door opened, and the two young sisters entered, carrying plates of food.

During her afternoon spent staring out into the garden from her bedroom window, Lyla had told herself she would not eat anything Noah offered her. Yet, upon smelling the rich aromas of roast meat and vegetables, her mouth watered, and her stomach yearned for food. She had not eaten anything since her wedding breakfast so many hours before, her lunch uneaten, in her room.

"I apologise for locking you in your room today. I really had hoped this would have gone a lot smoother," Noah said between mouthfuls of food. "It is not my intention to make you feel like you are a prisoner here."

Lyla put her fork down, the slice of roast duck falling off the tines and onto the plate. "I take it I am free to leave and go home then?"

Noah raised his head, cocking it slightly, and looked at her, a hint of a smile tugging at the corner of his mouth. "Well, no. You are my wife. This is your home now. Why would you want to leave?"

Lyla looked down at her plate. Instead of responding, she picked up her fork, stabbed the slice of duck, and resumed eating.

"I took the liberty of having some of your books brought over as well, and you will see, I have quite a broad selection of books myself. I do hope you will enjoy some time tonight reading with me in the library," he said, breaking the silence.

Lyla's attention peaked, and she risked a look at her husband. His dark blue dinner jacket hugged his chest tightly and complemented his skin tone. The collar of a pale green linen shirt peaked out above the jacket lapel.

'Green, like the colour of my dress,' she thought, and rolled her eyes, unimpressed at his attempt to unite them.

His brown hair was pulled back and tied at the nape of his neck, something Lyla had not seen him do before. Unfortunately, it showed off his jawline, and Lyla's eyes passed across his face, to his lips, and as they parted slightly, she felt her face flush as their eyes met.

He smiled as he stared intently into her eyes. Lyla watched as his gaze shifted down to her pink lips, and his smile broadened. "You really are breath-taking, Lyla," he said, his voice deep and smooth.

The way he spoke her name with such tenderness, such … longing, sent a quiver down her spine. Shaking her head, as if to expel the sensation, she dropped her eyes back to the table, to her plate, to her fingers holding the fork, anywhere but his face.

No! She would not fall for him. She would not allow herself to get swept away with the very man who held her sister hostage somewhere and killed her beloved Winston.

"I would like to return to my bedroom after dinner, please, Meg has my books waiting for me there."

"As you wish." He nodded respectfully but then added, "If it pleases you, we could take a walk around the grounds tomorrow morning. I have some wonderful areas of the garden I would like to show you." His deep voice lulled Lyla towards a sense of ease, to which she scowled quietly to herself.

"I shall see how I am feeling in the morning." Lyla resumed eating, finishing the food on her plate, and ignored the offering of fruit and cake that was placed in front of her.

"Are you not feeling well?" Noah asked with concern.

"It has been a long day," she responded politely yet with a hint of sorrow.

The tension in the air became more palpable, and Noah pushed his chair back as though sensing Lyla was no longer going to talk to him. Walking over to her, he offered her his hand. "Please. Let me escort you back to your room."

Eager to be out of Noah's company, Lyla accepted his hand and allowed him to pull out the chair as she stood. Placing his hand gently on her lower back, he guided Lyla out of the dining room and back into the foyer.

As they walked up the stairs together, Lyla kept her eyes focused in front of her. Reaching the landing, she stopped suddenly and stared at a large painting hanging on the wall. The painting depicted a delicate gold vase of white carnations standing on a round wooden table. In front of the vase, three blue iris flowers lay on their sides.

"It is beautiful, is it not?" Noah said, his hand still on her back.

Lyla nodded in agreement before she could stop herself. The picture was painted with such exquisite technique that she couldn't help but admire the scene with awe. The details of the petals were so precise, Lyla felt that if she touched the painting, the flowers would be real.

"I had it painted just for you as a wedding gift. Your favourite flower and Iris's favourite flower. Do you like it?"

Lyla did not know whether to laugh or cry. Was he mocking her with the painting, or was it in fact meant to be a genuine gift from a husband to his wife?

"It is … beautiful," she whispered as her hand slowly reached up, but quickly dropped back to her side when she realised touching it would not bring Iris to her. She turned slowly, moving away from the painting. Making her way back up the rest of the stairs and to her room, Noah followed, a few steps behind her.

Upon reaching her room, Noah paused at the doorway, grabbed Lyla's hand, and turned her around to face him. "I will send Meg up to help you get into your bedclothes. Although it is customary for a husband and wife to share their bed on the night of their wedding, I will allow this one time off. I know you are grieving the loss of Winston, and I would not force you to consummate the wedding if your heart is not truly in it."

Slipping his fingers under Lyla's chin, he tilted her face up and leant in, bringing his mouth close to hers, his breath warm against her lips and chin. They were so close that Lyla could see the candlelight flickering in his eyes. Not the same shade of blue as hers, but equally stunning. She blinked, trying to break the trance he had put her in.

"I do hope that perhaps tomorrow night, you will join me in my room and spend the night with me," his voice dropped to a whisper. "I very much look forward to seeing how much more of your body is beautiful. You are exquisite in every way." His left hand moved around her waist, and he pulled her closer to him.

Lyla stared hard into his eyes, mustering all the hatred that she could, but it did not discourage Noah at all. Instead, while holding her chin, he ran the tip of his thumb across Lyla's bottom lip, the sensation bringing an unwanted sigh of pleasure that threatened to break her composure. Before she could pull her head away, Noah lowered his lips onto hers and kissed her more deeply than he had this morning at the pulpit.

Struggling to maintain her composure, Lyla tried not to kiss him back, but the warmth in his lips softened hers. Deep within Lyla, her body struggled to fight the new sensations, which coursed through her veins. This was her first real kiss and as Lyla's lips responded to his touch, Noah moaned slightly, the sound adding to the overwhelming feeling.

At eighteen, Lyla had no experience with men. She remained pure, and her wedding night was the time to explore the world of intimacy. Her body reacted to Noah's kiss in a way she wished it did not, and without meaning to, she leant in closer to him. Taking it as an invitation, Noah wrapped his arm around her waist and pulled her tightly against him. With his free hand, he trailed it from her chin, down her neck and cupped the back of her neck, pressing their lips together as the passion in his kiss deepened.

Lyla's heart raced as she instinctively responded to his touch, her lips moving in motion with his, her body arching closer. Suddenly, regaining her senses, Lyla pressed her hand to his chest and pushed him away, breaking the connection.

Instantly, Lyla missed the feeling of Noah's lips on hers. A wanting and new desire flashed across her cheeks, reddening them. Panting slightly, Noah took a step backwards, his hands falling to his sides, and his eyes burning with lust. Lyla opened her mouth slightly to speak but instead, only a quickened and raspy breath escaped, which made Noah take a step closer to her again.

Frustration, confusion, and anger now coursed through her veins, and before she could make a terrible mistake, she stepped backwards into her room and quickly closed the door, blocking Noah from her view.

Breathing hard and fighting the tingling sensations she could feel building between her legs; Lyla spun and leaned back against the door. Closing her eyes, she forced herself to slow her breathing, slow her rapidly beating heart and dispel the rising desire in her body.

Hearing Noah chuckle behind the door only enraged Lyla's hatred of him. Within a few seconds, Lyla heard the door across the hall from hers close, and she felt her body relax a little.

Regaining her composure, Lyla opened her eyes, and her gaze fell on the large bed and suddenly, she wanted to do anything but be close to that specific piece of furniture.

"O, good grief, no!" she said aloud and rushed to the brocade chairs by the window, but this time, sat in the second chair, her back to the bed. How was she going to sleep tonight?

Feeling embarrassed by the way her body betrayed her in response to Noah's kiss, Lyla covered her face with her hands. What would happen tomorrow night when he took her to his room? What would her body do then if he laid her down on his bed?

Fighting back the tears, not wanting to feel weak and vulnerable, Lyla's thoughts turned to Winston. Had he been the one she'd married today; would they have already shared his bed? Would she be content and proud to have fulfilled her wifely duties?

A few nights before, Lyla's mama had sat her down and explained what would be expected of her on her wedding night—what she was required to do to consummate the marriage. From what her mama had said, Lyla had in fact wanted to share herself with her husband, but under these new circumstances, Lyla could not think of anything worse.

Against her will, her body continued to respond to the thoughts that now ran through her mind, to the things her mother had told her. Her heart rate picked up again, and her breathing quickened. Struggling to get a deep enough breath, Lyla stood and paced the room. Still unable to breathe deep enough, Lyla fought with her dress, undoing the buttons at the front of her bodice, and tried to loosen the corset underneath.

The memory of Noah's lips on hers made her face flush further. Unable to loosen the corset without help, Lyla shook her head and dropped her hands to her sides as she tried to push away the unwanted thoughts. When that didn't work, Lyla dug her fingernails into her palms, hoping the pain would divert her attention.

It did not.

Chapter 24

The morning brought a new awareness to Lyla. Different sounds travelled to her from within the house, and it took a few moments to remember where she was. Slowly, she sat up and looked around the room, *her* new bedroom, in *her* new house.

Throwing back the covers Lyla swung her legs over the edge of the bed. The mattress was so deep, her feet were still far off the ground. Shuffling forwards, Lyla allowed her toes to stretch down until they curled into the plush, cream rug which covered the wooden floor beneath her bed.

Planting her feet firmly on the rug, Lyla arched her back and stretched, relaxing her body after a long night of restless sleep. After finding Lyla dozing in the chair, her bodice undone but still dressed, Meg had helped Lyla change into her bedclothes and finally convinced her to climb into the bed, but despite the soft mattress and warm covers she could not find a comfortable position and spent the night tossing and turning.

Making her way to the washroom, Lyla splashed water on her face and wiped the night's frustrations away.

Moments later, she heard Meg's voice as she entered the room.

"Good morning, Lyla."

"I will be right out." Lyla quickly dried her face and ran her fingers through her long hair. Stepping back into the bedroom, Lyla broke into a smile when she saw Meg. It was a blessing indeed to have Meg still with her. Lyla was not sure if she would have coped if her handmaid were someone she did not know.

"I thought you might like to wear the blue dress today," Meg said as she pulled open the armoire and took out a dark blue dress, which matched Lyla's eyes.

"Sure, whichever one you think will look nice."

Meg turned and stared at Lyla. "They all look nice, hence why I brought them!" She smiled broadly at Lyla. Within moments, Lyla was sitting at the dressing table while Meg braided her hair, sweeping the plaits up into a stylish knot atop her head.

"Do you think I might get to see Iris today?" she asked, looking at her reflection.

"I'm not sure but remember what we said before. If you want to save Iris, you need to do whatever Noah says. Iris's safety is our priority."

"I know." Lyla studied her reflection in the mirror, and her thoughts turned to Noah calling her exquisite. She had thought herself pretty, but that was about it. Turning her head from side to side, Lyla studied the shape of her face, trying to see what Noah saw. Catching herself, she rolled her eyes and turned away from the mirror, as Meg finished her hair.

"Shall we head down to breakfast?" Meg asked, smoothing the silk on Lyla's dress.

"I guess so. I should not keep my *husband* waiting!" she said with a tone of sarcasm.

"Good husband or no, he is still your husband. You should not keep him waiting."

Lyla shook her head, took a deep breath, and walked out the door, her head held high.

Noah was once again waiting patiently for Lyla in the dining room. Upon her arrival, he walked up to her, kissed her tenderly on the cheek and guided her to her chair. Just like the night before, he sat opposite Lyla, and within a few minutes, plates of hot food were bought out. Again, Meg was led down to the kitchen to eat.

"I hope you slept well," Noah said as he cut his sausages.

"I did," Lyla lied, not wanting Noah to know otherwise.

"Good to hear. I did have concerns about you sleeping alone in this house for the first night."

"Well, I wasn't alone, was I? You were only across the hall." Her cold eyes met his.

"This is true." He smiled, and Lyla's heart skipped a beat. Mentally cursing herself for looking at his handsome face, she quickly dropped her eyes and focused on the plate of eggs, sausages, and boiled fish in front of her.

"Are you still up for a walk through the garden this morning?" Noah asked, resuming the conversation.

"Sure," Lyla responded curtly. Meg's words swam through her mind — think of Iris and her safety.

Needing a distraction to avoid looking at her husband, Lyla took in the dining room, which she had mostly ignored the night before. Eight chairs sat around the modest-sized mahogany table that filled the room without overtaking it. To the right of the table stood a large stone fireplace, it's hearth cold and unlit for now, the sunlight streaming through two elaborate glass doors, framed with deep red heavy curtains, was enough to warm the room.

Lyla noted the room was simple and lacked any ornamental touches. Although the walls were bare of any paintings or tapestries, the morning sunlight, which bounced off the fancy glass pendants hanging from the two silver chandeliers above the table, sent rainbows of twinkling light over the light cream walls with dark forest green cornices, and matching green half panels. The sight bringing a smile to Lyla.

The rest of breakfast passed without incident and minimal chatter, and once they finished and their plates and glasses cleared, Noah once again—a gentleman and gracious husband—offered Lyla his hand as she rose. Instead of leading her back into the front of the house, Noah took her to the large glass doors and opened them, allowing her to walk out towards the back garden.

The sight of the garden took Lyla's breath away. The morning air was scented with hundreds of brightly coloured flowers. Garden beds of lavender, roses, daffodils, and sweet peas lined the edge of the house. A deep green, neatly trimmed hedge ran parallel with the house and separated the gravel path from the lush green grass, which stretched to the back wall, at least a hundred meters away.

Directly in line with the opening in the hedge, Lyla could see a large stone fountain in the middle of the lawn, surrounded by a gravel footpath. The fountain sprayed clear water into the air, which then cascaded over two stone bowls, and finally pooling in the shallow basin below.

Closing her eyes, Lyla listened to the birds chirping from the two rows of trees lining the outside edges of the property. While the garden was nowhere near as big as her parent's and the lawn was only a fraction of the size, Lyla still found it impressive.

"Shall we?" Noah offered his arm. Hitching up her dress with one hand, Lyla rested her other hand atop his as they descended the steps.

As soon as they reached the gravel path, Lyla removed her hand from Noah's, took a step to the side, creating distance without seeming rude. Her simple blue satin shoes lightly crunched on the small stones of the path as Noah led them through the gap in the hedge and out onto the lawn.

A warm breeze rushed past Lyla as she made her way to the fountain and she tilted her face up, inhaling deeply. It was peaceful in the garden. The sound of the water trickling down over the fountain bowls soothed her more than she expected.

"We did not get a chance to talk enough at your Flowering Day, and because you chose Winston instead, I feel like we have so much to catch up on," Noah commented as Lyla sat on the edge of the stone fountain, her heart skipping a beat, hearing Winston's name.

While she did not want to engage in conversation with Noah, Lyla knew she inevitably had no choice.

"What would you like to know?" she asked, dropping her hand into the cool water and swirling it with her fingertips. Lyla could feel the intensity of Noah's gaze upon her as he strolled around the fountain.

"Do you like dogs?" he asked.

"I do."

"Any particular breed?" He kept walking, his hands shoved deep in his trouser pockets.

"I like Collies the most," she replied absently.

Noah nodded and smiled to himself. "Do you like to paint?"

"Yes," Lyla said, boredom brimming in her tone.

"And croquet? Do you play?"

Lyla looked up at him with the hint of a smile. "I'm very good at croquet, actually."

"Ah, we shall have to have a game later this afternoon then. I am quite good, myself," he gloated. Lyla's face softened as she thought about playing croquet with her family. She rarely lost, and her father refused to play with her, telling her she was just too clever at it.

"Cards? Do you play?" Noah asked as he continued to stride around the fountain, heading back to where Lyla was sitting.

"I enjoy Brag," she replied.

"I bet you do. Did you win against Jonathan, Emily, and Iris?"

Lyla's head snapped up, and her eyes darkened at hearing Iris's name. Noah stopped in his tracks, and from his stunned expression, Lyla knew he was aware he might have said the wrong thing.

"If you are not going to let me, see Iris, I would prefer you not utter her name!"

"My apologies." He put his hand on his chest. "I did not mean to upset you." Noah bowed slightly, lowering his head apologetically.

Lyla stood and pleaded with Noah. "Can you just let her go? You got what you wanted from me. I married you. Please, let her go home to my parents."

"I cannot. Not yet." His eyes softened as he stared at her.

"Noah! She is only twelve years old! She is no longer your bargaining tool. I will fulfil my duties and remain married to you. You need not worry about me leaving." Lyla tried to sound as convincing as she could. Despite the fact that every part of her wanted to flee from Noah, she stayed to fight for her sister's freedom.

"Every duty?" he questioned her, his eyes widening.

"Yes," she replied, knowing full well what he was referring to.

"Tonight. You will come to my room?" he asked, an eyebrow raised as though he believed she would decline.

Lyla swallowed thickly as she looked at him and nodded gently. His face lit up, and his lips parted in a happy smile. Unable to look at him, Lyla turned away, not wanting to blush again, not in front of him. Yet she couldn't stop the recollection of their kiss surging forward.

"Lyla, are you okay?" Noah asked as he stood before her.

"Yes. I am fine. The sun is just getting to me."

"Shall we head back inside? You said you liked to play Brag. Shall we have a game or two?"

Lyla nodded and walking side by side, they headed back towards the house. Just as they passed through the hedge, William briskly approached them.

"Sir, I am sorry to interrupt you." He motioned to Noah to move aside.

Lyla watched as the two men took a few steps away from her. The butler leaned in close and spoke to Noah, whispering so Lyla could not hear what he was saying. Trying not to stare, Lyla lowered her head but kept the two in her peripheral vision. With a slight nod from Noah, the butler hurried back to the manor.

"I apologise. I have some business to take care of, so I will not be able to play Brag with you now, but I do hope you will join me for dinner tonight." His face turned serious, and his eyes darkened.

"Is everything okay?" Lyla asked, wanting to know what would cause Noah to leave her.

"I just need to leave and sort a few … matters out. I shall be gone a few hours." He smiled at Lyla, but the smile only touched his lips. He did not look happy, and as he offered his arm to her, she took it lightly, and he escorted her back to the house.

Leaving her in the main sitting room, he bowed low, apologised again, and left the room. Shortly after, Lyla heard the carriage wheels crunch over the gravel driveway as he departed from the house.

"Where is he going in such a rush?" Meg asked as she entered the room. Lyla stood up quickly.

"I don't know. We were heading back to the house from the gardens when the butler interrupted. He seemed to be … concerned about something."

Meg sighed deeply as she sat on the other side of the baby blue velvet settee Lyla had been sitting on. "The staff here are very quiet people," Meg said. "It's rather … unnerving." Before Lyla could respond, a side door opened, and Regina came into the room, carrying a tray of cakes, biscuits, two teacups and a small pot of tea. She placed them on the table in front of them, bowed low and scurried back out the door, closing it quietly behind her.

"See what I mean?" Meg motioned with her hand. "It is like they are too scared to talk to us."

Lyla leant forward and grabbed a slice of fruitcake. "Are they like that when you have to eat with them in the kitchen?"

Meg nodded as she poured the tea into the two cups. "They nod and make room for me at the table, but they do not talk to me, ever. I try to make conversation, but they do not really answer me."

"Noah told me last night that he had only bought this house a few weeks ago. They could be unfamiliar staff, who are still getting used to working here."

Meg frowned. "What do you mean, he only just bought this house a few weeks ago?" She placed the teapot back down and stared at Lyla.

"He told me he only acquired it a few weeks ago, and there is still some work to be done to it. He has asked me to help him decorate it."

The pair of them glanced around the sitting room, taking in the space. A second settee sat opposite them, in front of a large window. Flanking the window, in the same matching blue velvet material as the settee, hung two heavy curtains. A tapestry carpet of blue, white, and cream lay under them, covering the deep brown wooden floorboards, the colours matching perfectly with the cream walls and blue furniture.

Two paintings hung on either side on the window. Landscape scenes, in hues and shades of soft blues, purples and greens bring the whole colour scheme of the room together.

On the wall opposite the window, stood a wonderful walnut credenza. Its large square mirror edged in a decorative frame of swirls and leaves. The same creative carvings trimmed the serpentine base. Bottles of colourful liquors and glasses adorned the white and grey marble top.

A square rosewood card table, with expertly carved detailing along the clawed foot and table edge, sat surrounded by four high-backed chairs, padded in a rich red velvet.

Smiling to herself, Lyla felt there would be no need to redecorate this room. It was perfect just as is.

But then a thought came to mind, and she turned to Meg. "Do you think this is a coincidence, that he had this house available? It is not just me overthinking this, is it?" Lyla asked.

"As in, you think maybe he had been planning this from the moment you picked Winston instead of him?"

"He did tell me I would regret not choosing him, but I don't recall him mentioning he owned a house at my ceremony."

"I am not sure. I would like to think that most of the men who were picked for your Flowering Day ceremony would have been looking to purchase a house of their own anyway. It may not be coincidental," Meg said honestly. Lyla shook her head, not agreeing with Meg.

"And taking Iris? How does that all play in this situation?" Lyla asked, turning her face away from Meg. "I could have prevented all this from happening if I had just picked him in the first place."

Meg leant over and placed her hand on Lyla's. "There is nothing you could have done. This is not your fault." Lyla turned back to look at Meg. "There was a reason you did not pick him at your Flowering Day ceremony. It could have been that your instincts knew something was not right. You could not have known he would do something like this."

A tear ran down Lyla's cheek. "He will not tell me where she is, and he will not let me see her. I am scared, Meg. Scared that he has done something horrible to her."

Chapter 25

Sitting alone in the carriage, Noah twisted his hands in frustration. Sighing deeply, he looked out the window as the wheels bounced along the gravel road, and his body swayed with the movement.

When Lyla closed the door in his face the night before, he admitted to himself, that this arrangement was not going the way he initially planned, yet at the same time, it was. Anger still pulsed through him every time he recalled seeing Lyla pick up Winston's rose instead of his iris. It should have been him she picked right from the beginning.

Noah reminded himself that he gave Lyla the chance to change her mind, twice in fact. Firstly, after she did not pick him at her Flowering Day and a few days ago when he had conveniently run into her in the park. Yet she had rejected him both times. Whatever she saw in Winston, over him, he could not tell. But this did not worry him anymore. Winston was no longer a problem.

With the carriage rumbling along, Noah thoughts wandered back to the night before the wedding and had to admit, Winston put up a good fight and died an honourable death. The death of a gentleman fighting for his love. The death of a man who unfortunately, was unable to match Noahs' skills with a rapier.

Noah had not intend for the duel to take as long as it did, but Winston, being a true gentleman, and refusing to give up, kept getting back on his feet, swinging his rapier around, frantically trying to fight, and Noah had to keep stabbing him, to make him stay down.

"Please," Noah whispered to him, as he lay on the bloody grass, "Stay down, you have lost the fight."

"No!" Winston replied, pushing Noah away and staggered to his feet, his balance weak.

"Come now Winston. You have fought a good fight but look at you." He motioned to Winston's blood-soaked shirt and pants. "Stay down," he said, stabbing Winston in the stomach again.

It was *not* Noah's fault he died slowly, bleeding out in the field, beside the forest edge.

"I wish you all the best in the afterlife Winston, may you rest in peace," he said as he knelt by his side, holding his hand. "I promised to take good care of Lyla. She will want for nothing with me. I will be the perfect husband," he'd whispered in Winston's ear.

Noah stayed long enough to watch Winston take his last breath, nodded respectfully to Winston's father and brother, who both attended the duel as witnesses, and left via horseback without a second glance, to get ready for the wedding.

Yesterday, the morning of the wedding, when Noah arrived early with a crateful of iris flowers, it had not been easy to convince Albert that Winston had gotten cold feet and inevitably approached Noah to take his place, stating he believed Noah was the better choice and Lyla had made an error in judgment. Understandably, Albert was shocked to believe Winston would not have said something first, considering he had lunched with Lyla the day before.

"I am sorry," Noah had said. "Winston approached me late yesterday afternoon, declaring he could not marry your daughter and asked if I would step in, to prevent any … implications and embarrassment your family might endure if Lyla did not get married."

"But Lyla did not indicate Winston was indeed getting cold feet, nor did he speak to me," Albert responded. "She came back from lunch happy and excited."

"What can I say, perhaps after their last time together, he realised he was … unfit for her, and perhaps too embarrassed to approach you."

Albert had paced the small sitting room while Noah stood patiently, finally agreeing it would be in the best interest of the family.

"I will of course need to inform Lyla and her mother first." Albert commented.

"No Albert, I do not think that would be wise. You would not want your daughter to get cold feet instead. The shame to your family, it might not be redeemable. I am here to save the day. Lyla will not mind. I was her second choice."

Feeling like he might not have full control over the new arrangements, and believing Albert might ruin things, Noah had already resorted to taking Iris as leverage, promising Albert she would be returned, unharmed once Lyla and he were married.

Conceding and agreeing with Noah, the shame would be unforgivable, Albert accepted Noah's offer and with the staff's help, removed the red roses, and replaced them with Noah's iris's. And knowing how much Iris liked him, that part of his plan fell into place very quickly.

Yet Noah, not feeling that he was one hundred percent in control of the situation, resorted to his backup plan and kidnapped Iris as his insurance that Lyla would not back out. And knowing how much Iris liked him, this part of his plan fell into place easily.

After an hour of travelling, the carriage pulled up to a small rundown house, hidden away in the forest. Getting out, Noah stretched his legs and arms and inhaled the damp, wet smell of the soil.

Utter silence greeted Noah. No birds sang in the trees surrounding him. Even the meandering river which ran behind the house ebbed quietly. Nodding to his driver, Noah held out his hand and accepted an old brass key then watched as the driver pushed the horse forward, and the carriage moved off towards a larger house, about one hundred meters from this small one.

Rotating the key in his hand, studying the intricate swirls and flourishes on the handle, Noah waited until the carriage came to a stop and the driver climbed down and entered the house. Once he disappeared, Noah approached the building.

There were very few people whom Noah trusted in this world, and his driver was one of them. But right now, he needed to be alone.

Slipping the key into the ancient-looking lock and turning it clockwise, Noah sighed, letting the weight of his problems fall away at the doorstep.

Pushing the door open, the smell of vomit, urine and body sweat hit him with such force that Noah had to turn away, to take in a breath of fresh air, as his own stomach churned. Closing his eyes and taking a second breath, he turned back and entered the large, darkened room, making sure to close the door tightly behind him.

The room was dull and dark. Old curtains, rotten and torn, hung limply over the small greasy window next to the door. The overgrown plants outside prevented the sunlight from coming through.

Allowing his eyes to adjust to the dim light, Noah glanced around the room, taking in the small house. Casting his eyes to the ground, Noah noticed a broken plate lying on the floor below a small dining table. The uneaten sandwich and thin slice of fruitcake were now mixed in with shards of broken porcelain, dirt, and ants.

Trailing his eyes across the dirty floor to the opposite side of the room, he saw a shattered glass lay near an unlit fireplace in a pool of water.

Sighing with contempt and squaring his shoulders, Noah's eyes eventually fell on the object of his visit.

Curled up in the corner of the room, on a small bed made of hay and linen, sat a young girl. Her hair was unruly and stuck to her damp forehead. Traces of dried vomit lay on her lavender-blue bridesmaid dress, and her face was puffy and swollen from crying. Shaking his head, Noah stared at the young girl.

"This behaviour is not very becoming of a young lady now, is it, Iris!"

Chapter 26

❧

"I want to go home!" Iris whispered.

"Now, now. You will not be here for long." He took a step closer to Iris and then paused mid step. Thinking better of it, he moved to the side of the door and gripping a worn fragile curtain, pulled it slowly across the window. The morning sun filtered through the dirty glass, illuminating the room and the many dust particles, swirling through the air.

"Why am I here?" Iris pleaded, squinting her eyes.

"Now, now. You will not be here for long." He took a step closer to Iris and then looking at the state of her dress, thought better of it and stood where he was.

"Why am I here?" Iris pleaded, her voice small and hoarse.

"You are here because I needed something from you," he said and watched as Iris frowned, her eyes darting across his face in confusion. "And I got what I needed," Noah added with a smile and flashed his left hand towards Iris, wiggling his fingers, so she could see the ring. "You will be happy to know your beloved sister Lyla is now my wife. She married me yesterday."

"She married you?" Her voice cracked and sounded weak from screaming out all night. Noah moved towards the table, pulled out a chair, and sat down. He leant forwards, placed his elbows on his knees, and stared intently at Iris.

"Of course! Just what you wanted her to do. Remember?" He smiled sweetly at Iris.

"So why could I not have been there to see it? I thought you said you needed me to do something for you," she asked a bit more boldly.

"I did, and you did exactly what I needed you to do. You got into the carriage and came here."

"But you never asked me to do that!" Iris raised her voice in frustration, but Noah ignored it.

"Well, maybe not in so many words." Noah looked at the floor, and towards the broken plate. He clicked his tongue against the back of his teeth. "You should not waste food, Iris. You should have eaten something. I cannot take you back … sick and weak. I do not need your family to think I am a monster."

"You *are* a monster," she said, raising herself to her knees. "You tricked me and stole me away from my family," her voice falling back to a whisper.

"As I recall, Iris. You came willingly! I did not steal someone who *chose* to get into the carriage."

Iris's eyes darkened, and she stared at him. Noah sniggered when he could see, Iris realised it was true.

When Noah saw Iris walking through the gardens in the front of the manor, yesterday morning, he saw an opportunity to set his plan in motion and approached her.

"Good morning, Iris," he said, his voice sweet and deliberate, through his eyes glinted with something unspoken.

"Noah," she replied and smiled, happy to see him.

"What are you doing out here in the garden, shouldn't you be getting ready for the wedding?"

"I am ready," she replied and motioned down to her bridesmaids dress. "I came out to pick some flowers for Lyla's room. Are you attending the wedding?" she asked.

"Yes," he replied, and turned towards the manor, his eyes searching for anyone watching their interaction. Satisfied they were alone, Noah lowered his voice and said, "I have something to share with you, but I must know if I can trust you first."

Iris, suddenly intrigued, nodded. "You can trust me," she replied, squaring her shoulders and lifting her chin towards him.

Noah placed his hand on her shoulder, giving it a little squeeze. "Good," he said and gently turned her around. "Shall we walk?"

Again, Iris nodded and matching his stride, walked along besides him.

Clasping his hands behind his back, Noah spoke with conviction. "Last night, Winston approached me and advised that he had reconsidered and no longer wished to proceed with the marriage to your sister. Naturally, I was surprised by this change of heart, as I had previously believed his acceptance of Lyla's offer to be sincere," he stated, his tone reflecting concern.

"Does Lyla know?" Iris asked, stopping abruptly in shock.

"No, I do not believe she does, which is why I need your help."

"My help?" she asked as Noah placed his hand on her back and gently ushered her forwards.

"Yes. I thought I would step up and marry Lyla today and I would like to hope I have *your* blessing to do so."

"Mine?" Iris asked, her expression displaying a subtle sense of pride.

"Yes, well I do hope you would still like me to marry Lyla, after all, you did tell me that at her Flowering Day ceremony, did you not?"

"I did," she said, her eyes bright with excitement.

"Well, seeing how Winston left late last night, I would hate to see Lyla and your family lose any respect in society, and knowing I was Lyla's second choice, I am going to step in his place today," he responded, studying Iris's reaction.

"So, how can I help?" she questioned, and Noah smirked, knowing she'd taken the bait.

"I thought, to help your sister, you might like to pick some special flowers that grow just outside on the main road."

Iris, wanting to please him, followed Noah to his carriage and quickly jumped in. Climbing in after her, and out of view, Noah rapidly bound her hands and feet and placed a rag over her mouth.

"So gullible!" he said, then kissed her on the forehead. With a tap on the roof, the carriage launched forwards, taking Iris and Noah away.

Now, Noah watched Iris lowered herself down and curl up in the corner of the bed pulling her dirty dress over her knees. Shifting on the bed, Iris never took her eyes off Noah.

"You lied to me," she said softly. "I wanted to see Lyla get married; I wanted to see her in her wedding dress."

"Yes, well, you can't have everything you want Iris," said Noah as he played with the gold band on his finger.

"Well, if Lyla married you, you could take me home then."

"That was the plan, but there has been a little … glitch," he groaned, his voice deepening slightly. Iris frowned. "I might need you to stay here another night."

"Why?" she asked, shifting forwards slightly.

Noah's gaze lifted, and he stared at a dark spot on the wall just above her head. "We didn't get the chance to consummate the wedding last night."

A small huff of humour escaped Iris's lips. Despite the fact that she was only twelve years old, Noah did not doubt Iris knew the procedures that took place on the first night of the wedding. Dropping his eyes back to Iris, he confirmed by her expression she knew what he meant.

"Why did it not happen? I thought …" Iris stopped talking, her cheeks flushing slightly at the topic of their conversation.

"Your sister refused me, if you must know." Noah replied firmly and sat back in the chair.

"But why should that stop me from going home to my family?" she asked.

"Because I need Lyla to do what is needed to make this marriage official!" Noah said, his voice rising in frustration. "It won't be valid until we …" he paused, rubbing his fingers over his temple. Taking deep breaths to calm himself down, Noah continued. "Once we have shared my bed tonight, you can return home."

"But that is not what the lady told me! She said that it would only be one night." Iris crossed her arms and looked at Noah in anger. "*Plus*, you just said you could not take me home sick and weak."

"That lady!" Noah spat out, keeping his voice level, "Is my cousin, and you shall address her as Miss Daisy."

"Daisy! Like the flower?" Iris's brow furrowed.

"Yes, just like your name. So, the two of you should get along very well." In an effort to compose himself, Noah drew circles in the dust on the table when the door suddenly opened behind him.

"I would be more than happy to be friends with her if she did not bite and kick so much."

Hearing a female's voice, Noah eyes lit up and standing abruptly, he spun on his heels and pushed the chair aside. Within four strides, he crossed the room and grasped the females hands, bringing them up to his lips as he pressed a kiss on them.

"Daisy, I am sorry if she is causing you trouble. She seemed to be so… mature a few days ago," he said, his voice softening.

"I am mature!" Iris demanded.

"If you were. Then you would have eaten the food I made for you, instead of throwing it on the floor!" Daisy said over Noah's shoulder.

"I would happily eat food you gave me if it were worth eating! I have no idea what you served me! It looked like something the pigs would eat!" Iris yelled, her face reddened in frustration.

"Noah." Daisey took her attention off Iris and stared at Noah. "This plan of yours will not work if I have to look after her."

"Don't worry." He kissed her hands again. "It will all work out. Lyla has married me and tonight, we will consummate the wedding. Tomorrow, I will return Iris and make my next move."

A small squeak escaped from Daisy and Noah knew that comment had hit her hard. "This plan to take her father's manor," she said, changing the subject. "It seems like a big thing. Do we really need to go through all this? We could just live somewhere else."

"No!" he yelled suddenly, making both Iris and Daisy jump. Dropping Daisy's hand, he rubbed his fingers over his forehead, trying to push away the building headache. "No," he repeated calmly, "this is how it has to be."

"Are you doing this to acquire my father's property?" Iris questioned.

Noah rolled his eyes and turning around slowly, he moved away from Daisy towards Iris, eventually stopping only a few feet away. Lowering himself down to her level, he looked at her, his blue eyes burning into hers.

"If you must know. Your father has an exceptionally large piece of property, which I would like to … obtain. And I very much doubt he will just give it to me. So, by marrying your sister, I will inherit the land when he dies."

Iris's eyes flicked between Noah and Daisy in confusion but settled back on Noah.

"Does Lyla know this?" she asked.

"Of course not, or she wouldn't have married me!" he said bluntly.

"Oh, that's why you took me, wasn't it. To make sure my sister married you?"

"Well look who just worked it out!" Noah mocked but narrowed his eyes when Iris smiled.

"You might have to wait a while. My father is in good health," Iris said proudly.

"Not if he dies sooner," Noah replied, a sinister tone lingering in his voice.

"You plan to kill him?" Iris's eyes widened in fear, the smug look on her face disappearing quickly.

"Well. He will be of no use to me now that Lyla is my wife, and once I consummate the wedding tonight … well." He smiled at her, his eyes bearing into hers with distaste.

"Once Lyla finds out, she will not bed you. She does not love you! She picked Winston!"

"And Winston wasn't there to marry her, was he?" he said pushing his face closer to Iris. "Tonight, she *will* bed me, and she doesn't have to love me to be mine completely."

He stood up abruptly, causing Iris to cower against the wall and moved back to Daisy, taking her face in his hands and gently kissed her forehead.

"Should you really be telling her all this?" Daisy questioned, her eyes searching Noah's.

Noah smiled. "No one will believe her. She's a child. Children lie and make up stories all the time."

A small giggle escaped Iris as though a sudden realisation hit her. "There is a flaw in your devious plan, Noah!"

He sighed and glanced back over his shoulder. "And what is wrong with my plan, Iris?" he asked, his deep voice sounded bored.

"Jonathan is next in line to the property, so you will have to wait until both my father and my brother die!" she said, with a hint of satisfaction.

"Well then, I guess there will be a double funeral soon!" He laughed loudly and turned away from Iris to kiss Daisy's cheek.

Daisy squeezed Noah's hands. "Oh, Noah, I hate to say this, but the young child is right. For you to take over the Peirson's manor and all the land he owns, Lyla will need to have a male heir, a son … your son, or you get nothing." Her hands trembled slightly in his.

Noah had not considered that. He had hoped his plan would be simple and easy. Now there was an obstruction, a complication, he had not foreseen.

"Once you kill my father and my brother and Lyla finds out, she will never have a child with you, let alone a son," Iris said boldly.

"Well, I guess I will have to make sure she never finds out, and tonight's consummation goes to plan, and in nine months' time, we'll see what happens after I hold my son."

"And if she does not birth a boy?" Iris asked meekly.

"Then I guess I could marry Emily. She will be eighteen soon. And if she fails to give me a son, I could always marry you. I'm sure you could give me an heir," he said with a smug look on his face.

"When Lyla and my father find out what you are planning ..."

Noah sighed deeply, and releasing Daisy's face, he turned back to face Iris. "No one is going to find out anything because you are not going to tell anyone. I think my dear Iris; you might have to stay here a little longer."

"No," she called out in fear.

"Noah," Daisy said softly. "I think we need to give up on this plan." She grabbed his hand and squeezed it.

Iris looked from Noah to Daisy, her gaze steady and observant. Realizing he had shared more information than intended and that Iris had noticed his interactions with Daisy, Noah turned away.

With a defiant sigh, Noah nodded to Daisy. Spinning on his heels, he opened the door, and ushered Daisy out. Without looking back, Noah closed the door, locking it firmly, once again, trapping Iris inside.

Watching Noah leave, Iris leapt up, rushed to the door, and tried in vain to open it, shouting for Noah or Daisy to return.

"Noah! Don't leave me here! Please, I won't say anything, I promise. Please Noah, let me go home. Noah? Daisy?"

Hearing Noah laugh; Iris moved away from the door and peered through the greasy, dirty window. Rubbing a small clean spot, Iris watched Noah and Daisy walk away.

Banging on the glass, Iris pulled at the rusty old latch, but the latch would not budge, the window would not open.

"Noah, I won't say anything, please," she cried out tearfully, but Noah did not stop, nor did he or Daisy turn to look at her. Feeling lost and alone and chastising herself for trusting in Noah and so willingly wanting to please him, Iris eventually returned to the straw bed, curled back up in a small ball, and cried until she fell asleep, wishing she had never met Noah.

Chapter 27

"How long do you intend to keep her here? I thought you were just going to hold her until you married Lyla!" Noah's cousin asked as they walked back to the main house and entered the kitchen.

"I know. I have complicated things a little more, haven't I?" he said as he sat down at the old worn kitchen table and slammed the key down in front of him. Staring into the flames of the fireplace on the opposite side of the room, Noah ran his fingers through his hair and sighed in frustration.

Daisy moved to the table, pulled out a chair, and sat down opposite Noah. "You said this would be a simple thing. That everything would go according to your plans. You take Iris as leverage, Lyla marries you, you take Iris home. Well? Now she knows more than she should. You should not have told her your plans, Noah."

Noah looked up at her, the setback showing in the glare of his eyes. "I know … I know."

"You did not tell me she is one hot-headed little brat!" Daisy said, pointing to the small house outside. "I swear she almost bit me!"

"Yes, she is, and so very gullible too." He smirked as the memory of how quickly she'd climbed in his carriage. "Has she eaten anything since you both arrived?" he asked, spinning the key over the table.

Daisy shook her head. "Refused to. Then cried and yelled herself to the point, she threw up! And I am not here to clean up after her!" Daisy turned her face away from Noah. She sat back in the chair, crossing her arms.

"Well, do you at least have another dress she can put on? The smell in the house is terrible."

"What? Give her one of my dresses! I do not even have a dress in her size!"

"Daisy!" Noah huffed, then softened his eyes. "I am not evil, and I understand this is not the most ideal situation we are in, but I will not allow someone to sit in their own filth. A simple nightdress is all she needs. I will talk to her about eating. Maybe arrange for a few other bits of clothing to accommodate her." Letting go of the key, he stood up and paced across the kitchen.

Daisy sighed, long and deep, the air whooshing from her nose. Wringing her fingers nervously, her eyes searched Noahs face.

"What?" he asked, sensing her discomfort.

"I was not aware you did not consummate the wedding last night," she said, with a hint of disappointment.

"Well, not everything went according to plan, did it? She was not in a very receptive mood last night."

"And what if you do not bed her tonight?"

"I know what has to be done Daisy, but I will not take her virginity by force. Not if I can help it." His voice rose in anger. Daisy glanced down at the worn table; her fingers now tracing the deep grooves in the wood.

"Daisy, he said, his voice softening as he knelt by her side. "I'm sorry I have to share my bed with Lyla. You know I would rather be with you instead, sharing our first night together, but if I want to take the Peirson manor, I must consummate the marriage."

"I know that Noah, and I do understand what you have to do, but I did not think you would have to get her pregnant. That changes everything, Noah." He watched as her eyes moistened. "What if she refuses you? It means Iris might be here for a few days. Her family will start looking for her." She raised her eyes to Noah, as the tears slid down her cheeks.

"I know. I had not thought of that. Iris is a little vixen!" He wiped away her tears, then stood abruptly, and made his way to the kitchen fireplace, relishing the light warmth the fire gave.

Daisy stared at his back, still wringing her hands. "And … I am not sure I can manage you having a child with *her*," she said, not wanting to say Lyla's name. "It should be me having your first child, your son, not her."

Noah stared into the flames. "I know, I know. It is a small price to pay for the grander picture, Daisy, and you will give me a son, plenty of them." He cocked his head and stared at her tenderly. "That house is massive; I would like nothing more than to fill it with *our* children." He smiled at her, his love for her undeniable.

"And what if after tonight, if she does lay with you, she is not with child, nor the month after? How long am I to wait? What if she births a daughter, you have to try again? This could take years," her voice quivered in sadness.

He sighed deeply. "Yes, I know, and I am sorry. It will make thinks harder and draw the plan out," he replied, wringing his own hands together, feeling cold, despite the flames at his back and legs.

"This plan better work, and you take Iris back home soon. I do not want to be visiting out here longer than needed. This house, this swamp … it is creepy." She looked around the room, a shiver running down her spine.

"It is not a swamp, Daisy. Just an abandoned property. I doubt anyone remembers it is even here." He paced the room again, deep in thought.

"How did you find it, anyway?" She asked as she watched him walk back and forth.

"It used to belong to a gentleman my father once knew, a long time ago. The children died of scarlet fever. After the parents moved away, no one ever came back."

Daisy jumped out of the chair and rushed to the centre of the room. "This house had scarlet fever?" Her hands flew to her mouth in horror, but then she lowered them quickly desperately trying to wipe them clean on her dress.

"Calm down." Noah stopped pacing. "This place has been abandoned for over five years. There is no more virus here."

Daisy inhaled a small breath. "It still gives me the creeps."

Noah rolled his eyes. "In the long run, visiting here will mean nothing once you move into the Pierson Manor. That place is opulence to the ultimate degree. And once we turn the grounds and grow crops, you will have a manor fit to behold a princess!" He held out his hand to Daisy. A small smile tugged at her lips. She stepped forward and placed her hand in his. He spun her around and pulled her in close.

"Well, I just wish you could make it happen faster. I do not need Mama and Papa getting suspicious every time I need to leave. It is hard enough to go anywhere unescorted."

He placed a light kiss on her forehead. "Tonight, I shall bed Lyla, and she will be with child. I know it. As soon as she delivers a boy, you will take care of my son and have the house." His smile curled at the corners, and his eyes darkened. "I cannot wait for my father to pass, no matter how unwell he is. He has nothing to his name, no property worth holding on to anyway. He will leave us all poor. Our manor is small, no bigger than this run-down heap, and our land," he laughed, "The soil cannot grow crops. It is useless. The Pierson manor is large, and with rich soil, we would make more money that we could dream of."

"And Lyla?" Daisy questioned as she stared into Noah's eyes. "What will happen to her? You said I would raise your son."

"And you will, as your very own. It is a shame that so many mothers do not survive after childbirth. I guess she will just be another one of those who did not make it." He shrugged and laughed aloud.

Daisy giggled like a nervous little girl. Noah knew she loved him with all her heart, and if this is what had to be done to ensure they got the Peirson manor for themselves, she would bear it. Daisy pushed herself out of Noah's arms, a little smile tipping her lips. "I guess I could go into town and buy a simple housedress, something like what the servants wear."

"That could work." Noah slipped his hand into his coat pocket and pulled out a few bills and passed them to Daisy. Escorting Daisy from the kitchen and into the sitting room, he could see why she did not like it. Time and weather had taken a toll on the house, and the furniture and drapes were torn and fading.

"If it makes it easier, the house staff can look after her tonight. That way, you will not need to visit again, and I only need to return tomorrow to take her home. You are right to think someone might become suspicious."

Daisy nodded in agreement. "And if she says anything about what happened to her here and what you told her?" asked Daisy.

"Then perhaps something bad shall happen to her too. So many children die in accidents. A drowning perhaps, in the lake? I will talk to her in the carriage on the way home tomorrow. Fear not Daisy. All will work out fine."

Noah smiled as Daisy nodded. He was well aware that Daisy's love for him blinded her vision, and he wanted nothing more than to spend the rest of his days with her at his side and *not* Lyla.

Daisy had turned eighteen the year before, and at the end of her own Flowering Day, she chose no one. Her parents tried to find five new suitors for Daisy, but each time she met them, she would turn them down, without even speaking to them. Within the year, they stopped trying.

Despite Noah being her first cousin, he knew her heart belonged to him. It always had, and it *always* would. Her parents wanted her to marry someone outside of the family; to establish a good financial arrangement with another wealthy family but Daisy had always wanted Noah.

For as long as Noah could remember, he reciprocated the feelings towards Daisy and had loved her for most of his life but to establish his own property, and to run the business he had dreamt of for years, Noah needed to marry someone who would come with the wealth and property size he needed. The two things Daisy's family did not have.

For Noah and Daisy, how society would view them was more important than anything, and for Noah, acquiring the Pierson manor was the only way he could see it happening.

From the day his parents agreed to Noah attending Lyla's Flowering Day, he'd promised Daisy that not only would he win her favour, but that as soon as he obtained the Pierson house, his marriage to Lyla would end and he would marry her. After all, he loved Daisy, not Lyla.

Although his plans were ever-changing, and not going to his original plan, Noah still knew the overall outcome would be in his favour, because Noah *always* got what he wanted!

Chapter 28

It was a few hours before Noah returned to the manor and found Lyla walking through the garden beds and around the fountain, her nose buried deep in a small book. Standing on the back verandah, hidden in the deep shadows, he watched her in silence. In a way, he did pity Lyla. It would be a shame to kill her in the end.

As he observed her, tucked against the manor wall to avoid being seen, Noah admired her beauty and while Lyla was not the most stunning female Noah had seen, her beauty was still enough to hold his breath. Watching her, he could not help but compare her appearance to Daisy.

Lyla's long straight blond hair was free and flowing down her back, glowing in the sun as a light breeze played with the loose strands. Daisy's hair was light brown and curly, falling just below her shoulders.

Lowering his gaze to Lyla's dark blue satin dress which picked up the sun's rays and shone as she moved, Noah admired the way it tapered in at her waist, pushed up her breasts, and exposed the soft pale skin on her arms. Daisy was slightly larger than Lyla, plumper around the waist, bigger breasted. She was right in stating none of her dresses would have fitted Iris's petite frame.

There was no denying the attraction he felt towards Lyla, and if the situation were different, Noah felt that he could have easily fallen in love with her, if he were not already in love with Daisy. Otherwise, Lyla could very well have been a perfect wife for him.

Spying on her, his heart quickened as he began thinking about what they would be doing tonight. Using the emotions that coursed through him, he walked quickly down the stairs, across the gravel path and through the hedge, towards Lyla. The sound of his shoes on the gravel caught Lyla's attention, and she looked up as he approached her with his most charming smile.

Noah watched her breath hitched when her eyes fell on his face, and he smiled to himself when she turned her face abruptly, hiding the light rosy blush that reddened her cheeks. Did she find him attractive? The thought amused Noah.

"Have you been here all day?" he asked with deliberate coolness as he approached and extended his hand to her. Lowering her book, Lyla accepted his gesture courteously, though she refrained from making eye contact.

"No. I have only just come back outside."

He kissed the back of her hand tenderly. "You look radiant." Lyla's eyes widened slightly and for a brief second, met his gaze "The sun is at the right position in the sky, and with you outside in the garden, you are glowing like an angel." He kissed her hand again.

His compliments deepened her blush, and she pulled her hand out from his. "Flattery will not excuse what you have done, Noah!" She turned slightly, angling her body away from his.

"And I truly am sorry." He bowed low. "What can I do to amend my errors?"

"Return my sister for a start and annul this sham of a marriage!"

"I cannot. At least not yet."

Lyla turned back to look at him. "What do you mean, not yet?" Her eyes blackened.

"This is a … complicated situation Lyla." Noah said softly.

"There is nothing complicated about this, Noah. I do not wish to keep repeating myself … but if you do not return my sister …"

Noah stepped forward, his eyes darkened as he towered over her. "Then what?" He stared hard at Lyla, cutting off her words. "What shall you do, Lyla?" He waited for her to answer. Lyla turned her face away from him and backed up a few steps. "Whatever do you think *you* could do to *me*?" he asked, a hint of rage edged his voice.

He took a few steps towards her, closing the gap again. Lyla kept her eyes lowered. "Yes, I did not think there was much you could do." He sighed loudly then softened his voice. "I promise you, if you just do what I need you to do as my wife, you will get your precious Iris back."

Rasing his hand, Noah touched Lyla's cheek. Slowly, he traced his fingers down her face and then cupped them under her chin, where he finally lifted it gently, bringing Lyla's eyes up to his.

Before Lyla could respond, he brought his mouth down to hers, crushing her lips against his. His other hand, slipped around her waist, pulling her against him. His kiss, although forced and hard, eventually softened, and as suddenly as it started, he abruptly pulled back.

"Please do not make this harder than it needs to be," he whispered as he closed his eyes and rested his forehead on hers. His breathing quickened, and each breath grazed along Lyla's mouth, quickening hers. Trying to catch her own breath, Lyla turned her face away, pulling out of Noah's grasp, but not out of his grip around her waist.

"Please come to me tonight," He said as he opened his eyes to gaze at Lyla. She glanced sideways at him but remained silent. "You *will* come to me tonight!" His voice deepened, and his grip around her waist tightened. Lyla nodded in agreement.

He sighed with relief and smiled. "Until then." He kissed her forehead, let go of her waist leaving Lyla's side, walked back through the hedge towards to Manor.

As soon as Noah disappeared from view, Lyla clutched her hands to her chest before she stumbled to the side and collapsed onto the rim of the fountain.

Struggling to breathe, Lyla dropped the book and clawed at the front of her dress, trying to open it. Finally, with shaking fingers, the ribbon snapped, and the corset gave slightly, allowing Lyla to get more air into her lungs. Tears of shame and sorrow flowed rapidly down her cheeks.

As though on cue, Meg came running through the garden and fell to her knees.

"Did he hurt you?" she cried out.

Lyla shook her head. "I just couldn't breathe," she replied as pushing the loosened corset against her skin. Meg reached up and wiped the tears from her cheeks.

"And why could you not breathe?"

"He is a monster!"

"Well, yes, we know this already." Meg stood began to slowly fix the front of Lyla's dress. "What did he do to you?"

Lyla sighed and looked at Meg trying to hide her embarrassment. "He kissed me!"

Meg paused and met Lyla's gaze, her eyebrows raised in surprise.

"He is a monster because he kissed you?" Meg queried, slightly confused.

"I did not ask to be kissed. He just did it of his own accord, and he was … rough. And told me I am to join him tonight in his bed. I do not know if I can do this, Meg. I do not want him to be my first." Fresh tears flowed as she struggled to maintain her poise.

"Now, now." Meg wiped the tears away. "I am sure we can find a reason for you not to join him."

"You want me to lie to him?"

"'Tis better to lie to him than to lie with him!" Meg said honestly.

"But the longer I hold him off, the longer he holds Iris. I couldn't bear it if anything happened to her. I would never forgive myself."

"Did Noah say anything about when Iris will return home?" Meg asked, helping Lyla stand.

"No. He just demanded that I do my wifely duties. Afterwards, he will see about her return."

"Okay then. Tonight, you will visit his bed, do what needs to be done. Once we get Iris back, we will leave. Head back to the manor." Meg stooped down and picked up Lyla's book. "Then we will have him arrested, and this whole drama will be over. Okay?"

Lyla took her arm, and nodded, although a sudden rush of nerves coursed through her, making her knees weak. As they headed back to the manor, a thought crossed Lyla's mind.

"You said you did not know the way here, that the curtains in the carriage were kept close. I certainly did not pay much attention to our directions. I was too distraught. How are we meant to get back home if we do not know which way to go?"

Meg suddenly stopped and tugged on Lyla's arm. Quickly glancing around the garden and through the hedge towards the manor, making sure no one was in view. Once she believed they were alone, she turned to Lyla.

"Do you remember, just before the two of you left, Noah invited your family to join you this weekend for a picnic lunch?" A smile formed on her lips.

"Yes," Lyla responded curiously.

"He will have to allow your family to join us. We can then just leave with them."

"Only if Iris has been returned. Otherwise, if I try to leave without her, I might never see Iris again."

Meg groaned with frustration. "We will see!"

Chapter 29

The rest of the afternoon passed by quietly, and to Lyla's relief, Noah made no effort to engage with her at all, preferring to work at the small writing desk in the sitting room.

Lyla kept Meg close by her side, unwilling to face any greater discomfort than was necessary. The evening ahead loomed over her, promising to be challenging enough without further complications. With Meg's reassuring presence, Lyla sought solace and support, determined to endure whatever the night might bring.

As the sun set, Meg encouraged her to change into a dark green dinner dress, with small, ruffled sleeves, and a tight corset, and carefully pulled her hair back off her face. She added a simple pearl necklace, and a dab of perfume, much to Lyla's annoyance—but Meg insisted.

"You may not like the position you are in, but as your maid-in-waiting, I will not have you dressing lower than you are entitled to. You are a lady. In fact, you are *the* lady of this house, and you will always look your best and smell your best. I do not dress you like this for *his* benefit. I dress you like this because *you* are worth it."

Lyla cried upon hearing these words. Meg has always been by her side and made sure Lyla looked her best, and in this situation, Lyla was ever more grateful to have her presence.

Finding Noah waiting for her outside her bedroom, Lyla struggled to not roll her eyes, knowing the smug look Meg would have displayed behind her when Noah complimented Lyla on her appearance.

Dinner with Noah was a sombre affair. Neither of them spoke more than a few words to each other, Lyla's nerves getting the better of her. Sitting across the table, she hoped he felt the same. Once dinner finished, Noah got up without a word and upon reaching Lyla, extended his arm towards her. Knowing she had no other option than to accept, Lyla allowed him to escort her out the dining room.

Believing this was the moment she feared, Lyla was surprised when Noah led her not to the grand staircase but towards the library.

Having declined the invitation the night before, retiring to her room instead, Lyla sighed softly, thankful Noah was not rushing the night, yet she was still apprehensive, knowing what she needed to do to get her Iris back.

Upon walking through the doors, Lyla's eyes widened, and she inhaled deeply. The familiar aroma of musty leather and old paper drifted towards her as Noah led her into the centre of the room. Dropping her hand, he stepped back, and she could feel him watching her as she looked around her.

Eager eyes soaked in every part of the room. Directly in front of Lyla stood a great stone fireplace, lit and crackling softly. The marble mantle was adorned with an oval mirror and flanked by two large paintings, both depicting vases of flowers and fruits. Raising her hand, Lyla ran her fingers over one of three pale green velvet, wingback chairs which sat between her and the fireplace, as her gaze fell to a large plush white rug carpeted the floor, before the hearth.

Shifting her gaze to the right, two floor-to-ceiling windows looked out towards the side of the house. The floor-length black curtains had not yet been drawn closed and the setting sun cast shadows across the garden outside.

A small mahogany table stood between the windows; topped with a vase filled with flowers from the garden. A Georgian fold over tea table stood in the corner of the room, between the fireplace and first window, complete with a polished silver serving tray, and matching silver tea set.

To Lyla's pleasure, an elegant Victorian writing desk, stood to Lyla's side with paper, ink and quill ready to be used. In the far-right corner, stood an opulent rosewood cabinet, filled with decanters filled with amber-coloured liquors and matching crystal glasses.

Tilting her head back, Lyla admired a beautiful crystal chandelier, its candles, illuminating the room in a soft yellow glow. The grand beauty of the room left Lyla speechless.

Leaving the best view till last, Lyla turned her head to the left and stared at an enormous wooden bookshelf, brimming with books, it's shelves running the full length of the wall. Noah told her he owned a few books of his own but there were more far more books in the library than Lyla had imagined.

Moving as if in a dream, Lyla approached the books taking in the different hews of blues, greens, reds, and browns of the leather and fabric that bound them, their spines, beautifully adorned with gold and silver writing. Gently, Lyla reached up and rang her fingertips across the spines, and she found herself smiling.

"This room is for you." Noah's deep voice broke the silence. His words made her jump a little and she turned to look back at him, forgetting he was there. "These books are … all yours."

"For me?" she said in awe, her smile widening. He bowed slightly, and Lyla returned the gesture with a slight nod. "Thank you," she said, touched by his gesture.

"Please, help yourself." He waved his hand towards the bookshelf.

"You collected all these for me?" she questioned, looking to the books, then back to Noah.

"Yes," he replied, though as he ducked his head, and turned slightly away from Lyla.

Lyla dismissed his movement and turned back to the bookshelf. As she inspected the titles, trying to pick something to read, Lyla heard Noah walk across the room and sit in the chair furthest away. Glancing over her shoulder, she watched him pick up a book from the side table and opening it mid-way, he began reading. As though sensing her gaze, Noah peered at her over the book and smiled. The look in his eyes quickened Lyla's pulse and she quickly turned her attention back to the books.

Eventually, after ten minutes of looking, Lyla selected a book with a deep red cover and sat in the chair closest to the bookshelf and as far from Noah as possible.

"Have you read that one?" Noah asked.

"No. I have not," Lyla responded politely as she smoothed out her dress.

"Would you like some tea?" he asked in another attempt at making small talk.

"No, thank you." Lyla shook her head, opened the book, and focused on reading, hopeful that Noah would take the hint.

After about an hour, Penelopy and Regina, the two servants Lyla met when she arrived, entered the library. Distracted from her novel, Lyla watched as one closed the curtains, as the another politely placed a tray loaded with tea and small cakes, on the tea table and with two curt nods, left as silently as they had arrived.

Standing quietly, Lyla moved to the table and poured herself a cup of tea and helped herself to the cakes, glancing at Noah while doing so. Although he did not look directly up, Lyla could saw that his gaze remained still, no longer reading.

Once she settled back down, Lyla struggled to read, or enjoy her tea, instead flicking timid glances at Noah over her book. His hair was loose, framing his face, and the golden lighting of the room made the dark blue material of his coat shimmer, defining his torso and muscular arms.

Lyla watched his chest rise and fall with each breath, a steady pace she unknowingly matched. In an ordinary situation, she considered that she could be happy married to him. His handsome features were annoyingly attractive, further complicating an already tricky situation. Lyla desperately wanted to dislike him, to hate him for what he had done. Yet, sitting with him, in the lavish library he'd curated just for her, Lyla could once again see the charm and easy-going quality she noted in him at her Flowering Day Ceremony, which appealed to her romantic side.

Another hour passed and the teapot sat empty, and only a scattering of crumbs remained of the cakes.

"Are you enjoying the book?" Noah's voice startled Lyla, pulling her from the story and back into the real world.

"Yes, very much, thank you." Lyla glanced up and looked at him. "Shall we retire for the night?" Noah asked.

Lyla swallowed nervously. She had used their time in the library to avoid the inevitable, but she knew there was no delaying it. Lyla wanted nothing more than to get Iris back, and if consummating the marriage made that happen, she felt like there was no other choice. Closing the book, Lyla placed it onto the table next to her.

Noah, taking this as a positive sign, placed his own book down as well. Standing up, he offered his hand. Lyla looked into his blue eyes and gave him a tentative smile. Slowly, she placed hers in his and stood. Noah stepped up closer to Lyla and took her face in his other hand. Gradually, not breaking eye contact with her, he lowered his face to just a few inches from hers.

Feeling his breath on her neck, Lyla heard him moan as he inhaled her perfume. At the same time standing so close to her husband, Lyla could smell Noah's cologne. Hints of spices and wood mix with lavender tickled her nose and instantly brought her back to when they danced at her birthday and as her heart fluttered, her own breath hitched. Sensing her reaction, Noah brought his lips down to hers, pressing them gently together.

This time, the kiss was different, it was soft and tender, nothing like his previous kisses and it took her by surprise. Melting into his embrace, Lyla kissed him back, her lips moving with his, her legs feeling weak. When Noah finally broke the kiss, Lyla's heart was racing, and she could feel the heat in her cheeks.

"Thank you," he murmured, the warmth of his breath teasing the tip of her nose. Lyla opened her eyes, overwhelmed with mixed emotions. Noah smiled tenderly and dropped his hand from her chin. Turning around, he led Lyla by the hand, out of the library, up the grand stairs and to his room. Pausing at his door, he looked at her, his eyes burning with desire.

"Will you join me?"

Swallowing the lump in her throat, Lyla nodded and with a smile, Noah pulled her into his room, closing the door behind them.

Chapter 30

Noah's room was only slightly larger than Lyla's. The layout was the same, just in reverse, but decorated in masculine tones of blue, dark green and gold.

The oil lamps were lit, and a low fire burned brightly in the fireplace, warming the room. Lyla's heart raced, as a new wave of nerves coursed through her.

As Noah led Lyla to the centre of the room, she tentatively stole glances towards the large bed set against the far wall, her mind filled with images of what was about to take place. Pausing mid step, Noah turned to face her and letting her go, once again cupped Lyla's face in his hands, and kissed her softly.

The kiss lasted longer this time, and Lyla could feel herself respond to his touch. She felt Noah's hesitation as he ended the kiss, his lips lingering over hers before he drew back. As she looked up at him, Lyla could see from the quickened rise and fall of his chest that his own rapid breathing now matched hers.

Without breaking their gaze, Noah began to untie her bodice. As he loosened the string and pulled the top of the dress apart, he lent back in and kissed her again, his passion taking over. Although Lyla did not want to respond to his touch, she found herself pushing his jacket off his shoulders before she realized what she was doing. No sooner had his jacket fallen to the floor, Lyla was already unbuttoning his shirt, their lips never parting.

With a final tug, Noah released Lyla from her bodice, and the dress fell to the floor, exposing her under garments. Only then did he break their kiss as he stepped back, kicking off his shoes and tugging his trousers off before throwing them across the room.

Lyla's face grew hot, not only from the way her body reacted to Noah, but because she was alone for the first time with a near-naked male. Unable to stop herself, Lyla ran her gaze over his body, her eyes trailing along his muscular arms and across his broad shoulders. With a shaky inhale, Lyla slowly dropped her gaze to his chest, then down to his white drawers. Everything about his body made her blush deepen as the realisation that this was really going to happen.

Lyla was about to become a woman.

Helping Lyla step over of her dress, where it had pooled at her feet, Noah gently led her towards the bed. Letting go of her hand, he ran his gaze up and down her body and the intensity of his expression brought on a new sense of wanting in her. Once again, he pulled her in close and kissed her, deeper this time, and Lyla responded without hesitation.

With his arms wrapped around her, Noah pulled her in tighter, sending a pulse of need through her. Lyla had never been this close to a male before and the heat and contours of his bare chest through her light cotton chemise, fuelled her desire further.

Breaking the kiss once more, Noah suddenly stepped back and removed his drawers, exposing himself completely to Lyla. Not daring to look, Lyla kept her attention on his face instead. Breathing rapidly, Noah carefully lowered the straps of Lyla's chemise off her shoulders, letting it fall to the floor. Kneeling before her, he took off her shoes, and slipped her stockings down, pulling them tenderly from her legs. Feeling vulnerable, Lyla automatically covered herself with her hands.

"Don't," Noah said softly as he clutched her wrists and pulled them away from her body as he stared up at her from his knees. "You look beautiful." He stood and glanced at her, Lyla sensing the warmth of his gaze as it moved over her. She felt both embarrassed and excited, and as though sensing her unease, Noah stood and wrapped his arms around her, pulling her back against his chest.

Lyla could feel the heat radiating off him as his mouth found hers again, and without hesitation, she responded to his kiss. She could feel every part of him pressed against her own skin and before she knew it, Noah lifted her up and placed her onto the bed. Pulling her up onto the pillows. Noah stared into her eyes, holding her gaze.

"You are radiant," he whispered as he lowered himself onto her.

Lyla closed her eyes.

For Iris, she said to herself. I am doing this for Iris.

Chapter 31

As Lyla opened her eyes to the faint morning sounds of the staff moving about the house, she could feel the heat of Noah's back pushed against her. Keeping still, she listened to the deep rhythmic sound of his breathing, and she sighed softly, relieved he was still asleep.

Listening to her own breaths, Lyla lay motionless for a few more minutes, contemplating what to do. Instead, memories of the previous night rushed forward, and Lyla closed her eyes praying it would somehow make them stop.

It didn't.

While Noah was gentle and took his time consummating their marriage, ensuring Lyla remained comfortable throughout the experience, she felt ashamed and embarrassed about what she did. Did everyone feel like that afterwards?

Lying beside Noah, Lyla assumed her first time would be with a man who loved her, and a man she loved back. A man who could never hurt her or the ones she loved. But Noah was not this man. She did not love Noah and Noah did not care for her, the way she believed Winston did.

Feeling her distain for Noah growing again, Lyla gently pushed the covers off, and eased herself away, hoping not to wake him. Making it to the edge of the bed, Lyla stood carefully and picking up her chamise, silently slipped it on, instantly feeling better, relieved she was no longer naked.

Knowing picking up her dress would make too much noise, Lyla left it and her other clothes on the floor and tiptoed across the room. Stealing one last look at Noah, his back still towards her, Lyla carefully opened the door. Peeking out into the corridor and making sure no-one was outside Noah's room, Lyla stepped out, closing the door behind her.

Ducked across the hallway to her room, and closing the door quietly behind her, Lyla rushed to her washroom. Not waiting for Meg to bring fresh hot water, she grabbed her washcloth and pear scented soap and removing her chamise, dropping the thin dress to the floor. Then, dipping her cloth in the chilly bowl of water, Lyla began to wash herself. Although Noah didn't hurt her, her body still felt tender and the dull ache between her legs worried her.

Halfway through her wash, there was a light knock at the door.

"Lyla? Are you in there?" Meg's sweet voice drifted into the room.

"Yes," Lyla replied as she straightened.

"Would you like some hot water?"

"No thank you, I am almost done."

"Okay, I'll wait for you out here," Meg replied, and Lyla heard her move away from the door. Grabbing the towel, which was draped over a small chair, she dried herself off. Looking down at herself, Lyla wondering if she appeared different. She felt different. More grown up, more mature, yet observing herself, she saw no difference.

Lyla wrapped the towel around herself and padded back into her bedroom where Meg waited patiently at her dressing table.

"Are you alright?" she asked, pulling out the chair so Lyla could sit.

She nodded. "I think so."

"Did you stay in his room the whole night?" Meg asked as she began combing Lyla's hair.

"I did," she replied quietly.

"And ..." Meg paused. "Did you, you know ... consummate the marriage?"

Lyla nodded again and Meg gave her shoulders a gentle squeeze. "I hope he was gentle." She resumed combing her hair.

"He was. Although, it still hurt."

"Yes. It does hurt the first time, but afterwards, it gets better."

Lyla turned around and looked at Meg, her eyebrows raised. "Have you?"

Meg smiled slightly, her cheeks flushing. "Maybe."

"I thought ... but you are not married."

"No, I am not. I haven't found a husband, and I doubt I will. My time is occupied with you, but I have had a few ... male companions, whom I have spent my nights with."

Lyla looked at Meg through the mirror with a cheeky smile but said nothing further. Instead, she watched as Meg continued to comb her hair, slowly plaiting it, before arranging it high on her head. While dressing, Lyla excitingly told Meg about the library.

"I know the library was nothing compared to the one at home, but the amount of books on that wall, oh Meg, I could stay in there for months and not get to read them all."

"It sounds very impressive," Meg replied, having finished her hair and was now slipping a dark pink dress over Lyla's head.

"Oh, it was, and the chairs in there," Lyla sighed. "They were so comfortable, and the fire, I was so relaxed and content," she rambled on, the words flowing quickly. Meg moved behind Lyla, smoothing her dress down, allowing Lyla to keep talking.

"I should very much like to return to the library today, perhaps finish the book I was reading," Lyla said as Meg encouraged her to step into her shoes.

Once dressed, Lyla stood before the full-length mirror. Turning herself left and right, she smiled, admiring her reflection. "Do you think I look older Meg?" she asked and spun on her heels to face her.

Moving forward, Meg grabbed Lyla's hands and pulled her gaze. With a slight smile, she sighed softly. "You look very mature Lyla, and quite the lady, but ..." she said raising her brow. "Do you think Noah will send Iris home today?"

"Oh, I hope so." Lyla said, squeezing Meg's hands. "I've fulfilled my duties, we are officially married, there should be no reason for him not to."

Glancing back to her reflection, Lyla noted her skin seemed to have a certain glow about it this morning. The dress Meg chose, made her skin look lighter and with her blonde hair elegantly plaited and positioned on her head like a crown, Lyla felt grown up suddenly, and considered perhaps she had changed after all.

"Well then, Milady." Meg said and curtsied as Lyla walked past.

"Please do not do that." Lyla said, her eyes widening in dismay.

"Well, you are a lady now," she smirked.

"I guess I am, but calling me that, makes me feel old."

"Fair enough, I shall never repeat it again."

Just as Lyla got to her bedroom door, she turned to face Meg. "I hope I never have to lay with him again," she said timidly, her youth and innocence showing.

"Hopefully not," Meg replied.

Meg stayed in the room while Lyla walked into the hallway. Noah's door was open, and she could see her clothes were no longer on the floor, and the bed was freshly made. Seeing his bed brought a rush of memories back from the previous night. Lyla's cheeks grew warm, and she quickly turned her gaze away.

Approaching the top of the stairs, Lyla paused when she saw Noah standing on the landing, waiting for her. His hair was tied back and the dark grey coat and trousers he wore looked more formal and business-like than usual. Holding her breath, she watched as his eyes trailed upwards from the skirt of her dress up to her face, a smile lighting up his expression. Lyla couldn't return it — she felt too confused. She had fulfilled her wifely duties, and the last thing she expected was to find Noah waiting for her with such a look of desire in his eyes.

"Good morning," he said, his deep voice causing an unexpected flutter in her stomach. He held out his hand towards her. Slowly Lyla walked down the steps and hesitantly took his hand.

"You look beautiful," Noah said as he lent forwards and kissed her lightly on the lips.

"Thank you." Lyla blushed at the kiss, immediately thinking about being alone with him in his bedroom.

"How are you feeling this morning?" he asked as they walked down the grand staircase. She turned to glance at him, finding him watching her, waiting for her to answer.

"I am good, thank you."

"I hope last night was … okay for you." The concern in his voice surprised Lyla. She nodded and gave him a weak smile. "I know the first time is always a bit … awkward. I hope the next time will be … better," he said with a reassuring smile.

Lyla just smiled politely back. Just as she'd said to Meg before, she had no intention of sleeping with Noah again.

Stepping off the staircase and onto the marble floor of the foyer, Noah stopped and turned to her.

"I have a surprise for you," he said, his voice full of such charm that Lyla felt her heart skip a beat.

Iris! she thought hopefully.

"Come with me." Noah smiled and instead of leading her to the dining room, pulled her in the opposite direction, towards the sitting room. Lyla's heart raced at the thought of being reunited with her dearest Iris, and together they could leave this house and return home.

Entering the small parlour, Lyla quickly scanned the room, searching for her sister, but her shoulders dropped in disappointment when she realised no one was there.

"Come," Noah said as he guided her around the sofa. Suddenly, her steps faulted, and she stopped in her tracks. Sitting in the middle of the dark yellow rug, sat a small puppy.

"She is yours," Noah said proudly as he moved over to the small collie.

"Mine?" Lyla was shocked. This was not what she anticipated. "You gave me a puppy?" She stood frozen in place.

"Yes. A wedding gift from me to you." He picked up the little pup and carried her to Lyla. "She needs a name." Lyla watched in bewilderment as he moved towards her.

Once he stood in front of her, Lyla lowered her eyes and stared at the puppy, her eyes drinking in the soft white and tan fur. Lyla's heart melted in an instant. She cradled the puppy's face and kissed her little head.

"Take her," Noah said softly and pushed the puppy into Lyla's arms. The pup eagerly licked Lyla's nose. "See, she loves you already." He stood by her side, wrapping an arm around her waist.

"She's really mine?" asked Lyla, turning to Noah in awe.

"Absolutely." He kissed her forehead.

Lyla buried her face in the puppy's warm fur and scratched behind her ears, She'd never owned her own dog and holding the puppy, Lyla's smiled as she cooed and fussed over her.

"Regrettably, I am unable to join you for breakfast this morning," Noah stated, "So I hope this little lady keeps you company. I shall be back after lunch, then, we could all take a walk in the gardens?" he asked and squeezed Lyla's waist.

Lyla nodded absentmindedly as she cuddled the puppy, her attention full. "Until this afternoon," he said, kissing her gently on the lips before walking out of the sitting room and back into the foyer.

It was not until she heard the front door close, that she turned around and walked to the dining room with the puppy in her arms. As she entered the room, she noticed the table has only been set for herself and on the floor, a small bowl of food for the dog. Tenderly, she placed the puppy on the ground and sat herself down.

"Good morning, madam. I trust you slept well," the butler said as he brought in her breakfast. Lyla glanced at him briefly, surprised by his greeting. Normally, he only nodded to her.

Seeing Noah's bed freshly made this morning, meant the sheets would have been changed also. Lyla felt embarrassed, certain the staff all knew what transpired the night before. Lyla's blood was on those sheets; the vital evidence she had lost her virginity last night. Now the marriage was officially unified, did they respect her?

"I did, thank you," she replied and waited for him to leave. With a curt nod, the butler disappeared back to the kitchen.

Lyla ate her breakfast in silence, with the only interruption the puppy, moving to lay down at her feet after she finished the small bowl of her own food. "Tuckered out already?" Lyla questioned and laughed to herself when she got no response.

Finishing her meal, Lyla wiped her mouth and placed the napkin on the table. Staring across the empty room, Lyla felt a rush of home sickness as she sat there alone. She was used to hearing her family chatter and laugh during meals, and the background sounds of the staff moving throughout the house. Here in this place, she was met with only silence and emptiness.

Realising she would have the morning to herself, Lyla decided to spend more time in the library, looking at all the books Noah had collected. Pushing her chair back and stepping away from the table, she bent down, picked up the puppy and cuddling her tight, strolled back to the library.

The familiar smell of the room generated an instant feeling of peace. As she made her way over to her chair, Lyla noticed a new thick blanket on the floor. Noah had thought of everything, and she wondered how long he had planned to get her a puppy. Thinking back to their conversation in the garden yesterday, Lyla remembered telling him she loved collies, and marvelled at the speed in which he organised her companion.

Laying the puppy on the blanket, she glanced to the bookshelf. The sheer number of books lining the shelves made her feel a little sad. Just like she'd said to Meg that morning, she'd love nothing more than to spend endless days, months, even years, sitting in the library and reading every book. Yet, she knew the reality. As soon as Iris was returned to, she would leave the manor, have Noah charged with Winston's murder and Iris's kidnapping and return to her parents.

Returning to her chair, Lyla picked up the book she was reading last night. She hadn't been reading long when Meg entered the room. "Wow, you weren't wrong. There are a lot of books in here!"

"I know," Lyla sighed, as she lay the book in her lap. "I could live happily in this room forever."

"Are you alone?" Meg questioned, as she looked around the large room with wide eyes.

"No, not really." A cheeky smile came over Lyla. She motioned for Meg to come to her side. "Look what Noah got me as a wedding present."

"Who is this?" Meg gasped as she saw the puppy curled up on the blanket.

"This is my little one," Lyla said as she slid off the chair and knelt next to the pup, scratching her head just behind the ear.

"He gave you a puppy?" Meg questioned her. "What about Iris?"

"He didn't mention her," Lyla sighed woefully. "Noah presented me with the puppy then said he needed to leave. What if he has left to get her now?" Lyla said as she smiled at the puppy who was wagging her tail with excitement. "I have to give her a name." Scooping the puppy up into her arms, Lyla looked at Meg. "How about Lucy, or Bonnie, or Annabelle?" she said, as she rubbed her nose against the puppy's.

Abruptly, Meg bent down and grabbed Lyla's arm, hurting her in the process. "Lyla! Can you not see what he is doing to you?" she said, frowned at her.

Lyla's brow furrowed in return. "What do you mean?" she asked trying to pull her arm free. "And you are hurting me."

Meg shook her head. "He is distracting you, Lyla. Giving you a beautiful library and now a puppy! What's next? A grand piano and riding lessons?" Letting go of Lyla, Meg flung her hands in the air in frustration.

"It is not like that! And I already know how to ride, Meg!" Lyla protested, nuzzling the dog again.

Meg walked away from her and towards the bookshelf, trailing a finger over the spines as she inspected them, before turning back to look at Lyla. "This would have cost a fortune Lyla. All these books. Some of these are incredibly old. I'm telling you; Noah is up to something. I do not trust him Lyla, and neither should you."

Lyla stopped snuggling the puppy long enough to stare at Meg. "I don't trust him either. I haven't forgotten what he has done to Winston or to Iris. But what am I meant to do? Fight him at every turn? I cannot risk Iris's safety."

"No, you cannot but I just want you to be aware of him. I just feel like he is up to something more … dangerous, than just marrying you."

Lyla dropped her eyes back down to the ball of fur in her arms, feeling her eyes sting with tears. "If I just do what he asks of me, I know he will bring Iris back. I must trust him!"

Meg sighed and crouched beside Lyla. "I didn't mean to upset you or hurt you, Lyla. I am just concerned." Running a hand through the puppy's fur, she smiled tenderly to Lyla and changed the subject. "Let us get this girl outside, before she makes a mess on the floor."

Chapter 32

Cantering away from the manor on his horse, Noah regretted leaving Lyla behind. Although it was never his intention to have any feelings for her, spending time with her and getting to know her more over the past two days, he admitted to himself he was starting to see her differently.

When Albert and Grace approached Noah and his parents to ask if he would be interested in being a suitor for Lyla, Noah had jumped at the opportunity. Within a few minutes, Noah surmised his plan to obtain a large manor with full staff and vast grounds to help fulfil his plans to become an entrepreneur, could play out well. He was very aware of Albert's reputation and knew about the large property he owned. And Lyla would simply be a small pawn in that plan.

His parents, although well off, had little in the way of a legacy to leave behind, and with his father being unwell, Noah didn't believe he would see the year out. His parents house only possessed a small garden and no place to keep a horse. The same was with Daisy's parents. They too owned a small house in the city, but both Noah and Daisy knew the city was not where they wanted to spend the rest of their lives together.

Daisy was also a keen lover of the outdoors. She loved tending to the gardens and being amongst nature, especially her horse, and Noah wanted nothing more, than to make her happy.

Noah was adamant he would not follow in his father's footsteps regarding his career. He was more of a hands-on man and not one to sit behind a desk. Banking did not appeal to him at all, and with Albert's property Noah saw the perfect opportunity to get what he wanted. What *they* wanted.

Only now, things were getting complicated. Firstly, Noah had no doubt that he would win Lyla over at her Flowering Day and was genuinely shocked when she did not pick his flower. Even poor Iris was visibly upset at Lyla's choice. He left that night seething, and by the time he got home, he was determined to do whatever was needed to change Lyla's mind or at the very least, marry her despite her chosen union with Winston.

Thankfully, his beloved Daisy completely supported his actions. Although, as he rode towards the forgotten homestead, Noah realised his role as Lyla's husband, was making this task a little bit harder — and he also knew it weighed on Daisy's mind. She was correct though — Noah would have preferred his first-born child, preferably a boy, to be Daisy's and not Lyla's.

In his initial plan, he assumed he would only have to bed her once; to consummate their union on the night of the wedding and that would be it. Daisy understood it was necessary for his plan to work, that he needed to sleep with Lyla to ensure the marriage was legal, and he swore to her it would mean nothing to him. It was merely an insignificant task in the grand scheme of things.

Noah and Daisy, although not yet married, had been intimate a few times now, and Noah took great pains to ensure she would not fall pregnant. He would not sully her name before they wed, and they both knew there could be a costly price to pay for their moments of weakness, if it were discovered she was no longer pure, but they could not stay away from each other.

Now that things were falling into place, and his plan was working, Noah worried his feeling for Lyla would grow stronger. The desire he felt for her made it difficult for him to concentrate on anything.

Pushing his horse to go faster, Noah tried to brush the thoughts of Lyla to the back of his mind. He needed a clear head when he returned to Daisy. While he didn't think he needed to worry about Daisy becoming jealous, Noah was all too aware he was asking a lot from her. Daisy was loyal and devoted to him, but walking away from Lyla this morning was hard. Every part of him longed to remain at her side, and as he reached the threshold of the front door, it took all his willpower not to turn around. Thankfully, the urgency of his reason to leave her won over.

Noah was well aware Lyla did not love him—she'd made no attempt to hide it from him, which gave him some relief. Having to change his plans to accommodate for Lyla needing to bear him a son, her lack of affection for him would make it easier, if he needed her to die. Noah hadn't considered that his own feelings would be the hindrance. Yet, seeing her standing naked before him last night, his heart raced for all the wrong reasons.

Although he had been slightly apprehensive, bedding Lyla was harder than he had imagined. Noah's plan was to do what he needed to do as quickly as possible. Instead, he found himself wishing the night would never end. As he drifted to sleep with Lyla in his arms, he found himself hoping she would still be there in the morning, willing to make love to him again. Instead, when he woke and found her gone from his bed, he felt a pang of despair — and longing.

Noah slowed his horse to a walk and navigating through a dark overgrown path, he desperately tried to shake off the intrusive visions of Lyla. Watching her face light up when she held the puppy this morning, or her look of complete awe when he showed her the library. Seeing her face glow with happiness and pure joy, made him smile, catching him by surprise.

Noah struggled to understand the sense of pride and elation he felt simply observing her. Despite his intentions, he couldn't deny his longing to be with her, to hold her, to smell her sweet vanilla and rose infused perfume or to run his fingers across her cheek. Her skin so soft and warm, and it excited him to see her slowly respond to his touch.

Noah shook his head firmly — he couldn't have feelings for her. Daisy was the woman he loved, the one who he wanted to spend the rest of his life with. *Not* Lyla. Everything he was doing, was for Daisy, for their happy future together.

But then again, what if he did fall in love with Lyla? If he took Iris home now, would it fix everything? Could it make Lyla fall in love with him? What if she did bear him a son, would he not still fulfill his dream, to own her father's manor, but with Lyla by his side and not Daisy?

Shaking his head in frustration and finally clearing his head of the thoughts which plagued his journey, Noah lead his horse past the small house where Iris was being kept and over to the old, dilapidated barn at the main house. Dismounting and tying his horse to a wooden pole, Noah peered back through the overgrown brush, to the small house. Feeling sure of what to do with her, Noah walked into the old manor and found the house maid in the kitchen.

"Good morning," he said cheerfully, grabbing an apple off the table and bit deeply into it. "How is my guest?" he asked.

The young house maid, a girl not much older than Iris herself, nodded and curtsied to Noah. "Still not eating sir."

Noah sighed heavily. "I will take something for her." He motioned for a plate of food, and the girl quickly grabbed another apple, a small block of cheese and a slice of bread. Handing the plate to Noah, she turned and resumed cleaning the tabletop.

"Are there any other issues I need to address?" he asked.

"No, sir," she responded quietly.

"The key," he said, holding out his hand with the apple still in it. Quickly the young girl walked to a kitchen drawer and took out the old key. Hooking it over Noah's extended finger, she kept her head lowered and stepped backwards.

"Please let the driver know I will need the carriage," Noah said and without waiting for the maids response, left the kitchen and returned to the front door. Standing on the porch, he glanced around the overgrown garden and back down towards the small house near the river. He could see why Daisy did not like to come here. The trees and bushes were wild and unkept and the path to the house was dark and overshadowed by branches and tall grass.

Thinking on how to manage the situation with Iris, Noah took another bite from the apple and slowly ambled his way to the run-down servant house. Surely, Iris would not give him anymore trouble.

On the night of Lyla's Flowering Day ceremony, Iris made it truly clear she wanted him to marry Lyla. Now that Lyla and he were married and the wedding consummated, Noah decided Iris could come home with him—so long as she kept her mouth closed about Noah's plans. All he needed to do, was to have a little chat with her in the carriage, and everything would be all right. Before he could stop himself, Noah smiled as he thought how happy Lyla would be to see her sister.

Finishing the apple, Noah threw the core out into the brush as he climbed the two steps to the door. Straightening his jacket, he flipped the key off his finger and into his hand and unlocked the door. As he slipped the key into his coat pocket, Noah pushed the door open.

Stepping quickly into the house and shutting the door behind him, he stood still and despite the curtain at the window having been opened, once again Noah allowed his eyes to adjust to the gloom.

The room was incredibly quiet. Too quiet.

"Iris!" his deep voice boomed through the house as his eyes trailed over to the small pile of blankets on the floor. The make-shift bed was empty. Glancing around the room, he could see the area was tidy. The table and chairs stood upright, and the broken plate and spoiled food gone. Though in its place sat a plate of uneaten eggs, sausages, and bread.

"Iris!" he called louder, inspecting every corner of the room. It was empty. Looking at the only other door which led to a small bedroom and washroom at the back of the house, Noah paced quickly to the table, put the plate down, and strode over to the closed door. Knocking on it once, he called out again.

"Iris, are you in here?" Silence was his only response. Opening the door, Noah face fell as he saw that not only was the small room empty bar an old rusty bed, but the window on the back wall was broken and Iris was nowhere to be seen.

Chapter 33

"No!" Noah screamed into the empty room. "Damn it! Iris!" he called out as he stormed through the house, pushing a dining chair out of the way before barging out the front door.

Picking up the pace, Noah rushed around to the back of the house, hoping to find Iris there. She was not. Turning around quickly, Noah scanned the area and called out again.

"Iris! Where are you?" Once again, there was no response. Even the birds had fallen silent.

Growling in anger, he dropped his head. The sunlight pushing its way through the branches and leaves above, shone on the broken shards of glass, which lay scattered under the window, the bright reflective light, hurting his eyes.

Noah frowned as he studied the shards and looking closer, found drops of blood on the grass. Bending down, he touched the blood with a fingertip and found that it was still slightly sticky. Glancing up at the broken window, Noah saw more blood on the sill, and traces on the broken glass still in the window.

Iris had hurt herself climbing out.

Straightening, Noah turned and stared deep into the brush and overgrown plants. "Iris, it's Noah. I'm here to take you home!"

Noah took a few steps forward, his eyes darting back and forth, looking for any signs of movement. Receiving no response, Noah looked back down at the grass and soil, trying to trace the blood. After a few steps he spotted some on the side of a small tree. Judging by the height and positioning of it, Noah surmised that Iris must have cut her hand.

"Iris, please, I'm not here to hurt you," he called out, the lie thick on his tongue. In his current state of mind, with an anger so deep he was almost shaking, he doubted Iris would make it home. "I have come to take you back to Lyla. Please, Iris. Come out." His deep voice cracked with anger and fear. If Iris were gone, his plan would crumble apart.

Walking towards the tree, Noah discovered two more blood splatters on the ground and another patch of blood on a tree close to the river.

Rushing over to it, Noah clearly saw two small footprints in the mud and followed them towards the water's edge. As his heart skipped painfully, Noah suddenly realised Iris had gone into the water.

"Iris!" Noah yelled, madly scanning up and down the stream. Although the water's current was not overly fast, it flowed steadily away from the house. "Damn it, Iris!"

Noah wiped his sweaty palms over his pants as an overwhelming sense of panic kicked in. Did Iris know how to swim?

Shaking his head in frustration, Noah turned and quickly ran back to the main house. Banging the front door open he called out to the house maid, who was still in the kitchen.

"Girl! Come here!" When the young girl stepped into the room, he stormed over to her, standing tall above her small frame. "Where is she?" he growled.

The young girl's gaze darted past Noah in the direction of the small house, as she frowned in confusion. Noah suddenly grabbed her face and turned it back to face his. "Where is she!" he demanded, his hot breath sputtering across her small face.

"I do not know, sir. She was there this morning when I took her breakfast." Noah squeezed her jaw harder, taking his anger out on her as her face contorted in agony.

"Useless!" He yanked his hand from her face and shoved her backwards towards the old fireplace. "She's gone! The back window is broken, and she has run away!"

"I am sorry, sir. I didn't know." The girl fell to her knees begging Noah to forgive her.

The raised voices alerted Leon, the male valet who Noah had employed to oversee Iris and the property. Running into the room, he halted as he looked from the girl on her knees to where Noah loomed, his fists clenched at his side and expression contorted in a snarl.

"Sir, what is the issue. Can I be of assistance?" Within seconds, Noah stood face to face with the older man.

"Where is the young girl who was in the house?" He pointed towards the dwelling outside.

"She should be inside it, sir," Leon replied with a frown.

"Well, she's not! She has escaped and you need to help me find her!"

"Yes, Sir. Of course." Leon took a step backwards and bowed slightly to Noah.

"The girl is particularly important to me and is bleeding. We need to find her. Now!" Noah turned around and ran his hand through his hair. Lyla would never forgive him if anything happened to Iris.

Closing his eyes, Noah sighed deeply; his plan had taken a very drastic turn, for the worst.

Chapter 34

When the young maid arrived at the run-down hut with breakfast, Iris demand to know when Noah would return, and when she was informed, he would be there within the next hour or two, Iris sensed she was no longer safe. Everything good she thought she saw in Noah, was a faded memory.

Iris realised she had to make a run for it, to get back home and warn her father of Noah's plans. Her only chance was to get away now, before Noah arrived.

As soon as the maid left, locking the door behind her, Iris, ignoring the plate of food despite her hunger, ran to the door and tried desperately to open it. Feeling frustrated, Iris listened as the maid walked off the porch and then spun around to face the room.

Moving quietly to the small room at the back of the hut, Iris stared at the broken wrought iron bed, the rotted wooden washstand, and rusty bucket on the floor. Glancing up to the small window above the bed, she knew this might be the only way to get out.

Closing the cracked wooden door, so that she did not draw attention to herself, Iris picked up the bucket and threw it against the window.

The glass shattered.

Iris stood still for a moment, her heart beating loudly, and listened for the front door to open, hoping the sound was not heard. When nothing happened, Iris climbed onto the bed and using the bent frame, scrambled out the window, slicing her hand on a large piece of glass still lodged in the windowsill.

Landing awkwardly on the ground outside, the glass shards littering the overgrown grass, Iris fort back her tears as she stared at the large gash across the palm of her hand. Biting her lower lip, Iris carefully picked up a piece of glass and being careful to not cut herself further, she sliced a ribbon off her petticoat and wrapped it tightly around her bleeding palm.

Once the wrapping was secure, Iris hid behind the small house and waited patiently, hoping the sound of the breaking glass was not heard by the young girl. Iris had no idea how far away the girl might be and the last thing she wanted right now was to be discovered.

Finally, after waiting a few minutes, she peeked around the side of the house and through the thick, dark trees. Far in the brush, Iris could make out an old looking manor, covered in vines. As she shuffled around to the other side of the house, Iris spied a pathway which lead from the main house, past her and down into the dense trees.

Understanding the path would lead Iris away from the house, she knew she could not risk the chance of being seen. Who knows what would happen if she ran into Noah while trying to escape.

Iris glanced around trying to find another route. Hearing water flowing somewhere nearby, she hoped it could be her best chance of escape.

Creeping away from the house, Iris fought her way through the overgrown bushes and trees as quietly as possible. Manoeuvring through the branches which grabbed at her dress, and with the blood seeping through her make-shift bandage, she struggled toward the bubbling stream.

Reaching the riverbank, Iris glanced behind her to make sure she was still hidden from the house that had been her prison.

Grateful no-one was behind her; Iris stared back at the flowing water of the stream and her heart gave a little jolt as a rush of nerves coursed through her. It was not the small bubbling stream she had imagined. Instead, the river was at least thirty meters wide, and as she watched the water flow by, Iris hoped it was much shallower than it looked.

Her father had often taken her to the lake behind their house, where they would swim and play in the water, and Iris was a decent swimmer like Johnathan, unlike Lyla and Emily, who would only stand in the water, no deeper than their knees.

Watching the water flow by, Iris surmised it would take her only a few minutes to swim across to the other side. With a final glance over her shoulder, Iris lifted the hem of her dress and walked through the soft layer of mud and into the cold flowing water.

Taking another step forward, as the water soaked into her dress, her pretty lavender silk shoes slipped off her feet, getting stuck in the mud underneath her. Wading further into the river, her breath hitched as the cool water enveloped her chest. Holding onto a low-lying branch, Iris allowed herself a moment to adjust to the frosty temperature before she finally pushed herself forward.

Gasping in horror, the weight of her waterlogged bridesmaid dress suddenly pulled her down as the water rushed over her shoulders and around her neck, and Iris kicked frantically as she realised, she could no longer to touch the riverbed.

Taking a deep, controlled breath, Iris kicked hard with her bare feet, and swishing her arms through the water, slowly inched her way towards the opposite bank. Yet, as she swam further out into the middle of the river, the speed of the flow took her by surprise. Instead of swimming straight across, Iris began to travel downstream.

Fear kicked in and she started to panic — her breathing quickened, and she almost called out for help. Losing her momentum, Iris's shoulders went under the water again, her head following soon after. The icy water now hit her face and in reaction to the shock, she inhaled a mouthful of water. Kicking harder and pulling her hands above her head, Iris managed to push her head back out, coughing and spluttering the water from her throat and lungs. Gasping deeply for a breath of air, Iris went under again.

The river pulled her down, spinning her body like a piece of broken driftwood. Twice Iris was able to break through the surface to gasp for air before the water pulled her back under. Just as she thought she was about to succumb to the depths, the river slowed, and Iris managed to keep her head above the surface. Summoning every bit of strength she had left, Iris sawm to the opposite bank.

Numb from the chilly water, Iris feebly grabbed onto the reeds growing along the bank. Slowly, she clambered and pulled her way out of the water and sprawled across a large overgrown patch, covered with reeds and long grass. Exhausted from the river crossing, Iris closed her eyes and fell asleep.

The sound of Noah calling out her name, abruptly woke her.

"Iris! Iris, please! I'm sorry. Please come back. I promise I'll take you home!" Noah's voice echoed through the air.

Iris buried herself deeper into the reeds, trying to make herself as small as possible. Although she could not see Noah on the other side of the river, his pleas sounding increasingly desperate each time he called her name.

Closing her eyes and breathing quietly through her nose, Iris lay as still as she could and focused on her throbbing hand. Although the blood was no longer oozing from the wound, it still stung.

When Iris could no longer hear Noah calling out for her, she carefully moved her stiffened legs. Grateful for the morning sun, Iris's clothes were mostly dry but laying on the ground after her struggles in the river, left her limbs aching.

Making as little noise as possible, Iris wiggled her toes and flexed her legs allowing the blood to flow back though her body, as she peeked through the long grass towards the other side.

Iris gasped loudly in surprise to see how far the current had taken her. No longer could she see the small house, nor the spot where she had entered the water, a bend in the river now blocked her view.

Unknowingly, when Iris slipped into the river and swam away from the old servant's house, it did not flow back towards her parents' manor like she'd hoped. Instead, it flowed in the opposite direction, so when Iris emerged from the cool water, she was further away from her home then when she started.

Keeping herself low, unsure if Noah was still searching for her, Iris crept through the grass away from the riverbank. As the grass and reeds thinned out, Iris trailed her eyes over a dusty gravel road, which ran adjacent to the river. The old road bent around a corner, a few hundred meters to the left, and to the right, the road ran straight, disappearing into a forest of thick trees.

In front of Iris, on the other side of the road, was a large open field, with no place to hide. Tentatively looking around, not wanting to be seen, but knowing she would need help to get home, she crept along to the left, in the same direction as the river flowed.

Making her way along the river, a further hundred meters from where she came out, a sob of relief escaped Iris when she spotted a small village up ahead. Knowing she would have to expose herself by straightening, she glanced around carefully, making sure there was no sign of Noah. Even though he was on the other side of the river, and she had not heard him call her name in a while, Iris had no idea how far down he might have searched.

She closed her eyes briefly, inhaling a few times as she willed the courage to stand up and run. After a few moments, telling herself it was now or never, Iris quickly stood, and without looking back, she hitched up her dress and took off down the gravel road as fast as her bare feet could take her.

<h1 style="text-align:center">Chapter 35</h1>

It was well after lunch before Noah arrived back at the house. Retuning his horse, along with the carriage to the stable, he walked slowly to the house, thoughts of what he would say to Lyla rushing through his mind. How was he going to tell her, he had lost her sister!

He found Lyla in the sitting room, playing a round of cards with Meg, the small puppy asleep at her feet. Lyla glanced up in his direction as he entered and he saw her look past him, searching for someone else. Iris. He felt a pang in his chest as he watched her expression sadden upon the realisation that she was alone. Noah braced himself, knowing he was about to face one of the hardest things he would have to do.

"Did your day go well?" Lyla asked politely, turning back to the cards in her hand. Noah hovered in the doorway, unsure of what to say. Staring at his wife, he looked at the pale skin of her elegant neck and desperately wanted to run his fingers down it. Regret and anger pulsed though his veins at the knowledge that he would ever touch her again.

Glancing down to his muddied shoes and trousers, he sighed. Without saying a word, Noah turned, walked back into the foyer and up the grand staircase.

Hearing his footsteps trail away, Lyla turned around to glance at the empty space. He had not brought Iris with him. But then again, nor had he promised too either. They had not discussed when he would return Iris to her, or send her home but nevertheless, she was disappointed.

"What more must I do? Why has he not brought Iris to me?" she asked Meg, her voice meek and sorrowful.

"I don't know." Meg smiled weakly. "I know this must be hard for you, Lyla. I wish there were something I could do," she added and played her turn.

"I don't think there is much more you can do then myself!" Lyla replied bluntly and rearranged her cards.

Continuing to play for a few more rounds, Lyla eventually threw her cards on the table in frustration.

Meg placed her cards on the table and laid her hand on Lyla's. "You need to go talk to him," she said bluntly.

"I beg your pardon?" Lyla was a bit taken back.

"You have made multiple mistakes in this game because you are not focused on the cards. You need to talk to him."

"If Noah has something to say to me, he can come here. He knows where I am." Lyla defiantly remained in the chair.

"Lyla, the longer Iris is missing, the more dangerous this situation becomes."

"You think I don't know that already!" Lyla suddenly stood up and stormed over to the window, her dress swishing behind her. "I am aware of how desperate this situation is becoming, but I don't know what it is he wants from me. I married him. I gave him my virginity!" she lowered her voice when she realised, she was yelling.

Meg stood and joined Lyla, placing her hands on her arm. "There is obviously something we are not seeing yet. If you were to ask him what he wants, you could get Iris back faster."

Lyla just stared out the window and into the garden, knowing Noah was the one calling all the shots. There was no way Lyla was going to beg for him to release Iris. She could not jeopardize her safety.

Meg sighed and calmly walked over to the puppy and picked her up.

"I am going to take Anabelle out for a walk and a toilet break; would you care to join us?" Lyla shook her head and stayed where she was. "Come on little girl," Meg whispered to the dog. Lyla stood at the window until she saw Meg walk down the stairs and head off along the gravel path.

Turning away from the window, Lyla made her way to the library, to the room she felt the most content and picked up the book she placed down the night before. Losing herself in her story, Lyla shut out the world. Her thoughts and desire to get Iris back, pulling deeply at her heart.

A few hours later, as Noah walked down the stairs, he watched as his butler walked into the library and politely interrupted Lyla.

"Dinner is ready, Ma'am," he said, his voice echoing across the foyer.

"I am not dressed for dinner," she replied, her sweet voice sending an unexpected tingle through Noah.

"You look perfectly wonderful to me," Noah said as he entered the library and extended a hand towards her. While he had changed out of his muddy clothes, he'd made a point not to dress in the usual dinner attire, opting for a casual pair of trousers and light blue linen shirt.

"Let us have a casual dinner tonight. No formalities needed," he said, and as Lyla hesitantly put her hand in his, he escorted her to the dining room. He smiled lightly to her, but his eyes did not shine. Tonight, he was sad and withdrawn, and seeing Lyla's questioning gaze, he realised she had noticed.

They entered the room and Noah politely pulled out her chair and waited for her to sit down, before moving to the other end of the table. As he sat quietly, Noah watched Lyla, his eyes tracing the shape of her face, the sprinkling of freckles across her nose and cheeks, and her delicate dusky pink lips.

Again, images of kissing her face, those freckles, her mouth last night, stirred in his mind, and a swell of desire coursed through him. Watching her from across the table, Noah could not deny the fact he was falling in love with her. Yet, at what cost? Iris was missing. She had run away, and no matter how long he searched for her earlier, he could not find her, and he feared that once he told Lyla, her hate for him would be tenfold.

Noah spent a few hours exploring the riverbanks trying to find where Iris might have come out of the water. The banks around the river and down steam were rough, overgrown, and dangerous for a young girl. With every swallow, his throat bobbed painfully, raw, and painful after calling out for Iris, over and over. Upon his return home, he'd felt deflated, angry, and worn out. But sitting opposite Lyla, his heart fluttered, and he forced himself to turn his face away, not wanting to see the sadness in her eyes or her lack of smile. Noah struggled with trying to find the words to tell her that her dear little sister was missing.

"I named the puppy Anabelle," Lyla finally spoke, breaking the silence at the table.

"That is a good name." Noah glanced up briefly, locking his eyes with hers, but for only a moment.

"I won three games of Brag against Meg," Lyla continued, but Noah sensed her attempt at trying to make conversation was only to appease him.

"You did say you were good at it." Noah did not pause while eating, and Lyla fell silent, leaving the two of them to continue eating in silence.

Once the servant removed the plates, Lyla stood up and stared at Noah. He did not look up to meet her gaze.

"If you don't mind, I might retire for the night," she said, and as Noah nodded silently, Lyla sighed and stepped away from the table.

"Lyla!" Noah said suddenly, his voice full of urgency. Yet, as she turned back to look at him, he found himself at a loss for words. "Goodnight," he murmured. Lyla raised an eyebrow in response before she turned and walked out of the room.

With tears streaming down her face, Lyla wondered what she had done to make Noah treat her so poorly. Climbing the staircase, Lyla shook her head, the confusion of Noah's behaviour overwhelming her. Noah had so desperately wanted to marry her, to make her his, but now, he could barely even look at her, let alone talk to her. Lyla felt confused, alone, and scared.

This is not what her marriage should be like. Admittedly, she did not want to be married to Noah for any longer than she needed to, yet the sudden distance between them unnerved him—it was vastly different from the affection he'd shown her before leaving her that morning. By the time she returned to her bedroom, Anabelle and Meg were already inside waiting for her. Lyla fell into Megs arms as her tears intensified.

"Come, come, Lyla. Tears will not do you any good here." Meg stroked her back lightly and passed her a handkerchief. "Dry your eyes. Tomorrow is a new day, and you will try again." She helped Lyla change into her bed clothes and placed Annabelle on the bed next to her. After hanging up her dress, and putting everything else away, Meg wished them both a good night sleep and closed the door behind her.

A few hours later, while cuddling with Annabelle, and reading a book by the light of the oil lamp next to her bed, Lyla paused as she heard footsteps travelling along the hallway before stopping outside her door. Her breath caught in her throat with the knowledge it was Noah, and she silently prayed that he would not come in. It felt like an eternity that passed as she awaited the dreaded knock or request to come in, but finally, she heard him cross the hall, followed by the closing of his own door. Lyla sighed with relief, her heart pounding.

Tonight, she would sleep alone.

Chapter 36

When Lyla woke the next morning, the house felt eerily quiet. No one came to wake her, and Anabelle was whimpering at the door, needing to go outside.

"Oh, hang on girl," Lyla said as she threw off her bedding. Quickly, Lyla put on her dressing gown and slippers, opened her bedroom door, and followed the puppy along the corridor, down the staircase and through to the kitchen.

"Sorry, sorry, coming through," Lyla called out as Anabelle sped through the small room and ran outside.

The kitchen staff nodded and smiled politely to her as she hovered at the back door, watching Annabelle run towards the grass, desperately needing to urinate. Trying to make eye contact, Lyla noted the house staff still didn't appear overly comfortable talking to her yet and she wondered how long it would take for them to accept her.

Growing up, all the staff in her house spoke to her and her family, like they were all friends. Hoping this would be the case here, Lyla turned and approached the cook.

"Excuse me Maryan have you seen Noah, I mean Mr. Valdez this morning?" she asked.

"No ma'am. He left early," she replied and promptly went back to chopping her vegetables.

"Thank you." Lyla started to make her way out the kitchen when Regina spoke up.

"Would you like some breakfast ma'am? I would be happy to bring some to the dining room, after you have dressed?"

Lyla paused and looked down at her attire, and feeling herself blush, she nodded. "That would be nice, thank you."

Swiftly she left the kitchen and made her way back though the house. Pausing at the bottom of the stairs, she wondered where Meg was. It wasn't like her to not wake Lyla, so she turned on her heels, Lyla walked back to the kitchen and approached. Regina

"Sorry to bother you Regina , but have you seen Meg this morning?"

"No sorry ma'am." The young girl shook her head.

"You can call me Lyla if you want," Lyla commented. "Ma'am makes me feel … old."

The girl blushed and turned her face away. The cook glanced up and spoke to Lyla instead.

"Mrs Valdez, Meg left early this morning with Mr Valdez."

Lyla turned and looked at Maryan, her eyebrows creasing with confusion. "They left together?"

"Yes, Ma'am."

"Thank you." Lyla sighed and turned slowly. Why would Meg go anywhere with Noah? Shaking her head a little, Lyla walked quietly back through the house and to her room where she made her way over to the window and looked out across the garden. Smiling, she watched Annabelle play with the gardener.

Raising her gaze, Lyla stared long into the distance. Whatever could Meg and Noah be up to? Meg did not like Noah any more than she did. Trying to brush the worrying thought from her head, Lyla undressed from her night clothes and slipped into a simple dress that required no assistance and headed back down to the dining room.

As promised, Lyla found an assortment of food waiting for her on the table. Sitting by herself, which felt odd as Lyla very rarely dined alone, she ate breakfast in silence, the memories of Noah's behaviour last night, still fresh in her mind. Despite her unwillingness to marry Noah in the first place, his behaviour was unsettling and now, she felt like the marriage was falling apart.

How much shame would she bring to herself and to her family, if she could not even make her marriage last a few days?

Trying to assess what had happened, Lyla assumed Noah realised his mistake and took Meg with him to fetch Iris. She knew Iris was not in this house or anywhere in the grounds. The times she was alone in the garden, Lyla had walked the length of the estate, and there was no other building where Noah could have hidden her.

Finishing her food, Lyla strolled to the library and sat in her chair closest to the bookshelf. Inhaling slightly, the light aroma of ash and smoke enveloped Lyla's sensors and she starred into the dark cavity of the cold fireplace. Lyla's brows furrowed as her eyes gaze fell on the charred wood piled at the bottom of the hearth.

Lyla realised Noah must have been in the library after she retired to her room and sat alone by the fire. Feeling a little ashamed of herself to have abandoned him when she could see he was unhappy, Lyla's head tilted slightly, and her eyes narrowed when she saw a small piece of paper amongst the ashes. Leaning forwards in the chair, she wondered if Noah had deliberately burn something.

Glancing around the edge of the wingback chair, making sure she was indeed alone, Lyla carefully eased herself off the chair and onto the floor, her curiosity getting the better of her. Shuffling towards the fireplace, the scent of the burnt wood grew stronger the closer she got.

Stopping at the front of the hearth, Lyla carefully plucked up a piece of paper which had not burned completely. As she read, 'Dear Mr Valdez,' her breath hitched, and she closed her eyes for a moment trying to steady her breathing. Lyla had no doubt that Noah had tried to burn a letter last night. But what would he try to hide? Did the letter have anything to do with Iris? Was it a clue as to where he had taken her?

Scanning through the ash, Lyla saw another piece close to edge of the mantle, and she carefully picked it up. She could see the words 'house by the' and below that, 'far away.' The rest of the sentences missing, the paper having been previously torn before thrown into the fire. Looking back into the fireplace, Lyla spied another piece of paper behind a portion of charred wood. Picking it up carefully so as not to cover her fingers in ash, Lyla turned the paper over and saw 'young girl who' and 'will require more money' written in the same handwriting as the other piece.

Clearly Noah was trying to burn evidence of some kind. Lyla quickly looked at the rest of the cold wood and ash but couldn't find any further readable pieces of paper.

Keeping a hold of the three small portions of paper, Lyla stood carefully, bracing herself against the mantlepiece, to steady her trembling legs. What could have happened to cause Noah to burn a letter? Lyla's imagination went to the worst-case situations. Something dreadful had happened to Iris; she felt it in her heart. Her sister was dead, which would explain why Noah's behaviour to her yesterday was cold and absent. Silent tears streamed down Lyla's cheeks.

If it were true, and Iris were dead, Noah would pay, Lyla would make sure of it. Killing Winston was bad enough, but the death of her sister … Noah would not see the end of this day! Lyla spun on her heels and stormed towards the front door. No matter what, Lyla needed to leave the house; she no longer felt safe.

Pulling the door open, Lyla was confronted with the back of a man she did not recognise, standing at the stoop, blocking her way out.

"Excuse me, please," she commented as she walked through the doorway and tried to pass him.

The older gentleman turned slightly, moving his arm out to prevent Lyla from passing. "Sorry, Ma'am, you need to stay inside."

"I beg your pardon?" Lyla asked in confusion and placed her hand on his arm to push it away. The man's arm locked into place, unmoveable.

In a quick motion, the man spun around to face her and stepped directly into her path. "I have been ordered, ma'am, to prevent you from leaving. Please forgive me, but I need you to step back inside." The man stood a full head taller than Lyla and spoke down to her. Not in an aggressive way, but with enough force in his tone to make sure Lyla complied.

"On who's orders?" Lyla asked but she already knew the answer.

"By Mr Valdez's orders, ma'am," he replied honestly. Lyla huffed with distain.

"You cannot prevent me from leaving. Now please, move out of the way. I need to go!" Lyla spoke with as much authority as she could manage, without raising her voice.

"I am sorry, Mrs Valdez. I cannot let you leave. Please step back into the house." He raised his hand, and although he did not place his hand on her, she understood. If needed, he would push her backwards. Taking another step back, Lyla stepped over the threshold and found herself back inside the house.

"Thank you, ma'am." The gentleman stepped forward, and grasped the door handle, pulling it towards him. Knowing she had no other choice, Lyla stepped to the side and allowed him to close the door. She couldn't believe she was now a prisoner in her own home!

Chapter 37

It was dark when Meg had been woken abruptly just after four in the morning.

"Meg," Noah whispered, gently shaking her shoulder. "Meg, wake up."

Opening her eyes, Meg was stunned to find Noah leaning over her, holding a candle.

"Mr Valdez?" she questioned, her speech thick from sleep.

"Meg, I need your help."

"Is Lyla okay?" she asked, rubbing her eyes.

"Lyla is fine, it's Iris, Meg, she's missing, and I need you to please help me." It took her a few minutes to understand what he was telling her, but once his words became clear, she shot straight out of bed, pushing Noah backwards.

Covering herself quickly with a blanket, ashamed to have a male in her room while she only wore her bed clothes, she tried to push past him and get herself to Lyla's room.

Before she even took a few steps, Noah grabbed her arm and held tight. "No. We cannot tell her. Not yet." Noah's eyes pleaded with her to not leave. "I cannot bear it."

"She has a right to know what you have done," Meg hissed as she tried to pull her arm free.

"I know. I know." He hung his head in shame. "I did not mean for it to turn out like this." He loosened his grip, his hand falling limply to his side.

"None of this should have happened, Noah. You will be the end of Lyla. She will die of a broken heart. Is this what you wanted for her?" She spat the words at him. Meg knew she disliked him from the moment the wedding ceremony ended, but now, the hate in her heart overwhelmed her. She slapped Noah hard across the face, not regretting it for one moment.

"That is from Lyla, on my behalf!" Meg said proudly, despite the sting in her hand. Noah closed his eyes as a red patch spread from his cheek to his eyes.

"Please. Please help me," his voice was quiet and filled with desperation.

"How am I meant to help you, if I cannot go to Lyla?" she questioned, sidestepping away from him.

"I need to you to come with me. Iris knows you. She will trust you."

Meg halted, her brows creased with confusion. "But you said she is missing! How can I help you if you don't know where she is?" She pulled the blanket around her tighter. Even though it was not cold, Meg felt a chill creep down her back.

"I know where she is … well was, and I am hoping she has not gone far. She may have even gone to the main house to hide from me, but she did not come when I called. I know she dislikes me, but she knows you, she might come to you instead."

"The main house?" Meg questioned him.

"I will explain it all on the way there, but please, I need you to help me." He gazed at Meg, his eyes softening, his plea desperate.

Meg crossed her arms through the blanket and stared coldly at him. "After what you did to Winston, and Lyla, you do not deserve help, but considering this involves Iris, who *you* kidnapped, I will help for her sake. And for Lyla's. But hear me now Noah, you will not get away with this. When we find Iris, I will make sure you get arrested!"

Noah's head hung down. "Thank you. Thank you." He hesitated before taking a step backwards. "I will let you get changed. I'll meet you in the kitchen, but please I beg you, do not go to Lyla. Not yet."

Meg sighed as she tightened her lips. "Fine."

Noah bowed quickly and stepped out of her room, closing the door behind him. Meg, struggling to hold the tears at bay, dressed quickly into her riding dress and sturdy boots. Sweeping her hair up into a high bun, she stepped out the door to find William waiting at her door.

"Are you ready?" he asked. Meg nodded. "He is waiting for us." Together Meg and the butler made their way quickly to the kitchen. Two gentlemen stood alongside Noah. He acknowledged Meg with a nod before he turned and led them briskly out the back door and to a carriage and two extra horses, waiting at the side of the house.

The sun had not yet risen, and in the dim light, Meg climbed into the carriage. Penelopy and a young man Meg did not recognise climbed in with her. Seconds later, the carriage jolted forwards and began moving away from the manor. Meg glanced out the window to find Noah and William on horseback, just a few meters behind. Within minutes, they left the estate and headed down a road, away from the rising sun.

Now, three hours after leaving the house, Meg was fighting her way through trees, low bushes, and ankle-deep mud as she followed the riverbank, calling out for Iris. Pleading her to come out from hiding.

Through investigative questions in the carriage, Meg discovered more of the events from the two companions with her.

"Could either of you tell me what is going on?" Meg asked. Penelopy glanced nervously between Meg and the young man. Sighing in frustration, Meg placed her hand on Penelopy's knee. "Penelopy, please, if you know what has happened, it will make this ride a lot easier."

With a gentle nod, Penelopy began to talk. "Mr Valdez informed us that Miss Iris ran away from the house she was staying in."

The young man scoffed at Penelopy's comment and Meg turned to him.

"Do you have something to add?" she asked bluntly.

"I wouldn't say Miss Iris was *staying* in the house, she was locked up in a small old servant house."

"And you know this how?" Meg asked, her anger peaking.

"I was asked to help look after her by Mr Valdez, until she was able to go home," he replied politely.

"And where exactly is this old servant house? Meg asked, unsure if she really wanted to know.

"Out in the swamp lands."

Penelopy gasped and Meg saw her flick her gaze to the young man. "Oh, the poor dear," she said and squeezed her lips closed. Meg could see she was on the verse of crying.

Now knowing the full story, that Noah had locked Iris away in an old house, in the middle of a swamp land, Meg despised him even more. Staring out the window, watching the dark scenery pass, Meg believed the slap she gave him earlier was nowhere near what he deserved.

Arriving at the old manor and servant house, and seeing the state of the neglected lands, Meg drew in a shallow breath as she climbed out the carriage. Taking in her surroundings, she blinked back her tears. The manor looked as though it had sat empty for a long time, and it was surrounded by unkept grounds. Lyla was right to have called Noah a monster. How could a man treat a young girl like this? How would Iris have felt being locked up in a place so cold and far away.

Seeing the overgrown trees and bushes, Meg instantly worried for Iris's safety.

But now, as the sun was slowly began to rise in the distance, Meg hoped the daylight would hopefully aid them in tracking Iris down.

Rushing straight to the worn-down servant's house, hoping Iris was inside, Noah burst through the door, with Meg on his heels,

"Iris?" he called out, his voice hopeful. Looking around the empty space, his shoulders drooped when he realised, she had not returned.

The fresh blankets and food on the table he'd instructed the young girl to supply yesterday, in case Iris returned, lay untouched.

Walking back outside, Noah passed between the other members of the search party and taking a deep breath, turned to the five of them, avoiding Meg's gaze now that she knew the full story.

"I know what I have done is a terrible thing, but I ask you all to please help me. I need to find Iris." He glanced at Meg, his gaze full of remorse. "My life will depend on it."

Swallowing the lump in his throat at the cold look she gave him, he continued. "I know she has been hurt; I've found traces of blood think she may have cut herself on the window she broke yesterday. I also found footprints leading towards the river." Noah paused, glancing over his shoulder in the direction of the river as he sighed fearfully. "I am certain, she went into the water — likely tried to swim to the other side."

Meg covered her mouth with her hands, and Noah felt a fresh wave of shame at her reaction.

"Can she swim?" he asked Meg.

"Yes." Meg's voice caught in her throat. Noah nodded, feeling a sliver of relief.

"I am hoping, with the six of us here, we will be able to track her. I have a small boat which myself, William and Daniel shall use to cross the river and search the other side." He motioned towards Leon. "If you, Meg, and Penelopy stay on this side, we can cover more ground." He turned to look at the young house maid and Phillip, the young man who rode with Meg and was about to address them, when a voice interrupted him.

"Is there anything I can do to help?" Noah's eyes shot up in surprise as he looked passed the group to find Daisy standing behind them. The others all turned around to look at the new arrival, and Noah saw Daisy's quick glance at Meg before she quickly averted her eyes back to his.

Daisy's unexpected appearance threw him off, and Noah wondered how much she knew of Iris's disappearance. "Stay at the manor with Phillip and Daphnie, in case she comes back," Noah said as he swiftly recovered, though he could hear the tension in his voice. Daisy, Phillip, and Daphnie nodded and together, they left the group, walking back to the manor.

"Right, Willam and Daniel, come with me."

"Iris!" Meg called into the dense trees. "Iris, it's Meg, please come out!" Her throat was dry and hurt painfully with every swallow. For the past two hours, Meg had called Iris's name to no avail.

No more tears fell down her cheeks, but her eyes felt puffy and sore, and her face was stained with dirt and grime from her soiled fingers and hands.

Meg's dress was torn and muddied from trampling through the thick bushes along the river's edge, desperately searching for Lyla's little sister. Her left knee was bleeding and throbbing painfully, after she tripped over a fallen log, tearing a large hole in the thick material. Thoughts of what the young maid Regina would think seeing her dress in its current state, Meg thought it might be kinder to just throw the dress away than to wash and repair it.

Sitting on a fallen tree trunk, Meg closed her eyes briefly, listening to the other voices, which echoed out through the thicket, calling out for Iris as well.

With a heavy weight sitting on her chest, Meg wondered how she could possibly tell Lyla that Iris was missing.

As the sun rose higher and the temperature climbed, feeling exhausted, in pain and with her energy levels low, Meg could no longer hold in the grief. She began to cry again. Iris's footsteps still showed she had gone into the water, but no matter how far down the river Meg investigated, she could not find any footsteps returning. Iris could be anywhere by now, hurt, and afraid. It boggled her, the lengths Noah had gone to, and yet it made no sense to her. Why would he do such terrible things? What was he up to?

Knowing Iris hurt herself while climbing out the window, Meg feared for her. Without food and clean water, Iris would be weak, and infection could set into her wound.

Staring out into the bush, Meg felt an overwhelming amount of sorrow. There was no way they were going to find Iris with only six people. Meg knew she needed to return to Lyla and let her know.

Suddenly, a male's voice pulled Meg's attention back towards the river. She glanced up to see Noah rowing the small boat back up the river by himself. With no sign of William or Daniel, Meg abruptly stood, her worry intensifying immediately. Why was Noah alone?

"We found footsteps!" he called out when he saw Meg. "Down further on the other side of the river." As he got closer to the riverbank, Penelopy joined Meg, but she hardly noticed. Her attention was on Noah, who looked as tired and filthy as Meg felt. As he guided the boat towards the riverbank, he bent over, trying to catch his breath as though his exhaustion had caught up with him. Yet Meg couldn't muster any sympathy for him.

"Where are the others?" Penelopy asked Noah.

"Searching the other side. I told them I would return with you three and the horses, so we can look further." As he looked at Meg, she stared back at him with a cold hatred. No matter what happened, she had every intention of telling Lyla everything as soon as they returned.

Noah was not going to get away with this!

Chapter 38

Rocking side to side as the carriage bounced along the uneven terrain, Meg felt her impatience growing as Leon had to lead them further down the river to reach the bridge that would allow them to cross.

A further ten minutes later, they caught up to Willam and Daniel, who unfortunately, had lost the small footsteps and were now no wiser as to where Iris may have gone.

"We searched along the road here but can't see which way she might have gone sir," William said. Meg sighed, feeling as tired and worn out as the butler.

Meg stood on the gravel road, flicking her gaze left and right. In the distance, Meg saw a village by the river's edge.

"Does this path lead there?" Meg asked as she followed the direction of the gravel path with her eyes.

"I assume so," Noah replied.

"I think paying them a visit is our best bet," said Meg, staring at Noah. "Wouldn't you agree?"

Noah nodded.

Climbing back into the carriage, with Penelopy and Leon, they headed towards the village where they split up and began politely knocking on doors, asking those who answered, if they might have seen a young girl. With every denial, Meg felt her desperation and sorrow amplify, and she wondered whether it was a case of no one seeing Iris, or if they had and refused to tell them.

Some folks allowed them to search their small barns and outhouses, but they still found no sign of Iris. After another hour passed, Meg eventually approached Noah.

"We cannot go on like this. We need more people looking for her. You must take me home to tell Lyla. She needs to tell her family!" Noah turned away from her. "Noah, please!" Meg begged him, her hand resting gently on his arm.

"Mr Valdez." Penelopy stepped forward, her young voice pleading for understanding. "Leave us the carriage and take Meg back." She motioned to the men. "We can keep looking for Iris, but Ms Meg is right. We need more than six people." The three men nodded their heads in agreement.

"Can you ride?" he asked as he looked at Meg, his dark expression unreadable.

"Yes, very well," Meg replied. She'd ridden horses most of her life. Without another word, she approached William's horse, and without hesitation, he helped her into the saddle before handing her the reins.

"Hold still while I shorten the stirrups, Meg." Willam worked quickly, pulling the straps shorter to make sure Meg's feet hung at the right length. "Her name is Bess; she is a good horse and will canter smoothly." Meg nodded in thanks, a little taken aback as it was the most William had said to her since she arrived at the manor.

"Ready?" Noah asked after he mounted his own horse. Meg nodded again.

"Keep looking for her," he instructed the rest of the group. "I will return as soon as I can with more people."

Without saying goodbye, Noah and Meg headed back down the road, over the bridge and cantered as fast as they could back to his manor. Time was of the essence now. Iris had been missing for over a day and a half.

Chapter 39

The front door flung open with a loud bang, startling both Lyla and Annabelle, who yelped loudly in protest.

"Annabelle, hush now." She leant over to stroke the puppy and calm her, wondering what the commotion was about.

"Lyla, I need to speak to you!" Meg called out, her voice full of urgency.

"No! Let me do this!" Noah yelled fiercely. "Lyla, where are you?"

Hearing Noah's voice, the tone worrying her, Lyla rose from her chair and began to cross the room. "I'm in the library!" she called out and as she opened the door into the main foyer, Meg spun on her heels at the base of the stairs.

Noticing Megs dirty tear-stained face and her torn and dirty riding dress, Lyla hesitantly stepped through the doorway, her heart racing.

"Lyla." Noah spoke her name with a tenderness; it took her by surprise, and she turned in his direction. Adding to her confusion, Lyla's took in his appearance. He too, was dirty, and the lower half of his blue trousers and shoes were caked in mud. Lyla's eyes darted between the two of them, her brow furrowing in confusion.

"What is going on?" she asked nervously, her palms beginning to sweat. As she focused on Meg's red and puffy face, Lyla felt a sinking feeling in the pit of her stomach. "What has happened?" she asked taking a step towards Meg, her hand outstretched.

"Lyla, my love." Noah reached for her as he stepped between the two women.

"I am not your love!" she snapped as she withdrew her hand, leaving him looking as though she had slapped him. Lyla didn't care; her attention was firmly on Meg and the tears streaming down her face.

"Is it ... Iris?" When Meg didn't answer, Lyla felt as though her legs were about to give way and her heart quickened. Bringing her hand to her mouth, Lyla shook her head as she fought off her own tears.

As Noah approached her, Lyla glared at him. "What have you done to my sister? Is she dead? Did you kill her too?" she asked, her voice quivering.

"Come." Meg slipped her hand into Lyla's and led her back towards the library where Annabella hovered at the threshold, her head tilted as she watched on with mild curiosity.

"Meg, tell me!" Lyla's voice was now a mere whisper.

"In a minute, you need to sit down." Meg led Lyla back to her chair. As she sat, Meg pulled up a small footstool and sat in front of her. Lyla glanced up at Noah as he followed and noted he was unable to keep eye contact with her,

"Lyla?" Meg said, reaching out and taking Lyla's hands in hers, and Lyla turned back to her. "Iris is missing."

"We know that!" Lyla said, feeling confused. "She's been missing since the wedding."

"This is different," Meg explained. "From the moment Iris went missing, Noah knew where she was. He was holding her captive ..."

"I was not holding her ..." Noah interjected before Meg shot him a look of pure hate, stopping him in his tracks. Lyla, following Megs gaze, stared at Noah, and watched as he hung his head.

For a moment, Lyla was certain that she stopped breathing as she sat motionless in the chair. Sensing her mood, Annabelle slipped between Lyla and Meg, and with a small whimper, lay at her feet.

Turning back to Lyla, Meg continued. "Lyla, Iris was being held *captive* in a small rundown servant's house. Sometime yesterday morning, she escaped. Unable to find her or see where she might have gone, Noah woke me early this morning to go back with him and resume the search."

"That's why you didn't wake me this morning," Lyla said slowly, and Meg nodded. "Did ... did you find her?"

"No." A tear ran down Meg's face. "We found her footprints, so we know she went into the river behind the house, and we also found footprints further down on the other side of the river, but we need more people to help."

Lyla's chest rose and dropped rapidly as her heart began to beat faster, and she felt like she couldn't breathe. "So, she is alive then?" her voice quivered, and tears began to fall rapidly down Lyla's cheeks.

"We think so," Noah pipped up, and Lyla snapped her head in his direction.

"You!" she spat. "You do *not* get to speak to me." She stood so suddenly that Annabelle jumped in fear, bumping into Meg causing her to fall backwards off the stool. In her rage and grief, Lyla stepped passed her and stormed towards Noah. He tried to back up a few steps but ended up with his back against the large bookcase, and Annabelle, sensing her mistress was in trouble, growled at his feet.

"If something bad has happened to Iris, Noah, by gods I will make you pay! If she is dead, you will be as well!" Lyla spat at him, her hands clutched into fists at her sides.

"I am sorry, Lyla. So deeply sorry. It was not meant to go like this," his voice trembled as he spoke.

"Sorry? I don't think you're sorry, Noah. You don't know the meaning of the word." Lyla paused, swallowing hard. "Why did you do all this? Kill Winston. Kidnap Iris. What do you *want* from me?" she shouted.

"I ..." Noah shook his head, as though trying to find the words to explain his reasons. "I made a mistake ... it ... it was never meant to ... play out this way," he fumbled over his own words.

"A mistake!" The words hit Lyla hard, like a punch to the stomach. Meg appeared behind her and placed her hand gentle on Lyla's arm.

"Lyla."

Lyla's began to laugh hysterically. "He made a mistake." She stared at Meg, unable to stop the laugh. "A mistake ..." The tears and laughter became uncontrollable, and Lyla doubled over, struggling to breathe.

Meg ran her hand over Lyla's back, trying to sooth her. "Breathe Lyla ... just breathe." She looked at Noah. "We need to tell her parents. We need to organise a search party for Iris, and we need to do it now!"

Noah nodded in agreement. "I will head off there."

Hearing Noah's suggestion, Lyla took in a few slow breaths and stood up. "You shall not go anywhere near my family. I will tell them, but I need to know where you took her and where to search for her."

Meg stepped in. "I know where to look. I can lead us there." Lyla glanced back to Meg and nodded. Trailing her eyes back to Noah, she took a step closer to him.

"You will find as many people as you can to help search for my sister. When she is found, and she *will* be found, you will go to jail." Turning her back on him, she grabbed Meg's arm and marched towards the door. Before she left, Lyla paused and looked over her shoulder. "As of this moment, Noah, *this marriage* - is over. Do you understand?"

Hearing her words, Lyla watched as Noah's face changed. A dark shadow seemed to pass over him; his light blue eyes darkened to a shade Lyla had never seen before. His cold stare bore into her and her breath hitched. Squaring his shoulders and straightening his back, Noah's stance seemed to loam over her, Taking a deliberate step towards her, Lyla shrank back momentarily.

"If you walk away from this marriage, Lyla, you will bring nothing but shame to your family. You will never marry again. Women who leave a marriage are forbidden to re marry. Is that really what you want?" Noah said, his voice devoid of emotion.

Lyla stared at his lips, watching the smirk tweak the corners of his mouth. Raising her chin to meet his glare, Lyla spoke with conviction. "I would rather spend the rest of my life single and living with my family, than remaining married to you!"

"Come," Meg said, cutting off the conversation as she squeezed Lyla's arm and pulled her away, Annabelle scampering alongside them. "We need to get to your parents' house as fast as possible," she said, the urgency in her voice.

"Meg, where did he take Iris?"

"I will tell you everything I know once we are on the way. I don't wish to delay any more time in finding Iris. We must hurry." Pulling Lyla outside the house, Meg called out to the stable hand. "We're ready."

The young boy nodded his head and clambered up onto the hay cart that he had harnessed and waiting.

"Where is the carriage?" Lyla asked curiously, staring at the cart.

"It was faster to ride here on horseback than bring the carriage home, so we left it, in case they find Iris." Meg replied, climbing up swiftly beside the young boy. Leaning over, Meg held Lyla's hand, pulling her up onto the bench. Desperate to follow, Annabelle whimpered painfully at the wheel, as she could not follow.

"No Annabelle, stay here," Lyla called out, as the horse jerked forwards, leading them away from the house.

Squeezing Megs hand, Lyla begged for answers. "I think you need to tell me everything, Meg."

Meg sighed as she tenderly held Lyla's hand, her gaze fixed ahead. "Noah woke me early this morning, telling me to get dressed as he needed my help. He told me that Iris escaped the house he held her in sometime yesterday morning and even though he looked for her, he couldn't find her. Against my wishes, Noah prevented me from waking you, though I wanted to. As soon as I was dressed, he led a group of us away from the house."

"She could just be hiding from him?" Lyla suggested hopefully but Meg shook her head.

"Noah told me he found her footprints leading to a river which runs alongside the property, and he believed she swam to the other side. Yet when he searched, he couldn't locate tracks exiting the river,"

Lyla sobbed, the speed of the cart wiping the tears away before she had the chance to. "I can't understand why Noah would do this to us. Why would he take her away from us and lock her up?" She tugged Meg's hand, forcing her to meet her stare. "Did he say anything to you about why he did this?"

"No." Meg shook her head. "He never said anything about his reasoning, just that we needed to find her."

"What if something bad has happened to her? I know she can swim. She is a strong swimmer. ... Lyla's voice trailed off, as thoughts of Iris swimming in a river, scared her.

"Yes, she is a strong swimmer. With the search we did this morning, Noah obtained a small boat and found more footprints. Although they are a fair way down stream, we know she made it out on the other side but cannot see where she went from there."

Lyla brushed away fresh tears, not allowing her imagination to wonder what that could mean. "So, where was he holding her?"

"In an old run-down servant house at an abandoned manor. It's deep in the forest and doesn't look as though anyone has lived there in an exceedingly long time. So overgrown and dark; Iris would have been so scared."

Lyla closed her eyes. Her bottom lip quivered as she imagined Iris locked up all alone in an old house. How scared she would have been, yet how brave to run away.

"Could she perhaps already be home?" Lyla asked opening her eyes to look down the road.

"I think not. The house she was taken to was at least an hour's ride away from here. The footprints on the other side of the river were farther downstream than we expected. I have no idea which way she went."

"There is a small village down the road from where we found footprints. We went around, knocking on doors, but no one claimed to have seen her. Yet I'm sure she would have headed that way," Meg said firmly. "Aside from the village, there was only a large field on the other side of the path, surrounded by tall trees. She wouldn't have gone across that, barefoot."

"Barefoot?" asked Lyla, bewildered.

"Yes, I saw her shoes stuck in the mud at the bank of the river," Meg replied.

Lyla shook her head in fear. "We must find her, Meg. I will never forgive myself for marrying Noah if something bad happens to her."

"It's not like you had much choice in the matter. Noah threatened to harm her if you refused, although, I did believe he would bring her back that night. I only think there must be a deeper reason behind his actions," Meg said.

"I couldn't agree more," Lyla said grimly.

For the rest of the journey back to Lyla's family home, the two of them remained silent, each lost in their thoughts as they clutched each other's hands. As she watched the countryside pass them by, taking no pleasure in it, Lyla could only hope that Noah remained true to his word; that he'd gather more people to join the search. The thought of Iris lost and alone terrified her.

Chapter 40

It took just under an hour for Lyla and Meg to return home. The moment Lyla glimpsed sight of the manor she began calling out for her Papa. As soon as the cart came to a halt out the front, Lyla hitched her dress up above her knees, leapt from the cart and ran towards the house. Before she even made it halfway up the stairs, the front door swung open.

"Lyla!" Albert called out, his bushy eyebrows raised. "Lyla. What are you doing here? We didn't expect to see you so soon after the wedding." Lyla crashed into her fathers' arms; her tear-stained face pressed against his chest as she tried to speak through the fresh torrent of tears.

"Lyla, what is it?" Albert asked as he gently took her by the shoulders stepped back, his gaze intense. Suddenly, Lyla saw a flash of dread cross his expression.

"Iris … Is Iris here?" she asked.

"No, Lyla. Should she be?"

Lyla wailed as she covered her hands with her face.

"She is missing," Meg spoke for her as she stepped forward.

"Yes, we know that, Meg," Albert said. She has been since the morning of the wedding."

"No, Papa," Lyla gasped through her tears. "Iris ran away from the house Noah took her to, where he was keeping her locked up." Albert looked to Meg, his brow creased.

"What is she talking about?"

"Sir," Meg said softly. "When Noah took Iris, he locked her up in the abandoned servant house at the old Rocklar mansion."

Alberts eyes widened. "The Rocklar mansion? No one has lived there for years." He turned back to Lyla and held her carefully. "I think you both need to come inside and tell me the whole story." As he turned to lead them inside, Lyla's mother stepped through the doorway, surprised to see both girls.

"Lyla! Meg! My goodness, look at the pair of you! What has got you both in such a state?" Grace asked.

"Let's discuss this inside, my dears," Albert said as he swept them across the threshold before turning to his attendant.

"Marcel, tea in the lounge, please."

"Right away, sir." Marcel backed away and hurried to the kitchen. Once Albert managed to get Lyla to sit on the plush rose-pink sofa, Grace rushed to her side and wrapped her arms around Lyla, pulling her head against her shoulder. Turning to face Meg and Albert, she frowned.

"What is going on?"

Between sobs, Meg and Lyla took turns in explaining the situation, from the murder of Winston, through to the search for Iris. By the time they finished, Graces's eyes were as red and puffy as Lyla's. Albert on the other hand, paced the room, his expression thunderous.

"He will not get away with this," he swore as he stormed past the fireplace for the seventh time. "Where is he now?" he asked Meg.

"Hopefully in town, gathering more people to help search. We came here to assemble as many people as we could to join us back at the old town near to the manor. We believe that's the route Iris would have taken to try and get home."

"Do you mean the village on the east side of the Similaris River?" Albert asked.

"Yes sir," Meg said with a nod.

"I know that village." A change came over Albert's face and his features softened. "Right. I will arrange some men from here and pick up more on the way. I'm sure Derek and his boys next door will help." He turned towards the women on the couch. "You three will stay here in case Iris comes home, but I dare say, we might be gone for a few hours at the very least."

Lyla looked up at her father, her eyes wet with tears. "I'm coming with you." She tried to stand but Grace placed her hand firmly on her knee.

"Your Papa is right, Lyla. As much as I would like to look for Iris too, here is the best place for us. Come. While your Papa gets ready to leave, let me help you to your room. You look so tired my dear," Grace smoothed Lyla's hair and ran her hand down her damp cheek, as she looked at Meg, and her dirty, torn dress.

Knowing her mama was right, Lyla stood slowly with Meg by her side. Together the three of them left the room and headed towards the foyer.

Pausing at the base of the grand staircase, Grace turning to Meg. "Meg, please take Lyla to her room. I will join you both soon, and I will send Belinda up with some hot water for you, and some clean clothes." Lyla nodded in gratitude and as Meg wrapped her arm around Lyla's waist, they walked up the stairs.

Grace turned to Albert. "Please find our little girl." Albert pulled Grace into a tender embrace.

"I will not come home without her," he whispered into her ear. Grace closed her eyes and buried her face against his chest. Albert squeezed her gently for a moment before he gently broke the embrace and placed his hand beneath her chin, raising her face to his. "Go and be with Lyla. She will need your strength now; I will talk to Belinda." He kissed her lovingly on the lips.

Grace nodded and with a lingering gaze, smiled tenderly to him. "Hurry back with our girl." She turned, the skirts of her dress twirling elegantly around her as she glided up the staircase to Lyla's room as Albert watched in admiration.

Then he rushed into to the kitchen and alerted the staff to the situation. Within fifteen minutes Albert, along with Johnathan and five male house staff, had mounted their horses and were galloping down the driveway.

Back in her old bedroom, Meg stripped Lyla of her dress and pulled a night gown over her head. "Try and get some rest," Meg said as Grace walked through the door. Nodding politely to Grace, Meg excused herself and left quietly, leaving Lyla alone with her mama.

Relieved that her daughter hadn't put up a fight, Grace sat on the edge of the bed.

"I'm so sorry," Lyla wept, her chest heaving in grief. "I wish I'd never met Noah Valdez."

"Come now, we were all fooled by that man. Close your eyes and rest. The events of the day have clearly taken a big toll on your emotions. Your father will do everything he can to bring Iris home," Grace said while she stroked her hair. Within minutes, Lyla was fast asleep.

Moments later, Emily poked her head into the room. "Mama? What is Lyla doing here?" she asked. Placing her finger to her lips, Grace quietly got up from the bed and walked briskly towards the door as she ushered Emily back out into the corridor.

"You know how we told you Iris was taken away by Noah?" Emily nodded. "Well, yesterday morning, she managed to escape from where he kept her prisoner. But now, unfortunately, no one seems to know where she is. Your Papa and Johnathan have gone out to search for her."

Emily's eyes widened. "What if something bad has happened to her?" she whispered.

"We are hoping that she has made her way to a small village nearby. Your father knows the place. My fingers are crossed someone there has her wrapped up nice and warm in their house."

"Is there anything I can do, Mama?"

"Just stay close to Lyla. She is going to need all the support she can get. Although none of this is her fault, I have no doubt that she feels that she's to blame." She hugged Emily tightly.

"Mama?" Emily spoke into her mother's shoulder, as though she didn't want to let her go.

"Yes, my dear?"

"How do we know that Noah didn't harm Iris? You did say that he threatened to hurt her or Lyla if anyone of us interfered."

Grace stepped back and tenderly studied Emily's young face. "I must believe that he hasn't. Early this morning, Noah asked Meg to help look for her—why would he do that if he'd hurt her. Meg said she saw the house Iris was kept in and saw her footprints head into the river. I believe Meg. She would never lie to us. I feel it in my heart that Iris is alive."

"Will Noah be arrested then?"

"I have no doubt your Papa will make sure of it." Grace kissed Emily gently on the forehead.

"But that would mean Lyla's marriage would be over, wouldn't it?" she asked.

"Yes, it would."

"And that would bring shame to our family," Emily said, biting her lip with worry.

"Emily ..." Grace started to say before Emily's eyes widened.

"Perhaps we could find Mr Stuart again, I am positive Lyla would be more than happy to marry him, after all, she did pick him in the first place. I know Winston would change his mind," she said with a smile.

Grace retuned the smile, but there was no love in it. Hugging Emily again, she spoke softly into her ear. "There are some things you are not aware of and now is not the time to discuss them." Stepping back, and running a tender hand across Emily's cheek, Grace smiled again, this time, with admiration. "There are a few things I must tend to. Watch you sister, okay?"

"Yes, Mama."

Grace kissed her cheek and turning on her heels, walked away. Emily, smoothing out her hair and pulling down on her dress, walked back into Lyla's bedroom and sat in one of the chairs by the window. Exhausted from the emotions she had bottled up since the day of the wedding, tears for her beloved little sister, began to roll down her face. Although Iris annoyed her terribly, the thought that something bad could have happened to her, shattered her walls.

Chapter 41

Glancing at the puzzled looks forming on the faces around him, Noah could see many were confused or unsure of what Albert had said to him. When he had gathered men to assist him, he only told them Iris was missing, not that he had been the reason she was gone.

And he certainly had not spoken about Winston.

As Noah watched the faces of the other men changed from curiosity to bewilderment and then shock and anger, his mood blackened.

Hearing their whispers, Noah felt a fury like he'd never had before. Iris had destroyed everything. Noah knew the only way forward was to find her before anyone else did. His reputation balanced on a knife's edge, and Noah realised he needed to make sure he could convince her to stand by his side and tell everyone it was a mere misunderstanding.

The moment the crowd turned their attention to Albert, to hear his plea, Noah used this opportunity to disappear and slowly ducked away from the gathering.

Moving quietly towards the back of the nearest house and without needing any prompting, his valet joined him.

"Well, that was fun!" Noah huffed, storming away from the building.

"What's next, sir?" his valet asked inquisitively.

Noah sighed, the weight of the events laying heavy on his shoulders. "I need to find Iris. I need to explain to her …" his voice trailed off. "This is all falling apart!" he growled in frustration. Furiously brushing his face, Noah sighed again. How was he meant to find Iris before the others? There were too many people now, and Iris could be anywhere.

Storming away from the action in the street, Noah kept himself behind the houses, and headed back up the road, towards the river.

Earlier this morning, he had spotted a building on the far side of the field, almost hidden by the trees, but thinking Iris would have gone to the village, he pushed the thought she might have hidden there away.

Now, not wanting to be scrutinised any more than needed, Noah and his valet disappeared up the road.

"What do you think will happen if they find Iris before you, sir?" the valet asked bravely.

"I would not like to stick around to find out!" Noah replied and quickened his pace and soon enough, was running towards the green field. With his valet by his side, Noah darted into the tall wheat sprouts. Although the sprouts were still young and far from ready to plough, they crunched under their feet as they both cut across the middle. Within a few minutes, weaving his way between the field and dense trees, Noah arrived at the homestead, his valet panting wildly behind him.

"Do you … think anyone … is home?" the valet asked between gulps of air.

"I hope not, to be honest." Noah approached the house cautiously. Creeping towards the front door, Noah looked tentatively over his shoulder and back towards the field they had crossed. As far as he could see, no one had followed them. Good, he thought to himself, if they do happen to find Iris, I will not be there for them to arrest.

Straightening, he moved towards the door and knocked three times. No one responded. Peeking into the window, a few paces from the door, Noah saw no movement from within. With another glance across the field, still worried they'd be followed, Noah moved away from the front of the building and briskly walked to the back. Just as he rounded the back corner of the house, he noticed a female walking into a small, weathered barn. Pulling himself back from view, he held his breath.

"Sir?" The valet looked at him with worry.

"Ha." A small laugh escaped Noah mouth.

"Sir, what is it?" The valet was now curious.

"Someone just went into a barn," Noah whispered.

"Was it Iris?" the valet whispered back.

"No, I don't think so. She wasn't wearing the same dress that Iris had on and looked a lot older."

"She could be the head of the household," the valet suggested.

"Perhaps. Shall we find out?" He glanced at the valet and a small grin crept onto his lips as the thought that the woman could be hiding Iris in the barn.

Crouching again, Noah took off towards the barn, making sure he was well out of sight of the door, his valet close behind. Reaching the side of the barn, Noah stood soundlessly against the wall, his heart pounding as he pressed his ear to the wood. Hearing voices, his eyes suddenly widened, and he raised his finger to his lips and motioned to his valet to stay where he was. With a simple nod, the valet took a step backwards.

Turning his attention back to the barn, Noah snuck along the wall and disappeared around the corner.

Grateful the door was still open, Noah inched his way silently inside, using the darkness to hide him. Allowing his eyes to adjust to the dim light, Noah could see the lady who walked in earlier, standing near some hay bales.

A deep grin spread across Noah face and he sighed with relief. Sitting on a bale, directly in front of her, was Iris.

"I think I should take you to the village," Noah heard the lady said to Iris. "I have a friend that might be able to help you get back to your home."

"Thank you," Iris replied, her young voice like music to Noah's ears.

Before he even realised what he was doing, Noah stood up and stepped fully into the centre of the barn door.

"No need to, Ma'am, I can take her home." Both Iris and the lady turned to look in the direction of the male's voice and Iris let out a small moan, her eyes bulging in fear.

"Noah!" she whispered.

"Hello, Iris." He took a few steps closer and smiled as sweetly as he could.

"Oh, you know this young girl?" the lady exclaimed.

Noah nodded. "She is the youngest sister of my wife. And she has had us worried for a few days now. She ran away from home." He stared at her, his blue eyes turning dark as he watched Iris's bottom lip quiver. Turning his attention to the lady, he walked briskly towards her and held out his hand.

"Thank you very much for finding her. I hope she was not too much trouble."

"No, not at all. I wish I could have done more, but my husband is away currently with our cart." Noah stepped up to the lady. Taking her hand tenderly in his, he carefully moved her away from Iris and towards to barn door.

"Her sister and family will be most appreciative of your help." Slipping his hand into his coat pocket, Noah withdrew some money. "Please." He slipped the notes into her hand, "Take this as a token of our thanks." He proceeded to walk her outside.

"Oh, I could not." She tried to hand the money back to Noah, but he insisted.

"Please. Her father would be most offended if you did not take the reward." With a simple smile, the lady closed her fingers around the money and slipped it into her apron pocket.

"Thank you again. I will take her straight home," Noah spoke politely.

With a small nod, the lady turned on her heels and walked back to the house. Turning his attention back to Iris, he noticed she had moved off the hay bale.

"Iris, Iris, Iris," he tutted at her, his voice stern. "Do you have any idea what you have done?" He watched as her wide eyes darted a desperate glance towards the door, but he knew that he blocked her exit.

"Your sister has been worried sick about you. Why would you run away like that?" He took a few steps closer to her, his fingers tingling with anger.

"You kidnapped me, Noah. I had to get away," she whispered back, and Noah noted there was no longer any of the bravery he'd seen in her previously. For the first time, Iris looked genuinely afraid.

Noah laughed, the sound filling the barn. "You silly girl. I came to get you yesterday morning to take you home to Lyla."

"You did?" Iris's eyes widened with shock.

"Of course," Noah replied, ensuring his tone was sweet and loving. Smiling, he tried to convey how happy he was to find her, as he took a few more steps, closing the gap between them. "You didn't think I was going to keep you away from Lyla for ever, did you?"

"Are … are you really going to take me to Lyla or back to the old house?" Iris asked, not looking in the least bit comforted by Noah's words.

"Home to Lyla, I promise," he said as he reached Iris, towering over her. Reaching forward, he placed a firm hand on her shoulder. "We just need to have a little chat first." The tone in his voice changed slightly.

"A chat about what?" her voice cracked as she gazed up at him, and Noah felt her tremble beneath his touch.

"About what you are going to tell everyone, when you do get home." He squeezed her shoulder, his fingertips pushing into her skin as he applied more pressure.

"How about the truth!" she blurted out, wincing at the pain.

Noah's smile was anything but genuine, and he enjoyed the shadow of fear that flashed across Iris's face. "The truth will be what I tell you to say. Remember the last conversation we had, Iris? You know what the consequences are if you do not co-operate!"

Iris squirmed under Noah's grip but could not free herself. "You are a monster!" she cried out when he dug his fingers in further.

"Only when I need to be," he said.

"Let me go!" Iris called out, as she kicked her foot towards Noah's legs.

"Come now, Iris. This really isn't how a young lady should behave!" He pursed his lips as he grabbed her arms and pushed her backwards towards the bales in frustration.

A sudden commotion outside distracted Noah for a second, and as he turned, Iris kicked him sharply in the shin. Barking with pain, he dropped one hand, reaching down to grab his lower leg. At the same time, Iris twisted out of his other hand, shoving him backwards as she darted to the side to get away.

Watching her run away, Noah's anger peaked, and he reached towards his coat. As Iris ran towards the barn door, a gunshot cracked through the air, forcing her to stop dead.

Chapter 42

For a moment, time seem to stand still for Iris. The gunshot had been loud, and it caught her off guard. She stood motionless in the middle of the barn, waiting for the pain to kick in. With rapid breaths, it took Iris a moment to realise she didn't feel anything—she had not been shot.

Spinning around quickly to see if Noah still aimed the gun at her, confusion set in when she saw his eyes as wide as hers and his hands empty of any weapon. Realising Noah hadn't been shot either, Iris turned to run but she'd hesitated too long, and in her delay, Noah lunged forward and grabbed her hair, yanking her back against him. Yelping in pain, tears streamed down Iris's face.

"Let me go! Let me go!" Iris screamed.

Noah shuffled backwards, dragging her feet across the dirt floor.

"Be quiet!" he growled into her ear.

Wrapping an arm around her waist, he slammed his other hand over her mouth, silencing her. Pulling Iris closer to the hay bales, he tried to determine where the gunshot came from.

Iris didn't give up as she squirmed and wriggled within his grasp, which he only tightened. Hearing footsteps outside the barn, Noah spun around and as he pulled Iris backwards, a dark silhouette stepped into the barn door, temporarily blocking out the light. Noah squinted as he tried to see who had walked into the barn.

"Let her go, Noah!" a male's voice boomed out.

"Whoever you are, this is none of your business. Leave now!" Noah yelled out.

The male figure stepped sideways, allowing the light to filter back into the barn. Noah stared at the young man who was currently pointing a pistol towards him.

"Damien?" he asked, unable to contain his surprise.

"Let her go," Damien spoke softly but firmly, as though trying not to scare Iris any more than she already was.

Noah's eyes flickered towards the gun in Damien's hand and then to the side of the barn where he had left his valet. "Did you just shoot my valet?" he asked a hint of mirth in his tone.

"Unfortunately, yes," he replied, not taking his eyes off Noah.

"He was unarmed, as am I. Are you going to kill me too?" Noah asked, his eyebrows raised as he drew Iris closer to himself like a shield.

"Your valet is not dead, just wounded. But if I must shoot you, I will." Damien took a few steps towards them, the gun still pointing directly at Noah.

"Go ahead. But if you hurt Iris, you will never get away with it." Noah tried to sidestep away from Damien's advance.

"I am not going to hurt you," Damien spoke to Iris, his voice full of reassurance that only infuriated Noah further. Returnng his gaze to Noah, he spoke softly, "You're scaring her, Noah."

Noah laughed. "I am not the one pointing a pistol at her!" He knew the longer he kept a hold of Iris, the less chance Damien had to shoot him.

"I'm not sure of what the situation is, or why you have Iris here in this barn, but if you just let her go, we can calmly talk about what is going on." Damien lowered his gun slightly.

"There is nothing to talk about, Damien. The reason I have Iris, is none of your concern. The best thing you can do for her, is to back up and leave."

"I cannot do that, Noah." Damien took another step forward. Noah pulled harder on Iris's waist, digging his fingers in her side, feeling her wince against him.

"Keep coming closer. You are only endangering Iris's life." Noah warned as he sidestepped closer to the side of the barn, Iris tripping on her own feet as he forced her along with him.

"I think you have already done that!" Damien stated.

Noah stared hard at Damien. Then with a frown, he tilted his head slightly. "How did you know where I was?"

"I followed you."

"You followed me?" Noah's brow raised in amusement.

"Yes. I watched you and your valet skulk away from the village. Plus, when I heard what you had done to Iris and Winston, I knew I couldn't let you out of my sight."

"What *I* did to Winston?" Noah commented casually.

"Yes, what *you* did, when you killed him," Damien stated.

A snigger escaped from Noah. "He made his choices. It isn't my fault I was a better swordsman than he was." Iris's shoulders slumped slightly at his words, and Noah tightened his grip again.

"You are a sick man, Noah. What did you hope to achieve in all this?" Damien lowered the gun but still held it at the ready.

"It doesn't matter, Damien. It was of no concern to you then and it still doesn't concern you now. Please leave. I need to get Iris home."

"I will be more than happy to take her." Damien raised his free hand towards Iris.

"No. I will take her. I found her. Not you." Noah took two more steps to the side, shuffling Iris along with him.

Damien laughed. "You think they will forgive you because you found her? You came straight here, like you knew exactly where she would be. How do I know you didn't plan this whole thing to make yourself look like the hero?"

Noah clenched his jaw, trying to hide his agitation. "It doesn't matter what you think!" he yelled, his voice booming throughout the barn. "You are interfering and if you are not careful, you will end up like Winston!"

"You going to kill me too? With what? You said you were unarmed!"

Noah said nothing, but he could feel the angry heat flush up his neck and into his cheeks.

"You will hang for these actions, Noah. Just hand her to me and the authorities can deal with you." He wiggled his outstretched fingers, beckoning Iris to come over.

"Back away, Damien!" Noah screamed as his eyes flicked towards the open door.

"Don't even think about it, Noah!" Damien warned as he took a step towards them, his pistol still lowered.

"Back off!" Noah screamed.

In his frustration, Noah suddenly flung Iris aside, throwing her into the barn wall as he launched forward. With a sickening crunch, Iris's head slammed into one of the solid wooden support pillars, her body crumpling to the ground like a limp doll.

Watching Damien turn to gape at Iris, Noah gravitated towards him instead of the door. Seizing the opportunity,

Noah lunged towards Damien's hand, desperately reaching for the gun. Unfortunately, Damien was too quick and repositioned his hand, moved the gun from Noah's reach. Catching him by surprise, Damien thrust his free hand against Noah's face, shoving him away.

"Iris, Iris!" Damien yelled across the barn. Iris did not respond.

Again, Noah took advantage of Damien's distraction and clutched at his wrist, doing everything he could to free the pistol.

Taking a sidestep, Damien twisted around, freeing his hand from Noah's clutches, but as he tried to raise the gun, Noah's left fist connected with Damien's jaw. The blow forced Damien backwards, his feet stumbling beneath him, but he did not fall. In the time it took Damien to steady himself, Noah lurched towards Damien again, frantically trying once more to take the pistol for himself.

Grabbing Damien's coat, Noah spun him around and slammed his chest against him, winding the man. As the breath whooshed out of Damien, and he lost focus, Noah used the opportunity to punched Damien again across the side of his face, sending a spray of blood from his mouth and nose.

Gasping for breath, Damien's legs gave out, and he fell to his knees. Within seconds, Noah threw his body on top of Damien, slamming him to the ground.

In a tangled mess of hands, feet, and wrestling bodies, the two men fought on the barn floor, puffs of dirt erupting around them. For the second time that afternoon, the sound of gunfire cracked through the air.

Chapter 43

Damien's eyes widened in shock as warm blood seeped across his chest.

Laying on the dirt ground, his ears rung with the echoes of the gunshot, deafening him against any other sound. Closing his eyes, he felt the weight of Noah holding him down, and Damien struggled to breath. After a few seconds, he turned his head, opened his eyes slowly and looked across the barn floor to where Iris lay motionless.

"Iris … Iris!" he pleaded, his voice just a whisper. Again, Iris did not respond. Struggling to move and expand his lungs under the weight of Noah, Damien tried desperately to push the man off him aside.

"Get off me," he growled, but Noah continued to lay over him, his hefty body, solid and unresponsive. Pain rippled through his back and stomach each time he tried to wriggle free and though sheer will and determination, Damien managed to squeeze his hands between Noah's shoulders and himself, and with a grunted thrust, pushed Noah off his chest and towards his waist.

To his relief, a large mouthful of air rushed into Damien lungs. Breathing rapidly, and feeling his head begin to clear, Damien heaved at Noah one last time and twisted his torso.

Noah's lifeless body slid off Damiens stomach, landing heavily on the ground behind him.

Pulling his legs up and rolling onto his knees, Damien stared at a large hole gapping in Noah's chest and watched as his blood spread across the barn floor.

Shifting his eyes to the gun laying at his knees, Damien sighed heavily. While wrestling on the ground, the pistol had gone off in Damien's hand. Unfortunately for Noah, the mussel had been again his chest at that moment. The accidental shot killed him instantly.

Scrambling weakly over the sandy floor, Damien made his way to Iris's limp body.

"Iris, can you hear me?" A pool of blood had seeped into the dirt beneath her temple. Damien carefully cradled Iris's head with a hand already stained in blood and brought her face to his. "Please, please, be okay," he mumbled against her cheek.

He lay his hand on her chest and through the silken fabric of her dress, could feel her chest rising and falling. Weak but rhythmic.

"Iris, wake up," he spoke softly yet earnestly, needing Iris to open her eyes. When she did not respond, he scooped her up in his arms and pulled her small body close to his chest. As Damien slowly stood and turned around to move towards the door, he glanced over to Noah's dead body.

"Come on Iris, it is time to get you home." he whispered to her as she lay in his arms, aware that Noah's blood on his coat was seeping into Iris's dress.

Damien walked slowly across the dirt floor, taking a wide birth from Noah. His legs felt weak and tired as the adrenaline slipped away from his own body. Passing through the doors and into the sunshine, he was surprised to see a crowd of men and horses rushing towards him, Albert in the lead.

"Iris!" Albert called out, his voice cracking as he leapt from his horse. "No, no, no! My little girl!" He ran the short distance to stand in front of Damien.

"She is alive, sir, just not responding." Damien replied holding her tightly against him.

"She's bleeding," Albert said as he inspected the blood on the side of her head, and the stain spreading across her waist.

"Yes, sir. She hit her head on a beam inside, but the bleeding has stopped."

"And here?" He indicated to the blood across her dress.

"Not hers," replied Damien.

"Are you hurt?" Albert asked, concern thick in his voice.

"No, sir." Albert frowned. "Noah's blood sir." Damien added, shifting Iris's weight in his arms.

Marcus, who had been by Albert's side, interrupting their conversation.

"Where is Noah?" he asked desperately.

"Inside." Damien nodded towards the barn. "He's dead." His eyes flicked to Albert's. "I am sorry, sir. I didn't mean to kill him."

"I am sure you did what was needed, Damien," Albert said as he gently lifted Iris from Damien's arms and turned towards the group of men who had followed him. "I need to get her home," he said quietly, "but I have no way of getting her there."

"I have a cart I can get from my house," a villager offered. "It won't take me long to bring it here." Albert nodded his thanks, and the gentleman took off back to the village on his horse.

"You can bring her into the house while you wait, sir," said the lady who had been with Iris when Noah had arrived and motioned for Albert to enter her house.

"Thank you." Albert, Damien, and Patrick followed the older lady into the house and through to the bedroom, where Albert lay Iris down on her bed.

"I can clean her up a bit, if that is okay, sir?" The lady stood at the doorway; her weathered hands clasped fast in front of her dress.

"Thank you. Your generosity is most welcomed." He frowned slightly to her. "I must apologise; I do not know your name." Albert said looking at her with a teary smile.

"My name is Mrs Amanda Brooster, Mr Pierson."

"Thank you, Mrs Brooster. You are exceedingly kind."

"Not a worry at all," she said softly. "I'll just fetch some water and clean rags from the kitchen." Albert stood by the bedside, watching Iris.

"I can head into town, sir, and bring the doctor back with me," Patrick offered, placing a comforting hand on Albert's shoulder.

"Thank you, Patrick. Meet us back at the house instead," Albert said without taking his eyes off Iris.

"Yes, sir." Patrick left without another word.

"Damien?" Albert said still looking at Iris.

"Yes, Mr. Pierson?"

"I think you might need to tell me everything that happened." He turned to look at Damien, who nodded. "Outside perhaps."

"Yes, sir. Whatever I can do to help."

"Mr. Pierson, may I sit with her?" Bram said as he appeared at the bedroom door. "In case she wakes while you are gone."

"Thank you, Bram." He patted him on the shoulder as he walked past, Damien following close behind.

They left the bedroom, Albert glancing back one last time towards his daughter. The thought of how close he had come to losing her tore at his heart.

"How did you know where she was?" Albert asked when they stood on the front porch, his gaze lost over the field.

"I didn't, sir. I saw Noah and his valet sneak away after you addressed everyone. I would have informed you, but I didn't want to lose sight of where he was headed."

"Understandable. Did he come straight here?" he asked but shifted his eyes and watched over the group of men who had come with him.

"It seemed to look that way."

"So, he knew where she was then?" he said, finally looking at Damien.

Damien shook his head. "I can't say for sure, sir, he wouldn't tell me when I questioned him."

"Did ..." A tear fell down Albert's cheek. "Did he hurt her?"

Again, Damien shook his head. "I don't believe so, sir. Other than throwing her out of his way to attack me. That was when she knocked her head on the wooden beam."

Albert frowned, turning his head slightly to look at Damien. "The blood, on your shirt!" He gestured down to Damiens chest. "Are you sure you're not hurt?"

"No, I'm fine. It's Noah's blood," Damien replied, and Albert could see from the way he avoided touching his blood-soaked coat and shirt that the knowledge made him uncomfortable.

"I see. And his death?" he questioned Damien.

"Accidental, sir. We were fighting over my pistol. We fell to the floor, and I guess in the struggle, it went off, and he landed on top of me. He died instantly." He hung his head in shame.

Albert, noting the movement, stepped up to him.

"Damien; do not feel guilty for what you did. Noah Valdez was a bad man. There was no better punishment for his crime than death itself. I do not condone murder, but you saved my daughter today. You will not be punished for this." He placed a comforting hand on Damien's shoulder.

"Thank you, sir."

Stepping away from Damien, Albert stared out into the field once more. "Did he happen to say anything to you, in regard to why he did any of this?"

"No, Mr Pierson. I did ask, but he refused to answer."

"Thank you, Damien." Albert continued to stare out over the field, a wave of emotions cutting through his voice.

"Sir?" Damien said tentatively.

"Yes, Damien?" Albert turned back to Damien.

"How did you find us?"

"The lady of this house; Mrs Brooster, came running through the field yelling for help. She told us there was a young girl in her barn with a man she felt was going to hurt her. Plus, we also heard two gunshots. The one that killed Noah, and I am guessing, a shot that wounded him?" Albert nodded towards the valet nursing a wound to his leg.

"Yes sir, he came at me, before I entered the barn."

Nodding in appreciation for Damien's honestly, Albert smiled softly. "Thank you, Damien," Albert said and hung his head.

"Mr Pierson, may I ask you another question?" Damien asked.

"Yes," Albert replied lifting his gaze.

"Did Noah really kill Winston and kidnap Iris?"

Albert nodded slowly. "I am afraid so. Noah came to Grace and myself early on the morning of the wedding. He lied to us, told us that Winston had changed his mind and no longer wanted to marry Lyla, and had asked Noah to step in his place, believing Noah was more worthy" He paused and sat heavily on a wooden bench under the window.

"When we questioned his story, he threatened Grace and myself. Noah reminded us that if Lyla didn't wish to bring shame on her family, she could marry him. When we still questioned him, he informed us he'd taken Iris as leverage and if Lyla did not marry him, he would harm Iris." Albert paused again, the grief in his chest, making it hard to breathe.

"I didn't want to cause any trouble, especially for Lyla. Her wedding was meant to be the best day of her life. It should have the best day for *all* of us. Yet, it wasn't, and we have been worried sick about Iris ever since."

"You did not go to the authorities and tell them?" Damien asked, taking a step towards him.

"No. Noah said Iris would be home within a day or two. That she would be well looked after, although we were both worried, we never believed anything would go wrong. He lied to us again!" He wiped a tear from his eye. "According to Meg, Lyla's lady's maid, Winston did not in fact ask Noah to marry Lyla. Noah killed Winston in a duel, the night before the wedding, because he refused to walk away from Lyla."

Damien hung his head. "I am so sorry, sir."

Sounds of wheels crunching on the gravel road alerted Albert to the approaching cart. He stood and turned to Damien. "That was a very brave thing you did, Mr Olsen." He held out his hand for Damien to shake, but seeing the blood on his hands, dropped his discretely.

"Thank you, sir." Damien said, not looking the least bit offended.

"May I suggest you see Mrs Brooster and get cleaned up a bit?"

"I will do, sir, but please wait for me, I'd like to escort Iris home with you."

With a nod, Albert walked back into the house and back to his daughter.

Chapter 44

Waking, stretching her legs, and running her fingers through Annabelle's fur, it took Lyla a moment to realise she was in her bedroom, in her parents' manor. A puzzled look fell across her face.

"Meg!" she called out.

"Right here." Meg jumped off the chair by the window and rushed to Lyla's side.

"Why am I in my old room and why is Annabelle here?"

"You were exhausted. You passed out as soon as your head hit the pillow, and you've been asleep for the past three hours, and Annabelle is here because I didn't want to leave her alone in that house anymore."

"Exhausted?" she questioned, not understanding what Meg was saying.

"From the ordeal with Noah. After he told you Iris was missing." Meg frowned slightly at Lyla.

It took only a few moments for the sudden rush of memories to filter back through Lyla's head. "Iris!" she exclaimed. Pushing the covers back, startling Annabelle, Lyla stood too quickly, and her head spun, causing her to sit back down.

"Easy does it." Meg carefully helped Lyla sit. "I think you might need something to eat."

"Is Iris here?" Lyla looked hopefully at Meg as Annabelle moved behind her and jumped to the floor.

Meg shook her head. "Put on some slippers and a dressing gown. We shall head down to the kitchen and see what the cook made."

"I can't eat anything right now." Her shoulders slumped with grief.

"Whether you want to or not, you need to," Meg said firmly. "It's been hours since breakfast, and I bet you didn't eat much then, either." Meg slipped a pair of slippers on Lyla's feet and brought the matching dressing gown which Emily dropped off after Lyla fell asleep. Gently assisting Lyla to stand, they walked slowly towards the kitchen, with Annabelle trotting close behind.

"Oh, you are awake." Emily stated as they ambled past the library.

"I am." Lyla replied but did not stop.

"Where are you heading?" she asked, rushing to her sisters side and grasping Lyla's hand. "Are you hurt?" she asked, stepping forward to offer some assistance.

Lyla gently brushed her hand away. "I am fine. Meg just wants me to eat something." She looked sideways to Meg with a grimace.

"You will need your strength," Meg responded cheerfully.

Making their way into the kitchen, they were greeted with a broad smile from the cook. "Ah, Lyla. So good to see you again." She bustled up to Lyla, giving her a tight hug. "Oh," she exclaimed, looking down at Annabelle. "And who is this?"

Lyla smiled with pride. "This is Annabelle, my puppy."

"Well as cute as she is, she cannot stay here." Turning to one of the scullery maids, she motioned for Annabelle to be taken outside. "What are you doing here anyway? Miss my cooking already?" She laughed as she stepped back to preparing the meal for dinner.

"Something like that," Meg interjected before Lyla could say anything. "Do you have a little something Lyla could eat please, Cook?"

Looking at Lyla, she smiled. "Of course I do. What a silly question that is." Within a few moments, Lyla had a plate ladened with a sandwich, some fruit, a freshly made piece of cherry pie and a cup of tea.

The three of them sat around Cook's table, Emily and Meg also acquiring a piece of pie and a cup of tea.

"I always loved to come in here when I was younger," said Lyla between mouthfuls of food. "It always smelt so good."

"And it was always a pleasure to have your company while I cooked," replied the cook.

"I didn't think you were hungry," Meg chuffed, and Lyla looked at her with distain upon realising how quickly she was eating.

"Maybe she just needed my cooking to remind her how good food is for her." The Cook laughed as she cleared Lyla's empty plate.

"I think that must be it," Lyla said.

"Well, if your new cook needs any tips on how to prepare you a good wholesome meal, you send her to me, understand?" she laughed again.

"I don't think that will be necessary, Cook. But thank you for the offer." Finishing her tea, Lyla stood and walked solemnly from the kitchen, Meg, and Emily in tow. As she passed through the front foyer, the sound of hooves and wheels crunching up the drive drifted through the open windows. Turning her head towards the door, her heart skipped a few beats, and she quickened her pace.

"Lyla, you cannot go out dressed like that!" Meg followed her, trying to pull Lyla back. Slipping from Megs grasp, Lyla swung open the large wooden door and watched as two horses pulling a hay cart flew up the drive. Flicking her eyes just to the left of the cart, she noticed her father sitting proudly on his own horse. Before Meg or Emily could stop her, Lyla was running down the stairs and out onto the gravel driveway.

"Papa!" she called out as Albert cantered faster, past the cart and straight towards Lyla. She broke out into a grin as she saw how relieved her papa looked. "Iris?" she questioned as he pulled up in front of her.

He nodded enthusiastically. "She's in the cart." At her father's words, Emily spun on her heels and ran back into the house calling out for their mother.

Dismounting, Albert pulled Lyla in for a tight hug, as he whispered into her ear. "Iris has been hurt, but she is home with us again." Lyla's face dropped and a shadow of fear came over her. "She will be okay. Patrick has gone to fetch the doctor, and I dare say, he will be here soon." The cart slowed down and came to a stop just behind Albert. By the time Lyla had made it to the back, Grace and Emily were standing at the door.

"Iris?" Grace called out, walking slowly towards the stairs, her hand laying tenderly over her heart.

"Yes, my love, she is home." Albert rushed up the stairs and wrapped his arms around his wife. "She is home."

Grace cried openly into Albert's chest. "Thank you, Albert. Thank you for finding her and bringing her back."

"Well, truth be told, it was not me who found her." He looked down at her. At that moment, Damien slid off the back of the cart, holding Iris in his arms.

"Iris, oh my sweet Iris!" Lyla cried as she cradled her sister's face in her hands.

"I am fine, Lyla," her voice whispered in reply.

"I am so sorry." Lyla laid her hand on Iris's head.

"Lyla. I am okay. It was not your fault."

"Oh, my goodness. You're bleeding. Quick!" she motioned towards Damien, not even realising it was him. "Bring her inside."

"Certainly, Mrs Valdez," he replied. She gave a quick nod of thanks, but it wasn't until she looked down at Iris that the recognition caught up with her. With wide eyes, she glanced back up into the man's gentle, brown eyes.

"Damien? What are you doing here?" Confusion and surprise rushed through her.

Before Damien had a chance to reply, Albert appeared at her side and wrapped his arm tenderly around Lyla's waist.

"Damien is the one who found Iris. I asked him to help me bring her home."

"You? You found her?" A tear of gratitude ran down her cheek.

"I did." He smiled tenderly. Albert pulled Lyla with him, towards the house. "Come, we need to get her inside, Lyla. Let Damien pass." Lyla stepped aside, allowing Damien to carry Iris into the house.

"She's bleeding!" Lyla said again, her reunion with Damien momentarily forgot as she remembered the blood on the side of Iris's face and across her ruined bridesmaid dress.

"Yes, she hit her head, but she is awake now and seems to be okay. We will see what the doctor says when he gets here." No sooner had Albert finished speaking that they heard the sound of carriage wheels approaching the manor.

"Head inside, Papa," Jonathan said, not long having dismounted his own horse. "I will bring the doctor to Iris's room."

"Thank you, my boy." With his arm still around Lyla's waist, he moved back up the stairs and into the manor.

Following Damien up the stairs to Iris room, Lyla watched as he carefully helped her to lay on her bed.

"My sweet, sweet girl." Grace hovered over Iris, covering her face with kisses.

"I'm okay, Mama," Iris whispered back. "Just tired."

Grace hugged Iris tight. "I am never letting you go again."

Damien stepped back, away from the bed. As he turned around gravitating towards the door, Lyla gasped when she saw his coat covered in blood.

"Damien!" she exclaimed. "You are hurt?" She rushed towards him and reached out for him her eyes wild with fear. Yet, before she could touch him, Damien grasped hold of her hand.

"I'm fine Lyla," he said, a small smile on his lips.

"No, no." She pushed harder trying to get to him, to see where the blood was coming from. "You're bleeding!" Damien grabbed her gently on the shoulder with his free hand, holding her back. "Stop, Lyla. It's all right. It is not my blood," he spoke firmly.

She stopped struggling and stared intently at him, noting the slight glints of gold flecks in his brown eyes. Curiosity now in her stare. "Not yours? Then who's? There is so much." Lyla's eyes widened in fear, and she brought her hand up, covering her gaped mouth. "Iris's?" she asked.

"It's Noah's blood Lyla," he said calmly, reassuring her he was not injured.

"Noah's!" A shudder coursed through her as she glanced from Damien to her father.

"It's true, Lyla. He's dead," her father confirmed.

Lyla swallowed hard.

"How?" she asked tentatively.

"Come, here is not the best place to talk." Damien nodded towards Iris. Lyla hesitated a moment, glancing back towards her sister.

"I am fine now, Lyla. Come back to me later." Iris nodded slowly, flashing Lyla a brave but weakened smile.

"I won't be long," Lyla responded, before she allowed Damien to lead them from the room. Upon entering the hallway, Jonathan and the doctor greeted them.

"Damien!" The doctor frowned. "Are you hurt as well?"

"No, Doctor Meeler. The blood isn't mine, sir. It belongs to Noah Valdez."

"Is he hurt? I must tend to him as well then," the doctor said, stepping closer to Iris's room. "I'll see him right after Miss Iris."

"No need to, sir. Mr Valdez is dead," Damien stated quietly.

The Doctor paused and nodded his head. "Ah, fair enough, but don't go far. I would still like to check you over, after I've tended to Iris."

Damien smiled. "Yes sir." Side stepping out the way, Damien and Lyla allowed the doctor and Jonathan to enter the room, while they headed downstairs to the sitting room.

With a sigh, Damian turned from Lyla and gazed out the large window, admiring the stunning view of the long expanding garden.

"Is it really true?" Lyla asked quietly. "Is Noah dead?"

Damien nodded and slowly turned back to face her. "I am sorry. I didn't mean to kill him."

"*You* killed him?" Her eyes widened with shock.

"Accidently …" He trailed off as though he couldn't find the words.

"Damien?" Lyla prompted, needing to know what happened.

"Noah tried to grab my pistol. We fell to the floor." He turned around again, as he continued. "The gun went off. I am not sure who pulled the trigger, but when Noah went limp …" He stopped and hung his head.

Lyla ran up behind him and wrapped her arm around his waist.

"Damien," she whispered moving her hand up towards his chest.

"No!" Damien grabbed her hand again. "Don't touch me, I am covered in his blood!" He turned slightly, pulling away from her. "I don't want you to get it on your hands."

Frowning, Lyla had a sudden realisation as she stepped back.

"Damien, how is it you killed Noah? What were you doing with him?" she asked with a curious tone.

Damien smiled. "Bram and I happened to be in town when your father's butler came in, asking for volunteers to help look for Iris. We didn't give it a second thought and rode with him and our fathers to the village."

Lyla's brow furrowed further. "Bram was there as well?" She moved to the sofa and sat down, her legs feeling weak.

"Yes. There would have been about twenty-seven volunteers, maybe more, searching for Iris."

"So many people," she whispered, a soft smile tugging at the corners of her mouth as Damien nodded. "Though I'm still confused how you came to be with Noah? And where was Iris?"

"To answer your first question, while we were at the village about to start the search, your father gave Noah quite the dressing down, and when your father turned to address the crowd, I noticed him slip away." A small scowl slipped across his face. "I didn't think he should be trusted, so I decided to follow him."

"So, did he lead you to Iris?" she asked.

"Yes and no," Damien said and began to pace. "He took off towards a large field a fair distance from the village and crept towards a house that was hidden in the trees. Iris happened to be inside a barn, which sat behind the house."

"He did know she was there?"

"That's what I don't know. When I confronted Noah and asked if he knew she was there, he wouldn't answer me."

"Is … is that where he … died?" Lyla felt tongue-tied as she tried to speak.

Damien slowly nodded his head. "Yes."

Lyla blinked rapidly, forcing the tears away. Hearing Noah was no longer alive, did not console her, and she turned her head, ashamed to feel a sense of loss towards her husband. Wringing her fingers she looked at Damien.

"And how did Iris get hurt?" She asked nervously, hoping it was not due to anything Damien might have done.

"Noah was holding her, using her …" He paused again and Lyla could see he was debating on how much to tell her.

"Using her how, Damien?" she coaxed.

"Using her as a shield, so that if I shot at him …" He trailed off and walked slowly towards another chair to sit down, before letting out a frustrated sigh as he glanced down at his blood-soaked clothes.

"Take it off," Lyla demanded as she stood and held her hand out towards Damien. He looked at her, an eyebrow raised. "Take off your coat." She wiggled her fingers at him, indicating she wanted him to remove the blood-soaked clothing.

"No. I told you, I don't want Noah's blood on your hands. He was your husband."

"Please do *not* call him that!" Lyla said sternly as she walked briskly towards him. "Whether he was my husband or not, you cannot keep wearing that coat. Or at least, I don't think I can keep looking at you while you have it on." With a sigh Damien began to undo the buttons. Despite the fact it was medium blue in colour, the blood had begun to dry, and the front of the coat looked almost black. Just as he slipped it off, and before he could hand it to Lyla, Johnathan walked into the room, followed closely by Albert.

"Ah, here you are," Albert stated glancing between Lyla and Damien.

"Papa." Lyla's attention suddenly moving to her father. "How is Iris? What did the Doctor say?" She took a step towards him, leaving Damien standing awkwardly with his coat in his outstretched hand.

"He is still with her." He placed a comforting hand on her arm. "If it is alright with you, I do need to speak to Mr Olsen."

Lyla jolted. "Yes of course." She glanced back to Damien. "Oh, your coat."

"I will take it," Johnathan stepped forwards, removing the coat from Damien's grasp. "I am not quite the same size as you, but I do have a shirt I can lend to you."

Lyla watched as Johnathan's eyes dropped to Damien's chest, just as Damien also peered down. The front of his cream shirt was also a dark shade of crimson from where the blood had soaked through his coat and seeped against his chest.

"Damn!" He blurted out, then suddenly looking up at Lyla. "Sorry. I shouldn't have sworn." Turning abruptly around, Damian fumbled with the buttons and Lyla felt her face flush at the thought of Damian seeing shirtless. As she glanced up at her father, her blush deepened at his bemused expression, like he was about to laugh at any moment.

"Go to Iris. You and Damien may finish your conversation later. Oh, and Lyla." He stepped closer to her, whispering in her ear. "You might want to put on something a little bit more ... appropriate."

Lyla glanced down at her own clothes and suddenly wished the floor would open and swallow her. She had completely forgotten she was still wearing her night dress and dressing gown. "Yes, Papa," she replied quietly, feeling utterly mortified as she left the room—but not before she snuck a last glance at Damien.

Chapter 45

By the time Lyla returned downstairs, the sun had set, and the chandeliers, candles, and oil lamps shone brightly throughout the manor. Hearing voices in the main lounge, Lyla tentatively tiptoed towards the room, unsure if she should enter.

As she neared, she recognised the voices as belonging to her parents, Damien, and two other gentlemen.

"You shall not be charged, Mr Olsen. At the moment, I cannot find a reason to hold you. What you have told us; the accident was in self-defence. What you did was unfortunate and as you were there to rescue Miss Pierson, I will let the matter drop." A deep male voice drifted out to where Lyla by the door.

"Thank you, Constable Walidan," Damien replied. A loud sigh escaped Lyla's lips, giving her position away.

"You may come in Lyla," her father said, and she detected a hint of mirth in his tone. Lyla slipped around the doorframe and looked sheepishly at her father. "No need to hide, I saw you coming down the stairs."

"Sorry, Papa. I didn't want to interrupt."

"I was just leaving anyway," commented Constable Walidan as he turned to face Lyla. "I do need to have a conversation with you though, Mrs Valdez. It doesn't need to be tonight, but we will need to discuss what happened to you, and your marriage to Mr Valdez."

Lyla looked nervously towards her parents. Albert stood and beckoned her over. "You haven't done anything wrong. We just need to hear your side of the story. Find out what Noah said to you, regarding Iris and what happened to Winston, but we can do that tomorrow."

"I'm not sure that I'll be much assistance. I know as much as you do," Lyla responded sadly.

"Whatever information you or your handmaid can provide, will be useful," Constable Walidan said politely. "I will return in the morning." Excusing himself, the Constable and his partner left the room, Albert escorting them.

"Sorry to interrupt Ma'am, dinner is ready," Patrick interjected after he slipped into the room.

Taking that as his queue, Damien stood. "I shall take my leave." Lyla studied the new shirt Damien now wore, and his clean hands. Luck had it be, it matched the same shade as the light blue dress she had changed into.

"I have prepared a place for you at the table if you wish to stay, Mr Olsen," Patrick uttered politely.

"That was very kind of you, but really, I should leave."

"I don't believe your clothes are ready yet, Damien," Grace pipped up. "You are most welcome to eat at our table tonight. It is the least we can do after you rescued our daughter." Grace moved to Damien and took his hand in hers and smiled sweetly up at him. "I shall not take no for an answer."

"Fair enough, Mrs Pierson. I shall stay."

"Wonderful. Shall we?" She stretched out her other hand to Lyla.

"Yes, Mama."

Making their way to the dining room, Grace offered Damien the seat next to Lyla. As they began to eat, Lyla leaned in closer to Damien.

"You still haven't told me how Iris was hurt," she whispered. Damien looked at her with bewilderment before he whispered back.

"I don't think this is the time or the place for that conversation."

"Will you tell me later?" she asked, keeping her voice low.

"Yes. I will," he promised.

Sitting back, Lyla ate the rest of her meal in silence. So much had happened in the past few days. Winston, the man she had chosen to be her husband, was killed the morning of her wedding. Her beloved little sister kidnapped mere hours before she walked down the aisle to find Noah standing at the pulpit, smiling at her like he had played no part in any of that morning's events.

Once dinner finished, Damien turned to Lyla. "Shall we take a walk in the garden?"

Lyla stared at her parents, waiting for one of them to stand and accompany her.

"You are a married woman now Lyla, you do not need someone to be with you," her mother commented, a small smile tipping the corners of her mouth.

Smiling herself, Lyla turned to Damien. "That would be wonderful, thank you," she said softly.

Bowing politely to Albert and Grace, Damien offered Lyla his arm and lead her out the dining room doors and onto the large marble back veranda. Guiding her down the stairs, they crossed the cobblestone path and stepped onto the dark green grass.

Looking up at the sky, Lyla squinted slightly, taking in the brightness of the full moon, so bright that it blocked out the stars. Yet, she still found the night sky breathtaking.

"Shall we sit?" Damien asked as they approached a stone bench.

"Thank you." Lyla let go of Damiens arm and sat back, placing her hands gently in her lap.

"It is a perfect night, is in not?" Damien commented as he sat next to Lyla.

"Is it?" she asked inquisitively.

"Yes. Summer has begun. The air is warm. The moon … a little too bright," he chuckled, making Lyla smile.

"You are not trying to avoid anything are you?"

"Meaning?" He stared at her.

"You're talking about the weather and the moon." Her eyebrows raised with amusement. He smiled broadly.

"Maybe." He leant back against the bench and looked back up to the moon, his gaze drifting off into the vast sky.

"Please tell me what happened to Iris." Lya placed a hand gently on Damiens knee, evoking a sigh from him as she felt the warmth of his skin through his trousers.

Tenderly, he placed his hand on hers. "When I entered the barn, I found Iris and Noah in a tense moment." He looked at her, holding her eyes. "He was holding her against his chest. It looked like they were struggling. When he saw me with the gun, he turned her around and used her as a shield to hide behind."

Lyla's hand tensed against his leg, and he gently rubbed his thumb along the top of her fingers, soothing them. "I asked him to let her go; he refused. As we spoke, he took slow steps along the side of the barn, towards the doors, pulling Iris along. Eventually, he must have seen an opportunity to try run out, so …" He paused, shifting on the bench as he turned to face Lyla.

"He threw Iris aside. Threw her, like she meant nothing to him. Because they were so close to the barn wall, Iris's head hit the edge of one of the support beams and she collapsed immediately. I'm sure she was unconscious before she hit the ground." He stopped, interlacing his fingers with hers, and Lyla felt her breath quicken.

"I am sorry. I didn't want to tell you as I knew it would upset you." Feeling foolish as she felt a tear drop onto her cheek, she pulled her hand out from under Damien's, to wipe it away, turning her face from him under the guise of staring out across the garden. "Did he … do anything else to her?" she asked anxiously, remembering the blood on her dress.

"No. He attacked me after she hit her head. I thought he was going to try run for the door, but he lunged at me instead. I was not able to get to Iris, to help her."

"Papa said she was now awake. What did that mean?" she turned her gaze to Damien. He was again staring at the moon.

"When I got to her, after Noah died, she would not respond to me. She had hit her head extremely hard. There was … a lot of blood." He stopped, sighing deeply. "It was not until we were in the cart coming home, that she regained consciousness." He turned his gaze back to Lyla.

"And her dress?"

"It was Noah's blood. It soaked into her dress from my coat when I picked her up and carried her out the barn."

"And her hand? It was wrapped up and looked bloody. Did Noah do that too?"

"No, I asked her in the cart what had happened, she told me she cut it, after climbing out of a window she broke, in the servant house where she was locked up in."

"Will she be alright?" Another tear rolled down her face.

"The doctor said she would be fine. She has a mild concussion, and he has cleaned and stitched the wounds on her head and palm, but she does need to rest."

"And you? Did the doctor look at you too?"

"Yes." He grinned.

"What?" she asked, noting the humour on his face.

"Nothing. He said I was fine too. I never got hurt." He stood up and took a few steps away from Lyla.

She watched him as he stood in the garden, his black hair glinting in the moonlight. There was something about him she had not seen during her Flowering Day ceremony. Lyla had felt so angry with her parents for picking him as a suitor, that she'd blinded herself to his kindness and generosity.

Observing him now, she ran her eyes over his body, admiring the way her brothers shirt hugged his muscular back and how his black trousers highlighted the shape of his legs. She stared at his hands that were clasped tightly behind his back, her eyes lingering on his fingers and remembering how they felt holding hers only a few short moments ago. Lyla was surprised to find that she suddenly longed for them to be intertwined with hers again.

"It is rude to stare you know!' he spoke, jolting Lyla from her thoughts. Blushing with embarrassment, she realised that he was watching her from over his shoulder, and Lyla felt grateful they were sitting in the moonlight.

"Sorry." She stood abruptly and began walking away, scolding herself for her stupidity.

"Lyla, wait!" Damien launched towards her, grasping her fingers in his. Lyla paused mid step, her shoulders dropping as a small moan escaped her. The warmth of his hand against hers took her breath away. "I didn't mean to embarrass you."

With his free hand, he tilted her face towards him, yet she refused to look at him. Instead, she placed her hand on his chest.

"Thank you," she whispered. "Thank you for saving my sister." Lyla reached up and kissed him briefly on the cheek before she pulled her hand from his and strode quickly back to the manor, leaving Damien alone in the garden.

Chapter 46

The following morning, true to his word, Constable Walidan returned to the house to get a formal statement from both Lyla and Meg.

"Thank you, Mrs Valdez." Lyla winced slightly at the name. "I understand you knew very little about what your husband intentions were, is that right?"

"Yes, sir."

"To let you know, I had spoken to Mr Stuart's family the day he died. It was my understanding that he was in a duel with your husband. Is that correct?"

Lyla shuddered again. Meg held tightly to Lylas's hand, comforting her. "Yes. Noah …" She paused. Saying his name, caused a pang of sorrow in her heart. Despite wanting her marriage to Noah annulled, she never wanted him dead, not really. "Noah told me in the carriage on the way to his house, right after we got married, that he had asked Winston to walk away to allow him to marry me. When Winston refused, Noah would not give up. That was when Winston challenged him to a duel."

"Understandable. Unfortunately, we know the outcome." He stated factually. "And Iris. What did he tell you about her?"

She ran the tip of her tongue over her dry lips. Reaching forwards, she grabbed a glass of water and took a sip. "Sorry," she muttered as she placed the glass back.

"No need to apologise, ma'am, I am aware this is not easy to talk about, take your time."

"He told me he had taken Iris as leverage; to ensure that I married him. He said he would bring her home soon." She shook her head, embarrassed. "And I believed him."

"Did he?"

"No."

"Ms Meg." Meg glanced up at him. "Does that match what he told you?"

"Yes. Pretty much."

"Did either of you know where he was keeping her?"

"No." Lyla and Meg shook their heads at the same time. "He didn't tell us anything," Meg stated.

"Ms Meg," the constable continued, "When did you find out where Iris was being held?"

"Yesterday morning, when Noah woke me early to ask for my help in looking for her."

"And he took you directly to her?"

"Well, to the house he held her in, but she was no longer there."

"Thank you." He paused, his hands clasped tightly over his stomach. "Mrs Valdez."

"Please call me Lyla," she interjected.

"Ma'am. I do not wish to alarm you, but there is something I do need to share with you." Lyla sat straighter in the chair, her eyes flicking to her parents in curiosity. He walked over to a spare seat and sat down. "It would be my understanding, that you would not have been aware Mr

Valdez; your husband, was in fact in a relationship with someone else before you married him."

He looked at her earnestly, watching her reaction.

"Excuse me?" Lyla asked, her eyes wide and her mouth agape.

"Mr Valdez was already promised to a Miss Daisy Marrion, his cousin." Lyla swallowed a lump in her throat; her eyebrows raised in disbelief. "Although they had not as yet married, he had intentions of marrying her ..." He paused, his voice trailing off as he shot a nervous glance at Albert.

"Yes?" Albert questioned.

"After he had acquired this manor," he voiced sternly as he swept his hand around the room.

"I don't understand," Grace spoke up.

"Mr Valdez and Miss Marrion intended to take control of the property, the house, the gardens—all of it."

"And *how* did they intend to do that?" Albert asked, his voice full of annoyance and disbelief.

The constable turned back to Lyla. "By marrying you. He believed he would become the new owner, after the death of ..." Again, he paused and looked at Albert. "You, sir."

"That makes no sense, Constable Walidan. Lyla would not have overseen this house anyway after she married. This house, this property, will go to Jonathan, he's the next male heir of the family as per tradition. No offence my sweetheart." He looked lovingly towards Lyla.

"No offence taken, Papa," she replied quietly.

"Correct, sir and Iris, being the clever young girl she is, apparently reminded Mr Valdez, that only the next *male* family member in the bloodline would take that position." He paused again, allowing everyone in the room to absorb what he was saying.

"So, he changed his mind, readjusted his plans, and bedded you, in the hope you bore him a son, and after your

…" he paused again, small beads of sweat forming across his brow. "… untimely death after delivering the child, he would take ownership, until his son was of age." He finished with a huff, as though the revelation had exhausted him.

Grace yelped as her hand flew to her throat. Lyla felt like she was about to faint.

"What!" Albert exclaimed and as Lyla looked to her father, she saw his entire body was rigid with rage.

Constable Walidan wrung his fingers together as Albert stood and stormed across the room, too agitated to sit.

"Yes, well. There is a bit more to the story I am afraid," the Constable continued, following Alberts movements.

"More!" Grace licked her own lips. "I do not think I could take anymore." Her hand fluttered over her heart.

"It is my understanding, from what I have been told, Noah intended for both Albert and Jonathan to die, thus, leaving your son," he motioned back to Lyla. "As sole heir to the property."

"Good gracious!" Albert exclaimed as he braced himself against the mantle. Running his hand over his chin he stared across the room and out the window. After a moment, he turned back to Constable Walidan, his forehead creased. "Who told you all this?"

"Miss Marrion. She turned up at the police station after she heard of Mr Valdez's death. She wanted Mr Olsen to be charged with his murder. But, because I spoke to Iris yesterday, and she informed me that Mr Valdez had told her exactly what he was planning, I was able to get Miss Marrion, to confess to everything. By questioning the two of you today, Ms Lyla and Ms Meg, I had hoped you could confirm these statements to be true." He continued to wring his hands in his lap, as though he didn't know what else to do with them.

Albert strolled slowly back to the chair and resumed his position next to Grace, gently taking her hand in his. "Well, I am not sure how to take all of this."

"That is understandable, sir." The constable stood silently but hesitated, as though there was still more to the story.

"Before I leave, there is one more thing I do need to share with you, Ms Lyla."

"Me?" Lyla questioned, her voice barely a whisper.

"Yes. The house Mr Valdez took you to, after your wedding, did you know about it, or recognise it?" the Constable asked.

"No ... should I have?"

The Constable shook his head. "The house belonged to an elderly couple. A Mr and Mrs Benjamin Fielding. A week before your wedding, the couple died, and the house was then sold to Mr Valdez. It all happened rather quickly, and their deaths were deemed somewhat suspicious, but there was no investigation, as there was no family to request one. Yet Miss Marrion, during her confession informed us that Mr Valdez had in fact poisoned them both, and using his banking skills, took possession of the house. Then he presented it to you, as his wedding gift."

Lyla grasped Meg's hand and squeezed it hard, her body trembling as the whole picture finally came into view.

No wonder the house was so opulent and filled with furniture and books, the staff so quiet and withdrawn. Noah truly was a monster and would stop at nothing to get what he wanted.

To allow the family to absorb the information, Constable Walidan prepared himself to leave. "I believe that is everything I needed to share with you and thank you both, for your statements, Ma'am." He looked directly at Lyla. "I am sorry for your loss. For both Mr Stuart and Mr Valdez. I'm certain it wasn't how you expected your wedding to play out." He added. With a slight nod of his head, he started to leave the room.

"Thank you, Constable Walidan." Albert rose and shook the Constables hand.

"What will happen to Miss Marrion?" Lyla asked curiously as the Constable ambled towards the door, her father at his side.

"She will be charged with conspiring to murder and the kidnaping of Iris … Miss Pierson," he corrected himself.

"Wait. Miss Marrion met Iris?" Grace questioned.

"Yes. She informed me that she had visited her in the old house. Gave her food." Shaking her head, Lyla looked at her mother and saw silent tears streaming down her cheeks, the shock of everything finally setting in.

"Daisy Marrion will be questioned further, but I do believe she will be sent away," The constable added, and with a final nod, he left the room and made his way with Albert up to Iris's room.

"I am so sorry." Lyla began to cry uncontrollably, wailing into her hands. "This is all my fault!" Grace rushed over to her, wrapping her arms around her tightly.

"Oh, my girl. This was *not* your fault. There is nothing you did wrong. Noah threated all of us if you or we, did not comply to his wishes. None of us knew what his true intentions were." She kissed Lyla tenderly on her forehead.

"Your mama is right, Lyla." Meg stood behind Grace. "None of us knew what he was capable of. All we know now, is that we have escaped his terror and are home together. Safe. He will never be able to harm anyone else again."

<h1 style="text-align:center">Chapter 47</h1>

"Lyla!" Iris's shrill voice called out, her sweet voice trailing musically on the breeze. Lyla smiled. How little things had changed. "Lyla!" Iris's voice deepened with frustration.

"I'm here, near the pond," Lyla called back with a smile.

"There you are! You are always hiding from me." Iris's breathless voice cooed as she ran up to Lyla and dropped herself down on the picnic rug beside her.

"That's because you're always irritating me," Lyla teased as she tapped Iris's pert nose with her finger as she grinned at her little sister.

"You have a guest!" Iris looked at her with annoyance.

"I do?" Lyla straightened. "Who?" Her hand flew to her hair, carefully combing back the strands that had come free from her plait.

Iris sighed dramatically and rolled her eyes. "Mr Olsen is here to see you … again."

"Damien!" Lyla's eyes widened. She started to get to her feet but paused when she heard his deep voice behind her.

"Stay where you are, I will join you." He rounded the large willow tree Lyla had been sitting under, reading a book, and enjoying the tranquillity of the quiet lake.

Lyla turned her head to watch as Damien strolled towards her, a small posy of flowers in his hand.

"May I?" he asked politely, gesturing to the space on the rug.

"Yes, please." Lyla moved her legs slightly, pulling her white and cream day dress over, allowing more space for Damien to occupy.

"For you." He handed her the brightly coloured flowers as he sat down, and Lyla raised them to her nose and inhaled their sweet scent.

"Ew," Iris said as she rolled her eyes again.

"You don't need to stay, if this bothers you," Lyla teased.

"I think I have changed my mind," Iris said as she stood and smoothed the skirt of her yellow summer dress. "I do not *ever* want to be in love." Giving Lyla and Damien a sneer, she giggled and took off, running back through the garden.

"Is someone in love?" Damien asked playfully.

Lyla shot him a sideways glance, her heart fluttering in affection as she locked eyes with his. "Thank you for the flowers. They are beautiful," she said, changing the subject.

"You have picked a fine spot here, Lyla," Damien remarked as he stretched out his legs, leaned back on his elbows, and stared out over the lake.

"I've always loved it here." She followed his gaze out over the sparkling water.

They sat in silence for a while, neither needing to speak. The ducks swam lazily over the surface, leaving small ripples in their wake. Small brown birds flew across the soft blue sky, their silent flaps mesmerising to watch.

Slowly Damien sat and turned to face Lyla.

"It has been two months now, since … you know." He hesitated, searching her eyes with his own.

"I do. And?" Lyla responded softly, resting the flowers in her lap.

"And … maybe it's time to let your heart heal." Raising his hand, he reached over and tucked a stray strand of hair behind Lylas's ear before gently grazing his fingers over her cheek. Lyla's eyes closed as the touch sent a small shiver through her.

"I cannot, Damien."

"You can if you want to. And I know you do." His fingers tenderly traced down the side of her throat.

Smiling against her will, she pulled her head away a fraction, breaking the contact. "You know I cannot move forward, Damien. I won't marry again. It will bring shame to my family."

He dropped his hand and turn around completely to face her. Crossing his legs, he took her hand in his.

She could feel the heat of his knee as it rested against her thigh. The thin material of her dress, and the light woven brown fabric of his trousers, were the only thing between their skin. Her heart raced at his touch.

"Lyla." His voice crooned and she closed her eyes again. "You will not bring disgrace to your family. You have not left your marriage, nor are you a divorcee. You are a widow. Your husband died."

Lyla shuddered, an involuntary movement which sent a ripple of goosebumps down her arms, and she turned her face away. "My father would not allow it," she stated, a hint of sorrow in her tone.

Damien placed his fingers gently under Lyla's chin and pulled her face towards his. "The clergyman who performed your wedding has been informed of the situation, and has annulled the wedding, and both our parents have already given us their blessings," he said tenderly.

"What?" Lyla frowned, confused at his words.

Damien smiled and grabbed her hand. "Why do you think I have been visiting you all these weeks? Your mourning time was over a month ago. I have not been coming to see you, just because I want to make sure you are all right." He smiled and looked at her with wide eyes. "I have been visiting you, because I am in love with you."

"Our parents gave us their blessings?" She stared at him in awe.

"Yes, weeks ago. We've all been waiting for you to perhaps; indicate you wanted something formal to be announced between us. Assuming you were interested in me. I mean, I thought you were. You always seemed so happy to see me." His eyes darted over her face.

The realisation of what he said, slowly hit her. "You love me?"

"Yes, very much, and I sincerely hope you love me too, or this is one very awkward conversation we are having." He tried not to laugh.

Lyla giggled. "I do," she whispered. "I had just thought ..." her voice trailed off. "I did not think ..." She paused again, lost for words. Instead, Lyla pulled her hand out from his and picked up the posy in her lap, absently playing with the flowers.

"You are a widow, Lyla. You are free to marry whomever you choose or choose not to marry ever again if that is what you prefer. But if you marry again, it will not bring any shame to you nor to your family. If anything, we are all hoping it will help you to heal." She glanced up to see him staring at her so intently, she felt her heart skip a beat.

"But ... Jonathan," Lyla muttered then dropped her eyes, her heart feeling torn. Regardless of whether or not their parents approved Lyla's ability to marry again without sullying her family name, Jonathan had asked her *not* to pick him, *not* to marry him. Could she destroy her relationship with him just to find happiness?

Damien placed his hand tenderly on her knee. "Lyla," he said and waited for her to look at him. "Jonathan was the first person who gave me his approval.

"What?"

Damien chuckled. "After bringing Iris home, Jonathan has been nothing but grateful. It has been him the whole time, encouraging me to visit. Pushing me towards you. Helping you through your grief."

Ducking her head again, her heart racing, she focused again on the flowers in her lap, a small smile playing across her lips. "So, you want to marry me?" she asked still not looking at him, though she could feel his eyes on her.

"Yes, I do," he replied firmly, and Lyla couldn't have stopped her smile from widening even if she'd wanted to. "And *my* father has approved the marriage?"

"Yes, he has."

"Well, then," Lyla said as she finally looked up at him, and staring into his dark blues eyes, brought her hand up and spoke softly. "Mr Damien Olsen. Would you be my friend, my lover, and my husband, till death do us part?"

Damien lowered his eyes to see a white carnation between Lyla's fingers that she'd plucked from the posy.

Smiling like he'd just receive the best present in the world; he accepted the flower.

"It would be my honour."

The End

Acknowledgments.

Once again, I would like to thank my sister, Lana for being the first person to read this book and giving me the feedback I needed to make the book better. Your input, suggestions, honesty, and support are muchly appreciated, and I would be lost without you.

To my editor, Liz Butcher. Thank you again for helping me fine tune this novel. Your help and advice is scary, and overwhelming but necessary in helping me be a better writer. I know I still have a long way to go.

To my parents, for being amazingly supportive and eager to help. Thank you, dad, for being the last proofreader and finding the little errors.

To my children, Peta, and Travis, for your ongoing support. I may be distant and distracted but you are both never far from my thoughts, I love you both dearly.

To our two fur baby cats, Leo and Oni and our dearest kitty Nox who passed away while I was writing this book, your cuddles, endless amounts of fur and persistent mewls, have been a welcome distraction.

And finally, to you, the readers. If you read my first book and came back to read this one, thank you, thank you, thank you. Your support in this adventure of mine is most appreciated, and I will be forever grateful. If you have discovered me for the first time, I hope you enjoyed this book, my second published novel and stick with me as I write more. As a new writer, trying to get my novels into the vast world of story making, has been a long scary road, but I have loved every moment.